The Tory Lover

The Tory Lover
Sarah Orne Jewett

MINT EDITIONS

The Tory Lover was first published in 1900.

This edition published by Mint Editions 2021.

ISBN 9781513279893 | E-ISBN 9781513284910

Published by Mint Editions®

MINT
EDITIONS

minteditionbooks.com

Publishing Director: Jennifer Newens
Design & Production: Rachel Lopez Metzger
Project Manager: Micaela Clark
Typesetting: Westchester Publishing Services

Contents

I

The Sea Wolf

"By all you love most, war and this sweet lady."

The last day of October in 1777, Colonel Jonathan Hamilton came out of his high house on the river bank with a handsome, impatient company of guests, all Berwick gentlemen. They stood on the flagstones, watching a coming boat that was just within sight under the shadow of the pines of the farther shore, and eagerly passed from hand to hand a spyglass covered with worn red morocco leather. The sun had just gone down; the quick-gathering dusk of the short day was already veiling the sky before they could see the steady lift and dip of long oars, and make sure of the boat's company. While it was still a long distance away, the gentlemen turned westward and went slowly down through the terraced garden, to wait again with much formality by the gate at the garden foot.

Beside the master of the house was Judge Chadbourne, an old man of singular dignity and kindliness of look, and near them stood General Goodwin, owner of the next estate, and Major Tilly Haggens of the Indian wars, a tall, heavily made person, clumsily built, but not without a certain elegance like an old bottle of Burgundy. There was a small group behind these foremost men,—a red cloak here and a touch of dark velvet on a shoulder beyond, with plenty of well-plaited ruffles to grace the wearers. Hamilton's young associate, John Lord, merchant and gentleman, stood alone, trim-wigged and serious, with a look of discretion almost too great for his natural boyish grace. Quite the most impressive figure among them was the minister, a man of high ecclesiastical lineage, very well dressed in a three-cornered beaver hat, a large single-breasted coat sweeping down with ample curves over a long waistcoat with huge pockets and lappets, and a great white stock that held his chin high in air. This was fastened behind with a silver buckle to match the buckles on his tight knee breeches, and other buckles large and flat on his square-toed shoes; somehow he looked as like a serious book with clasps as a man could look, with an outward completeness that mated with his inner equipment of fixed Arminian opinions.

As for Colonel Hamilton, the host, a strong-looking, bright-colored man in the middle thirties, the softness of a suit of brown, and his own hair well dressed and powdered, did not lessen a certain hardness in his face, a grave determination, and maturity of appearance far beyond the due of his years. Hamilton had easily enough won the place of chief shipping merchant and prince of money-makers in that respectable group, and until these dark days of war almost every venture by land or sea had added to his fortunes. The noble house that he had built was still new enough to be the chief show and glory of a rich provincial neighborhood. With all his power of money-making,—and there were those who counted him a second Sir William Pepperrell,—Hamilton was no easy friend-maker like that great citizen of the District of Maine, nor even like his own beautiful younger sister, the house's mistress. Some strain of good blood, which they had inherited, seemed to have been saved through generations to nourish this one lovely existence, and make her seem like the single flower upon their family tree. They had come from but a meagre childhood to live here in state and luxury beside the river.

The broad green fields of Hamilton's estate climbed a long hill behind the house, hedged in by stately rows of elms and tufted by young orchards; at the western side a strong mountain stream came down its deep channel over noisy falls and rapids to meet the salt tide in the bay below. This broad sea inlet and inland harborage was too well filled in an anxious year with freightless vessels both small and great: heavy seagoing craft and lateen-sailed gundalows for the river traffic; idle enough now, and careened on the mud at half tide in picturesque confusion.

The opposite shore was high, with farmhouses above the fields. There were many persons to be seen coming down toward the water, and when Colonel Hamilton and his guests appeared on the garden terraces, a loud cry went alongshore, and instantly the noise of mallets ceased in the shipyard beyond, where some carpenters were late at work. There was an eager, buzzing crowd growing fast about the boat landing and the wharf and warehouses which the gentlemen at the high-urned gateway looked down upon. The boat was coming up steadily, but in the middle distance it seemed to lag; the long stretch of water was greater than could be measured by the eye. Two West Indian fellows in the crowd fell to scuffling, having trodden upon each other's rights, and the on-lookers, quickly diverted from their first interest, cheered them on, and wedged themselves closer together to see the fun. Old Cæsar, the majestic negro who had attended Hamilton at respectful distance, made it his welcome duty to approach the quarrel with loud rebukes; usually the authority of this great person in matters pertaining to the estate was only second to his master's, but in such a moment of high festival and gladiatorial combat all commands fell upon deaf ears. Major Tilly Haggens burst into a hearty laugh, glad of a chance to break the tiresome formalities of his associates, and being a great admirer of a skillful fight. On any serious occasion the major always seemed a little uneasy, as if restless with unspoken jokes.

In the meantime the boat had taken its shoreward curve, and was now so near that even through the dusk the figures of the oarsmen, and of an officer, sitting alone at the stern in full uniform, could be plainly seen. The next moment the wrestling Tobago men sprang to their feet, forgetting their affront, and ran to the landing-place with the rest.

The new flag of the Congress with its unfamiliar stripes was trailing at the boat's stern; the officer bore himself with dignity, and made his salutations with much politeness. All the gentlemen on the terrace came down together to the water's edge, without haste, but with exact deference and timeliness; the officer rose quickly in the boat, and stepped ashore with ready foot and no undignified loss of balance. He wore the pleased look of a willing guest, and was gayly dressed in a bright new uniform of blue coat and breeches, with red lapels and a red waistcoat trimmed with lace. There was a noisy cheering, and the spectators fell back on either hand and made way for this very elegant company to turn again and go their ways up the river shore.

Captain Paul Jones of the Ranger bowed as a well-practiced sovereign might as he walked along, a little stiffly at first, being often vexed by boat-cramp, as he now explained cheerfully to his host. There was an eager restless look in his clear-cut sailor's face, with quick eyes that seemed not to observe things that were near by, but to look often and hopefully toward the horizon. He was a small man, but already bent in the shoulders from living between decks; his sword was long for his height and touched the ground as he walked, dragging along a gathered handful of fallen poplar leaves with its scabbard tip.

It was growing dark as they went up the long garden; a thin white mist was gathering on the river, and blurred the fields where there were marshy spots or springs. The two brigs at the moorings had strung up their dull oil lanterns to the rigging, where they twinkled like setting stars, and made faint reflections below in the rippling current. The huge elms that stood along the river shore were full of shadows, while above, the large house was growing bright with candlelight, and taking on a cheerful air of invitation. As the master and his friends went up to the wide south door, there stepped out to meet them the lovely figure of a girl, tall and charming, and ready with a gay welcome to chide the captain for his delay. She spoke affectionately to each of the others, though she avoided young Mr. Lord's beseeching eyes. The elder men had hardly time for a second look to reassure themselves of her bright beauty, before she had vanished along the lighted hall. By the time their cocked hats and plainer head gear were safely deposited, old Cæsar with a great flourish of invitation had thrown open the door of the dining parlor.

II

The Parting Feast

"A little nation, but made great by liberty."

The faces gathered about the table were serious and full of character. They wore the look of men who would lay down their lives for the young country whose sons they were, and though provincial enough for the most part, so looked most of the men who sat in Parliament at Westminster, and there was no more patrician head than the old judge's to be seen upon the English bench. They were for no self-furtherance in public matters, but conscious in their hearts of some national ideas that a Greek might have cherished in his clear brain, or any citizen of the great days of Rome. They were men of a single-hearted faith in Liberty that shone bright and unassailable; there were men as good as they in a hundred other towns. It was a simple senate of New England, ready and able to serve her cause in small things and great.

The next moment after the minister had said a proper grace, the old judge had a question to ask.

"Where is Miss Mary Hamilton?" said he. "Shall we not have the pleasure of her company?"

"My sister looks for some young friends later," explained the host, but with a touch of coldness in his voice. "She begs us to join her then in her drawing-room, knowing that we are now likely to have business together and much discussion of public affairs. I bid you all welcome to my table, gentlemen; may we be here to greet Captain Paul Jones on his glorious return, as we speed him now on so high an errand!"

"You have made your house very pleasant to a homeless man, Colonel Hamilton," returned the captain, with great feeling. "And Miss Hamilton is as good a patriot as her generous brother. May Massachusetts and the Province of Maine never lack such sons and daughters! There are many of my men taking their farewell supper on either shore of your river this night. I have received my dispatches, and it is settled that we sail for France to-morrow morning at the turn of tide."

"To-morrow morning!" they exclaimed in chorus. The captain's manner gave the best of news; there was an instant shout of approval and congratulation. His own satisfaction at being finally ordered to sea after many trying delays was understood by every one, since for many months, while the Ranger was on the stocks at Portsmouth, Paul Jones had bitterly lamented the indecisions of a young government, and regretted the slipping away of great opportunities abroad and at home. To say that he had made himself as vexing as a wasp were to say the truth, but he had already proved himself a born leader with a heart on fire with patriotism and deep desire for glory, and there were those present who eagerly recognized his power and were ready to further his best endeavors. Young men had flocked to his side, sailors born and bred on the river shores, and in Portsmouth town, who could serve their country well. Berwick was in the thick of the fight from the very beginning; her company of soldiers had been among the first at Bunker's Hill, and the alarm at Lexington had shaken her very hills at home. Twin sister of Portsmouth in age, and sharer of her worldly conditions, the old ease and wealth of the town were sadly troubled now; there was many a new black gown in the parson's great parish, and many a mother's son lay dead, or suffered in an English prison. Yet the sea still beckoned with white hands, and Paul Jones might have shipped his crew on the river many times over. The ease of teaching England to let the colonies alone was not spoken of with such bold certainty as at first, and some late offenses were believed to be best revenged by such a voyage as the Ranger was about to make.

Captain Paul Jones knew his work; he was full of righteous wrath toward England, and professed a large readiness to accept the offered friendliness of France.

Colonel Jonathan Hamilton could entertain like a prince. The feast was fit for the room in which it was served, and the huge cellar beneath was well stored with casks of wine that had come from France and Spain, or from England while her ports were still home ports for the colonies. Being a Scotsman, the guest of honor was not unmindful of excellent claret, and now set down his fluted silver tumbler after a first deep draught, and paid his host a handsome compliment.

"You live like a Virginia gentleman, sir, here in your Northern home. They little know in Great Britain what stately living is among us. The noble Countess of Selkirk thought that I was come to live among the savages, instead of gratifying my wishes for that calm contemplation and poetic ease which, alas, I have ever been denied."

SARAH ORNE JEWETT

"They affect to wonder at the existence of American gentlemen," returned the judge. "When my father went to Court in '22, and they hinted the like, he reminded them that since they had sent over some of the best of their own gentlefolk to found the colonies, it would be strange if none but boors and clowns came back."

"In Virginia they consider that they breed the only gentlemen; that is the great pity," said Parson Tompson. "Some of my classmates at Cambridge arrived at college with far too proud a spirit. They were pleased to be amused, at first, because so many of us at the North were destined for the ministry."

"You will remember that Don Quixote speaks of the Church, the Sea, and the Court for his Spanish gentlemen," said Major Tilly Haggens, casting a glance across at the old judge. "We have had the two first to choose from in New England, if we lacked the third." The world was much with the major, and he was nothing if not eager spoken. "People forget to look at the antecedents of our various colonists; 't is the only way to understand them. In these Piscataqua neighborhoods we do not differ so much from those of Virginia; 'tis not the same pious stock as made Connecticut and the settlements of Massachusetts Bay. We are children of the Norman blood in New England and Virginia, at any rate. 'T is the Saxons who try to rule England now; there is the cause of all our troubles. Norman and Saxon have never yet learned to agree."

"You give me a new thought," said the captain.

"For me," explained the major, "I am of fighting and praying Huguenot blood, and here comes in another strain to our nation's making. I might have been a parson myself if there had not been a stray French gallant to my grandfather, who ran away with a saintly Huguenot maiden; his ghost still walks by night and puts the devil into me so that I forget my decent hymns. My family name is Huyghens; 't was a noble house of the Low Countries. Christian Huyghens, author of the Cosmotheoros, was my father's kinsman, and I was christened for the famous General Tilly of stern faith, but the gay Frenchman will ever rule me. 'Tis all settled by our antecedents," and he turned to Captain Paul Jones. "I'm for the flower-de-luce, sir; if I were a younger man I'd sail with you to-morrow! 'T is very hard for us aging men with boys' hearts in us to stay decently at home. I should have been born in France!"

"France is your country's friend, sir," said Paul Jones, bowing across the table. "Let us drink to France, gentlemen!" and the company drank the toast. Old Cæsar bowed with the rest as he stood behind his master's chair, and smacked his lips with pathetic relish of the wine which he had tasted only in imagination. The captain's quick eyes caught sight of him.

"By your leave, Colonel Hamilton!" he exclaimed heartily. "This is a toast that every American should share the pleasure of drinking. I observe that my old friend Cæsar has joined us in spirit," and he turned with a courtly bow and gave a glass to the serving man.

"You have as much at stake as we in this great enterprise," he said gently, in a tone that moved the hearts of all the supper company. "May I drink with you to France, our country's ally?"

A lesser soul might have babbled thanks, but Cæsar, who had been born a Guinea prince, drank in silence, stepped back to his place behind his master, and stood there like a king. His underlings went and came serving the supper; he ruled them like a great commander on the field of battle, and hardly demeaned himself to move again until the board was cleared.

"I seldom see a black face without remembering the worst of my boyish days when I sailed in the Two Friends, slaver," said the captain gravely, but with easy power of continuance. "Our neighbor town of Dumfries was in the tobacco trade, and all their cargoes were unloaded in Carsethorn Bay, close by my father's house. I was easily enough tempted to follow the sea; I was trading in the Betsey at seventeen, and felt myself a man of experience. I have observed too many idle young lads hanging about your Portsmouth wharves who ought to be put to sea under a smart captain. They are ready to cheer or to jeer at strangers, and take no pains to be manly. I began to follow the sea when I was but a child, yet I was always ambitious of command, and ever thinking how I might best study the art of navigation."

"There were few idlers along this river once," said General Goodwin regretfully. "The times grow worse and worse."

"You referred to the slaver, Two Friends," interrupted the minister, who had seen a shadow of disapproval on the faces of two of his parishioners (one being Colonel Hamilton's) at the captain's tone. "May I observe that there has seemed to be some manifestation of a kind Providence in bringing so many heathen souls to the influence of a Christian country?"

The fierce temper of the captain flamed to his face; he looked up at old Cæsar who well remembered the passage from his native land, and saw that black countenance set like an iron mask.

"I must beg your reverence's kind pardon if I contradict you," said Paul Jones, with scornful bitterness.

There was a murmur of protest about the table; the captain's reply was not counted to be in the best of taste. Society resents being disturbed at its pleasures, and the man who had offended was now made conscious of his rudeness. He looked up, however, and saw Miss Hamilton standing near the open doorway that led into the hall. She was gazing at him with no relic of that indifference which had lately distressed his heart, and smiled at him as she colored deeply, and disappeared.

The captain took on a more spirited manner than before, and began to speak of politics, of the late news from Long Island, where a son of old Berwick, General John Sullivan, had taken the place of Lee, and was now next in command to Washington himself. This night Paul Jones seemed to be in no danger of those fierce outbursts of temper with which he was apt to startle his more amiable and prosaic companions. There was some discussion of immediate affairs, and one of the company, Mr. Wentworth, fell upon the inevitable subject of the Tories; a topic sure to rouse much bitterness of feeling. Whatever his own principles, every man present had some tie of friendship or bond of kindred with those who were Loyalists for conscience' sake, and could easily be made ill at ease.

The moment seemed peculiarly unfortunate for such trespass, and when there came an angry lull in the storm of talk, Mr. Lord somewhat anxiously called attention to a pair of great silver candlesticks which graced the feast, and by way of compliment begged to be told their history. It was not unknown that they had been brought from England a few summers before in one of Hamilton's own ships, and that he was not without his fancy for such things as gave his house a look of rich ancestry; a stranger might well have thought himself in a good country house of Queen Anne's time near London. But this placid interlude did not rouse any genuine interest, and old Judge Chadbourne broke another awkward pause and harked back to safer ground in the conversation.

"I shall hereafter make some discrimination against men of color. I have suffered a great trial of the spirit this day," he began seriously. "I ask the kind sympathy of each friend present. I had promised my friend, President Hancock, some of our Berwick elms to plant near his house on Boston Common; he has much admired the fine natural growth of that tree in our good town here, and the beauty it lends to our high ridges of land. I gave directions to my man Ajax, known to some of you as a competent but lazy soul, and as I was leaving home he ran after me, shouting to inquire where he should find the trees. 'Oh, get them anywhere!' said I, impatient at the detention, and full of some difficult matters which were coming up at our term in York. And this morning on my return from court, I missed a well-started row of young elms, which I had selected myself and planted along the outer border of my gardens. Ajax had taken the most accessible, and they had all gone down river by the packet. I shall have a good laugh with Hancock by and by. I remember that he once praised these very trees and professed to covet them."

"'T was the evil eye," suggested Mr. Hill, laughing; but the minister slowly shook his head, contemptuous of such superstitious.

"I saw that one of our neighbor Madam Wallingford's favorite oaks was sadly broken by the recent gale," said Mr. Wentworth unguardedly, and this was sufficient to make a new name fairly leap into the conversation,—that of Mr. Roger Wallingford, the son of a widowed lady of great fortune, whose house stood not far distant, on the other side of the river in Somersworth.

General Goodwin at once dropped his voice regretfully. "I am afraid that we can have no doubt now of the young man's sympathy with our oppressors," said he. "I hear that he has been seen within a week coming out of the Earl of Halifax tavern in Portsmouth, late at night, as if from a secret conference. A friend of mine heard him say openly on the Parade that Mr. Benjamin Thompson of old Rumford had been unfairly driven to seek Royalist protection, and to flee his country, leaving wife and infant child behind him; that 't was all from the base suspicions and hounding of his neighbors, whose worst taunt had ever been that he loved and sought the company of gentlemen. 'I pity him from my heart,' says Wallingford in a loud voice; as if pity could ever belong to so vile a traitor!"

"But I fear that this was true," said Judge Chadbourne, the soundest of patriots, gravely interrupting. "They drove young Thompson away in hot haste when his country was in sorest need of all such naturally chivalrous and able men. He meant no disloyalty until his crisis came, and proved his rash young spirit too weak to meet it. He will be a great man some day, if I read men aright; we shall be proud of him in spite of everything. He had his foolish follies, and the wrong road never leads to the right place, but the taunts of the narrow-minded would have made many an older man fling himself out of reach. 'T is a sad mischance of war. Young Wallingford is a proud fellow, and has his follies too: his kindred in Boston thought themselves bound to the King; they are his elders and have been his guardians, and youth may forbid his seeing the fallacy of their arguments. Our country is above our King in such a time as this, yet I myself was of those who could not lightly throw off the allegiance of a lifetime."

"I have always said that we must have patience with such lads and not try to drive them," said Major Haggens, the least patient of all the gentlemen. Captain Paul Jones drummed on the table with one hand and rattled the links of his sword hilt with the other. The minister looked dark and unconvinced, but the old judge stood first among his parishioners; he did not answer, but threw an imploring glance toward Hamilton at the head of the table.

"We are beginning to lose the very last of our patience now with those who cry that our country is too young and poor to go alone, and urge that we should bear our wrongs and be tied to the skirts of England for fifty years more. What about our poor sailors dying like sheep in the English jails?" said Hamilton harshly. "He that is not for us is against us, and so the people feel."

"The true patriot is the man who risks all for love of country," said the minister, following fast behind.

"They have little to risk, some of the loudest of them," insisted Major Haggens scornfully. "They would not brook the thought of conciliation, but fire and sword and other men's money are their only sinews of war. I mean that some of those dare-devils in Boston have often made matters worse than there was any need," he added, in a calmer tone.

Paul Jones cast a look of contempt upon such a complaining old soldier.

"You must remember that many discomforts accompany a great struggle," he answered. "The lower classes, as some are pleased to call certain citizens of our Republic, must serve Liberty in their own fashion. They are used to homespun shirt-sleeves and not to lace ruffles, but they make good fighters, and their hearts are true. Sometimes their instinct gives them to see farther ahead than we can. I fear indeed that there is trouble brewing for some of your valued neighbors who are not willing to be outspoken. A certain young gentleman has of late shown some humble desires to put himself into an honorable position for safety's sake."

"You mistake us, sir," said the old judge, hastening to speak. "But we are not served in our struggle by such lawlessness of behavior; we are only hindered by it. General George Washington is our proper model, and not those men whose manners and language are not worthy of civilization."

The guest of the evening looked frankly bored, and Major Tilly Haggens came to the rescue. The captain's dark hint had set them all staring at one another.

"Some of our leaders in this struggle make me think of an old Scottish story I got from McIntire in York," said he. "There was an old farmer went to the elders to get his tokens for the Sacrament, and they propounded him his questions. 'What's your view of Adam?' says they: 'what kind of a mon?' 'Well,' says the farmer, 'I think Adam was like Jack Simpson the horse trader. Varra few got anything by him, an' a mony lost.'"

The captain laughed gayly as if with a sense of proprietorship in the joke. "'T is old Scotland all over," he acknowledged, and then his face grew stern again.

"Your loud talkers are the gadflies that hurry the slowest oxen," he warned the little audience. "And we have to remember that if those who would rob America of her liberties should still prevail, we all sit here with halters round our necks!" Which caused the spirits of the company to sink so low that again the cheerful major tried to succor it.

"Shall we drink to The Ladies?" he suggested, with fine though unexpected courtesy; and they drank as if it were the first toast of the evening.

"We are in the middle of a great war now, and must do the best we can," said Hamilton, as if he wished to make peace about his table. "Last summer when things were at the darkest, Sam Adams came riding down to Exeter to plead with Mr. Gilman for money and troops on the part of their Rockingham towns. The Treasurer was away, and his wife saw Adams's great anxiety and the tears rolling down his cheeks, and heard him groan aloud as he paced to and fro in the room. '*O my God!*' says he, '*and must we give it all up!*' When the good lady told me there were tears in her own eyes, and I vow that I was fired as I had never been before,—I have loved the man ever since; I called him a stirrer up of frenzies once, but it fell upon my heart that, after all, it is men like Sam Adams who hold us to our duty."

"I cannot envy Sam Curwen his travels in rural England, or Gray that he moves in the best London society, but Mr. Hancock writes me 'tis thought all our best men have left us," said Judge Chadbourne.

"'T is a very genteel company now at Bristol," said John Lord.

"I hear that the East India Company is in terrible difficulties, and her warehouses in London are crammed to bursting with the tea that we have refused to drink. If they only had sense enough to lift the tax and give us liberty for our own trade, we should soon drink all their troubles dry," said Colonel Hamilton.

"'T is not because we hate England, but because we love her that we are hurt so deep," said Mr. Hill. "When a man's mother is jealous because he prospers, and turns against him, it is worst of all."

"Send your young men to sea!" cried Captain Paul Jones, who had no patience with the resettling of questions already left far behind. "Send me thoroughbred lads like your dainty young Wallingford! You must all understand how little can be done with this poor basket of a Ranger against a well-furnished British man-of-war. My reverend friend here has his heart in the matter. I myself have flung away friends and fortune for my adopted country, and she has been but a stingy young stepmother to me. I go to fight her cause on the shores that gave me birth; I trample some dear recollections under foot, and she haggles with me all summer over a paltry vessel none too smart for a fisherman, and sends me to sea in her with my gallant crew. You all know that the Ranger is crank built, and her timbers not first class,—her thin sails are but coarse hessings, with neither a spare sheet, nor stuff to make it, and there's not even room aboard for all her guns. I sent four six-pounders ashore out of her this very day so that we can train the rest. 'T is some of your pretty Tories that have picked our knots as fast as we tied them, and some jealous hand chose poor planking for our decks and rotten red-oak knees for the frame. But, thank God, she's a vessel at last! I would sail for France in a gundalow, so help me Heaven! and once in France I shall have a proper man-of-war."

There was a chorus of approval and applause; the listeners were deeply touched and roused; they all wished to hear something of the captain's plans, but he returned to the silver tumbler of claret, and sat for a moment as if considering; his head was held high, and his eyes flashed with excitement as he looked up at the high cornice of the room. He had borne the name of the Sea Wolf; in that moment of excitement he looked ready to spring upon any foe, but to the disappointment of every one he said no more.

"The country is drained now of ready money," said young Lord despondently; "this war goes on, as it must go on, at great sacrifice. The reserves must come out,—those who make excuse and the only sons, and even men like me, turned off at first for lack of health. We meet the strain sadly in this little town; we have done the best we could on the river, sir, in fitting out your frigate, but you must reflect upon our situation."

The captain could not resist a comprehensive glance at the richly furnished table and stately dining-room of his host, and there was not a man who saw it who did not flush with resentment.

"We are poorly off for stores," he said bitterly, "and nothing takes down the courage of a seaman like poor fare. I found to-day that we had only thirty gallons of spirits for the whole crew." At which melancholy information Major Haggens's kind heart could not forbear a groan.

General Goodwin waved his hand and took his turn to speak with much dignity.

"This is the first time that we have all been guests at this hospitable board in many long weeks," he announced gravely. "There is no doubt about the propriety of republican simplicity, or our readiness to submit to it, though our ancient Berwick traditions have taught us otherwise. But I see reason to agree with our friend and former townsman, Judge Sullivan, who lately answered John Adams for his upbraiding of President Hancock's generous way of doing things. He insists that such open hospitality is to be praised when consistent with the means of the host, and that when the people are anxious and depressed it is important to the public cheerfulness."

"'T is true. James Sullivan is right," said Major Haggens; "we are not at Poverty's back door either. You will still find a glass of decent wine in every gentleman's house in old Barvick and a mug of honest cider by every farmer's fireside. We may lack foreign luxuries, but we can well sustain ourselves. This summer has found many women active in the fields, where our men have dropped the hoe to take their old swords again that were busy in the earlier ways."

"We have quelled the savage, but the wars of civilization are not less to be dreaded," said the good minister.

"War is but war," said Colonel Hamilton. "Let us drink to Peace, gentlemen!" and they all drank heartily; but Paul Jones looked startled; as if the war might really end without having served his own ambitions.

"Nature has made a hero of him," said the judge to his neighbor, as they saw and read the emotion of the captain's look. "Circumstances have now given him the command of men and a great opportunity. We shall see the result."

"Yet 't is a contemptible force of ship and men, to think of striking terror along the strong coasts of England," observed Mr. Hill to the parson, who answered him with sympathy; and the talk broke up and was only between man and man, while the chief thought of every one was upon the venison,—a fine saddle that had come down the week before from the north country about the Saco intervales.

III

A Character of Honor

"Sad was I, even to pain deprest,
Importunate and heavy load!
The comforter hath found me here
Upon this lonely road!"

Your friend General Sullivan has had his defamers but he goes to prove himself one of our ablest men," said Paul Jones to Hamilton. "I grieve to see that his old father, that lofty spirit and fine wit, is not with us to-night. Sullivan is a soldier born."

"There is something in descent," said Hamilton eagerly. "They come of a line of fighting men famous in the Irish struggles. John Sullivan's grandfather was with Patrick Sarsfield, the great Earl of Lucan, at Limerick, and the master himself, if all tales are true, was much involved in the early plots of the old Pretender. No, sir, he was not out in the '15; he was a student at that time in France, but I dare say ready to lend himself to anything that brought revenge upon England."

"Commend me to your ancient sage the master," said the captain. "I wish we might have had him here to-night. When we last dined here together he talked not only of our unfortunate King James, but of the great Prince of Conti and Louis Quatorze as if he had seen them yesterday. He was close to many great events in France."

"You speak of our old Master Sullivan," said Major Haggens eagerly, edging his chair a little nearer. "Yes, he knew all those great Frenchmen as he knows his Virgil and Tally; we are all his pupils here, old men and young; he is master of a little school on Pine Hill; there is no better scholar and gentleman in New England."

"Or Old England either," added Judge Chadbourne.

"They say that he had four countesses to his grandmothers, and that his grandfathers were lords of Beare and Bantry, and princes of Ireland," said the major. "His father was banished to France by the Stuarts, and died from a duel there, and the master was brought up in one of their great colleges in Paris where his house held a scholarship. He was reared among the best Frenchmen of his time. As for his coming here, there are many old stories; some say 't was being found in some treasonable plot, and some that 't was for the sake of a lady whom his mother would not let him stoop to marry. He vowed that she should never see his face again; all his fortunes depended on his mother, so he fled the country.

"With the lady?" asked the captain, with interest, and pushing along the decanter of Madeira.

"No," said the major, stopping to fill his own glass as if it were a pledge of remembrance. "No, he came to old York a bachelor, to the farm of the McIntires, Royalist exiles in the old Cromwell times, and worked there with his hands until some one asked him if he could write a letter, and he wrote it in seven languages. Then the minister, old Mr. Moody, planted him in our grammar school. There had been great lack of classical teaching in all this region for those who would be college bred, and since that early year he has kept his school for lads and now and then for a bright girl or two like Miss Mary Hamilton, and her mother before her."

"One such man who knows the world and holds that rarest jewel, the teacher's gift, can uplift a whole community," said the captain, with enthusiasm. "I see now the cause of such difference between your own and other early planted towns. Master Sullivan has proved himself a nobler prince and leader than any of his ancestry. But what of the lady? I heard many tales of him before I possessed the pleasure of his acquaintance, and so heard them with indifference."

"He had to wife a pretty child of the ship's company, an orphan whom he befriended, and later married. She was sprightly and of great beauty in her youth, and was dowered with all the energy in practical things that he had been denied," said the judge. "She came of plain peasant stock, but the poor soul has a noble heart. She flouts his idleness at one moment, and bewails their poverty, and then falls on her knees to worship him the next, and is as proud as if she had married the lord of the manor at home. The master lacked any true companionship until he bred it for himself. It has been a solitary life and hermitage for either an Irish adventurer or a French scholar and courtier."

"The master can rarely be tempted now from the little south window where he sits with his few books," said Hamilton. "I lived neighbor to him all my young days. Not long ago he went to visit his son James, and walked out with him to see the village at the falls of the Saco. There was an old woman lately come over from Ireland with her grandchildren; they said she remembered things in Charles the Second's time, and was above a hundred years of age. James Sullivan, the judge, thinking to amuse his father, stopped before the house, and out came the old creature, and fell upon her knees. 'My God! 't is the young Prince of Ardea!' says she. 'Oh, I mind me well of your lady mother, sir; 't was in Derry I was born, but I lived a year in Ardea, and yourself was a pretty boy busy with your courting!' The old man burst into tears. 'Let us go, James,' says he, 'or this will break my heart!' but he stopped and said a few words to her in a whisper, and gave the old body his blessing and all that was in his poor purse. He would listen to her no more. 'We need not speak of youth,' he told her; 'we remember it only too well!' A man told me this who stood by and heard the whole."

"'Twas most affecting; it spurs the imagination," said the captain. "If I had but an hour to spare I should ride to see him once more, even by night. You will carry the master my best respects, some of you.

"One last glass, gentlemen, to our noble cause! We may never sit in pleasant company again," he added, and they all rose in their places and stood about the table.

"*Haud heigh*, my old auntie used to say to me at home. Aim high's the English of it. She was of the bold clan of the MacDuffs, and 't is my own motto in these anxious days. Good-by, gentlemen all!" said the little captain. "I ask for your kind wishes and your prayers."

They all looked at Hamilton, and then at one another, but nobody took it upon himself to speak, so they shook hands warmly and drank their last toast in silence and with deep feeling. It was time to join the ladies; already there was a sound of music across the hall in a great room which had been cleared for the dancing.

IV

The Flowering of whose Face

"Dear love, for nothing less than thee
Would I have broke this happy dream,

* * * * *

Therefore thou wak'dst me wisely; yet
My dream thou breakest not, but continuest it."

While the guests went in to supper, Mary Hamilton, safe in the shelter of friendly shadows, went hurrying along the upper hall of the house to her own chamber. The coming moon was already brightening the eastern sky, so that when she opened the door the large room with its white hangings was all dimly lighted from without, and she could see the figure of a girl standing at one of the windows.

"Oh, you are here!" she cried, with sharp anxiety, and then they leaned out together, with their arms about each other's shoulders, looking down at the dark cove and at the height beyond where the tops of tall pines were silvered like a cloud. They could hear the men's voices, as if they were all talking together, in the room below.

Mary looked at her friend's face in the dim light. There were some who counted Miss Elizabeth Wyat as great a beauty as Miss Hamilton.

"Oh, Betsey dear, I can hardly bear to ask, but tell me quick now what you have heard! I must go down to Peggy; she has attempted everything for this last feast, and I promised her to trim the game pie for its proud appearing, and the great plum cake. One of her maids is ill, and she is in such a flurry!"

"'T was our own maids talking," answered Betsey Wyat slowly. "They were on the bleaching-green with their linen this morning, the sun was so hot, and I was near by among the barberry bushes in the garden. Thankful Grant was sobbing, in great distress. She said that her young man had put himself in danger; he was under a vow to come out with the mob from Dover any night now that the signal called them, to attack Madam Wallingford's house and make Mr. Roger declare his principles. They were sure he was a Tory fast enough, and they meant to knock the old nest to pieces; they are bidden to be ready with their tools; their axes, she said, and something for a torch. Thankful begged him to feign illness, but he said he did not dare, and would go with the rest at any rate. She said she fronted him with the remembrance how madam had paid his wages all last summer when he was laid by, though the hurt he got was not done in her service, but in breaking his own colt on a Sunday. Yet nothing changed him; he said he was all for Liberty, and would not play the sneak now."

"Oh, how cruel! when nobody has been so kind and generous as Madam Wallingford, so full of kind thought for the poor!" exclaimed Mary. "And Roger"—

"He would like it better if you thought first of him, not of his mother," said Betsey Wyat reproachfully.

"What can be done? It may be this very night," said Mary, in a voice of despair.

"The only thing left is to declare his principles. Things have gone so far now, they will never give him any peace. Many have come to the belief that he is in close league with our enemies."

"That he has never been!" said Mary hotly.

"He must prove it to the doubting Patriots, then; so my father says."

"But not to a mob of rascals, who will be disappointed if they cannot vex their betters, and ruin an innocent woman's home, and spoil her peace only to show their power. Oh, Betsey, what in the world shall we do? There is no place left for those who will take neither side. Oh, help me to think what we shall do; the mob may be there this very night! There was a strange crowd about the Landing just now, when the captain came. I dare not send any one across the river with such a message but old Cæsar or Peggy, and they are not to be spared from the house. I trust none of the younger people, black or white, when it comes to this."

"But he was safe in Portsmouth to-day; they will watch for his being at home; it will not be to-night, then," said Betsey Wyat hopefully. "I think that he should have spoken long ago, if only to protect his mother."

"Get ready now, dear Betty, and make yourself very fine," said Mary at last. "The people will all be coming for the dance long before supper is done. My brother was angry when I told him I should not sit at the table, but I could not. There is nobody to make it gay afterward with our beaux all gone to the army; but Captain Paul Jones begged hard for some dancing, and all the girls are coming,—the Hills and Rights, and the Lords from Somersworth. I must manage to tell my brother of this danger, but to openly protect Madam Wallingford would be openly taking the wrong side, and who will follow him in such a step?"

"I could not pass the great window on the stairs without looking out in fear that Madam's house would be all ablaze," whispered Betsey Wyat, shuddering. "There have been such dreadful things done against the Tories in Salem and Boston!"

"My heart is stone cold with fear," said Mary Hamilton; "yet if it only does not come to-night, there may be something done."

There was a silence between the friends; they clung to each other; it was not the first time that youth and beauty knew the harsh blows of war. The loud noise of the river falls came beating into the room, echoing back from the high pines across the water.

"We must make us fine, dear, and get ready for the dancing; I have no heart for it now, I am so frightened," said Mary sadly. "But get you ready; we must do the best we can."

"You are the only one who can do anything," said little Betsey Wyat, holding her back a moment from the door. They were both silent again as a great peal of laughter sounded from below. Just then the moon came up, clear of the eastern hill, and flooded all the room.

V

The Challenge

"Thou source of all my bliss and all my woe."

An hour later there was a soft night wind blowing through the garden trees, flavored with the salt scent of the tide and the fragrance of the upland pastures and pine woods. Mary Hamilton came alone to a great arched window of the drawing-room. The lights were bright, the house looked eager for its gayeties, and there was a steady sound of voices at the supper, but she put them all behind her with impatience. She stood hesitating for a moment, and then sat down on the broad window seat to breathe the pleasant air. Betsey Wyat in the north parlor was softly touching the notes of some old country song on the spinet.

The young mistress of the house leaned her head wearily on her hand as she looked down the garden terraces to the river. She wished the long evening were at an end, but she must somehow manage to go through its perils and further all the difficult gayeties of the hour. She looked back once into the handsome empty room, and turned again toward the quiet garden. Below, on the second terrace, it was dark with shadows; there were some huge plants of box that stood solid and black, while the rosebushes and young peach-trees were but a gray mist of twigs. At the end of the terrace were some thick lilacs with a few leaves still clinging in the mild weather to shelter a man who stood there, watching Mary Hamilton as she watched the shadows and the brightening river.

There was the sharp crying of a violin from the slaves' dwellings over beyond the house. It was plain to any person of experience that the brief time of rest and informality after the evening feast would soon be over, and that the dancing was about to begin. The call of the fiddle seemed to have been heard not only through the house, but in all its neighborhood. There were voices coming down the hill and a rowboat rounding the point with a merry party. From the rooms above, gay voices helped to break the silence, while the last touches were being given to high-dressed heads and gay-colored evening gowns. But Mary Hamilton did not move until she saw a tall figure step out from among the lilacs into the white moonlight and come quickly along the lower

SARAH ORNE JEWETT

terrace and up the steps toward the window where she was sitting. It was Mr. Roger Wallingford.

"I must speak with you," said he, forgetting to speak softly in his eagerness. "I waited for a minute to be sure there was nobody with you; I am in no trim to make one of your gay company to-night. Quick, Mary; I must speak to you alone!"

The girl had started as one does when a face comes suddenly out of the dark. She stood up and pushed away the curtain for a moment and looked behind her, then shrank into a deep alcove at the side, within the arch. She stepped forward next moment, and held the window-sill with one hand as if she feared to let go her hold. The young man bent his head and kissed her tense fingers.

"I cannot talk with you now. You are sure to be found here; I hoped that you were still in Portsmouth. Go,—it is your only safety to go away!" she protested.

"What has happened? Oh, come out to me for a moment, Mary," he answered, speaking quietly enough, but with much insistence in his imploring tone. "I must see you to-night; it is my only chance."

She nodded and warned him back, and tossed aside the curtain, turning again toward the lighted room, where sudden footsteps had startled her.

There were several guests coming in, a little perplexed, to seek their hostess, but the slight figure of Captain Paul Jones in his brilliant uniform was first at hand. The fair head turned toward him not without eagerness, and the watcher outside saw his lady smile and go readily away. It was hard enough to have patience outside in the moonlight night, until the first country dances could reach their weary end. He stood for a moment full in the light that shone from the window, his heart beating within him in heavy strokes, and then, as if there were no need of prudence, went straight along the terrace to the broad grassy court at the house's front. There was a white balustrade along the farther side, at the steep edge of the bank, and he passed the end of it and went a few steps down. The river shone below under the elms, the tide was just at the beginning of its full flood, there was a short hour at best before the ebb. Roger Wallingford folded his arms, and stood waiting with what plain patience he could gather. The shrill music jarred harshly upon his ear.

The dancing went on; there were gay girls enough, but little Betsey Wyat, that dear and happy heart, had only solemn old Jack Hamilton to her partner, and pretty Martha Hill was coquetting with the venerable judge. These were also the works of war, and some of the poor lads who had left their ladies, to fight for the rights of the colonies, would never again tread a measure in the great room at Hamilton's. Perhaps Roger Wallingford himself might not take his place at the dancing any more. He walked to and fro with his eyes ever upon the doorway, and two by two the company came in turn to stand there and to look out upon the broad river and the moon. The fiddles had a trivial sound, and the slow night breeze and the heavy monotone of the falls mocked at them, while from far down the river there came a cry of herons disturbed in their early sleep about the fishing weirs, and the mocking laughter of a loon. Nature seemed to be looking on contemptuously at the silly pleasantries of men. Nature was aware of graver things than fiddles and the dance; it seemed that night as if the time for such childish follies had passed forever from the earth.

There must have been many a moment when Mary Hamilton could have slipped away, and a cold impatience vexed the watcher's heart. At last, looking up toward the bright house, his eyes were held by a light figure that was coming round from the courtyard that lay between the house and its long row of outbuildings. He was quickly up the bank, but the figure had already flitted across the open space a little way beyond.

"Roger!" he heard her call to him. "Where are you?" and he hurried along the bank to meet her.

"Let us go farther down," she said sharply; "they may find us if they come straying out between the dances to see the moon;" and she passed him quickly, running down the bank and out beyond the edge of the elm-trees' shadow to the great rock that broke the curving shore. Here she stood and faced him, against the wide background of the river; her dress glimmered strangely white, and he could see the bright paste buckle in one of her dancing-shoes as the moonlight touched her. He came a step nearer, perplexed by such silence and unwonted coldness, but waited for her to speak, though he had begged this moment for his own errand.

"What do you want, Roger?" she asked impatiently; but the young man could not see that she was pressing both hands against her heart. She was out of breath and excited as she never had been before, but she stood there insistent as he, and held herself remote in dignity from their every-day ease and life-long habit of companionship.

"Oh, Mary!" said young Roger, his voice breaking with the uncertainty of his sorrow, "have you no kind word for me? I have had a terrible day in Portsmouth, and I came to tell you;" but still she did not speak, and he hung his head.

"Forgive me, dear," he said, "I do not understand you; but whatever it is, forgive me, so we may be friends again."

"I forgive you," said the girl. "How is it with your own conscience; can you find it so easy to forgive yourself?"

"I am ashamed of nothing," said Wallingford, and he lifted his handsome head proudly and gazed at her in wonder. "But tell me my fault, and I shall do my best to mend. Perhaps a man in such love and trouble as I"—

"You shall not speak to me of love," said Mary Hamilton, drawing back; then she came nearer with a reckless step, as if to show him how little she thought of his presence. "You are bringing sorrow and danger to those who should count upon your manliness. In another hour your mother's house may be in flames. Do not speak to me of your poor scruples any more; and as for love"—

"But it is all I have to say!" pleaded the young man. "It is all my life and thought! I do not know what you mean by these wild tales of danger. I am not going to be driven away from my rights; I must stand my own ground."

"Give me some proof that you are your country's friend and not her foe. I am tired of the old arguments! I am the last to have you cry upon patriotism because you are afraid. I cannot tell you all I know, but, indeed, there is danger; I beg you to declare yourself now; this very night! Oh, Roger, *it is the only way!*" and Mary could speak no more. She was trembling with fright and passion; something shook her so that she could hardly give sound to her voice; all her usual steadiness was gone.

"My love has come to be the whole of life," said Roger Wallingford slowly. "I am here to show you how much I love you, though you think that I have been putting you to shame. All day I have been closeted with Mr. Langdon and his officers in Portsmouth. I have told them the truth, that my heart and my principles were all against this war, and I would not be driven by any man living; but I have come to see that since there is a war and a division my place is with my countrymen. Listen, dear! I shall take your challenge since you throw it down," and his face grew hard and pale. "I am going to sail on board the Ranger, and she sails to-morrow. There was a commission still in Mr. Langdon's hands, and he gave it me, though your noble captain took it upon himself to object. I have been ready to give it up at every step when I was alone again, riding home from Portsmouth; I could not beg any man's permission, and we parted in a heat. Now I go to say farewell to my poor mother, and I fear 't will break her heart. I can even make my peace with the commander, if it is your pleasure. Will this prove to you that I am a true American? I came to tell you this."

"To-morrow, to sail on board the Ranger," she repeated under her breath. She gave a strange sigh of relief, and looked up at the lighted house as if she were dreaming. Then a thought came over her and turned her sick with dread. If Paul Jones should refuse; if he should say that he dared not risk the presence of a man who was believed to be so close to the Tory plots! The very necessities of danger must hold her resolute while she shrank, womanlike, from the harsh immediateness of decision. For if Paul Jones should refuse this officer, and being in power should turn him back at the very last, there lay ready the awful opportunity of the mob, and Roger Wallingford was a ruined man and an exile from that time.

"You shall not give one thought to that adventurer!" cried the angry lover, whose quick instinct knew where Mary's thoughts had gone. "He has boldness enough, but only for his own advance. He makes light jokes of those"—

"Stop; I must hear no more!" said the young queen coldly. "It would ill befit you now. Farewell for the present; I go to speak with the captain. I have duties to my guests;" but the tears shone in her eyes. She was for flitting past him like a fawn, as they climbed the high bank together. The pebbles rattled down under their hurrying feet, and the dry elm twigs snapped as if with fire, but Wallingford kept close at her side.

"Oh, my darling!" he said, and his changed voice easily enough touched her heart and made her stand still. "Do not forgive me, then, until you have better reason to trust me. Only do not say that I must never speak. We may be together now for the last time; I may never see you again."

"If you can bear you like a man, if you can take a man's brave part"— and again her voice fell silent.

"Then I may come?"

"Then you may come, Mr. Wallingford," she answered proudly.

For one moment his heart was warm with the happiness of hope,— she herself stood irresolute,—but they heard heavy footsteps, and she was gone from his vision like a flash of light.

Then the pain and seizure of his fate were upon him, the break with his old life and all its conditions. Love would now walk ever by his side, though Mary Hamilton herself had gone. She had not even given him her dear hand at parting.

VI

THE CAPTAIN SPEAKS

"The Hous of Fame to descrive,—
Thou shalt see me go as blyve
Unto the next laure I see
And kisse it, for it is thy tree."

A t this moment the drawing-room was lively enough, whatever anxieties might have been known under the elms, and two deep-arched windows on either side of the great fireplace were filled with ladies who looked on at the dancing. A fine group of elderly gentlewomen, dressed in the highest French fashion of five years back, sat together, with nodding turbans and swaying fans, and faced the doorway as Miss Hamilton came in. They had begun to comment upon her absence, but something could be forgiven a young hostess who might be having a thoughtful eye to her trays of refreshment.

There was still an anxious look on many faces, as if this show of finery and gayety were out of keeping with the country's sad distresses. Though Hamilton, like Nero, fiddled while Rome was burning, everybody had come to look on: the surrender of Burgoyne had put new heart into everybody, and the evening was a pleasant relief to the dark apprehension and cheerless economies of many lives. Most persons were rich in anticipation of the success of Paul Jones's enterprise; as if he were a sort of lucky lottery in which every one was sure of a handsome prize. The winning of large prize money in the capture of richly laden British vessels had already been a very heartening incident of this most difficult and dreary time of war.

When Mary Hamilton came in, there happened to be a pause between the dances, and an instant murmur of delight ran from chair to chair of those who were seated about the room. She had looked pale and downcast in the early evening, but was rosy-cheeked now, and there was a new light in her eyes; it seemed as if the charm of her beauty had never shone so bright. She crossed the open space of the floor, unconscious as a child, and Captain Paul Jones stepped out to meet her. The pink brocaded flowers of her shimmering satin gown bloomed the better for the evening air, and a fall of splendid lace of a light, frosty pattern only half hid her white throat. It was her brother's pleasure to command such marvels of French gowns, and to send orders by his captains for Mary's adorning; she was part of the splendor of his house, moreover, and his heart was filled with perfect satisfaction as she went down the room.

The simpler figures of the first dances were over, the country dances and reels, and now Mr. Lord and Miss Betsey Wyat took their places with Mary and the captain, and made their courtesies at the beginning of an old French dance of great elegance which was known to be the favorite of the old Judge. They stood before him in a pretty row, like courtiers who would offer pleasure to their rightful king, and made their obeisance, all living color and fine clothes and affectionate intent. The captain was scarcely so tall as his partner, but gallant enough in his uniform, and took his steps with beautiful grace and the least fling of carelessness, while Mr. John Lord moved with the precision of a French abbé, always responsible for outward decorum whatever might be the fire within his heart.

The captain was taking his fill of pleasure for once; he had danced many a time with Mary Hamilton, that spring, in the great houses of Portsmouth and York, and still oftener here in Berwick, where he had never felt his hostess so charming or so approachable as to-night. At last, when the music stopped, they left the room together, while their companions were still blushing at so much applause, and went out through the crowded hall. There was a cry of admiration as they passed among the guests; they were carried on the swift current of this evident delight and their own excitement. It is easy for any girl to make a hero of a gallant sailor,—for any girl who is wholly a patriot at heart to do honor to the cordial ally of her country.

They walked together out of the south door, where Mary had so lately entered alone, and went across the broad terrace to the balustrade which overhung the steep bank of the river. Mary Hamilton was most exquisite to see in the moonlight; her dress softened and shimmered the more, and her eyes had a brightness now that was lost in the lighted room. The captain was always a man of impulse; in one moment more he could have dared to kiss the face that shone, eager, warm, and blooming like a flower, close to his own. He was not unskilled in love-making, but he had never been so fettered by the spell of love itself or the royalty of beauty as he was that night.

"This air is very sweet after an arduous day," said he, looking up for an instant through the elm boughs to the moon.

"You must be much fatigued, Sir Captain," said Mary kindly; she looked at the moon longer than he, but looked at him at last.

"'No, noble mistress, 't is fresh morning with me,'" he answered gently, and added the rest of the lovely words under his breath, as if he said them only to himself.

"I think that you will never have any mistress save Glory," said Mary. She knew The Tempest, too; but this brave little man, this world-circling sailor, what Calibans and Ariels might he not have known!

"This is my last night on land," he answered, with affecting directness. "Will you bid me go my lonely way unblest, or shall I dare to say what is in my heart now, my dear and noble mistress?"

Mary looked at him with most straightforward earnestness as he spoke; there was so great a force in her shining eyes that this time it was his own that turned away.

"Will you do a great kindness, if I ask you now?" she begged him; and he promised with his hand upon his heart.

"You sail to-morrow?"

"Yes, and your image shall go always with me, and smile at me in a thousand gloomy hours. I am often a sad and lonely man upon the sea."

"There has been talk of Mr. Wallingford's taking the last commission."

"How have you learned what only a few trusted men were told?" the captain demanded fiercely, forgetting his play of lover in a jealous guarding of high affairs.

"I know, and by no man's wrongful betraying. I give you my deepest proof of friendship now," said the eager girl. "I ask now if you will befriend our neighbor, my dear friend and playmate in childhood. He has been much misjudged and has come to stand in danger, with his dear mother whom I love almost as my own."

"Not your young rascal of a Tory!" the captain interrupted, in a towering rage. "I know him to be a rascal and a spy, madam!"

"A loyal gentleman I believe him in my heart," said Mary proudly, but she took a step backward as they faced each other,—"a loyal gentleman who will serve our cause with entire devotion since he gives his word. His hesitations have been the fault of his advisers, old men who cannot but hold to early prejudice and narrow views. With you at sea, his own right instincts must be confirmed; he will serve his country well. I come to you to beg from my very heart that you will stand his friend."

She stood waiting for assurance: there was a lovely smile on her face; it would be like refusing some easy benefaction to a child. Mary Hamilton knew her country's troubles, great and small; she had listened to the most serious plans and secret conferences at her brother's side: but the captain forgot all this, and only hated to crush so innocent a childish hope. He also moved a step backward, with an impatient gesture; she did not know what she was asking; then, still looking at her, he drew nearer than before. The captain was a man of quick decisions. He put his arm about her as if she were a child indeed. She shrank from this, but stood still and waited for him to speak.

"My dear," he said, speaking eagerly, so that she must listen and would not draw away, "my dear, you ask an almost impossible thing; you should see that a suspected man were better left ashore, on such a voyage as this. Do you not discern that he may even turn my crew against me? He has been the young squire and benefactor of a good third of my men, and can you not see that I must always be on my guard?"

"But we must not distrust his word," begged Mary again, a little shaken.

"I have followed the sea, boy and man, since I was twelve years old. I have been a seafarer all my days," said Paul Jones. "I know all the sad experiences of human nature that a man may learn. I trust no man in war and danger and these days of self-advancement, so far that I am not always on the alert against treachery. Too many have failed me whom I counted my sure friends. I am going out now, only half trusted here at home, to the coasts where treason can hurt me most. I myself am still a suspected and envied man by those beneath me. I am given only this poor ship, after many generous promises. I fear a curse goes with it."

"You shall have our hopes and prayers," faltered Mary, with a quivering lip. The bitterness of his speech moved her deepest feelings; she was overstrung, and she was but a girl, and they stood in the moonlight together.

"Do not ask me again what I must only deny you, even in this happy moment of nearness," he said sadly, and watched her face fall and all the light go out of it. He knew all that she knew, and even more, of Wallingford's dangerous position, and pitied her for a single moment with all the pity that belonged to his heart. A lonely man, solitary in his very nature, and always foreboding with a kind of hopelessness the sorrows that must fall to him by reason of an unkindness that his nature stirred in the hearts of his fellows, his very soul had lain bare to her trusting look.

He stood there for one moment self-arraigned before Mary Hamilton, and knowing that what he lacked was love. He was the captain of the Ranger; it was true that Glory was his mistress. In that moment the heavens had opened, and his own hand had shut the gates.

The smile came back to Mary's face, so strange a flash of tenderness had brightened his own. When that unforgettable light went out, she did not know that all the jealousy of a lonely heart began to burn within him.

"I have changed my mind. I will take your friend," he said suddenly, with a new tone of authority and coldness. "And I shall endeavor to remember that he is your friend. May I win your faith and patience, 't is a hard ploy."

Then Mary, of her own accord, put her hand into the captain's and he bent and kissed it.

"I shall watch a star in the sky for you every night," she told him, "and say my prayers for the Ranger till you come sailing home."

"God grant I may tread the deck of another and a better ship," said the captain hastily. Now he was himself again, and again they both heard the music in the house.

"Will you keep this ring for me, and give me yours?" he asked. "'T will be but a talisman to keep me to my best. I am humble, and I ask no more."

"No," said the girl, whose awakened feeling assured her of his own. She was light-headed with happiness; she could have thrown herself into the arms of such a hero,—of a man so noble, who had done a hard and unwelcome thing for her poor asking. She had failed to do him rightful honor until now, and this beautiful kindness was his revenge. "No," she entreated him, "not your own ring; you have done too much for me; but if you wish it, I shall give you mine. 'T is but a poor ring when you have done so great a kindness."

She gave it as a child might give away a treasure; not as a woman gives, who loves and gives a ring for token. The captain sighed; being no victor after all, his face grew sombre. He must try what a great conqueror might do when he came back next year with Glory all his own; and yet again he lingered to plead with her once more.

"Dear Mary," he said, as he lifted her hand again, "you will not forget me? I shall be far from this to-morrow night, and you will remember that a wanderer like me must sometimes be cruel to his own heart, and cold to the one woman he truly loves."

Something stirred now in Mary Hamilton's breast that had always slept before, and, frightened and disturbed, she drew her hand away. She was like a snared bird that he could have pinched to death a moment before: now a fury of disappointment possessed him, for she was as far away as if she had flown into the open sky beyond his reach.

"Glory is your mistress; it is Glory whom you must win," she whispered, thinking to comfort him.

"When I come back," he said sadly, "if I come back, I hope that you will have a welcome for me." He spoke formally now, and there was a haggard look upon his face. There had come into his heart a strange longing to forget ambition. The thought of his past had strangely afflicted him in that clear moment of life and vision; but the light faded, the dark current of his life flowed on, and there was no reflection upon it of Mary Hamilton's sweet eyes. "If I carry that cursed young Tory away to sea," he said to himself, "I shall know where he is; not here, at any rate, to have this angel for his asking!"

They were on their way to the house again.

"Alas," said Paul Jones once more, with a sad bitterness in his voice, "a home like this can never be for me: the Fates are my enemies; let us hope 't is for the happiness of others that they lure me on!"

Mary cast a piteous, appealing glance at this lonely hero. He was no more the Sea Wolf or the chief among pleasure-makers ashore, but an unloved, unloving man, conscious of heavy burdens and vexed by his very dreams. At least he could remember this last kindness and her grateful heart.

COLONEL HAMILTON WAS STANDING IN the wide hall with a group of friends about him. Old Cæsar and his underservants were busy with some heavy-laden silver trays. The captain approached his host with outstretched hands, to speak his farewells.

"I must be off, gentlemen. I must take my boat," said he, in a manly tone that was heard and repeated along the rooms. It brought many of the company to their feet and to surround him, with a new sense of his high commission and authority. "I ask again for your kind wishes, Colonel Hamilton, and yours, Mr. Justice, and for your blessing on my voyage, reverend sir;" and saluting those of the elder ladies who had been most kind, and kissing his hand to some younger friends and partners of the dance, he turned to go. Then, with his fine laced hat in hand, the captain waved for silence and hushed the friendly voices that would speak a last word of confidence in his high success.

"These friends of his and mine who are assembled here should know that your neighbor, Mr. Wallingford, sails with me in the morning. I count my crew well, now, from your noble river! Farewell, dear ladies; farewell, my good friends and gentlemen."

There was a sudden shout in the hushed house, and a loud murmur of talk among the guests, and Hamilton himself stepped forward and began to speak excitedly; but the captain stayed for neither question nor answer, and they saw him go away hurriedly, bowing stiffly to either hand on his way toward the door. Mary had been standing there, with a proud smile and gentle dignity in her look of attendance, since they had come in together, and he stopped one moment more to take her hand with a low and formal bow, to lift it to his lips, and give one quick regretful look at her happy face. Then Hamilton and some of the younger men followed him down through the gardens to the boat landing. The fleet tide of the river was setting seaward; the captain's boat swept quickly out from shore, and the oars flashed away in the moonlight. There were ladies on the terrace, and on the broad lookout of the housetop within the high railing; there were rounds upon rounds of cheers from the men who stood on the shore, black and white together. The captain turned once when he was well out into the river bay and waved his hand. It was as if the spectators were standing on the edge of a great future, to bid a hero hail and farewell.

The whole countryside was awake and busy in the moonlight. So late at night as this there were lights still shining in one low farmhouse after another, as the captain went away. The large new boat of the Ranger was rowed by man-of-war's men in trim rig, who were leaving their homes on the river shores for perhaps the last time; a second boat was to join them at Stiles's Cove, heaped with sea chests and sailors' bags. The great stream lay shining and still under the moon, a glorious track of light lay ready to lead them on, and the dark pines stood high on the eastern shore to watch them pass. The little captain, wrapped in his boat cloak, sat thoughtful and gloomy at the stern. The gold lace glittered on his hat, and the new flag trailed aft. This was the first reach of a voyage that would go down in history. He was not familiar with many of his men, but in this hour he saw their young faces before him, and remembered his own going from home. The Scottish bay of Carsethom, the laird's house at Arbigland, the far heights of the Cumberland coast, rose again to the vision of a hopeful young adventurer to Virginia and the southern seas.

They could still hear the music, faint and far away; perhaps the girls were dancing again, and not weeping for poor Jack, the sailor; but as the men pulled at their oars, light in the channel's flow, and looked back at the bright house, they saw a fire shining on the shore at Hamilton's. Word had been passed that the captain was going down; the crowd had gathered again; they were cheering like mad, and the boys in the boat yelled themselves hoarse, while some one drifting in a skiff near by fired a heavy pistol, which roused all the river birds and echoed in the river pines from shore to shore. Huzza! they were bringing refuse from the shipyard now, and piling it on the flame! The bonfire towered high, and lighted the shipping and the reefed sails of the gundalows. The steep roof of the house with its high dormer windows, the leafless elms, were all like glowing gold against the blue height of the sky. The eagles waked, and flew crying above the river in the strange light. Somebody was swinging a lantern from the roof of Hamilton house, and then there came a light to an upper window that had been dark before, and another, and another, till all the great house was lit and seemed to tower into the skies. The boat's crew leaned upon their oars, drifting and losing way as they tried to shout back. It cheered their brave hearts, and sent them gayly on their dark journey; a moment before they had thought heavily that some could play and dance ashore while others must go off into the night, leaving all but the thought of Glory behind them.

The whole river country was up. The old Piscataqua plantations had not been so stirred since the news came, many months before, of the peril of Boston and the fight at Lexington, when a company had started from Saco and marched across country, gathering like a rolling snowball on its way, and with Eben Sullivan and Nathan Lord's Berwick men had reached the great Bunker Hill fight in good season. Captain Moulton's company had taken the post road out of old York to join them; there was running to and fro in the country then, and a frenzy of haste, of bawling orders, of piteous leavetakings, of noisy drums and fifes and all the confusion of war. But this was felt to be almost as great a moment, and to mark a still bolder challenge to the foreign foe. There were bonfires on all the river points, and hardly a farmer whose beacon did not answer to his neighbor's. There were shadowy groups of women standing on the high banks against the dim sky, and crying shrill farewells to the boys in the boats: "God speed the Ranger! God bless you, Captain Paul!" and one voice after another took up the cry. "Good-by, boys! Good-by, boys!" they heard the girls calling after them all down the river, and saw new firelights brighten as they came.

The boat now felt the swift seagoing current more and more; they had passed High Point and the Devil's Reach and the old Hodgdon Farm and the mouth of Dover River, and at Hodgdon's Landing they had taken off young Humphry Lord with his little chest, and his mother's tears wet upon his coat; they swept faster still down past Dover Point and the mouth of Great Bay, where a new current caught them again like a mill race. The fires were bright along the Kittery shore, and the sound of old Portsmouth bells came up along the water, and soon they saw the lights at Rice's Ferry and all the leafless forest of idle shipping, and came at last to the dark crank-looking hull of the Ranger lying in midstream.

VII

The Sailing of the Ranger

*"Go you with your Don Quixote to your adventures, and leave us to
our ill fortunes! God will better them for us if we deserve it!"*

It was a gray, cold morning, windy and wet after the mild southerly airs of the night before. When the day broke and the heavy clouds changed to a paler hue, there were already many persons to be seen waiting on the Portsmouth wharves. There was a subdued excitement as the crowd gathered, and the hull and heavy spars of the Ranger out in the gray river were hardly imposing enough to be the centre of such general interest. She might have been one of the less noticeable merchantmen of that busy port, well used to its tugging tides and racing currents, and looked like a clumsy trading-vessel, until one came near enough to see that she was built with a gun deck, and that her ports were the many shrewd eyes of a warship, bent upon aggression as well as defense.

At that early hour there was a continual coming and going between the frigate and the shore, and an ever increasing cluster of boats surrounded her. There was loud shouting on the river and from the pier heads, and now and then a round of cheers from some excited portion of the admiring multitude. There were sad partings between the sailors and their wives and mothers at the water's edge, and there were sudden gusts of laughter among the idle lookers-on. The people had come out of the houses on Badger's Island, while from Newington and upper Kittery the wherries were coming down in a hurry, most of them strongly rowed by women with the short cross-handed stroke that jerked such boats steadily ahead against the wind, or through any river tide or set of current. The old market women bound for the Spring Market in Portsmouth, with their autumn freight of geese and chickens and high-priced eggs, rested on their crossed oars, and waited in midstream to see what came of this great excitement. Though they might be late to catch the best of their early traffic, some of them drove a thriving trade, and their hard red apples were tossed from boat to boat by rollicking customers, while those that missed their aim went bobbing, gay and shining on the cold water, out to sea.

The tide had now turned, and the noise of voices grew louder; there was a cold waft of air from the rising northerly wind, and suddenly everybody heard a shrill whistle on the ship and a cheer, and there was a yell from the tangled boats, before those on shore could see that the Ranger's men were lying out along the yards, and her sails were being spread. Then there were cheers indeed; then there were handkerchiefs and hats a-waving; then every boy and every man who wished in his heart to go and fight Great Britain on her own coasts split his throat with trying to cheer louder than the rest, while even those who had counseled prudence and delay felt the natural joy of seeing a great ship spread her wings to go to sea.

Almost every man and woman who looked on knew some lad or man who was sailing, and now there was great shouting and running near the slip where a last boat was putting off in haste. There was a young man aboard her, and many persons of dignity and position were bidding him farewell. The cheering grew louder; at that moment the slow bells began to ring in St. John's steeple and the old North Church; there was not a man who knew his story who did not honor young Mr. Wallingford for his bold and manly step. Word had been passed that he had taken a commission and was sailing with the rest, but few believed it. He was bound by family ties, he was endangering all future inheritance from old Loyalist relatives who would rather see him in jail than bent upon this thing: the only son of his mother, and she a Tory widow, there were reasons enough to keep any hero back upon the narrow neutral ground that still remained. And Roger Wallingford was not a hero,—only a plain gentleman, with a good heart and steady sense of honor.

He talked soberly with his old friends, and listened to Mr. Langdon's instructions and messages to France, and put some thick letters safely into the pockets of his uniform, which, having been made on a venture, with those for other officers, fitted him but awkwardly. As he stood in the boat nearing the frigate's side, there could hardly be a more gallant-looking fellow of his age. There was in his face all the high breeding and character of his house, with much personal courage and youthful expectancy. A handsome sword that had been his grandfather's hung heavy from the belt that dragged at his thin waist, and furrowed deep the stiff new cloth of his coat. More than one rough-cheeked market woman, in that bitter morning air, felt an unwonted slackening in her throat, and could not speak, but blessed him over and over in her warm heart, as her tears sprung quick to blur this last sight of young Wallingford going to the wars. Here was a chapter of romance, though some things in the great struggle with England were prosaic enough; there was as much rebellion now against raising men and money as there had ever been against the Stamp Act or the hated duties. The states were trying to excuse themselves, and to extort from one another; the selfish and cold-hearted are ever to be pushed forward to their public duties, and here in Portsmouth the patriots had many a day grown faint-hearted with despair.

The anchor broke ground at last; the Ranger swung free and began to drift; the creak of the cables and the chanty that helped to wind them mingled now with the noise of church bells and the firing of guns on the seaward forts at Newcastle. As Wallingford went up the vessel's side and stepped to the deck, it happened that the Ranger fired her own parting gun, and the powder smoke blew thick in his face. When it cleared away he saw the captain close beside him, and made his proper salute. Then he turned quickly for a last glimpse of his friends; the boat was still close under the quarter, and they waved to him and shouted last words that he could not hear. They had been his father's friends, every one,—they wished to be going, too, those good gentlemen; it was a splendid errand, and they were all brave men.

"Mr. Langdon and his friends bade me say to you and to Lieutenant Simpson that they meant to come aboard again, sir; they were sorry to be too late; they would have me take breakfast and wait while they finished these last dispatches which they send you for Mr. Franklin and Mr. Adams. I was late from home; it has been a sudden start for me," said the young man impulsively. "I thank you for your welcome message, which I got at two o'clock by the courier," he added, with a wistful appeal in the friendliness of his tone, as one gentleman might speak with another in such case.

"I had further business with them!" exclaimed the superior officer. "They owed it to me to board me long ago, instead of dallying with your breakfast. Damn your breakfast, Mr. Wallingford!" he said angrily, and turned his back. "I left them and the shore at three in the morning; I have been at my affairs all night. Go below, sir!" he commanded the new lieutenant fiercely. "Now you have no gray-headed pomposities to wait upon and admire you, you had best begin to learn something of your duties. Get you down and fall to work, sir! Go to Simpson for orders!"

Wallingford looked like an icicle under the droop of the great mainsail; he gazed with wonder and pity at the piqued and wearied little man; then his face grew crimson, and, saluting the captain stiffly, he went at once below. There was many a friendly greeting and warm handshake waiting for him between decks, but these could please him little just then; he made his way to the narrow cabin, cluttered and piled high with his sea kit and hasty provisionings, and sat there in the dim light until right-mindedness prevailed. When he came on deck again, they were going out of the lower harbor, with a following wind, straight to sea. He may have gone below a boy, but he came on deck a man.

Sir William Pepperrell's stately gambrel-roofed house, with the deer park and gardens and row of already decaying warehouses, looked drowsy with age on Kittery Point, and opposite, hiding away in Little Harbor, was the rambling, huge old mansion of the Wentworths, with its fine council chamber and handsome card-rooms, where he had danced many a night with the pretty Portsmouth girls. All Roger Wallingford's youth and pleasantries were left behind him now; the summer nights were ended; the winter feasts, if there were any that dreary year, must go on without him. The Isles of Shoals lay ahead like pieces of frozen drift ill the early morning light, and the great sea stretched away to the horizon, bleak and cold and far, a stormy road to France.

The ship, heading out into the waste of water, took a steady movement between wind and wave, and a swinging gait that seemed to deny at every moment the possibility of return. The gray shore sank and narrowed to a line behind her. At last the long blue hill in Northwood and the three hills of Agamenticus were seen like islands, and long before noon these also had sunk behind the waves, and the Ranger was well at sea.

VIII

The Major's Hospitalities

"But see how merciful Heaven sends relief in the greatest distresses,
for now comes Don Gayferos!"

The Haggens house, with its square chimneys, and a broad middle-
aged look of comfort, like those who were sheltered under its
roof, stood facing the whole southern country just where the two
roads joined from the upper settlements. A double stream of travel
and traffic flowed steadily by this well-known corner, toward the upper
and lower landings of the tide river. From the huge square stone that
floored a pointed porch of severely classic design could be seen a fine
sweep of land from the Butlers' Hill on the left, over the high oak
woods of a second height to the deep pasture valleys. Major Hight's
new house and huge sentinel pines stood on a ridge beyond, with the
river itself showing a gleam of silver here and there all along the low
lands toward Portsmouth. Across the country westward was the top
of Garrison Hill at Dover; to the south was the dark pine-forested
region of the Rocky Hills. It was a wide and splendid prospect even on
a bleak autumn day, and Major Haggens, the socially minded master
of the house, was trying hard to enjoy it as he sat in the morning wind,
wrapped in his red cloak and longing for proper companionship. He
cast imploring glances across the way to the habitation of his only
near neighbor, Mr. Rogers, but he could see the old gentleman sitting
fast asleep at that ridiculous hour of the morning, behind a closed
window. There was no one to be seen up the road, where Mr. Jenkins's
place of business was apt to attract the idle, especially in the harvest
time of his famous early apples. These were dull days; before the war
there were few mornings of the year when the broad space before the
major's house lacked either carriages or foot-travelers for half an hour.
In winter the two roads were blocked as far as a man could see with
the long processions of ox teams laden with heavy timber, which had
come from fifty or even a hundred miles back in the north country.
There were hundreds of trees standing yet in the great forests of the
White Hills that were marked with the deeply cut King's arrow, but

the winter snows of many years to come were likely to find these timber pines for the King's shipyards still standing.

The busy, quick-enriching days of the past seemed to be gone forever, and poverty and uncertainty had replaced them. There was no such market anywhere for Berwick timber as England had always been; the Berwick merchants would be prosperous no more; the town must live long now upon their hoarded gains, and then seek for some other means of living. The gay-hearted old major looked downcast, and gave a deep sigh. He had no such remembrance of the earlier wars, when Old England and New England had fought together against a common enemy. Those battles had been exciting enough, and a short and evident path to glory, where his fellow colonists had felt something of the happy certainties of the Old Testament Jews, and went out boldly to hew Agag in pieces and to smite the Amalekites hip and thigh. It appeared now as if, with all its hardships, war had been a not unwelcome relief to a dull level of prosperity and the narrowness of a domestic horizon. War gave a man the pleasures of travel, it was a man's natural business and outlet of energy; but war with moral enemies, and for opinion's sake, lacked the old color, and made the faces of those who stayed at home grow sullen. They were backbiting Hamilton in many a pious household, that morning, for giving a farewell feast to Paul Jones. 'T was all of a piece with Roundhead days, and christening a child by such names as must have depressed Praise-God Barebones, and little Hate-Evil Kilgore who was a neighbor of the major's, down the Landing hill.

The major's sound but lately unpracticed head was a little heavy from the last night's supper, and the world seemed to him badly out of joint. He was a patriot at heart, but one who stood among the moderates. He seemed uneasy in his wooden armchair, and pushed the ferule of his stout old ivory-headed cane angrily into a crevice below one of the Corinthian pillars of the porch. His tall sister, who, by virtue of two years' precedence in age, resolutely maintained the position of superior officer, had already once or twice opened the door behind to advise him to come in out of the cold wind; the chill might very well send him an attack of gout in the stomach.

"I've got no gout to send, nor any stomach to send it to," returned the major angrily. "What's the use of a stomach, when a man can get nothing decent to put into it, and has not even a dog to keep him company? I'd welcome even a tax gatherer!" The great door was shut again with decision enough to clack the oval brass knocker, and the major finished some protests against fate deep in his own disparaged interior, and punctuated his inarticulate grumbles by angry bobs of the head. He was really too cold, but he would not submit to Nancy, or let her think that she could rule him, as she seemed to wish.

Suddenly there was something moving down at the end of the street; it came up quickly over the slope into the full appearance of a horse and rider, and hope filled the major's once sorrowful mind.

"Jack Hamilton, by zounds!" laughed the old gentleman. "He's late on his way up country. I'll stretch a point: we'll make it an hour earlier, and have our toddy now; it must be after ten."

Hamilton presently declared that he was too much belated; he must go to the far regions of Tow-wow, where he owned great tracts of woodland; he really must not vex his conscience by loitering.

"Here, you, Cuffee! here, 'Pollo, you lazy dog!" the major called, merely turning his head, so that his voice might reach round the house through the long yard to his barns; and after a moment's consideration, Hamilton dismounted unwillingly. The gay creature he had ridden sidled away, and whinnied fretfully, as if she also objected to such an interruption of their plans.

"Keep her here; I shall not stop long," said the colonel to a black namesake of the great god Apollo, who was the first to arrive, and, although breathless, began to walk to and fro sentry fashion, as if by automatic impulse. The already heated young mare was nosing his shoulder with an air of intimacy, and nipping at the edge of his frayed hat.

"You'll be just far enough from both dinner and breakfast now," insisted the major, stamping along through the handsome cold hall of the house, with its elaborate panelings of clear, uupainted pine. "You'll get to Tow-wow, or Lebanon, as the new folks want to call it, all the sooner for this delay. You've pounded the first wind out of that colt already; you'd have had her sobbing on Plaisted's Hill. What we can't find in eatables we'll make up in drinkables. Nancy, Nancy, where's my spirit case? You're so precise I never can find anything where I leave it!"

"The case is on the top of the sideboard, directly in the middle, brother Tilly," said Miss Nancy, politely coming out of the room on the right, and looking after him, with her knitting in hand.

Mr. Hamilton turned, and she dropped a somewhat informal curtsy. She wore a plain turban which gave her a severe but most distinguished air. Miss Haggens was quite the great lady, and even more French in her appearance than the major himself.

"I was sorry to miss the gayeties last night," she said. "The major is boyish enough for anything, and can answer every beck and call, but I felt that I must not venture. I was sorry when it proved so fine an evening."

"No becks and calls to answer in these days," insisted the busy host. "'T would do you good, Nancy, as it did all the rest of us. Let's have it in the breakfast-room; I left a good fire there. If there's no hot water, I'll heat some quick enough in a porringer."

Hamilton, following, seated himself slowly in an armchair by the fireplace. The processes of hospitality would be swifter if quietly acquiesced in, and now that the slim decanter of Santa Cruz was opened the odor was not unwelcome. He bad been busy enough since daybreak, but wore an amused look, though somewhat tired and worried, as the major flew about like a captive bumblebee. Miss Nancy's prim turban got shifted over one ear, and one white and two black handmaidens joined her in the course of such important affairs. At last the major reappeared, victorious and irate, with a steaming porringer which had just begun to heat in the kitchen fireplace, and splashed it all the way along the floor. He went down stiffly on his knees in the breakfast-room to blow the coals, with such mighty puffs that a film of ashes at once covered the water and retarded its rise of temperature. Miss Nancy and Colonel Hamilton looked at each other across his broad back and laughed.

"There, there, major! The steam's rising, and 't will do already," urged the colonel. "I'd rather not take my drink too hot, and go out again to face the wind."

"I felt the wind myself," acknowledged the major, looking up pleasantly. "My fore door, where I like to sit, is well sheltered, but I felt the wind." Miss Nancy so far descended from her usual lofty dignity as to make a little face, which Hamilton, being a man, did not exactly understand.

"I like to have the water boiling hot; then you can let it cool away, and the flavor 's well brought out," explained the major. Phoebe, the old slave woman who looked over his shoulder, now pronounced with satisfaction that the water was minnying, with the steam all in it, to which her master agreed. Miss Nancy put out a strong hand and helped him to his feet.

"You've set your turban all awry, sister," the major remarked politely by way of revenge, and the little company burst into a hearty laugh. Miss

Nancy produced a gay china plate of pound cakes from the cupboard, and sat by in silence, discreetly knitting, until the toddy was not only made, but half gone down the gentlemen's throats.

"And so Roger Wallingford's gone to sea, and those who would burn him in his house for a Tory are robbed of a great pleasure," she said at last. "I wonder what their feelings are to-day! My heart aches for his mother; 't will be a deathblow to all her pride."

"It will indeed," said Hamilton seriously.

"I was sore afraid of his joining the other side only yesterday," said the major, "but this news has lain heavy as lead on me all the morning. There are those aboard the Ranger who will only have him for a spy. I heard a whisper of this last night, before we parted. I was even glad to think that the poor boy has plenty of old family friends in England, who can serve him if worst comes to worst."

"'T was in my mind, too," agreed the colonel. "John Lord was hinting at trouble, in my counting-room, this morning early. I fancied him more than half glad on his own account that Wallingford is gone; the lads have looked upon each other as rivals, and I have suspected that 't was Roger who was leading in the race." The colonel's wind-freshened cheeks brightened still more as he spoke, and looked up with an expectant smile at Miss Nancy, who did not reply except by giving two or three solemn nods of her turbaned head.

"Everybody loves the boy," she said presently, "but 't is of his dear mother I am thinking most. 'T is a sad heart alone in her great house to front the winter weather. She told me last week that she had a mind not to make the usual change to her house in town. There were like to be disturbances, and she had no mind for anything but quiet. I shall write, myself, to her young cousins in Boston, or to the Sherburnes, who are near friends, and beg them to visit her; 'tis none so cheerful in Boston either, now. We were always together in our youth, but age makes us poor winter comrades. Sit ye down," said Miss Nancy Haggens affectionately, as Hamilton rose and put by his empty glass. "And how is our dear Mary?" she asked, as she rose also, finding him determined. There was an eager look in the old lady's eyes.

"I have not seen my sister," answered Hamilton, looking grave. "I was very early by the riverside with my old brig Pactolus going downstream, and everything and everybody tardy. I shall lay her up for the winter by Christian Shore; but, as things look now, I fear 't is the last voyage of the good old vessel. I stood and watched her away, and when she made the turn past Pine Point it seemed as if her old topmasts were looking back at me wishfully above the woods."

The major made a sound which was meant for sympathy; he was very warm and peaceful now before the fire.

"My sister will not be long seeking such a friend as you," said Hamilton, with sudden change of tone, and looking at Miss Nancy with an unwonted show of sentiment and concern in his usually impassive face. "I slept but little last night, and my fears, small and great, did not sleep at all. 'T is heavy news from the army, and I am perplexed as to Mary's real feelings. The captain counts upon success; as for the step that Roger Wallingford has taken, it has no doubt averted a very real danger of the moment."

"She must go at once to see his mother. I wish that she might go to-day. You may tell Mary this, with the love of an old friend," said Miss Nancy warningly. "She has great reserve of feeling with all her pretty frankness. But young hearts are not easy reading."

"I must be gone all day," said Hamilton gravely.

For once the major listened and had no opinion ready. All the troubles of life had been lifted in the exercise of such instant hospitality.

"We must leave all to Time," he announced cheerfully. "No man regrets more than I our country's sad situation. And mark ye both: the captain of the Ranger's got all the makings of a hero. Lord bless me," he exclaimed, as he followed Hamilton along the hall, "I could have shed tears as I caught his fire, at thinking I was too old and heavy to ship with him myself! I might be useful yet with his raw marines and in the land attacks. I felt last night, as our talk went on, that I should be as good for soldiering as ever."

"Brother Tilly!" Miss Nancy was crying from the breakfast-room in despair. "Oh, don't go out into the wind, and you so warm with your toddy! Wait, I command you, Tilly! Phoebe's coming with your hat and cloak!" But the old campaigner was already out beyond the lilacs in the front yard, with the rising northwester lifting his gray locks.

SARAH ORNE JEWETT

IX

BROTHER AND SISTER

"All thoughts, all passions, all delights,
Whatever stirs this mortal frame,
All are but ministers of Love,
And feed his sacred flame."

That same afternoon of the first of November, one might have
thought that the adventurers on board the Ranger had taken all
the pleasant weather away with them, and all the pleasure and interest
of life; only endurance and the bleak chilliness of autumn seemed to be
left ashore. The wind changed into the east as night drew on, and a cold
fog, gathered along the coast, came drifting up the river with the tide,
until rain began to fall with the early dark. The poplars and elms looked
shrunken about the gardens at Hamilton's, and the house but ill lighted.
The great rooms themselves were cold and empty.

Colonel Hamilton, gloomy with further bad news from the army on
Long Island, sat alone reviewing some accounts, shaking his head over
a great ledger which had been brought up from the counting-house,
and lay before him on a table in the west room. The large Russian stove
was lighted for the first time that year, and the tiny grate glowed bright
in its tall prison-like front, which was as slow to give out any heat as a
New England winter to give place to spring. The pair of candles gave a
dull yellow light, and the very air of the west room looked misty about
them in a sort of halo, as Mary Hamilton opened the door. She was rosy
with color from an afternoon ride, while her brother looked tired and
dull. All the long day she had been so much in his anxious thoughts that
he glanced over his shoulder with apprehension. In spite of his grave
face and unyielding temper, he had a quick imagination, and, for the
few persons whom he loved, a most tender heart.

To his blank surprise, his young sister had never worn a more
spirited or cheerful look. She was no lovelorn maiden, and had come to
him for neither pity nor anxious confidence. She came instead to stand
close beside him, with a firm warm hand on his shoulder, and smiling
looked into his upturned face.

"Well, sir, have you made the most of a bad day?" she asked, in the tone of comradeship which always went straight to Hamilton's heart, and made him feel like a lover. "They must have had a good offshore wind for many hours," she added before he could answer. "The Ranger must be safe off the coast by this time, and out of this hindering fog."

"She must indeed," answered Hamilton, lending himself comfortably to her mood. "The wind was free all day out of the northwest until this easterly chill at sundown. They will not like to drift in a long calm and easterly fog."

"Come, you look miserable here; you are pale with cold yourself, Jack," she urged kindly. "Let us poke this slow contrivance for a fire! I like to see a broad blaze. Cæsar kept me a fine hoard of pitch-pine roots when they cleared that thicket of the upper pasture, and I made a noble heat with them just now in my own room. I told him to look after your stove here, but he was sulky; he seems to think 't is a volcano in a box, and may wreck the house and all his happiness. See, it was full of ashes at the draught. Sir, may I ask what you are laughing at?"

"I thought you would be like Niobe, all tears," he answered boldly, giving her a half amused, half curious glance. "And here you praise the wind that blows your lover seaward, and make yourself snug ashore."

The firelight flashed in Mary's face at that moment, and something else flashed back to meet it. She was kneeling close to the small iron door, as if she were before a confessional; but she looked over her shoulder for a moment with a quick smile that had great sweetness and power to charm.

"Let us be happy together, my dear," she said. "They go to serve our country; it should be a day for high hopes, and not for mourning. I look for great gallantry on board the Ranger!"

She stood facing her brother a moment later, and looked straight in his face, as if she had no fears of any curious gaze, simply unconscious of self, as if no great shock had touched her heart in either new-found happiness or sense of loss. It seemed as if her cheerful self-possession were putting a bar to all confidence.

"I cannot understand you!" he exclaimed sharply.

"You are cold and tired, my poor old man! Come, I shall have no more figuring," and she slid away the ledger beyond his reach on the smooth polished oak of the table top. "Let us make a bit of hot drink for so cold a man!" and was swiftly gone across the hall to the great kitchen, leaving the doors wide open behind her. It seemed warmer at once, and presently the sound of laughter and a coaxing voice made Hamilton's heart a little gayer. Old Peggy and her young mistress were in the midst of a lively encounter, and presently a noise of open war made him cross the hall with boyish eagerness to see the fray.

Peggy was having a glorious moment of proud resistance, and did not deign to notice the spectator. The combatants stood facing each other in front of the huge fireplace, where there was a high heap of ashes and but faint glow of fire. The old woman's voice was harsh, and she looked pale and desperate; there was always a black day for the household after such a masterpiece of a feast as Peggy had set before her master's guests the night before. The fire of energy was low in her gaunt frame, except for a saving spark that still moved the engines of her tongue. She stood like a thin old Boadicea with arms akimbo, and Mary Hamilton faced her all abloom, with a face full of laughter, and in exactly the same attitude; it was a pleasing sight to Hamilton at the door of the side hall. The usually populous kitchen was deserted of all Peggy's minions except Cæsar, and there were no signs of any preliminaries of even the latest supper.

"Oh, Peggy, what a cross old thing you are!" sighed Mary, at the end of Peggy's remarks upon the text of there being nobody in the house to do anything save herself. "I should really love to stay and have a good battle to warm us up, except that we should both be near to weeping when it was done, and you would be sorrier than you need, and cook something much too nice for supper, tired as you are." Then she dropped her hands and relaxed her mocking pose. "Come, Peggy dear, the colonel's here, and he's ridden the whole length of Beech Ridge and the Tow-wow woods since morning with his surveyors; he's very cold and down-hearted, and I only want a spatter of mulled wine for him. Come, find me a little skillet and we'll heat it here on the coals. See, they're winking bright under that hill of ashes. Where are all the maids?"

"In their beds, I suppose, black and white alike, and getting their first sleep like ladies," grumbled Peggy. "I told them the master would be late, and would sup at Pine Hill, as he said this morning. 'T is no matter about me; Cæsar and me, we're old and tough," and the stern features relaxed a little. "Why did n't you tell me 't was for the master, an' he'd no supper after such a day, with the clock far past seven, and you yourself with nothing but bread and milk to stay you? Truth to tell, I was asleep in the corner of the settle here, and a spark's burnt me a hole in this good apron and spoilt my temper. You have too much patience with poor old Peggy," she muttered, bending over the ashes and raking them open to their bright life with her hard brown hand.

Mary stood watching her for a moment; a quick change came over her face, and she turned away silently, and went toward the window as if to look up the river.

"What was you designin' to get for supper?" old Cæsar humbly inquired at this auspicious moment. "I mought be a-layin' of the table." But Peggy did not notice him. He was still in a place of safety behind the settle, his gray head just appearing over the high back.

"We might finish the pigeon pie," the young mistress suggested; "the colonel will like a bit of cheese afterward and plenty of bread. Mind, Peggy, 'tis only a cold supper!"

"Was you es-pectin' any of the quality aside yo'selves, missy?" politely demanded Cæsar, in the simple exercise of his duty.

"Don't you keep a-askin' questions; 't ain't no way to converse with human creatur's!" said Peggy severely.

"Laws, Peggy, I feels an int'rist!" said poor Cæsar humbly.

"No, you don't neither; you're full to bu'stin' of cur'osity, an' it's a fault that grows by feedin' of it. Let your mind dwell on that, now, next Sabbath mornin' up in your gallery, 'stid o' rollin' your eyes at the meetin' folks an' whisp'rin' with Cato Lord!" and Peggy laughed in spite of herself. "Come out from there, an' fetch me some dry pine chips, if 't won't demean your dignity. I'll ax you some questions you don't know no answers to, if you be an Afriky potentate!"

The master of the house had tiptoed back across the hall like a pleased schoolboy, and was busy with the ledger when his sister came back, a few minutes later, with a steaming porringer. She proceeded to mix a most fragrant potion in a large gayly flowered glass, while Hamilton described his morning entertainment by the major; then an old dog came loitering in, and watched his master enviously, as he drank, and stirred again, and praised the warm drink, and grew every moment more cheerful.

Mary Hamilton stood leaning against the Russian stove. "It is just getting warm now, this dull old idol of yours," she said, "and we cannot cool it before spring. We'll sit in the dining parlor to-night after supper; you shall smoke your pipe there, and I can see the good firelight. We are lonesome after a gay day and night like yesterday; we have had no word of gossip yet about our ball. I have many things to tell you."

Hamilton nodded amiably; the color had come back into his face, and driven away the worn and worried look that had fallen on him before his time. He had made so light of care that care made light of him, and was beginning to weigh his spirit down early in middle life.

"I came across the river at the Great Falls," he said, not without effort, and looking at his young sister, "the roads were so heavy through the woods by Cranberry Meadow."

"So you did n't stop to give Granny Sullivan the money?" asked Mary, as if she were disappointed.

"Yes, on my way this morning. She knew more about last night than I could sweep together to tell her if I had stayed an hour."

"The birds tell granny everything," said Mary, laughing. "She gave me a handsome scolding the other day because Peggy's rack of spiced hams had fallen in the ashes that very morning. How was the master?"

"Very absentminded, and reading his Horace as if the old poet were new. He did not even look up while she thanked me for the money the judge had sent. 'I'm knitting every minute I'm not working or eating, for my poor lame lad Jamie,' she said. 'Now, he has nothing to do but read his law books, an' tell others what's in them, and grow rich! 'T is all because his father's such a gentleman!'"

"How proud she is, the dear old woman!" said Mary warmly.

"Yes, and they have the sense to be proud of her," said Hamilton, settling into his chair more comfortably and putting his empty glass aside.

"I rode to the Rocky Hills myself late this afternoon. I heard that Elder Shackley had been ill. I liked the fresh wind and wet after last night's warmth and a busy morning here in the house. I meant at first to ride north to meet you; but it was better not, since you crossed at the Falls."

"I thought you would go another way," said Hamilton seriously. There were moments when he seemed old enough to be her father; there were, indeed, many years between them. "There is a sad heart and a lonely one across the river to-night, while we seem gay enough together."

Mary's face changed quickly; she stepped toward him, and seated herself on the broad arm of the chair, and drew her brother's head close against her side.

"What is it that you wish to say to me?" she asked. "I have been thinking of dear Madam Wallingford all day long," and Hamilton could feel her young heart beating quick like a bird's, close to his ear.

"She was in my mind, too. I came down that side of the river to see her, but it grew so rainy and late that I gave up my thought of stopping except to leave a message. My mare was very hot and spent," he explained, in a matter-of-fact way. "As I came toward the house I saw my lady standing at a window, and she beckoned me. She came herself to the door, and the wind blew her to and fro like a flag. She had been weeping terribly. 'I longed to see a friend,' she told me, and could say no more... I feared that she might bear us much ill will."

Hamilton was so full of feeling that his own voice failed him, and Mary did not speak at first.

"Well, dear brother?" she asked a moment later, knowing that he had more to say.

"She wished to send you a message; 't was her reason for calling me in. She asked if you would not come to see her to-morrow, late in the afternoon. Earlier she has business of the estate to manage, in place of her son. There are men coming down from the Lake."

"Oh yes, yes, I shall go!" said Mary, with a sob. "Oh, I am so glad; I feared that her heart was broken, and that she would only hate us!"

"I was afraid, too," returned Hamilton, and he took his sister's hand gently in his own, and would have spoken something that she could not bear to hear.

She moved away quickly. "Come, dear man," she said, "you must throw off these muddy clothes; you are warm again now, and they will soon be calling us to supper."

He sighed, and looked at her in bewilderment as he obeyed. She had gone to the window and pushed the shutter back, and was gazing out into the dark night. He looked at her again as he was going out of the room, but still she did not speak. Was it the captain, after all, who had gone away with her heart? She had not even mentioned his name!

She was not always so silent about her lovers; they had been many, and she sometimes spoke frankly enough when he and she were alone together like this, and the troubles and veils of every-day intercourse were all put aside. But who could read a woman's heart? Certainly not a poor bachelor, who had never yet learned to read his own!

SARAH ORNE JEWETT

X

AGAINST WIND AND TIDE

"Whose daughters ye are as long as ye do well and are not afraid with any amazement."

Late the next afternoon Mary Hamilton appeared at the north door of the house, and went quickly down the steep garden side toward the water. In the shallow slip between two large wharves lay some idle rowboats, which belonged to workmen who came every morning from up and down the river. The day's short hurry was nearly over; there was still a noise of heavy adzes hewing at a solid piece of oak timber, but a group of men had begun to cluster about a storehouse door to talk over the day's news.

The tide was going out, and a birch canoe which the young mistress had bespoken was already left high on the shore. She gave no anxious glance for her boatman, but got into a stranded skiff, and, reaching with a strong hand, caught the canoe and dragged it down along the slippery mud until she had it well afloat; then, stepping lightly aboard, took up her carved paddle, and looked before her to mark her course across the swift current. Wind and current and tide were all going seaward together with a determined rush.

There was a heavy gundalow floating down the stream toward the lower warehouse, to be loaded with potatoes for the Portsmouth market, and this was coming across the slip. The men on board gave a warning cry as they caught sight of a slender figure in the fragile craft; but Mary only laughed, and, with sufficient strength to court the emergency, struck her paddle deep into the water and shot out into the channel right across their bow. The current served well to keep her out of reach; the men had been holding back their clumsy great boat lest it should pass the wharf. One of them ran forward anxiously with his long sweep, as if he expected to see the canoe in distress like a drowning fly; but Miss Hamilton, without looking back, was pushing on across the river to gain the eddy on the farther side.

"She might ha' held back a minute; she was liable to be catched an' ploughed right under! A gal's just young enough to do that; men that's met danger don't see no sport in them tricks," grumbled the boatman.

"Some fools would ha' tried to run astarn," said old Mr. Philpot, his companion, "an' the suck o' the water would ha' catched 'em side up ag'in' us; no, she knowed what she was about. Kind of scairt me, though. Look at her set her paddle, strong as a man! Lord, she's a beauty, an' 's good 's they make 'em!"

"Folks all thinks, down our way, she'll take it master hard the way young Wallin'ford went off, 'thout note or warnin'. They've b'en a-hoverin' round all ready to fall to love-makin', till this objection got roused 'bout his favorin' the Tories. There'd b'en trouble a'ready if he'd stayed to home. I misdoubt they'd smoked him out within half a week's time. Some o' them fellows that hangs about Dover Landin' and Christian Shore was bent on it, an' they'd had some better men 'long of 'em."

"Then 't would have been as black a wrong as ever was done on this river!" exclaimed the elder man indignantly, looking back over his shoulder toward the long house of the Wallingfords, that stood peaceful in the autumn sunshine high above the river. "They've been good folks in all their generations. The lad was young, an' had n't formed his mind. As for Madam,—why, women folks is natural Tories; they hold by the past, same as men are fain to reach out and want change. She's feeble and fearful since the judge was taken away, an' can't grope out to nothin' new. I heared tell that one o' her own brothers is different from the rest as all holds by the King, an' has given as much as any man in Boston to carry on this war. There ain't no Loyalist inside my skin, but I despise to see a low lot o' fools think smart o' theirselves for bein' sassy to their betters."

The other man looked a little crestfallen. "There's those as has it that the cap'n o' the Ranger would n't let nobody look at young miss whilst he was by," he hastened to say. "Folks say they're good as promised an' have changed rings. I al'ays heared he was a gre't man for the ladies; loves 'em an' leaves 'em. I knowed men that had sailed with him in times past, an' they said he kept the highest company in every port. But if all tales is true"—

"Mostly they ain't," retorted old Mr. Philpot scornfully.

"I don't know nothin' 't all about it; that's what folks say," answered his mate. "He's got the look of a bold commander, anyway, and a voice an' eye that would wile a bird from a bush." But at this moment the gundalow bumped heavily against the wharf, and there was no more time for general conversation. Mary Hamilton paddled steadily up river in the smooth water of the eddy, now and then working hard to get round some rocky point that bit into the hurrying stream. The wind was driving the ebbing tide before it, so that the water had fallen quickly, and sometimes the still dripping boughs of overhanging alders and oaks swept the canoe from end to end, and spattered the kneeling girl with a cold shower by way of greeting. Sometimes a musquash splashed into the water or scuttled into his chilly hole under the bank, clattering an untidy heap of empty mussel shells as he went. All the shy little beasts, weasels and minks and squirrels, made haste to disappear before this harmless voyager, and came back again as she passed. The great fishhawks and crows sailed high overhead, secure but curious, and harder for civilization to dispossess of their rights than wild creatures that lived aground.

The air was dry and sweet, as if snow were coming, and all the falling leaves were down. Here and there might linger a tuft of latest frost flowers in a sheltered place, and the witch-hazel in the thickets was still sprinkled with bright bloom. Mary stopped once under the shore where a bough of this strange, spring-in-autumn flower grew over the water, and broke some twigs to lay gently before her in the canoe. The old Indian, last descendant of the chief Passaconaway, who had made the light craft and taught her to guide it, had taught her many other things of his wild and wise inheritance. This flower of mystery brought up deep associations with that gentle-hearted old friend, the child of savagery and a shadowy past.

The river broadened now at Madam's Cove. There was a great roaring in the main channel beyond, where the river was vexed by rocky falls; inside the cove there was little water left except in the straight channel that led to the landing-place and quaint heavy-timbered boat-house. From the shore a grassy avenue went winding up to the house above. Against the northwestern sky the old home of the Wallingfords looked sad and lonely; its windows were like anxious eyes that followed the river's course toward a dark sea where its master had gone adventuring.

Mary stood on land, looking back the way she had come; her heart was beating fast, but it was not from any effort of fighting against wind or tide. She did not know why she began to remember with strange vividness the solemn pageant of Judge Wallingford's funeral, which had followed the water highway from Portsmouth, one summer evening, on the flood tide. It was only six years before, when she was already the young and anxious mistress of her brother's house, careful and troubled about many things like Martha, in spite of her gentler name. She had looked out of an upper window to see the black procession of boats with slow-moving oars come curving and winding across the bay; the muffled black of mourning trailed from the sides; there were soldiers of the judge's regiment, sitting straight in their bright uniforms, for pallbearers, and they sounded a solemn tap of drum as they came.

They drew nearer: the large coffin with its tasseled pall, the long train of boats which followed filled with sorrowing friends,—the President of the Province and many of the chief men,—had all passed slowly by.

The tears rushed to Mary's eyes, that day, when she saw her brother's serious young head among the elder gentlemen, and close beside him was the fair tear-reddened face and blond uncovered hair of the fatherless son. Roger Wallingford was but a boy then; his father had been the kind friend and generous founder of all her brother's fortunes. She remembered how she had thanked him from a grateful heart, and meant to be unsparing in her service and unfailing in duty toward the good man's widow and son. They had read prayers for him in the Queen's Chapel at Portsmouth; they were but bringing him to his own plot of ground in Somersworth, at eventide, and Mary Hamilton prayed for him out of a full heart as his funeral went by. The color came in her young cheeks at the remembrance. What had she dared to do, what responsibility had she not taken upon her now? She was but an ignorant girl, and driven by the whip of Fate. A strange enthusiasm, for which she could not in this dark moment defend herself, had led her on. It was like the moment of helpless agony that comes with a bad dream.

She turned again and faced the house; and the house, like a great conscious creature on the hillside, seemed to wait for her quietly and with patience. She was standing on Wallingford's ground, and bent upon a most difficult errand. There was neither any wish for escape, in her heart, nor any thought of it, and yet for one moment she trembled as if the wind shook her as it shook the naked trees. Then she went her way, young and strong-footed, up the long slope. It was one of the strange symbolic correspondences of life that her path led steadily up the hill.

THE GREAT DOOR OF THE house opened wide before her, as if the whole future must have room to enter; old Rodney, the chief house servant, stood within, as if he had been watching for succor. In the

SARAH ORNE JEWETT

spacious hall the portraits looked proud and serene, as if they were still capable of all hospitalities save that of speech.

"Will you say that Miss Hamilton waits upon Madam Wallingford?" said Mary; and the white-headed old man bowed with much ceremony, and went up the broad stairway, still nodding, and pausing once, with his hand on the high banister, to look back at so spirited and beautiful a guest. A faithful heart ached within him to see her look so young, so fresh-blooming, so untouched by sorrow, and to think of his stricken mistress. Yet she had come into the chilly house like a brave, warm reassurance, and all Rodney's resentment was swift to fade. The quick instincts of his race were confronted by something that had power to master them; he comprehended the truth because it was a simple truth and his was a simple heart.

He disappeared at the turn of the staircase into the upper hall, and Mary took a few impatient steps to and fro. On the great moose antlers was flung some of the young master's riding gear; there was his rack of whips below, and a pair of leather gloves with his own firm grasp still showing in the rounded fingers. There were his rods and guns; even his old dog leash and the silver whistle. She knew them all as well as he, with their significance of past activities and the joys of life and combat. They made their owner seem so close at hand, and the pleasures of his youth all snatched away. Oh, what a sharp longing for the old lively companionship was in her heart! It was like knowing that poor Roger was dead instead of gone away to sea. He would come no more in the winter evenings to tell his hunter's tales of what had happened at the lakes, or to plan a snowshoe journey up the country. Mary stamped her foot impatiently; was she going to fall into helpless weakness now, when she had most need to be quiet and to keep her steadiness? Old Rodney was stepping carefully down the stairs again; she wore a paler look than when they had parted. Somehow, she felt like a stranger in the familiar house.

Once Rodney would have been a mere reflection of his mistress's ready welcome, but now he came close to Miss Hamilton's side and spoke in an anxious whisper.

"You'll be monst'ous gentle to her dis day, young mistis?" he asked pleadingly. "Oh yis, mistis; her heart's done broke!"

Then he shuffled away to the dining-room to move the tankards on the great sideboard. One could feel everything, but an old black man, born in the jungle and stolen by a slaver's crew, knew when he had said enough.

XI

THAT TIME OF YEAR

"Come, Sorrow! put thy sweet arms round my neck,
For none are left to do this, only thou."

The low afternoon sun slanted its rays into the stately chamber, and brightened the dull East Indian red of some old pictured cottons that made the tasseled hangings. There were glowing coals in the deep fireplace, and Madam Wallingford sat at the left, in one of those great easy-chairs that seem to offer refuge to both illness and sorrow. She had turned away so that she could not see the river, and even the wistful sunshine was all behind her. There was a slender light-stand with some white knitting-work at her side, but her hands were lying idle in her lap. She had never been called beautiful; she had no great learning, though on a shelf near by she had gathered a little treasury of good books. She had manner rather than manners; she was plainly enough that unmistakable and easily recognized person, a great lady. They are but few in every generation, but the simplicity and royalty of their lovely succession have never disappeared from an admiring world.

"Come in, Mary," said Madam Wallingford, with a wan look of gentleness and patience. "'Here I and Sorrow sit!'"

She motioned toward a chair which her attendant, an ancient countrywoman, was placing near. Mary crossed the room quickly, and took her appointed place; then she clasped her hands tight together, and her head drooped. At that moment patriotism and all its high resolves may have seemed too high; she forgot everything except that she was in the presence of a lonely woman, sad and old and bereft. She saw the woeful change that grief had made in this Tory mother of a Patriot son. She could but sit in silence with maidenly self-effacement, and a wistful affectionateness that was like the timidest caress,—this young creature of high spirit, who had so lately thrown down her bold challenge of a man's loyalty. She sat there before the fire, afraid of nothing but her own insistent tears; she could not conquer a sudden dumbness that had forgotten speech. She could not bear to look again at the piteous beloved face of Madam Wallingford. The march of events had withered the elder woman and trampled her underfoot, like a flower in the road that every wheel went over; she had grown old in two short days, while the girl who sat before her had only changed into brighter bloom.

"You may leave us now, Susan," said Madam Wallingford; and with many an anxious glance the old serving woman went away.

STILL THERE FELL SILENCE BETWEEN the two. The wind was droning its perpetual complaining note in the chimney; a belated song sparrow lifted its happy little tune outside the southern windows, and they both listened to the very end. Then their eyes turned to each other's faces; the bird had spoken first in the wintry air. Then Mary Hamilton, with a quick cry, took a hurried step, and fell upon her knees at the mother's side, and took her in her arms, hiding her own face from sight.

"What can I say? Oh, what can I say?" she cried again. "It will break my heart if you love me no more!"

The elder woman shrank for a moment; there was a quick flash in her eyes; then she drew Mary still nearer and held her fast. The comfort of a warm young life so close to her shivering loneliness, the sense of her own weakness and that Mary was the stronger, kept her from breaking now into the stern speech of which her heart was full. She said nothing for a long time but sat waiting; and now and then she laid her hand on the girl's soft hair, until Mary's fit of weeping had passed.

"Bring the little footstool here and sit by me; we must talk of many things together," she gave command at last; and Mary, doing the errand like a child, lingered by the window, and then returned with calmness to her old friend's side. The childish sense of distance between them had strangely returned, and yet she was conscious that she must take a new charge upon herself, and keep nearer than ever to this sad heart.

"I did not know his plans until that very night," she said to Madam Wallingford, looking bravely and sweetly now into the mother's face. "I could not understand at first why there was such excitement in the very air. Then I found out that the mob was ready to come and ruin you, and to drag him out to answer them, as they did the Loyalists in Boston. And there were many strangers on our side of the river. I heard a horrid humming in the crowd that gathered when the captain came; they kept together after he was in the house, and I feared that they were bent upon a worse errand. I was thankful to know that Roger was in Portsmouth, so nothing could be done that night. When he came to me suddenly a little later,"—the girl's voice began to falter,—"I was angry with him at first; I thought only of you. I see now that I was cruel."

"My son has been taught to honor and to serve his King," said Madam Wallingford coldly.

"He has put his country above his King, now," answered Mary Hamilton, who had steadied herself and could go on: yet something hindered her from saying more, and the wind kept up its steady plaint in the chimney, but in this difficult moment the little bird was still.

"To us, our King and country have been but one. I own that the colonies have suffered hardship, and not alone through willfulness; but to give the reins of government to unfit men, to put high matters into the hands of rioters and lawbreakers, can only bring ruin. I could not find it in my heart to blame him, even after the hasty Declaration, when he would not join with English troops to fight the colonies; but to join the rebels to fight England should shame a house like this. Our government is held a high profession among the wise of England; these foolish people will bring us all upon the quicksands. If my son had sailed with officers and gentlemen, such"—

"He has sailed with a hero," said Mary hotly, "and in company with good men of our own neighborhood, in whom he can put his trust."

"Let us not quarrel," answered the lady more gently. She leaned her head against the chair side, and looked strangely pale and old. "'T is true I sent for you to accuse you, and now you are here I only long for comfort. I am the mother of an only son; I am a widow,—little you know what that can mean,—and my prop has gone. Yet I would have sent him proudly to the wars, like a mother of ancient days, did I but think the quarrel just. I could but bless him when he wakened me and knelt beside my bed, and looked so noble, telling his eager story. I did not think his own heart altogether fixed upon this change until he said his country would have need of him. 'All your country, boy!' I begged him then, 'not alone this willful portion of our heritage. Can you forget that you are English born?'

"Then he rose up and stood upon his feet, and I saw that I had looked my last upon his boyish days. 'No, dear mother,' he told me, 'I am beginning to remember it!' and he stooped and kissed me, and stood between the curtains looking down at me, till I myself could see his face no more, I was so blind with tears. Then he kissed me yet again, and went quick away, and I could hear him sobbing in the hall. I would not have him break his word though my own heart should break instead, and I rose then and put on my double-gown, and I called to Susan, who wept aloud,—I even chid her at last for that, and her foolish questions; and all through the dead of night we gathered the poor child's hasty plenishings. Now I can only weep for things forgotten. 'T was still dark when he rode away; when the tide turned, the river cried all along its banks, as it did that long night when his father lay dead in the house. I prayed; I even lingered, hoping that he might be too late, and the ship gone to sea. When he unpacks the chest, he will not see the tears that fell there. I cannot think of our parting, it hurts my heart so... He bade me give his love to you; he said that God could not be so cruel as to forbid his return.

"Mary Hamilton!" and suddenly, as she spoke, all the plaintive bewailing of her voice, all the regretful memories, were left behind. "Oh, Mary Hamilton, tell me why you have done this! All my children are in their graves save this one youngest son. Since I was widowed I have gathered age even beyond my years, and a heavy burden of care belongs to this masterless house. I am a woman full of fears and weak in body. My own forefathers and my husband's house alike have never refused their loyal service to church and state. Who can stand in my son's place now? He was early and late at his business; the poor boy's one ambition was to make his father less missed by those who look to us for help. What is a little soldiering, a trading vessel sunk or an English town affrighted, to the service he could give at home? Had you only thought of this, had you only listened to those who are wiser than we, had you remembered that these troubles must be, in the end, put down, you could not have been unjust. I never dreamed that the worst blow that could fall upon me, except my dear son had died, could be struck me by your hand. Had you no pity, that you urged my boy to go? Tell me why you were willing. Tell me, I command you, why you have done this!"

Mary was standing, white as a flower now, before her dear accuser. The quick scarlet flickered for one moment in her cheeks; her frightened eyes never for one moment left Madam Wallingford's face.

"You must answer me!" the old mother cried again, shaken with passion and despair.

"Because I loved you," said the girl then, and a flash of light was on her face that matched the thrill in her voice. "God forgive me, I had no other reason," she answered, as if she were a prisoner at the bar, and her very life hung upon the words.

Madam Wallingford had spent all the life that was in her. Sleepless nights had robbed her of her strength; she was withered by her grief into something like the very looks of death. All the long nights, all the long hours since she had lost her son, she had said these things over to herself, that she might say them clear to those who ought to listen. They had now been said, and her poor brain that had shot its force of anger and misery to another heart was cold like the firelock that has sped its ball. She sank back into the chair, faint with weakness; she put out her hands as if she groped for help. "Oh, Mary, Mary!" she entreated now; and again Mary, forgetting all, was ready with fond heart to comfort her.

"It is of no use!" exclaimed Madam Wallingford, rousing herself at last, and speaking more coldly than before. "I can only keep to one thought,—that my son has gone. 'T is Love brings all our pain; this is what it means to have a child; my joy and my sorrow are one, and the light of my life casts its shadow! And I have always loved you; I have wished many a time, in the old days, that you were my own little girl. And now I am told that this adventurer has won your heart,—this man who speaks much of Glory, lest Glory should forget to speak of him; that you have even made my son a sacrifice to pride and ambition!"

Mary's cheeks flamed, her eyes grew dark and angry; she tried to speak, but she looked in her accuser's face, and first a natural rage, and then a sudden pity and the old love, held her dumb.

"Forgive me, then," said Madam Wallingford, looking at her, and into her heart there crept unwonted shame.

"You do me wrong; you would wrong both your son and me!" and Mary had sprung away next moment from her side. "I have told only the truth. I was harsh to Roger when I had never known him false, and I almost hated him because he seemed unsettled in his course. I even thought that the rising against the Loyalists had frighted him, and I hated him when I thought he was seeking shelter. He came that very night to tell me that he was for the Patriots, and was doing all a brave man could, and standing for Liberty with the rest of us. Then I knew better than he how far the distrust of him had gone, and I took it upon myself to plead with the captain of the Ranger. I knew too well that if, already prejudiced by envious tales, he turned the commission down, the mob would quick take the signal. 'T was for love of my friends I acted; something drove me past myself, that night. If Roger should die, if indeed I have robbed you of your son, this was the part I took. I would not have done otherwise. He has taken a man's part for Liberty, and I thank God. Now I have told you all."

They were facing each other again. Mary's voice was broken; she could say no more. Then, with a quick change of look and with a splendid gesture, Madam Wallingford rose from her place like a queen. Her face shone with sudden knowledge of new happiness; she held out her arms,—no queen and no accuser, but only a bereft woman, a loving heart that had been beggared of all comfort. "Come, my darling," she whispered; "you must forgive me everything, and love me the more for my poor weakness; you will help me to have patience all these weary months."

THE SUN BROKE OUT AGAIN from behind a thick, low-hanging cloud, and flooded all the dark chamber. Again the Indian stuffs looked warm and bright; the fire sprang on the hearth as if upon an altar: it was as if Heaven's own light had smiled into the room. Poor Mary's young pride was sore hurt and distressed, but her old friend's wonted look of kindness was strangely coming back; she showed all her familiar affectionateness as if she had passed a great crisis. As for the lad whom they had wept and quarreled over, and for whose sake they had come back again to each other's hearts, he was far out upon the gray and tumbling sea; every hour took him farther and farther from home.

And now Madam Wallingford must talk of him with Mary, and tell her everything; how he had chosen but two books,—his Bible and an old volume of French essays that Master Sullivan had given him when he went to college. "'T was his copy of Shakespeare's plays," said she, "that he wanted most; but in all our hurry, and with dull candlelight, we could find it nowhere, and yesterday I saw it lying here on my chest of drawers. 'T is not so many days since he read me a pretty piece of The Tempest, as we sat together. I can hear his voice now as he read: 't was like a lover, the way he said '*my noble mistress!*' and I could but smile to hear him. He saw the great Garrick in his best characters, when he was in London. Roger was ever a pretty reader when he was a boy. 'T is a gift the dullest child might learn from Master Sullivan."

The mother spoke fondly between smiles and tears; the old book lay open on her knee, and something dropped to the floor,—a twig of faded witch-hazel blossoms that her son had held in his fingers as he read, and left between the leaves for a marker; a twig of witch-hazel, perhaps from the same bough that Mary had broken as she came. It were easy to count it for a message where some one else might think of but a pretty accident. Mary stooped and picked the withered twig of blossoms from the floor, and played with it, smiling as Madam Wallingford talked on, and they sat together late into the autumn twilight. The poor lady was like one who, by force of habit, takes up the life of every day again when death has been in the house. The familiar presence of her young neighbor had cured her for the moment of the pain of loneliness, but the sharp words she had spoken in her distress would ache for many a day in Mary's heart.

Mary could not understand that strange moment when she had been forgiven. Yet the hardest soul might have compassion for a poor woman so overwrought and defeated; she was still staggering from a heavy blow.

It was dark when they parted, and Madam Wallingford showed a strange solicitude after her earlier reproaches, and forbade Mary when she would have crossed the river alone. She took a new air of rightful command, and Rodney must send two of the men with their own boat, and put by the canoe until morning. The stars were bright and quick as diamonds overhead, and it was light enough on the water, as they crossed. The candlelight in the upper chamber on the hill looked dim, as if there were illness in the house.

Indeed, Madam Wallingford was trembling with cold since her young guest had gone. Susan wrapped her in an old cloak of soft fur, as she sat beside the fire, and turned often to look at her anxiously, as she piled the fagots and logs on the hearth until their flame towered high.

"Dear child, dear child," the poor lady said over and over in her heart. "I think she does not know it yet, but I believe she loves my son."

THAT NIGHT OLD SUSAN HOVERED about her mistress, altering the droop of the bed curtains and untwisting the balls of their fringe with a businesslike air; then she put some heavy knots of wood on the fire for the night, and built it solidly together, until the leaping lights and shadows played fast about the room. She glanced as often as she dared at the tired face on the pillow.

"'T is a wild night, Susan," said Madam Wallingford. "I thought the wind was going down with the sun. How often I have watched for my dear man such nights as this, when he was kept late in Portsmouth! 'T was well we lived in town those latest winters. You remember that Rodney always kept the fire bright in the dining parlor ('t is a cosy place in winter), and put a tankard of mulled wine inside the fender; 't would bring back the color to his face all chilled with winter rain, and the light into his eyes. And Roger would come in with him, holding his father's hand; he would ever run out bareheaded in the wet, while I called to them from the door to come in and let the horse go to stable, and they laughed at me for my fears. Where is Roger to-night, I wonder, Susan? They cannot be in port for a long time yet. I hate to think of him on the sea!"

"Maybe 't is morning there, and the sun out, madam."

"Susan," said Madam Wallingford, "you used to sing to him when he was a baby; sit near the fire awhile,—there is no more for you to do. Sing one of your old hymns, so that I may go to sleep; perhaps it will quiet his heart, too, if we are quiet and try to be at peace."

The very shadows grew stiller, as if to listen, as the patient old handmaiden came and sat beside the bed and began to sing, moving her foot as if she still held the restless baby who had grown to be a man. There were quavering notes in her voice, but when she had sung all her pious verses of the Cradle Hymn to their very end Madam Wallingford was fast asleep.

XII

BETWEEN DECKS

"But when shall I see Athens and the Acropolis again?'

*"'Wretched man! doth not that satisfy thee which thou seest every day?
Hast thou aught better or greater to see than the sun, the moon, the
stars, the common earth, the sea?'"*

"Who would Hercules have been if he had sat at home?"

The Ranger was under full sail, and ran like a hound; she had cleared
the Banks with all their snow squalls and thick nights, without
let or hindrance. The captain's boast that he would land his dispatches
and spread the news of Burgoyne's surrender in France in thirty days
seemed likely to come true. The men were already beginning to show
effects of constant vigilance and overwork; but whatever discomforts
might arrive, the splendid seamanship of Paul Jones could only be
admired by such thorough-going sailors as made up the greater portion
of his crew. The younger members of the ship's company were full of
gayety if the wind and work eased ever so little, and at any time, by
night or day, some hearty voice might be heard practicing the strains
of a stirring song new made by one of the midshipmen:—

> *"That is why we Brave the Blast
> To carry the news to Lon-don."*

There were plenty of rival factions and jealousies. The river men were
against all strangers; and even the river men had their own divisions,
their warm friendships and cold aversions, so that now and then some
smouldering fire came perilously near an outbreak. The tremendous
pressure of work alow and aloft, the driving wind, the heavy tumbling
seas, the constant exposure and strain in such trying duty and incessant
service of the sails, put upon every man all that he could well bear, and
sent him to his berth as tired as a dog.

It takes but little while for a good shipmaster to discover who are the
difficult men in his crew, the sea lawyers and breeders of dissatisfaction.

The captain of the Ranger was a man of astonishing readiness both to blame and praise; nobody could resist his inspiriting enthusiasm and dominating presence, but in absence he was often proved wrong, and roundly cursed, as captains are, with solid satisfaction of resentment. Everybody cheered when he boldly declared against flogging, and even tossed that horrid sea-going implement, the cat, lightly over the ship's side. Even in this surprising moment, one of the old seamen had growled that when you saw a man too good, it was the time to look out for him.

"I dasen't say but it's about time to get a fuss going," said one of these mariners to a friend, later on. "Ginerally takes about ten days to start a row atween decks, 'less you're extra eased off with good weather."

"THIS BAD WEATHER'S ALL ALONG o' Dickson," ventured his comrade; "if they'd known what they was about, he'd been the fust man they'd hasted to set ashore. I know him; I've knowed him ever since he was a boy. I see him get a black stripe o' rage acrost his face when he seen Mr. Wallin'ford come aboard, that mornin'. Wallin'ford's folks cotched him thievin' when he had his fat chance o' surveyor up country, after the old judge died. He cut their growth on his own account and done a sight o' tricks, and Madam dismissed him, and would ha' jailed him but for pity of his folks. I always wished she'd done it; 't would ha' stamped him plain, if he'd seen the inside o' old York jail for a couple o' years. As 't was, he had his own story to tell, and made out how he was the injured one; so there was some o' them fools that likes to be on the off side that went an' upheld him. Oh, Dickson's smart, and some calls him pious, but I wish you'd seen him the day Madam Wallin'ford sent for him to speak her mind! That mornin' we was sailin' out o' Porchmouth, I see him watch the young man as if he was layin' for him like a tiger! There he is now, comin' out o' the cabin. I guess the cap'n's been rakin' him fore an' aft. He hates him; an' Simpson hates him, too, but not so bad. Simpson don't jibe with the cap'n hisself, so he demeans himself to hark to Dickson more 'n he otherwise would. Lord, what a cur'ous world this is!"

"What's that n'ise risin' out o' the fo'c's'le now, Cooper? Le' 's go see!" and the two old comrades made haste to go below.

PAUL JONES GAVE A HEARTY sigh, as he sat alone in his cabin, and struck his fist into the empty air. He also could hear the sound of a loud quarrel from the gun deck, and for a moment indulged a fierce hope that somebody might be well punished, or even killed, just to lessen the number of citizens in this wrangling village with which he had put to sea. They had brought aboard all the unsettled rivalries and jealousies of a most independent neighborhood.

He looked about him as he sat; then rose and impatiently closed one of his lockers where there was an untidy fold of crumpled clothing hanging out. What miserable surroundings and conditions for a man of inborn fastidiousness and refinement of nature!

Yet this new ship, so fast growing toward the disgusting squalor of an old one; these men, with their cheap suspicions and narrow ambitions, were the strong tools ready to his hand. It was a manly crew as crews go, and like-minded in respect to their country's wrongs.

"I feel it in my breast that I shall some day be master in a great sea fight!" said the little captain as he sat alone, while the Ranger labored against the waves, and the light of heroic endurance came back to his eyes as he saw again the splendid vision that had ever led him on.

"Curse that scoundrel Dickson!" and his look darkened. "Patience, patience! If I were a better sleeper, I could face everything that can come in a man's day; I could face the devil himself. The wind's in the right quarter now, and the sea's going down. I'll go on deck and give all hands some grog,—I'll give it them myself; the poor fellows are cold and wet, and they serve me like men. We're getting past the worst," and again Paul Jones fell to studying his charts as if they were love letters writ by his lady's hand.

Cooper and Hanscom had come below to join the rest of their watch, and still sat side by side, being old shipmates and friends. There was an easy sort of comfort in being together. Just now they spoke again in low voices of young Mr. Wallingford.

"Young master looks wamble-cropped to me," said Hanscom. "Don't fancy privateerin' so well as ridin' a blood horse on Porchmouth Parade, and bein' courted by the Tory big-bugs. Looks wintry in the face to me."

"Lord bless us, when he's old 's we are, he'll l'arn that spring al'ays gets round again long's a creatur' 's alive," answered Cooper, who instinctively gave a general turn to the discussion. "Ary thing that's livin' knows its four seasons, an' I've long maintained that after the wust o' winter, spring usu'lly doos come follerin' right on."

"I don't know but it's so," agreed his mate politely. Cooper would have these fanciful notions, while Hanscom was a plain-spoken man.

"What I'd like to know," said he, "yes, what I'd like to ascertain, is what young Squire Wallin'ford ever come for; 't ain't in his blood to fight on our side, an' he's too straight-minded to play the sneak. Also, he never come from cowardice. No, I can't make it out noway. Sometimes folks mistakes their duty, and risks their all. Bain't spyin' round to do no hurt, is he?—or *is* he?"

There was a sharp suggestion in the way this question was put, and Cooper turned fiercely upon his companion.

"Hunscom, I be ashamed of you!" he said scornfully, and said no more. There was a dull warmth of color in his hard, sea-smitten face; he was an elderly, quiet man, with a round, pleasant countenance unaltered in the worst of weather, and a look of kindly tolerance.

"There's b'en some consid'able changin' o' sides in our neighborhood, as you know," he said, a few moments later, in his usual tone. "Young Wallin'ford went to school to Master Sullivan, and the old master l'arnt everybody he could l'arn to be honest an' square, to hold by their word, an' be afeard o' nothin'."

"Pity 't was that Dickson could n't ha' got a term o' such schoolin'," said Hanscom, as they beheld that shipmate's unwelcome face peering down the companion.

"Sometimes I wish I was to home again," announced Cooper, in an unexpected fit of despondency. "I don' know why; 'tain't usual with me to have such feelin's in the outset of a v'y'ge. I grow sicker every day o' this flat, strivin' sea. I was raised on a good hill. I don' know how I ever come to foller the sea, anyway!"

The forecastle was a forlorn abiding-place at best, and crowded at any hour almost past endurance. The one hint of homeliness and decency was in the well-made sea chests, which had not been out of place against a steadier wall in the farmhouses whence most of them had come. They were of plain wood, with a touch of art in their rude carving; many of them were painted dull green or blue. There were others with really handsome escutcheons of wrought iron, and all were graced with fine turk's-heads to their rope handles, and every ingenuity of sailors' fancywork.

There was a grumbling company of able seamen, their owners, who had no better place to sit than the chest tops, or to stretch at idle length with these treasures to lean against. The cold sea was nearer to a man than when he was on deck and could reassure himself of freedom by a look at the sky. The hammocks were here and there sagging with the rounded bulk of a sleeping owner, and all jerked uneasily as the vessel pitched and rolled by turns. The air was close and heavy with dampness and tobacco smoke.

At this moment the great sea boots of Simon Staples were seen descending from the deck above, and stumbling dangerously on the slippery straight ladder.

"Handsomely, handsomely," urged a spectator, with deep solicitude.

"She's goin' large now, ain't she? How's she headin' now?" asked a man named Grant.

"She's full an' by, an' headin' east by south half east,—same 's we struck out past the Isles o' Shoals," was the mirthful answer. "She can't keep to nothin', an' the cap'n 's got to make another night on't. But she 's full an' by, just now, all you lazy larbowlines," he repeated cheerfully, at last getting his head down under decks as 'his foot found the last step. "She's been on a good leadin' wind this half hour back, an' he's got the stu'n'sails set again; 'tis all luff an' touch her, this v'y'ge."

There was a loud groan from the listeners. The captain insisted upon spreading every rag the ship could stagger under, and while they admired his persistent daring, it was sometimes too much for flesh and blood.

Staples was looking ruefully at his yarn mittens. They were far beyond the possibility of repair, and he took off first one and then the other of these cherished reminders of much logging experience, and, sitting on his sea chest, began to ravel what broken gray yarn was left and to wind it into a ball.

"Goin' to knit you another pair?" inquired Hanscom. "That's clever; empl'y your idle moments."

"Mend up his stockin's, you fool!" explained Grant, who was evidently gifted with some sympathetic imagination.

"I wish they was thumbs up on the stakes o' my old wood-sled," said Staples. "There, when I'm to sea I wish 's how I was lumberin', an' when I'm in the woods I'm plottin' how to git to sea again; ain't no suitin' of me neither way. I al'ays wanted to be aboard a fast sailer, an' here I be thrashin' along, an' lamentin' 'cause my mittins is wore out the fust fortnight."

"My! I wish old Master Hackett that built her could see how she runs!" he exclaimed next moment, as if a warm admiration still had power to cheer him. "I marked her lines for a beauty the day I see her launched: 't was what drove me here. There was plenty a-watchin' her on Lungdon's Island that hoped she'd stick in the stays, but she took the water like a young duck."

"He'd best not carry so much sail when she's clawin' to wind'ard close hauled," growled James Chase, an old Nantucket seaman, with a warning shake of the head. "'T won't take much to lay her clear down, I can tell him! I never see a ship drove so, in my time. Lord help every soul aboard if she wa'n't so weatherly!"

Fernald and Sherburne, old Portsmouth sailors, wagged their sage heads in solemn agreement; but William Young, a Dover man, with a responsible look, was waiting with some impatience for Chase to stand out of the poor supply of light that came down the narrow hatchway. Young was reading an old copy of the New Hampshire Gazette that had already been the solace of every reading man aboard.

"What in time 's been the matter amongst ye?" Staples now inquired, with interest. "I heard as how there was a fuss goin' down below; ain't ary bully-raggin' as I can see; dull as meetin'!" Hanscom and Cooper looked up eagerly; some of the other men only laughed for answer; but Chase signified that the trouble lay with their messmate Starbuck, who appeared to be surly, and sat with his back to the company. He now turned and displayed a much-disfigured countenance, but said nothing.

"What's the cap'n about now?" Chase hastened to inquire pointedly.

"He's up there a-cunnin' the ship," answered Staples. "He's workin' the life out o' Grosvenor at the wheel. I just come from the maintop; my arms aches as if they'd been broke with a crowbar. I lost my holt o' the life line whilst we was settin' the stu'n's'l there on the maintops'l yard, an' I give me a dreadful wrench. He had n't ought to send them green boys to such places, neither; pore little Johnny Downes was makin' out to do his stent like a man, but the halyards got fouled in the jewel blocks, an' for all he's so willin'-hearted the tears was a-runnin' down his cheeks when he come back. I was skeert the wind'd blow him off like a whirligig off a stick, an' I spoke sharp to him so 's to brace him, an' give him a good boxed ear when I got him in reach. He was about beat, an' half froze anyway; his fingers looked like the p'ints o' parsnips. When he got back he laid right over acrost the cap. I left him up there a-clingin' on."

"He worked as handsome a pair o' man-rope knots as I ever see, settin' here this mornin'," said Cooper, compassionately. "He'll make a good smart sailor, but he needs to grow; he's dreadful small to send aloft in a spell o' weather. The cap'n don't save himself, this v'y'ge, nor nobody else."

"Come, you'd as good 's hear what Starbuck's b'en saying," said Chase, with a wink. He had been waiting impatiently for this digression to end.

"That spry-tempered admiral o' yourn don't know how to treat a crew!" Starbuck burst forth, at this convenient opportunity. "Some on us gits a whack ivery time he parades the deck. He's re'lly too outdacious for decent folks. This arternoon I was a-loungin' on the gratin's an' got sort o' drowsin' off, an' I niver heared him comin' nor knowed he was there. Along he come like some upstropelous poppet an' give me a cuff side o' my head. I dodged the next one, an' spoke up smart 'fore I knowed what I was doin'. 'Damn ye, le' me be!' says I, an' he fetched me another on my nose here; most stunded me.

"'I'll l'arn ye to make yourself sca'ce! Keep to the port-hand side where ye belong! Remember you're aboard a man-o'-war!' says he, hollerin' like a crowin' pullet. 'T ain't no fishin' smack! Go forrard! Out o' the way with ye!' says he, same 's I was a stray dog. I run to the side, my nose was a-bleedin' so, an' I fumbled arter somethin' to serve me for a hankicher.

"'Here 's mine,' says he, 'but you've got to understand there's discipline on this frigate,' says he. Joseph Fernald knows where I was," continued the sufferer; "you see me, Joseph, when you come past. 'Twa'n't larboard nor starboard; 'twas right 'midships, 'less I may have rolled one way or t'other. I could ha' squinched him so all the friends he'd ever needed 'd be clargy an' saxon, an' then to pass me his linning handkicher's if I was a young lady! I dove into my pockets an' come upon this old piece o' callamink I'd wropped up some 'baccy in. I never give a look at him; I d' know but he gallded me more when he was pleasant 'n when he fetched me the clip. I ketched up a lingum-vitæ marlinspike I see by me an' took arter him. I should ha' hit him good, but he niver turned to look arter me, an' I come to reason. If I'd had time, I'd ha' hit him, if I'd made the rest o' this v'y'ge in irons."

"Lord sakes! don't you bluster no more!" advised old Mr. Cooper soothingly, with a disapproving glance at the pleased audience. "Shipmasters like him ain't goin' to ask ye every mornin' how seafarin' agrees with ye. He ain't goin' to treat hisself nor none on us like passengers.

He ain't had three hours sleep a night sence this v'y'ge begun. He's been studyin' his charts this day, with his head set to 'em on the cabin table's if they showed the path to heaven. They was English charts, too, 'long by Bristol an' up there in the Irish Sea. I see 'em through the skylight."

"I'll bate he's figurin' to lay outside some o' them very ports an' cut out some han'some prizes," said Falls, one of the gunners, looking down out of his hammock. Falls was a young man full of enthusiasm, who played the fiddle.

"You'll find 't will be all glory for him, an' no prizes for you, my young musicianer!" answered Starbuck, who was a discouraged person by nature. Now that he had a real grievance his spirits seemed to rise. "Up hammocks all! Show a leg!" he gayly ordered the gunner.

"Wall, I seldom seen so good a navigator as the cap'n in my time," insisted Staples. "He knows every man's duty well's his own, an' that he knows to a maracle."

"I'll bate any man in this fo'c's'le that he's a gre't fighter; you wait an' see the little wasp when he's gittin' into action!" exclaimed Chase, who had been with Paul Jones on the Alfred. "He knows no fear an' he sticks at nothin'! You hold on till we're safe in Channel, an' sight one o' them fat-bellied old West Injyinen lo'ded deep an' headed up for London. Then you'll see Gre't Works in a way you niver expected."

This local allusion was not lost upon most members of the larboard watch, and Starbuck's wrongs, with the increasing size of his once useful nose, were quite disregarded in the hopeful laughter which followed.

"Hand me the keerds," said one of the men lazily. "Falls, there, knows a couple o' rale queer tricks."

"You keep 'em dowsed; if he thinks we ain't sleepin' or eatin', so 's to git our courage up," said Staples, "he'll have every soul on us aloft. Le' 's set here where 't 's warm an' put some kecklin' on Starbuck; the cap'n 's 'n all places to once, with eyes like gimblets, an' the wind 's a-blowin' up there round the lubber holes like the mouth o' hell."

Chase, the Nantucket sailor, looked at him, with a laugh.

"What a farmer you be," he exclaimed. "Makes me think of a countryman, shipmate o' mine on the brig Polly Dunn. We was whaling in the South Seas, an' it come on to blow like fury; we was rollin' rails under, an' I was well skeert myself; feared I could n't keep my holt; him an' me was on the fore yard together. He looked dreadful easy an' pleasant. I thought he'd be skeert too, if he knowed enough, an' I kind o' swore at the fool an' axed him what he was a-thinkin' of. 'Why, 't is the 20th o' May,' says he; 'all the caows goes to pastur' to-day, to home in Eppin'!'"

There was a cheerful chuckle from the audience. Grant alone looked much perplexed.

"Why, 't is the day, ain't it?" he protested. "What be you all a-laughin' at?"

At this moment there was a strange lull; the wind fell, and the Ranger stopped rolling, and then staggered as if she balked at some unexpected danger. One of the elder seamen gave an odd warning cry. A monstrous hammer seemed to strike the side, and a great wave swept over as if to bury them forever in the sea. The water came pouring down and flooded the forecastle knee-deep. There was an outcry on deck, and an instant later three loud knocks on the scuttle.

"All the larboard watch ahoy!" bawled John Dougall. "Hear the news, can't ye? All hands up! All hands on deck!"

XIII

The Mind of the Doctor

"Or rather no arte, but a divine and heavenly instinct, not to be gotten by labour and learning, but adorned by both."

There was one man, at least, on board the Ranger who was a lover of peace: this was the ship's surgeon, Dr. Ezra Green. With a strong and hearty crew, and the voyage just beginning, his professional duties had naturally been but light; he had no more concern with the working of the ship than if he were sitting in his office at home in Dover, and eagerly assented to the captain's proposal that he should act as the Ranger's purser.

The surgeon's tiny cabin was stuffed with books; this was a good chance to go on with his studies, and, being a good sailor and a cheerful man, the whole ship's company took pleasure in his presence. There was an amiable seriousness about his every-day demeanor that calmed even the activities of the captain's temper; he seemed to be surgeon and purser and chaplain all in one, and to be fit, as one of his calling should be, to minister to both souls and bodies. It was known on board that he was unusually liberal in his views of religion, and was provided with some works upon theology as well as medicine, and could argue well for the Arminian doctrines against Dickson, who, like many men of his type, was pretentious of great religious zeal, and declared himself a Calvinist of the severest order. Dickson was pleased to consider the surgeon very lax and heretical; as if that would make the world think himself a good man, and the surgeon a bad one, which was, for evident proof and reason, quite impossible.

On this dark night, after the terrible sea of the afternoon had gone down, and poor Solomon Hutchings, the first victim of the voyage, had been made as comfortable as possible under the circumstances of a badly broken leg, the surgeon was sitting alone, with a pleasant sense of having been useful. He gave a sigh at the sound of Dickson's voice outside. Dickson would be ready, as usual, for an altercation, and was one of those men who always come into a room as if they expect to be kicked out of it.

Green was writing,—he kept a careful journal of the voyage,—and now looked over his shoulder impatiently, as if he did not wish to be interrupted.

Dickson wore a look of patient persistence.

The surgeon pointed to a seat with his long quill, and finished the writing of a sentence. He could not honestly welcome a man whom he liked so little, and usually treated him as if he were a patient who had come to seek advice.

"I only dropped in for a chat," explained the visitor reprovingly, as his host looked up again. "Have you heard how the captain blew at young Wallingford, just before dark? Well, sir, they are at supper together now. Wallingford must be a tame kitten. I suppose he crept down to the table as if he wanted to be stroked."

"He is a good fellow and a gentleman," said Ezra Green slowly. "The captain has hardly left the deck since yesterday noon, when this gale began." The surgeon was a young man, but he had a grave, middle-aged manner which Dickson's sneering smoothness seemed always to insult.

"You always take Jones's part," ventured the guest.

"We are not living in a tavern ashore," retorted the surgeon. "The officer you speak of is our captain, and commands an American man-of-war. That must be understood. I cannot discuss these matters again."

"Some of the best sailors vow they will desert him in the first French port," said Dickson.

"Then they make themselves liable to be shot for desertion whenever they are caught," replied Green coolly, "and you must take every opportunity to tell them so. Those who are here simply to make a little dirty money had better have stayed ashore and traded their country produce with the British ships. They say there was a fine-paying business on foot, out at the Isles of Shoals."

This advice struck home, as the speaker desired. Dickson swallowed hard once or twice, and then looked meek and stubborn; he watched the surgeon slyly before he spoke again.

"Yes, it is a very difficult crew to command," he agreed; "we have plenty of good loyal men aboard, but they want revenge for their country's wrongs, as you and I do, I hope!"

"War is one thing, and has law and order to dignify it; common piracy and thievery are of another breed. Some of our men need education in these matters, not to say all the discipline they can get. The captain is much wronged and insulted by the spirit that has begun to spread between decks. I believe that he has the right view of his duty; his methods are sometimes his own."

"As in the case of Mr. Wallingford," blandly suggested Dickson, swift to seize his opportunity. "Even you would have thought the captain outrageous in his choice of words."

"The captain is a man easily provoked, and has suffered certain provocations such as no man of spirit could brook. I believe he was very wrong to vent his spite on Mr. Wallingford, who has proved as respectful of others and forgetful of himself as any man on board. I say this without knowing the present circumstances, but Wallingford has made a nobler sacrifice than any of us."

"He would have been chased to his own kind among the Tories in another week," sneered the other. "You know it as well as I. Wallingford hesitated just as long as he dared, and there's the truth! He's a good mate to Ben Thompson,—both of 'em courtiers of the Wentworths; and both of 'em had to hurry at the last, one way or the other, whichever served."

"Plenty of our best citizens clung to the hope that delay would bring some proper arbitration and concession. No good citizen went to war lightly and without a pang. A man who has seen carnage must always dread it; such glory as we win must reckon upon groans and weeping behind the loudest cheers. But war once declared, men of clear conscience and decent character may accept their lot, and in the end serve their country best," said the doctor.

"You are sentimental to-night," scoffed Dickson.

"I have been thinking much of home," said the surgeon, with deep feeling. "I may never see my home again, nor may you. We are near shore now: in a few days this ship may be smeared with blood, and these poor fellows who snarl and bargain, and discuss the captain's orders and the chance of prize money, may come under my hands, bleeding and torn and suffering their last agony. We must face these things as best we may; we do not know what war means yet; the captain will spare none of us. He is like a creature in a cage now, fretted by his bounds and all their petty conditions; but when the moment of freedom comes he will seek action. He is fit by nature to leap to the greatest opportunities, and to do what the best of us could never dream of. No, not you, sir, nor Simpson either, though he aims to supplant him!" grumbled the surgeon, under his voice.

"Perhaps his gift is too great for so small a command as this," Dickson returned, with an evil smile. "It is understood that he must be transferred to a more sufficient frigate, if France sees fit," he added, in a pious tone. "I shall strive to do my own duty in either case." At which Dr. Green looked up and smiled.

Dickson laughed back; he was quick to feel the change of mood in his companion. For a moment they were like two schoolboys, but there was a flicker of malice in Dickson's eyes; no one likes being laughed at.

"Shall we take a hand at cards, sir?" he asked hastily. "All these great things will soon be settled when we get to France."

The surgeon did not offer to get the cards, which lay on the nearest shelf. He was clasping his hands across his broad breast, and leaning back in a comfortable, tolerant sort of way in his corner seat. They both knew perfectly well that they were in for a long evening together, and might as well make the best of it. It was too much trouble to fight with a cur. Somehow, the current of general interest did not set as usual toward theological opinions.

"I was called to a patient down on Sligo Point, beyond the Gulf Road, just before we sailed," said Green presently, in a more friendly tone. "'T was an old woman of unsteady brain, but of no common-place fancy, who was under one of her wildest spells, and had mounted the house roof to sell all her neighbors at auction. She was amusing enough,—'t is a pretty wit when she is sane; but I heard roars of laughter as I rode up the lane, and saw a flock of listeners at the orchard edge. She had knocked off the minister and both deacons, the lot for ninepence, and was running her lame neighbor Paul to seventy thousand pounds."

"I heard that they called the minister to pray with her when her fit was coming on, and she chased him down the lane, and would have driven him into the river, if there had not been some men at fall ploughing in a field near by. She was a fixed Calvinist in her prime, and always thought him lax," said Dickson, with relish, continuing the tale. "They had told the good man to come dressed in his gown and bands, thinking it would impress her mind."

"Which it certainly seemed to do," agreed the doctor. "At any rate, she knocked him down for nine-pence. 'T was a good sample of the valuation most of us put upon our neighbors. She likes to hear her neighbor Paul play the fiddle; sometimes he can make her forget all her poor distresses, and fall asleep like a baby. The minister had somehow vexed her. Our standards are just as personal here aboard ship. The Great Day will sum up men at their true value,—we shall never do it before; 't would ask too much of poor human nature."

Dickson drummed on the bulkhead before he spoke. "Some men are taken at less than their true value."

"And some at more, especially by themselves. Don't let things go too far with Simpson. He's a good man, but can easily be led into making trouble," said the surgeon; and Dickson half rose, and then sat down again, with his face showing an angry red.

"We must be patient," added the surgeon a moment later, without having looked again at his companion. "'T is just like a cage of beasts here: fierce and harmless are shut in together. Tame creatures are sometimes forced to show their teeth. We must not fret about petty things, either; 't is a great errand we have come out upon, and the honest doing of it is all the business we have in common."

"True, sir," said Dickson, with a touch of insolent flattery. "Shall we take a hand at cards?"

XIV

To add More Grief

"O garlands, hanging by these doors, now stay,
Nor from your leaves too quickly shake away
My dew of tears. (How many such, ah me!
A lover's eyes must shed!)"

Captain Paul Jones was waiting, a most affable and dignified host, to greet his guest. Wallingford stood before him, with a faint flush of anger brightening his cheeks.

"You commanded me, sir," he said shortly.

"Oh, come, Wallingford!" exclaimed the captain, never so friendly before, and keeping that pleasant voice and manner which at once claimed comradeship from men and admiring affection from women. "I'll drop the commander when we're by ourselves, if you'll consent, and we'll say what we like. I wanted you to sup with me. I've got a bottle of good wine for us,—some of Hamilton's Madeira."

Wallingford hesitated; after all, what did it matter? The captain was the captain; there was a vigorous sort of refreshment in this life on shipboard; a man could not judge his associates by the one final test of their being gentlemen, but only expect of each that he should follow after his kind. Outside society there lies humanity.

The lieutenant seated himself under the swinging lamp, and took the glass that was held out to him. They drank together to the flag they carried, and to their lucky landfall on the morrow.

"To France!" said the captain gallantly. It was plainly expected that all personal misunderstandings should be drowned in the good wine. Wallingford knew the flavor well enough, and even from which cask in Hamilton's cellar it had been drawn. Then the captain was quickly on his feet again, and took the four steps to and fro which were all his cabin permitted. He did not even appear to be impatient, though supper was slow in coming. His hands were clasped behind him, and he smiled once or twice, but did not speak, and seemed to be lost in thought. As for the guest, his thoughts were with Mary Hamilton. The flavor of wine, like the fragrance of a flower, can be a quick spur to memory. He saw her bright face and sweet, expectant eyes, as if they were sitting together at Hamilton's own table.

The process of this evening meal at sea was not a long one; and when the two men had dispatched their food with businesslike haste, the steward was dismissed, and they were left alone with Hamilton's Madeira at better than half tide in the bottle between them, a plate of biscuit and some raisins, and the usual pack of cards. Paul Jones covered these with a forbidding hand, and presently pushed them aside altogether, and added a handful of pipes to the provisioning of the plain dessert. He wished to speak of serious things, and could not make too long an evening away from his papers. It seemed incredible that the voyage was so near its end. He refilled his own glass and Mr. Wallingford's.

"I foresee much annoyance now, on board this ship. I must at once post to Paris, and here they will have time to finish their machinations at their leisure, without me to drive them up to duty. Have you long known this man Dickson?" asked the captain, lowering his voice and fixing his eyes upon the lieutenant.

"I have always known him. He was once in our own employ and much trusted, but was afterward dismissed, and for the worst of reasons," said Wallingford.

"What reputation has he borne in the neighborhood?"

"He is called a sharp man of business, quick to see his own advantage, and generous in buying the good will of those who can serve his purpose. He is a stirring, money-getting fellow, very close-fisted; but he has been unlucky in his larger ventures, as if fortune did not much incline to favor him."

"I despised the fellow from the first," said the captain, with engaging frankness, "but I have no fear that I cannot master him; he is much cleverer than many a better man, yet 't is not well to forget that a cripple in the right road can beat a racer in the wrong. He has been sure these last days that he possesses my confidence, but I have made him serve some good turns. Now he is making trouble as fast as he can between Simpson and me. Simpson knows little of human nature; he would as soon have Dickson's praise as yours or mine. He cannot wait to supplant me in this command, and he frets to gather prizes off these rich seas. There's no harm in prizes; but I sometimes think that no soul on board has any real comprehension of the larger duties of our voyage, and the ends it may serve in furthering an alliance with France. They all begin, well instructed by Dickson, to look upon me as hardly more than a passenger. 'T is true that I look for a French frigate very soon, as Dickson tells them; but he adds that it is to Simpson they must look for success, while if he could rid himself of Simpson he would do it. I must have a fleet if I can, and as soon as I can, and be master of it, too. I have my plans all well laid! Dickson is full of plots of his own, but to tell such a man the truth about himself is to give him the blackest of insults."

Wallingford made a gesture of impatience. The captain's face relaxed, and he laughed as he leaned across the table.

"Dickson took his commission for the sake of prize money," he said. "A pirate, a pirate, that's what he is, but oh, how pious in his speech!"

> "*Unpitying hears the captive's moans*
> *Or e'en a dying brother's groans!*'"

"There's a hymn for him!" exclaimed the captain, with bitter emphasis. "No, he has no gleam of true patriotism in his cold heart; he is full of deliberate insincerities; 'a mitten for any hand,' as they say in Portsmouth. I believe he would risk a mutiny, if he had time enough; and having gained his own ends of putting better men to shame, he would pose as the queller of it. A low-lived, self-seeking man; you can see it for yourself, Mr. Wallingford."

"True, sir. I did not need to come to sea to learn that man's character," and Wallingford finished his glass and set it down, but still held it with one hand stretched out upon the table, while he leaned back comfortably against the bulkhead.

"If our enterprise has any value in the sight of the nations, or any true power against our oppressors, it lies in our noble cause and in our own unselfishness," said Paul Jones, his eyes kindling. "This man and his fellows would have us sneak about the shores of Great Britain, picking up an old man and a lad and a squalling woman from some coastwise trading smack, and plundering what weak craft we can find to stuff our pockets with ha'pennies. We have a small ship, it is true; but it is war we follow, not thievery. I hear there's grumbling between decks about ourselves getting nothing by this voyage. 'T is our country we have put to sea for, not ourselves. No man has it in his heart more than I to confront the enemy: but Dickson would like to creep along the coast forever after small game, and count up by night what he has taken by day, like a petty shopkeeper. I look for larger things, or we might have stopped at home. I have my plans, sir; the Marine Committee have promised me my proper ship. One thing that I cannot brook is a man's perfidy. I have good men aboard, but Dickson is not among them. I feel sometimes as if I trod on caltrops. I am outdone, Mr. Wallingford. I have hardly slept these three nights. You have my apology, sir."

The lieutenant bowed with respectful courtesy, but said nothing. The captain opened his eyes a little wider, and looked amused; then he quickly grew grave and observed his guest with fresh attention. There was a fine unassailable dignity in Wallingford's bearing at this moment.

"Since you are aware that there is some disaffection, sir," he said deliberately, "I can only answer that it seems to me there is but one course to follow, and you must not overrate the opposition. They will always sit in judgment upon your orders, and discuss your measures, and express their minds freely. I have long since seen that our natural independence of spirit in New England makes individual opinion appear of too great consequence,—'t is the way they fall upon the parson's sermon ashore, every Monday morning. As for Lieutenant Simpson, I think him a very honest-hearted man, though capable of being influenced. He has the reputation in Portsmouth of an excellent seaman, but high-tempered. Among the men here, he has the advantage of great powers of self-command."

Wallingford paused, as if to make his words more emphatic, and then repeated them: "He has the mastery of his temper, sir, and the men fear him; he can stop to think even when he is angry. His gifts are perhaps not great, but they have that real advantage."

Paul Jones blazed with sudden fury. He sprang to his feet, and stood light and steady there beyond the table, in spite of the swaying ship.

"Forgive me, sir," said Roger Wallingford, "but you bade us speak together like friends to-night. I think you a far greater man and master than when we left Portsmouth; I am not so small-minded as to forget to honor my superiors. I see plainly that you are too much vexed with these men,—I respect and admire you enough to say so; you must not expect from them what you demand from yourself. In the worst weather you could not have had a better crew: you have confessed to that. I believe you must have patience with the small affairs which have so deeply vexed you. The men are right at heart; you ought to be able to hold them better than Dickson!"

The captain's rage had burnt out like a straw fire, and he was himself again.

"Speak on, Mr. Lieutenant; you mean kindly," he said, and took his seat. The sweat stood on his forehead, and his hands twitched.

"I think we have it in our power to intimidate the enemy, poorly fitted out as we are," he said, with calmness, "but we must act like one man. At least we all pity our countrymen, who are starving in filthy prisons. Since Parliament, now two years agone, authorized the King to treat all Americans taken under arms at sea as pirates and felons, they have been stuffing their dungeons with the innocent and guilty together. What man seeing his enemy approach does not arm himself in defense? We have made no retaliation such as I shall make now. I have my plans, but I cannot risk losing a man here and a man there, out of a crew like this, before I adventure a hearty blow; this cuts me off from prize-hunting. And the commander of an American man-of-war cannot hobnob with his sailors, like the leader of a gang of pirates. I am no Captain Kidd, nor am I another Blackboard. I can easily be blocked in carrying out my purposes. Dickson will not consent to serve his country unless he can fill his pockets. Simpson cannot see the justice of obeying my orders, and lets his inferiors see that he resents them. I wish Dickson were in the blackest pit of Plymouth jail. If I were the pirate he would like to have me, I'd yard-arm him quick enough!"

"We may be overheard, sir," pleaded Wallingford. "We each have our ambitions," he continued bravely, while his father's noble looks came to his face. "Mine are certainly not Dickson's, nor do I look forward to a life at sea, like yourself. This may be the last time we can speak together on the terms you commanded that we should speak to-night. I look for no promotion; I am humble enough about my fitness to serve; the navy is but an accident, as you know, in my career. I beg you to command my hearty service, such as it is; you have a right to it, and you shall not find me wanting. I know that you have been very hard placed."

And now the captain bowed courteously in his turn, and received the pledge with gratitude, but he kept his eyes upon the young man with growing curiosity. Wallingford had turned pale, and spoke with much effort.

"My heart leaps within me when I think that I shall soon stand upon the shore of France," Paul Jones went on, for his guest kept silence. "Within a few days I shall see the Duke of Chartres, if he be within reach. No man ever took such hold of my affections at first acquaintance as that French prince. We knew each other first at Hampton Roads, where he was with Kersaint, the French commodore. My only thought in boarding him was to serve our own young navy and get information for our ship-building, but I was rewarded by a noble gift of friendship. 'T is now two years since we have met, but I cannot believe that I shall find him changed; I can feel my hand in his already. He will give our enterprise what help he can. He met me on his deck that day like a brother; we were friends from the first. I told him my errand, and he showed me everything about his new ship, and even had copies made for me of her plans. 'T was before France and England had come to open trouble, and he was dealing with a rebel, but he helped me all he could. I had loaded my sloop with the best I had on my plantation; 't was May, and the gardens very forward. I knew their vessels had been long at sea, and could ship a whole salad garden. I would not go to ask for favors then without trying to make some pleasure in return, but we were friends from the first. He is a very noble gentleman; you shall see him soon, I hope, and judge for yourself."

Wallingford listened, but the captain was still puzzled by a look on the young man's face.

"I must make my confession," said the lieutenant. "When I hear you speak of such a friend, I know that I have done wrong in keeping silence, sir. I put myself into your hands. When I took my commission, I openly took the side of our colonies against the Crown. I am at heart among the Neutrals: 't is ever an ignominious part to take. I never could bring myself to take the King's side against the country that bore me. I should rather curse those who insisted, on either side, upon this unnatural and unnecessary war. Now I am here; I put myself very low; I am at your mercy, Captain Paul Jones. I cannot explain to you my immediate reasons, but I have gone against my own principles for the sake of one I love and honor. You may put irons on me, or set me ashore without mercy, or believe that I still mean to keep the oath I took. Since I came on board this ship I have begun to see that the colonies are in the right; my heart is with my oath as it was not in the beginning."

"By Heaven!" exclaimed the captain, staring. "Wallingford, do you mean this?" The captain sprang to his feet again. "By Heaven! I could not have believed this from another, but I know you can speak the truth! Give me your hand, sir! Give me your hand, I say, Wallingford! I have known men enough who would fight for their principles, and fight well, but you are the first I ever saw who would fight against them for love and honor's sake. This is what I shall do," he went on rapidly. "I shall not iron you or set you ashore; I shall hold you to your oath. I have no fear that you will ever fail to carry out my orders as an officer of this ship. Now we have indeed spoken together like friends!"

They seated themselves once more, face to face.

There was a heavy trampling overhead. Wallingford had a sudden fear lest this best hour of the voyage might be at an end, and some unexpected event summon them to the deck, but it was only some usual duty of the sailors. His heart was full of admiration for the great traits of the captain. He had come to know Paul Jones at last; their former disastrous attempts at fellowship were all forgotten. A man might well keep difficult promises to such a chief; the responsibilities of his life were in a strong and by no means unjust hand. The confession was made; the confessor had proved to be a man of noble charity.

There was a strange look of gentleness and compassion on the captain's face; his thought was always leading him away from the past moment, the narrow lodging and poor comfort of the ship.

"We have great dangers before us," he reflected, "and only our poor human nature to count upon; 't is the shame and failures of past years that make us wince at such a time as this. We can but offer ourselves upon the altar of duty, and hope to be accepted. I have kept a promise, too, since I came to sea. I was mighty near to breaking it this very day," he added simply.

The lieutenant had but a dim sense of these words; something urged him to make a still greater confidence. He was ready to speak with utter frankness now, to such a listener, of the reasons why he had come to sea, of the one he loved best, and of all his manly hopes; to tell the captain everything.

At this moment, the captain himself, deeply moved by his own thoughts, reached a cordial hand across the table. Wallingford was quick to grasp it and to pledge his friendship as he never had done before.

Suddenly he drew back, startled, and caught his hand away. There was a ring shining on Paul Jones's hand, and the ring was Mary Hamilton's.

XV

The Coast of France

"They goe very neer to ungratefulnesse."

Next day, in the Channel, every heart was rejoiced by the easy taking of two prizes, rich fruit-laden vessels from Madeira and Malaga. With these in either hand the Ranger came in sight of land, after a quick passage and little in debt to time, when the rough seas and the many difficulties of handling a new ship were fairly considered.

The coast lay like a low and heavy cloud to the east and north; there were plenty of small craft to be seen, and the Ranger ran within short distance of a three-decker frigate that looked like an Englishman. She was standing by to go about, and looked majestic, and a worthy defender of the British Isles. Every man on board was in a fury to fight and sink this enemy; but she was far too powerful, and much nobler in size than the Ranger. They crowded to the rail. There was plenty of grumbling alow and aloft lest Captain Paul Jones should not dare to try his chances. A moment later he was himself in a passion because the great Invincible had passed easily out of reach, as if with insolent unconsciousness of having been in any danger.

Dickson, who stood on deck, maintained his usual expression of aggravating amiability, and only ventured to smile a little more openly as the captain railed in greater desperation. Dickson had a new grievance to store away in his rich remembrance, because he had been overlooked in the choice of prize masters to bring the two merchantmen into port.

"Do not let us stand in your way, sir," he said affably. "Some illustrious sea fights have been won before this by the smaller craft against the greater."

"There was the Revenge, and the great San Philip with her Spanish fleet behind her, in the well-known fight at Flores," answered Paul Jones, on the instant. "That story will go down to the end of time; but you know the little Revenge sank to the bottom of the sea, with all her men who were left alive. Their glory could not sink, but I did not know you ever shipped for glory's sake, Mr. Dickson." And Dickson turned a leaden color under his sallow skin, but said nothing.

"At least, our first duty now is to be prudent," continued the captain. "I must only fight to win; my first duty is to make my way to port, before we venture upon too much bravery. There'll be fighting soon enough, and I hope glory enough for all of us this day four weeks. I own it grieves me to see that frigate leave us. She's almost hull down already!" he exclaimed regretfully, with a seaward glance, as he went to his cabin.

Presently he appeared again, as if he thought no more of the three-decker, with a favorite worn copy of Thomson's poems in hand, and began to walk the deck to and fro as he read. On this fair winter morning the ship drove busily along; the wind was out of the west; they were running along the Breton coast, and there was more and more pleasure and relief at finding the hard voyage so near its end. The men were all on deck or clustered thick in the rigging; they made a good strong-looking ship's company. The captain on his quarter-deck was pacing off his exercise with great spirit, and repeating some lines of poetry aloud:—

> *"With such mad seas the daring Gama fought,*
> *For many a day and many a dreadful night;*
> *Incessant lab'ring round the stormy Cape*
> *By bold ambition led"*—

> *"The wide enlivening air is full of fate."*

Then he paused a moment, still waving the book at arm's length, as if he were following the metre silently in his own mind.

> *"On Sarum's plain I met a wandering fair,*
> *The look of Sorrow, lovely still she bore"*—

"He's gettin' ready to meet the ladies!" said Cooper, who was within listening distance, polishing a piece of brass on one of the guns. "I can't say as we've had much po'try at sea this v'y'ge, sir," he continued to Lieutenant Wallingford, who crossed the deck toward him, as the captain disappeared above on his forward stretch. Cooper and Wallingford were old friends ashore, with many memories in common. The lieutenant was pale and severe; the ready smile that made him seem more boyish than his years was strangely absent; he had suddenly taken on the looks of a much-displeased man.

SARAH ORNE JEWETT

"Ain't you feelin' well, sir?" asked Cooper, with solicitude. "Things is all doin' well, though there's those aboard that won't have us think so, if they can help it. When I was on watch, I see you writin' very late these nights past. You will excuse my boldness, but we all want the little sleep we get; 't is a strain on a man unused to life at sea."

"I shall write no more this voyage," said Wallingford, touched by the kindness of old Cooper's feeling, but impatient at the boyish relation with an older man, and dreading a word about home affairs. He was an officer now, and must resent such things. Then the color rushed to his face; he was afraid that tears would shame him. With a sudden impulse he drew from his pocket a package of letters, tied together ready for sending home, and flung them overboard with an angry toss. It was as if his heart went after them. It was a poor return for Cooper's innocent kindness; the good man had known him since he had been in the world. Old Susan, his elder sister, was chief among the household at home. This was a most distressing moment, and the lieutenant turned aside, and leaned his elbow on the gun, bending a little as if to see under the sail whether the three-decker were still in sight.

The little package of letters was on its slow way down through the pale green water; the fishes were dodging as it sank to the dim depths where it must lie and drown, and tiny shells would fasten upon the slow-wasting substance of its folds. The words that he had written would but darken a little salt water with their useless ink; he had written them as he could never write again, in those long lonely hours at sea, under the dim lamp in his close cabin,—those hours made warm and shining with the thought and promise of love that also hoped and waited. All a young man's dream was there; there were tiny sketches of the Ranger's decks and the men in the rigging done into the close text. Alas, there was his mother's letter, too; he had written them both the letters they would be looking and longing for, and sent them to the bottom of the sea. If he had them back, Mary Hamilton's should go to her, to show her what she had done. And in this unexpected moment he felt her wondering eyes upon him, and covered his face with his hands. It was all he could do to keep from sobbing over the gun. He had seen the ring!

"'Tis ashore headache coming on with this sun-blink over the water," said Cooper, still watching him. "I'd go and lie in the dark a bit." It was not like Mr. Wallingford, but there had been plenty of drinking the night before, and gaming too,—the boy might have got into trouble.

"The Lusitanian prince, who Heaven-inspired
To love of useful Glory roused mankind."

They both heard the captain at his loud orations; but he stopped for a moment and looked down at the lieutenant as if about to speak, and then turned on his heel and paced away again.

THE SHORE SEEMED TO MOVE a long step nearer with every hour. The old seafarers among the crew gave knowing glances at the coast, and were full of wisest information in regard to the harbor of Nantes, toward which they were making all possible speed. Dickson, who was in command, came now to reprimand Cooper for his idleness, and set him to his duty sharply, being a great lover of authority.

Wallingford left his place by the trunnion, and disappeared below.

"On the sick list?" inquired Dickson of the captain, who reappeared, and again glanced down; but the captain shrugged his shoulders and made no reply. He was sincerely sorry to have somehow put a bar between himself and his young officer just at this moment. Wallingford was a noble-looking fellow, and as good a gentleman as the Duke of Chartres himself. The sight of such a second would lend credit to their enterprise among the Frenchmen. Simpson was bringing in one of the prizes; and as for Dickson, he was a common, trading sort of sneak.

The dispatches from Congress to announce the surrender of Burgoyne lay ready to the captain's hand: for the bringing of such welcome news to the American commissioners, and to France herself, he should certainly have a place among good French seamen and officers. He stamped his foot impatiently; the moment he was on shore he must post to Paris to lay the dispatches in Mr. Franklin's hand. They were directed to Glory herself in sympathetic ink, on the part of the captain of the Ranger; but this could not be read by common eyes, above the titles of the Philadelphia envoy at his lodgings in Passy.

After reflecting upon these things, Paul Jones, again in a tender mood, took a paper out of his pocketbook, and reread a song of Allan Ramsay's,—

"At setting day and rising moon,"

which a young Virginia girl had copied for him in a neat, painful little hand.

"Poor maid!" he said, with gentle affectionateness, as he folded the paper again carefully. "Poor maid! I shall not forget to do her some great kindness, if my hopes come true and my life continues. Now I must send for Wallingford and speak with him."

XVI

It is the Soul that Sees

"When good and faire in one person meet—"

E very-day life at Colonel Hamilton's house went on with as steady current as the great river that passed its walls. The raising of men and money for a distressed army, with what survived of his duties toward a great shipping business, kept Hamilton himself ceaselessly busy. Often there came an anxious company of citizens riding down the lane to consult upon public affairs; there was an increasing number of guests of humbler condition who sought a rich man's house to plead their poverty. The winter looked long and resourceless to these troubled souls. There were old mothers, who had been left on lonely farms when their sons had gone to war. There was a continued asking of unanswerable questions about the soldiers' return, while younger women came, pale and desperate, with little troops of children pulling at their skirts. When one appealing group left the door, another might be seen coming to take its place. The improvident suffered first and made loudest complaint; later there were discoveries of want that had been too uncomplainingly borne. The well-to-do families of Berwick were sometimes brought to straits themselves, in their effort to succor their poorer neighbors.

Mary Hamilton looked graver and older. All the bright elation of her heart had gone, as if a long arctic night were setting in instead of a plain New England winter, with its lengthening days and bright January sun at no great distance. She could not put Madam Wallingford's sorrow out of mind; she was thankful to be so busy in the great house, like a new Dorcas with her gifts of garments, but the shadow of war seemed more and more to give these days a deeper darkness.

There was no snow on the ground, so late in the sad year; there was still a touch of faded greenness on the fields. One afternoon Mary came across the flagstoned court toward the stables, tempted by the milder air to take a holiday, though the vane still held by the northwest. That great wind was not dead, but only drowsy in the early afternoon, and now and then a breath of it swept down the country.

Old Peggy had followed her young mistress to the door, and still stood there watching with affectionate eyes.

"My poor darlin'!" said the good soul to herself, and Mary turned to look back at her with a smile. She thought Peggy was at her usual grumbling.

"Bless ye, we've all got to have patience!" said the old housekeeper, again looking wistfully at the girl, whose tired face had touched her very heart. As if this quick wave of unwonted feeling were spread to all the air about, Mary's own eyes filled with tears; she tried to go on, and then turned and ran back. She put her arms round Peggy, there in the doorway.

"I am only going for a ride. Kiss me, Peggy,—kiss me just as you did when I was a little girl; things do worry me so. Oh, Peggy dear, you don't know; I can't tell anybody!"

"There, there, darlin', somebody 'll see you! Don't you go to huggin' this dry old thrashin' o' straw; no, don't you take notice 'bout an old withered corn shuck like me!" she protested, but her face shone with tenderness. "Go have your ride, an' I'm goin' to make ye a pretty cake; 't will be all nice and crusty; I was goin' to make you one, anyway. I tell ye things is all comin' right in the end. There, le' me button your little cape!" And so they parted.

Peggy marched back into the great kitchen without her accustomed looks of disapproval at the maids, and dropped into the corner of the settle next the fire. She put out her lame foot in its shuffling shoe, and looked at it as if there were no other object of commiseration in the world.

"'T is a shame to be wearin' out, so fine made as I was. The Lord give me a good smart body, but 'tis beginnin' to fail an' go," said the old woman impatiently. "Once't would ha' took twice yisterday's work to tire foot or back o' me."

"I'm dreadful spent myself, bein' up 'arly an' late. We car'ied an upstropelous sight o' dishes to an' fro. Don't see no vally in feedin' a whole neighborhood, when best part on 'em 's only too lazy to provide theirselves," murmured one of the younger handmaidens, who was languidly scouring a great pewter platter. Whereat Peggy rose in her wrath, and set the complainer a stint of afternoon work sufficient to cast a heavy shadow over the freshest spirit of industry.

THE MISTRESS OF THESE HAD gone her way to the long stables, where a saddle was being put on her favorite horse, and stood in the wide doorway looking down the river. The tide was out; the last brown leaves of the poplars were flying off some close lower branches; there was a touch of north in the wind, but the sun was clear and bright for the time of year. Mary was dressed in a warm habit of green cloth, with a close hood like a child's tied under her chin; the long skirt was full of sharp creases where it had lain all summer in one of the brass-nailed East Indian chests, and a fragrance of camphor and Eastern spices blew out as the heavy folds came to the air. The old coachman was busy with the last girth, and soothed the young horse as he circled about the floor: then, with a last fond stroke of a shining shoulder, he gave Mary his hand, and mounted her light as a feather to the saddle. "He's terrible fresh!" said the old master of horse, as he drew the riding skirt in place with a careful touch. "Have a care, missy!"

Mary thanked the old man with a gentle smile, and took heed that the horse walked quietly away. When she turned the corner beyond the shipyard she dropped the curb rein, and the strong young creature flew straight away like an arrow from the bowstring. "Mind your first wind, now. 'T is a good thing to keep!" said the rider gayly, and leaned forward, as they slackened pace for a moment on the pitch of the hill, to pat the horse's neck and toss a handful of flying mane back to its place. Until the first pleasure and impulse of speed were past there was no time to think, or even to remember any trouble of mind. For the first time in many days all the motive power of life did not seem to come from herself.

The fields of Berwick were already beginning to wear that look of hand-shaped smoothness which belongs only to long-tilled lands in an old country. The first colonists and pilgrims of a hundred and fifty years before might now return to find their dreams had borne fair fruit in this likeness to England, that had come upon a landscape hard wrung from the wilderness. The long slopes, the gently rounded knolls that seemed to gather and to hold the wintry sunshine, the bushy field corners and hedgerows of wild cherry that crossed the shoulders of the higher hills, would be pleasant to those homesick English eyes in the new country they had toiled so hard to win. The river that made its way by shelter and covert of the hilly country of field and pasture,—the river must for many a year have been looked at wistfully, because it was the only road home. Portsmouth might have been all for this world, while Plymouth was all for the next; but the Berwick farms were made by home-makers, neither easy to transplant in the first place, nor easy now to uproot again.

The northern mountains were as blue as if it were a day in spring. They looked as if the warm mist of April hung over them; as if they were the outposts of another world, whose climate and cares were of another and gentler sort, and there was no more fretting or losing, and no more war either by land or sea.

The road was up and down all the way over the hills, winding and turning among the upper farms that lay along the riverside above the Salmon Fall. Now and then a wood road or footpath shortened the way, dark under the black hemlocks, and sunshiny again past the old garrison houses. Goodwins, Plaisteds, Spencers, Keays, and Wentworths had all sent their captives through the winter snows to Canada, in the old French, and Indian wars, and had stood in their lot and place for many a generation to suffer attacks by savage stealth at their quiet ploughing, or confront an army's strength and fury of firebrand and organized assault.

There was the ford to cross at Wooster's River,—that noisy stream which can never be silent, as if the horror of a great battle fought upon its bank could never be told. Here there was always a good modern moment of excitement: the young horse must whirl about and rear, and show horror in his turn, as if the ghosts of Hertel and his French and Indians stood upon the historic spot of their victory over the poor settlers; finally the Duke stepped trembling into the bright shallow water, and then stopped midway with perfect composure, for a drink. Then they journeyed up the steep battleground, and presently caught the sound of roaring water at the Great Falls, heavy with the latter rains.

On the crest of the hill Mary overtook a woman, who was wearily carrying a child that looked large enough to walk alone; but his cheeks were streaked with tears, and there were no shoes on his little feet to tread the frozen road: only some worn rags wrapped them clumsily about. Mary held back her horse, and reached down for the poor little thing, to take him before her on the saddle. The child twisted determinedly in her arms to get a look at her face, and then cuddled against his new friend with great content. He took fast hold of the right arm which held him, and looked proudly down at his mother, who, relieved of her extra burden, stepped briskly alongside.

"Goin' up country to stay with my folks," she answered Mary's question of her journey. "Ain't nothin' else I can do; my man's with the army at Valley Forge. 'God forbid you're any poorer than I be!' he last sent me word. 'I've got no pay and no clothes to speak of, an' here's winter comin' right on.' This mornin' I looked round the house an' see how bare it was, an' I locked the door an' left it. The baby cried good after his cat, but I could n't lug 'em both. She's a pretty creatur' an' smart. I don't know but she'll make out; there's plenty o' squirrels. Cats is better off than women folks."

"I'll ride there some day and get her, if I can, and keep her until you come home," offered Mary kindly.

"Rich folks like you can do everything," said the woman bitterly, with a look at the beautiful horse which easily outstepped her.

"Alas, we can't do everything!" said Mary sadly; and there was something in her voice which touched the complainer's heart.

"I guess you would if you could," she answered simply; and then Mary's own heart was warmed again.

The road still led northward along the high uplands above the river; all the northern hills and the mountains of Ossipee looked dark now, in a solemn row. Mary turned her horse into a narrow track off the highroad, and leaned over to give the comforted child into his mother's arms. He slipped to ground of his own accord, and trotted gayly along.

"Look at them pore little feet! I wisht he had some shoes; he can't git fur afore he'll be cryin' again for me to take an' car' him," said the mother ruefully. "You see them furthest peaks? I've got to git there somehow 'n other, with this lo'd on my back an' that pore baby. But I know folks on the road; pore's they be, they'll take me in, if I can hold out to do the travelin'. War 's hard on pore folks. We've got a good little farm, an' my man didn't want to leave it. He held out 'count o' me till the bounty tempted him. We could n't be no porer than we be, now I tell ye!"

"Go to the store on the hill and get some shoes for the baby," said Mary eagerly, as if to try to cheer her fellow traveler. "Get some warm little shoes, and tell the storekeeper 't was I who bade you come." And so they parted; but Mary's head drooped sorrowfully as she rode among the gray birches, on her shorter way to the high slopes of Pine Hill.

This piece of country had, years before, furnished some of the noblest masts that were ever landed on English shores. The ruined stump of that great pine which was the wonder of the King's dockyards, and had loaded one of the old mastships with its tons of timber, could still be seen, though shrunken and soft with moss. A fox, large in his new winter fur, went sneaking across the way; and the young horse pranced gayly at the sight of him, while Mary noticed his track and the way it led, for her brother's sake, and turned aside across the half-wooded pasture, until she had a sportsman's satisfaction in seeing the fox make toward a rough, ledgy bit of ground, and warm thicket of underbrush at a spring head. This would be good news for poor old Jack, who might take no time for hunting, but could dream of it any night after supper, like a happy dog before his own fire.

On the heights of the great ridge some of the elder generation of trees were still standing, left because they were crooked and unfit for the mastships' cargoes. They were monarchs of the whole landscape, and waved their long boughs in the wintry wind. Mary Hamilton had known them in her earliest childhood, and looked toward them now with happy recognition, as if within their hard seasoned shapes their hearts were conscious of other existences, and affection like her own. She stopped the fleet horse on the top of the hill, and laid her hand upon the bark of a huge pine; then she looked off at the lower country. The sight of it was a challenge to adventure; a great horizon sets the boundaries of the inner life of man wider to match itself, and something that had bound the girl's heart too closely seemed to slip easily away.

She smiled and took a long breath, and, turning, rode down the rough pasture again, and along the field toward the river. Her heavy riding dress filled and flew with the cold northwest wind, and a bright color came back to her cheeks. To stand on the bleak height had freed her spirit, and sent her back to the lower countries of life happier than she came: it was said long ago that one may not sweep away a fog, but one may climb the hills of life and look over it altogether.

She leaped the horse lightly over some bars that gave a surly sort of entrance to a poor-looking farm, and rode toward the low house. Suddenly from behind a thorn bush there appeared a strange figure, short-skirted and bent almost double under a stack of dry beanstalks. The bearer seemed to have uprooted her clumsy burden in a fury. She tramped along, while the horse took to shying at the sight, and had to be pacified with much firmness and patience.

The bean stack at last ceased its angry progress, and stood still.

"What's all that thromping? Keep away wit' yourself, then, whoiver ye are! I can only see the ground by me two feet. Ye'll not ride over me; keep back now till I'm gone!" screamed the shrill voice of an old woman.

"It is I, Mary Hamilton," said the girl, laughing. "You've frightened the Duke almost to death, Mrs. Sullivan! I can hold him, but do let me get by before you bob at him again."

There was a scornful laugh out of the moving ambush.

"Get out of me road, then, the two of ye!" and the bean stack moved angrily away, its transfixing pole piercing the air like a disguised unicorn. The two small feet below were well shod and sturdy like a boy's; the whole figure was so short that the dry frost-bitten vines trailed on the ground more and more, until it appeared as if the tangled mass were rolling uphill by its own volition.

Mary went on with the trembling horse. A moment later she walked quickly up the slope to the gray wooden house. There was the handsome head of a very old man, reading, close to the window, as she passed; but he did not look up until she had shut the door behind her and stood within the little room.

Then Master Sullivan, the exile, closed his book and sprang to his feet, a tall and ancient figure with the manners of a prince. He bent to kiss the hand of his guest, and looked at her silently before he spoke, with an unconscious eagerness of affection equal to her own.

"A thousand welcomes!" he said at last. "I should have seen you coming; you have had no one to serve you. I was on the Sabine farm with Horace; 't is far enough away!" he added, with a smile.

"I like to fasten my horse myself," answered Mary. "'T is best I should; he makes it a point of honor then to stand still and wait for me, and resents a stranger's hand, being young and impatient."

Mary looked bright and smiling; she threw back her close green hood, and her face bloomed out of it like a flower, as she stood before the gallant, frail old man. "There was a terrible little bean stack that came up the hill beside us," she went on, as if to amuse him, "and I heard a voice out of it, and saw two steady feet that I knew to be Mrs. Sullivan's; but my black Duke was pleased to be frightened out of his wits, and so we have all parted on bad terms, this dark day."

"She will shine upon you like a May morning when she comes in, then!" said Master Sullivan. "She's in a huge toil the day, with sure news of a great storm that's coming. 'Stay a while,' I begged her, 'stay a while, my dear; the wind is in a fury, and to-morrow'"—

"An' to-morrow indeed!" cried the master's wife, bursting in at the door, half a wild brownie and half a tame enough grandmotherly old soul. "An' to-morrow! I've heard nothing but to-morrow from ye all my life long, an' here 's the hand of winter upon us again, an' thank God all me poor little crops is under cover, an' no praise to yourself."

The old man held out his slender hand; she did not take it, but her face began to shine with affection.

"Thank God, 't is yourself, Miss Mary Hamilton, my dear!" she exclaimed, dropping a curtsy. "My old gentleman here has been sorrowing for a sight of your fair face these many days. 'T is in December like this we do be sighing after the May. I don't know, have ye brought any news yet from the ship?"

"Oh no, not yet," said Mary. "No, there is no news yet from the Ranger."

"I have had good dreams of her, then," announced the old creature with triumph. "Listen: there's quarrels amongst 'em, but they'll come safe to shore, with gold in everybody's two hands."

She crossed the room, and drew her lesser wheel close to her knee and began to spin busily.

XVII

The Remnant of Another Time

"Simple and true I share with all
The treasures of a kindly mind;

And in my cottage, poor and small,
The great a welcome find.

"I vex not Gods, nor patron friend,
For larger gifts or ampler store;

My modest Sabine farm can lend
All that I want, and more."

They sat in silence,—it was pleasure enough to be together,—and Mary knew that she must wait until Master Sullivan himself made opportunity for speaking of the things which filled her heart.

"Have I ever told you that my father was a friend, in his young days, of Christopher Milton, brother to the great poet, but opposite in politics?" he asked, as if this were the one important fact to be made clear. "A Stuart partisan, a violent Churchman, and a most hot-headed Tory," and the old master laughed with sincere amusement, as Mary looked up, eager to hear more.

"Voltaire, too, had just such a contradiction of a brother, credulous and full of superstitions,—a perfect Jansenist of those days. Yes, I was reading Horace when you came, but for very homesickness; he can make a man forget all his own affairs, such are his polite hospitalities of the mind! These dark autumn days mind me every year of Paris, when they come, as April weather makes me weep for childhood and the tears and smiles of Ireland."

"The old days in your Collége Louis-le-Grand," Mary prompted him, in the moment's silence. "Those are your Paris days I love the best."

"Oh, the men I have known!" he answered. "I can sit here in my chair and watch them all go by again down the narrow streets. I have seen the Abbé de Châteauneuf pass, with his inseparable copy of Racine sticking out of his pocket; I often hid from him, too, in the shadow of an archway, with a young boy, his pupil and my own schoolfellow, who had run away from his tasks. He was four years younger than I. *Le petit Arouet* we called him then, who proves now to be the very great Voltaire! Ah, 't was an idle flock of us that ranged the old cloisters in cap and gown; 't was the best blood in France! I have seen the illustrious Duke de Boufflers handsomely flogged for shooting peas at dull old Lejay, the professor. (We were the same age, Monsieur de Boufflers and I; we were great friends, and often flogged in company for our deviltries.) He was a colonel of the French army in that moment, and bore the title of Governor of Flanders; but on the day of the pea-shooting they flogged him so that I cried out at the sight, and turned to the wall, sick at heart. As for him, he sobbed all night afterward, and caught his breath in misery next morning while we read our Epictetus from the same book. We knelt together before the high altar and vowed to kill Lejay by dagger or poison before the month's end. 'T was a good vow, but well broken."

The old man laughed again, and made a gay French gesture. Mary laughed with him, and they had a fine moment together.

"You were not always like that,—you must have learned your lessons; it was not all idleness," Mary protested, to lead him on.

"The old fathers taught us with all their power to gain some skill in the use of words," reflected the master soberly. "Yes, and I learned to fence, too, at the college. A student of Louis-le-Grand could always speak like a gentleman, but we had to play with our words; 't was the most important of all our science. 'Les sottises, toujours les sottises,'" grumbled the old man. "Yes, they made a high profession then of talking nonsense, though France was whipped at Blenheim and lost the great fight at Malplaquet. They could laugh at the ruined convent of Port Royal and the distresses of saintly souls, but they taught us to talk nonsense, and to dress with elegance, and to be agreeable to ladies. The end is not yet; the throne of France will shake, some day, until heads fall in the dust like fruit that nobody stoops to gather."

The master fell a-whispering to himself, as if he had forgotten that he had a listener.

"I saw some signs of it, too. I knew there, when I was a lad, Le Tellier, the King's confessor, who was the true ruler of France. I rode to St. Denis myself, the day of the old King's funeral, and it was like a fair: people were singing and drinking in the booths, and no one all along the way but had his gibe at Le Tellier, whose day was over, thank God!

Ah, but I was a gay lad then; I knew no country but France, and I cannot but love her yet; I was only a Frenchman of my gay and reckless time. There was saving grace for me, and I passed it by; for I knew the great Fénelon, and God forgive my sins, but I have been his poor parishioner from those days to these. I knew his nephew, the Abbé de Beaumont, and I rode with him in the holidays to Cambrai,—a tiresome journey; but we were young, and we stayed in the good archbishop's house, and heard him preach and say mass. He was the best of Christians: I might have been a worse man but for that noble saint. Yes, I have seen the face of the great Fénelon," and Master Sullivan bent his head and blessed himself. The unconscious habit of his youth served best to express the reverence which lay deep in his aged heart.

"I think now, as I look back on those far days, that my good archbishop was the greatest prince and saint of them all, my dear child," said the old teacher, looking up gently from his reverie into Mary Hamilton's face.

"You belong to another world, mon maître," said the girl affectionately. "How much you could teach us, if we were but fit to learn!"

The old man gave an impatient fling of his hand.

"I am past eighty years old, my darling," he answered. "God knows I have not been fit to learn of the best of men, else I might now be one of the wisest of mankind. I have lived in the great days of France, but I tell you plain, I have lived in none that are fuller of the seeds of greatness than these. I live now in my sons, and our Irish veins are full of soldier's blood. 'T is Tir-nan-Og here,—the country of the young. My boys have their mother's energy, thank God! As for me, my little school is more alive than I. There is always a bright child in every flock, for whose furthering a man may well spend himself. 'T is a long look back; the light of life shone bright with me in its beginning, but the oil in the old lamp is burning low. My forbears were all short-lived, but the rest of their brief days are added to the length of mine."

"'T is not every man has made so many others fit to take their part in life," said Mary. "Think of your own sons, master!"

"Ay, my sons," said the old man, pleased to the heart, "and they have their mother's beauty and energy to couple with their sad old father's gift of dreams. The princes of Beare and Bantry are cousins to the Banshee, and she whispers me many things. I sometimes fear that my son John, the general, has too much prudence. The Whisperer and Prudence are not of kin."

There was a new silence then; and when Master Sullivan spoke again, it was with a sharp, questioning look in his eyes.

"What said your little admiral at parting? I heard that he was fretted with the poor outfitting of his ship, and sailed away with scant thanks to the authorities. Prudence cannot deal with such a man as that. What of our boy Roger? How fares the poor mother since she lost him out of her sight? 'T was anxious news they brought me of his going; when my first pride had blazed down, you might have seen an old man's tears."

Mary looked up; she flushed and made as if she would speak, but remained silent.

"You'll never make soldier or sailor of him, boy or man; the Lord meant him for a country gentleman," said the master warningly; and at this moment all Mary's hopes of reassurance fell to the ground.

"My son John is a soldier born," he continued coldly; "he could tell you where the troops were placed in every battle, from old Troy down to the siege of Louisburg."

Mary began to speak, and again something ailed her throat. She turned and looked toward the fireside, where the old housemother was knitting now, and humming a strange old Irish tune to herself; she had left them to themselves as much as if she were miles away.

"Incipit vita nova," said the master under his breath, and went on as if he were unobservant of Mary's startled look.

"Captain Paul Jones is a man of the world, and Wallingford is a country gentleman of the best sort," he continued; "they may not understand each other at these close quarters. I mind me of pushing adventurers in my old days who came from the back corner of nowhere, and yet knew the worst and the best of Paris. How they would wink at their fellows when some noble boy came to see the world, from one of the poor and proud châteaux of Brittany or the far south!"

"Roger is college-bred, and you have called him your own best scholar of these later days," insisted Mary, with a touch of indignation. "With such kindred in Boston, and the company of his father's friends from childhood, he is not so new to the world."

"Ecce Deus fortior me qui veniens dominabitur mihi," the old man repeated softly, as if he were saying a short prayer; then glanced again at the girl's beautiful young face and pleading eyes. "Well, the gallant lads have sailed!" he exclaimed, with delighted eagerness, and no apparent concern for his listener's opinion. "They'll be in good season, too, in spite of all delays. What say the loud Patriots now, who are so full of fighting, and yet find good excuse for staying at home? They are an evil-minded chorus! but the young man Wallingford will serve them for a text no more. His father was a man of parts, of the same type as Washington himself, an I mistake not that great leader, though never put to the proof by so high a summonsing of opportunity. Our Roger is born out of his father's clear brain rather than his fiery heart. I see in him the growing scholarliness and quiet authority of the judge's best days upon the bench, not the strong soldier of the Indian wars. And there is something in the boy that holds by the past; he may be a persuaded Patriot, but a Tory ghost of a conscience plucks him by the sleeve. He does not lack greatness of soul, but I doubt if he does any great things except to stand honestly in his place, a scholar and a gentleman; and that is enough."

Mary listened, with her eyes fixed upon Master Sullivan's face.

"God bless the poor lads, every one! We must send our prayers after them. Wallingford will fall upon evil days; 't will try him in blood and bone when they suspect him, as they surely will. God help an old ruin like me! If I were there, and but a younger man!" and the master clenched the arms of his chair, while something Mary never had seen before flashed in his eyes.

"I have seen much fighting in my time," he said the next moment to Mary, falling to a gentler mood. "My mind is often with those lads on the ship." And the startled girl smiled back at him expectantly.

"I am glad when I think that now Roger will see France again, as a grown man. He will remember many things I have told him. I wish that I might have seen him ere he went away so suddenly. Wherever he is, he has good thoughts in his head; he always loved his Latin, and can even stumble through the orchard ground and smell the trodden thyme with old Theocritus. I wish I had been there at your parting feast. 'T was a glory to the house's mistress, and that merchant prince, the good master of the river."

"Peggy has another opinion of me. 'Go you an' deck the tables, an it please you, child,' she says, 'an' leave me to give my orders;' but we hold some grave consultations for all that," insisted Mary modestly. "She is very stern on feast days with us all, is Peggy."

"Lenient in the main," urged Master Sullivan, smiling. "She found convoy for a basket of her best wares only yesterday, with a message that she had cooked too much for Portsmouth gentlemen, guests who failed in their visit. Margery and I feasted in high hall together. There was a grand bottle of claret."

"My brother chose it himself from the cellar," said Mary, much pleased, but still there was a look of trouble in her eyes.

"You will give him my thanks, and say that it made a young French gallant of me for a pleasant hour. The only fault I found was that I had not its giver to drink share and share with me. Margery, my wife, heard tales from me which had not vexed the air these fifty years, and, being as warm as a lady abbess with such good cheer, she fell asleep in the middle of the best tale, over her worsted knitting! 'Sure,' she waked to tell me, 'if these be true, 't was time you were snatched out of France like a brand from the burning, and got the likes o' poor me to straighten ye!'" and the old man looked at Mary, with a twinkle in his eyes.

"They said you danced all night with the little captain, and that he spoke his love on the terrace in the sight of more than one of the company," said the master gayly. "'T is another heart you've broke, I suppose, and sent him sad away. Or was it his uniform that won ye?" They both laughed, but Mary blushed, and wished she were away herself.

"I have no right to ask what passed between ye," he said then, with grave sweetness that won her back to him. "I find him a man of great power. He has the thoughts and manners of a gentleman, and now he goes to face his opportunity," added the old Irish rebel.

"'Tis said everywhere that your great captain is an earl's son," said Margery unexpectedly, from the fireside. But Master Sullivan slowly shook his head. The old wife was impatient of contradiction at the best of times, and now launched forth into an argument. He treated her, in these late days, as if she were a princess; but 't was a trying moment to him now, and luckily the old volume of Horace fell from his lap to the floor.

Mary picked it up quickly, and old Margery's withered cheeks flushed crimson at this reminder of the sad day when she had thrown one of his few dear books to the flames, in furious revenge for what she thought his willful idleness and indifference to their poverty, and her children's needs. "*Himself cried*," she always mourned in passionate remorse, when anything reminded her of that black day. She fancied even yet, when she saw the master stand before his little bookshelf, that he was missing the lost volume. "*Himself cried*," she muttered new, and was silent; and the old man saw her lips moving, and gave her one of those looks of touching affection that had kept her for fifty years his happy slave.

"He is a bold adventurer, your little captain," he went on, "but a man of very marked qualities."

"I believe that he will prove a great captain," said Mary.

"Yes, he is all that; I have seen much of men," and the master turned to look out of the window, far down the winter fields.

"His heart is set upon the future of our country," said Mary, with eagerness. "He speaks with eloquence of our wrongs. He agrees 't is the hindering of our own natural development, and the forbidding of our industries in the past, that has brought all these troubles; not any present tyranny or special taxes, as some insist. He speaks like a New Englander, one of ourselves, and he has new ideas; I heard him say that every village should govern itself, and our government be solely for those necessities common to all, and this would do away with tyranny. He was very angry when Major Haggens laughed and pounded the table, and said that our villages must keep to the same laws, and not vex one another."

"Your captain has been reading that new writer, Monsieur Rousseau," said the master sagaciously, and with much interest. "Rousseau is something of a genius. My son James brought me his book from Boston, and I sat up all night to read it. Yes, he is a genius at his best, but at his worst no greater fool ever sneaked or flaunted along a French road. 'T is like the old donkey in Skibbereen, that was a lion by night with his bold braying, and when the sun shone hung his head and cried to everybody, '*Don't beat me!*' I pray God that no pupil of mine makes the mistake of these people, who can see no difference between the church of their own day and Christianity itself. My old Voltaire has been his master, this Rousseau. There have been few greater men in the world than le petit Arouet, but 't was a bit of a rascal, too! My son James and I have threshed these subjects lately, until the flails came too near our own heads. I have seen more of the world than he, but my son James always held the opinions of a gentleman."

"These subjects are far too large for me," Mary acknowledged humbly.

"'T is only that our opinions are too small for the subjects,—even mine and those of my son James," said Master Sullivan, smiling; "yet every man who puts his whole heart into them helps to bring the light a little nearer. Your captain is a good French scholar; we had some good talk together, and I learned to honor the man. I hope he will be friendly to our lad at sea, and be large-hearted in such a case. I have much pity for the Loyalists, now I am an old man that was a hot enough rebel in my youth. They have many true reasons on their side for not breaking with England, and they cling to sentiment, the best of them, without which life is but a strange machine. Yet they have taken the wrong side; they will find it out to their sorrow. You had much to do with Roger's going, my child; 't was a brave thing to start him in the right road, but I could wish he and his mother had been a sorrowing pair of that eleven hundred who went out of Boston with the English troops. They would have been among their fellows then, and those who were like-minded. God help me for this faint-heartedness!"

To this moment had the long talk come; to this clear-spoken anxiety had Mary Hamilton herself led the way. She could not part from so wise a friend until he spoke his mind, and now she stood piteous and dismayed before his searching look. It was not that the old man did not know how hard his words had been.

"I could not bear that he should be disloyal to the country that gave him birth, and every low soul be given the right to sneer at him. And the mob was ready to burn his mother's house; the terror and danger would have been her death," said Mary. "All this you know."

"The boy has talked much with me this summer," answered the schoolmaster, "and he put me questions which I, a rebel, and the son of rebels against England, could not answer him. I am an exile here, with my birthright gone, my place among men left empty, because I did not think as he thinks now when I was young, and yet I could not answer him. 'I could as soon forsake my mother in her gathering age as forsake England now,' he told me, one day in the summer. He stood on this floor before me, where you stand now, and looked every inch a man. Now he has changed his mind; now he puts to sea in an American man-of-war, with those to whom the gentle arts of piracy are not unknown, and he must fain be of their company who go to make England suffer. He has done this only that he may win your heart."

The master's blue eyes were black and blazing with excitement, and Mary fronted him.

"You cannot think him a rascal!" she cried. "You must believe that his very nature has changed. It has changed, and he may fight with a heavy heart, but he has come to think our quarrel just. I should break my own heart did I not think this true. Has he not sworn his oath? Then you must not blame him; you must blame me if all this course was wrong. I did push him forward to the step. God help me, master, I could not bear we should be ashamed of him. You do not mean that 't were better he had fled with the Loyalists, and thrown his duty down?"

She fell to her knees beside the old man's chair, and her hot forehead was touching his thin hand. He laid his right hand on her head then as if in blessing, but he did not speak.

At last he made her rise, and they stood side by side in the room.

"We must not share this anxious hour with Margery," he told her gently. "Go away, dear child, while she still sleeps. I did not know the sword of war had struck your heart so deep. You must wait for much time to pass now; you must have patience and must hear bad news. They will call Roger Wallingford a spy, and he may even flinch when the moment of trial comes. I do not think he will flinch; 't is the woe of his own soul that I sorrow for; there is that in him which forbids the traitor's act. Yet either way life looks to him but treacherous. The thought of his love shines like a single star above the two roads, and that alone can succor him. Forgive the hardness of my thoughts, yes, and keep you close to his poor mother with all patience. If the boy gets into trouble, I have still some ancient friendships that will serve him, for my sake, in England. God grant me now to live until the ship comes back! I trust the man he sails with, but he has his own ends to serve. I fear he is of the *Brevipennes*, the short-winged; they can run better for what wings they have, but they cannot win to fly clear of the earth."

"I COULD TELL YOU MANY a tale now that I have shut close in my heart from every one for more than sixty years," said Master Sullivan slowly, with an impulse of love and pity that he could not forbid. "I was a poor scholar in some things, in my young days, but I made sure of one lesson that was learnt through pain. The best friends of a human soul are Courage and her sister Patience!"

The old man's beautiful voice had a strange thrill in it. He looked as if he were a king, to the girl who watched him; all the mystery of his early days, the unexplained self-denial and indifference to luxury, seemed at this moment more incomprehensible than ever. The dark little room, the unequal companionship with the wife who slept by the fire, the friendship of his heart with a few imperial books, and the traditions of a high ancestry made evident in the noble careers and present standing of his sons, were enough to touch any imagination. And Mary Hamilton, from her early childhood, had found him the best and wisest man she knew. He had set the humblest Berwick children their copies, and taught them to read and spell, and shared his St. Augustine and Homer and Horace with those few who could claim the right. She stood beside him now in her day of trouble; she turned, with a look of deep love on her face, and kissed him on the brow. Whatever the cause had been, he had taken upon himself the harsh penalty of exile.

"Dear friend, I must be gone," said Mary, with beautiful womanliness and dignity. "You have helped me again who have never failed me; do not forget me in these days, and let us pray for Roger Wallingford, that he may be steadfast. Good-by, dear master."

Then, a minute later, the old man heard the horse's quick feet go away down the hill.

It was twilight in the room. "I believe she will love the boy," whispered the old schoolmaster to himself. "I thought the captain might wake her heart with all his gallantry. The springs of love are living in her heart, but 't is winter still,—'t is winter still! Love frights at first more than it can delight; 't will fright my little lady ere it comes!"

The heavy book slipped unheeded to the floor again. The tired old woman slept on by the dying fire, and Master Sullivan was lost in his lonely thoughts, until Hope came again to his side, bright shining in a dream.

XVIII

Oh Had I wist!—

"You need not go into a desert and fast, a crowd is often more lonely than a wilderness and small things harder to do than great."

The ship had run between Belle Isle and the low curving shores of Quiberon. The land was in sight all along by St. Nazaire, where they could see the gray-green of winter fields, and the dotted fruit trees about the farmhouses, and bits of bushy woodland. Out of the waste of waters the swift way-wise little Ranger came heading safely in at the mouth of the Loire. She ran among all the shoals and sand banks by Paimboeuf, and past the shipyards of the river shores, until she came to harbor and let her anchor go.

There was something homelike about being in a river. At first sight the Loire wore a look of recent settlement, rather than of the approach to a city already famous in old Roman times; the shifting sand dunes and the empty flats, the poor scattered handfuls of houses and the works of shipbuilding, all wore a temporary look. These shiftless, primitive contrivances of men sparsely strewed a not too solid-looking shore, and the newcomers could see little of the inland country behind it. It was a strange contrast to their own river below Portsmouth, where gray ledges ribbed the earth and bolted it down into an unchangeable permanence of outline. The heights and hollows of the seaward points of Newcastle and the Kittery shore stood plain before his mind's eye as Wallingford came on deck, and these strange banks of the Loire seemed only to mask reality and confuse his vision. Farther up the stream they could see the gray walls of Nantes itself, high over the water, with the huge towered cathedral, and the lesser bulk of the castle topping all the roofs. It was a mild day, with little air moving.

Dickson came along the deck, looking much displeased. That morning he had received the attention of being kicked down the companion way by the captain, and nothing could soften such an event, not even the suggestion from his conscience that he had well deserved the insult. It seemed more and more, to those who were nearest him, as if Dickson were at heart the general enemy of mankind,—jealous and bitter toward those who stood above him, and scornful of his inferiors. He loved to defeat the hopes of other people, to throw discredit upon sincerity; like some swift-creeping thing that brings needless discomfort everywhere, and dismay, and an impartial sting. He was not clever enough to be a maker of large schemes, but rather destructive, crafty, and evil-minded,—a disturber of the plans of others. All this was in his face; a fixed habit of smiling only added to his mean appearance. What was worst of all, being a great maker of promises, he was not without influence, and had his following.

The fresh air from the land, the frosty smell of the fields, made Wallingford feel the more despondent. The certainty had now come to his mind that Paul Jones would never have consented to his gaining the commission of lieutenant, would never have brought him, so untried and untrained, to sea, but for jealousy, and to hinder his being at Mary Hamilton's side. This was the keenest hurt to his pride; the thought had stabbed him like a knife. Again he made a desperate plunge into the sea of his disasters, and was unconscious even of the man who was near by, watching him. He was for the moment blind and deaf to all reality, as he stood looking along the water toward the Breton town.

"All ready to go ashore, sir?" asked Dickson, behind him, in an ingratiating tone; but Wallingford gave an impatient shrug of his shoulders.

"'T is not so wintry here as the shore must look at home," continued Dickson. "Damn that coxcomb on the quarter-deck! he's more than the devil himself could stand for company!"

Wallingford, instead of agreeing in his present disaffection, turned about, and stood fronting the speaker. He looked Dickson straight in the eye, as if daring him to speak again, whereat Dickson remained silent. The lieutenant stood like a prince.

"I see that I intrude," said the other, rallying his self-consequence. "You have even less obligation to Captain Paul Jones than you may think," he continued, dropping his voice and playing his last trump. "I overheard, by accident, some talk of his on the terrace with a certain young lady whom your high loftiness might not allow me to mention. He called you a cursed young spy and a Tory, and she implored him to protect you. She said you was her old playmate, and that she wanted you got out o' the way o' trouble. He had his arm round her, and he said he might be ruined by you; he cursed you up hill and down, while she was a-pleadin'. 'Twas all for her sake, and your mother's bein' brought into distress"—

Dickson spoke rapidly, and edged a step or two away; but his shoulder was clutched as if a panther's teeth had it instead of a man's hand.

"I'll kill you if you give me another word!" said Roger Wallingford. "If I knew you told the whole truth, I should be just as ready to drop you overboard."

"I have told the truth," said Dickson.

"I know you are n't above eavesdropping," answered Wallingford, with contempt. "If you desire to know what I think of your sneaking on the outside of a man's house where you have been denied entrance, I am willing to tell you. I heard you were there that night."

"You were outside yourself, to keep me company, and I'm as good a gentleman as Jack Hamilton," protested Dickson. "He went the rounds of the farms with a shoemaker's kit, in the start of his high fortunes."

"Mr. Hamilton would mend a shoe as honestly in his young poverty as he would sit in council now. So he has come to be a rich merchant and a trusted man." There was something in Wallingford's calm manner that had power to fire even Dickson's cold and sluggish blood.

"I take no insults from you, Mr. Lieutenant!" he exclaimed, in a black rage, and passed along the deck to escape further conversation.

There had been men of the crew within hearing. Dickson had said what he wished to say, and a moment later he was thinking no less highly of himself than ever. He would yet compass the downfall of the two men whom he hated. He had already set them well on their way to compass the downfall of each other. It made a man chuckle with savage joy to think of looking on at the game.

Wallingford went below again, and set himself to some work in his own cabin. Character and the habit of self-possession could carry a man through many trying instances, but life now seemed in a worse confusion than before. This was impossible to bear; he brushed his papers to the floor with a sweep of his arm. His heart was as heavy as lead within him. Alas, he had seen the ring! "Perhaps—perhaps"—he said next moment to himself—"she might do even that, if she loved a man; she could think of nothing then but that I must be got away to sea!"

SARAH ORNE JEWETT

"Poor little girl! O God, how I love her!" and he bent his head sorrowfully, while an agony of grief and dismay mastered him. He had never yet been put to such awful misery of mind.

"'T is my great trial that has come upon me," he said humbly. "I'll stick to my duty,—'tis all that I can do,—and Heaven help me to bear the rest. Thank God, I have my duty to the ship!"

XIX

The Best-laid Plans

*"Artists have come to study from these marbles. . . Boys have flung
stones against the sculptured and unmindful devils."*

As soon as the Ranger was at Nantes, and the formalities of the
port could be left in the hands of his officers, Captain Paul Jones
set forth in haste toward Paris to deliver his despatches. He was only
sixty hours upon the road, passing over the country as if he saw it from
a balloon, and at last had the supreme disappointment of finding that
his proud errand was forestalled. He had driven himself and his ship
for nothing; the news of Burgoyne's surrender had been carried by a
messenger from Boston, on a fast-sailing French vessel, and placed in
the hands of the Commissioners a few hours before his own arrival. It
was understood some time before, between the Marine Committee of
the colonies and Captain Paul Jones, that he was to take command
of the fine frigate L'Indien, which was then building in Amsterdam;
but he received no felicitations now for his rapid voyage, and found
no delightful accumulations of important work, and was by no means
acknowledged as the chief and captain of a great enterprise. As the
Ranger had come into harbor like any ordinary vessel from the high
seas, unheralded and without greeting, so Paul Jones now found
himself of no public consequence or interest in Paris. What was to be
done must all be done by himself. The Commissioners had their hands
full of other affairs, and the captain stood in the position of a man who
brought news to deaf ears. They listened to his eager talk and well-
matured plans with some wonder, and even a forced attention, as if he
were but an interruption, and not a leader for any enterprise they had in
hand. To him, it had almost seemed as if his great projects were already
accomplished.

It was in every way a most difficult situation. The ownership of the
Indien frigate had been carefully concealed. Paul Jones himself had
furnished the plans for her, and the Commissioners in France had
made contracts under other signatures for her building in the neutral
port of Amsterdam. It was indispensable that the secret of her destiny

should be kept from England; but at the moment when she was ready to be put into commission, and Paul Jones was on the sea, with the full expectation of finding his ship ready when he came to France, some one in the secret had betrayed it, and the British officials at Amsterdam spoke openly to the government of the Netherlands, and demanded that the frigate should be detained for breach of neutrality, she being destined for an American ship of war. There was nothing to be done. The Commissioners had made some efforts to hold the frigate, but in the end France had come forward and stood their friend by buying her, and at a good price. This had happened only a few days before, so Captain Paul Jones must hear the sorry tale when he came to Paris and saw the three American Commissioners.

He stood before them, a sea-tanned and weary little hero, with his eyes flashing fire. One of the three Commissioners, Arthur Lee, could not meet his aggrieved and angry looks. To be sure, the money was in hand again, and they could buy another ship; but the Indien, the Indien was irrecoverable.

"If I had been there, gentlemen," cried Paul Jones, with a mighty oath, "nothing would have held me long in port! I'd have sailed her across dry ground, but I'd have got her safe to sea! She was ours in the sight of Heaven, and all the nations in the world could not prevent me!"

Mr. Franklin looked on with approval at so noble and forgivable a rage; the others wore a wearied and disgusted look, and Mr. Arthur Lee set himself to the careful mending of a pen. It was a sorry hour for good men; and without getting any definite promise, and having bestowed many unavailing reproaches, at last Paul Jones could only fling himself out of Paris again, and in black despair post back to the Ranger at Nantes. He had the solitary comfort, before he left, of a friendly and compassionate interview granted by Mr. Franklin, who, over-burdened though he was, and much vexed by a younger man's accusations, had yet the largeness of mind to see things from the captain's side. There was nothing for it but patience, until affairs should take a turn, as the Commissioner most patiently explained.

All the captain's high hopes and ceaseless industry in regard to his own plans were scattered like straws in the wind. He must set his mind now to the present possibilities. Worst of all, he had made an enemy in his quick mistrust and scorn of Mr. Arthur Lee, a man who would block many another plan, and hinder him in the end as a great sea captain and hero had never been worse hindered since the world began.

Dickson stood on the deck of the Ranger, by the gangway, when the captain came aboard, fatigued and disappointed; it might be that some creature of Lee's sending had already spoken with Dickson and prepared him for what was to come. He made a most handsome salutation, however, and Lieutenant Simpson, hoping for news of his own promotion, stepped forward with an honest welcome.

"Gentlemen, I have much to tell you, and of an unwelcome sort," said the captain, with unusual dignity of bearing. "There is one blessing: our defeat of Burgoyne has brought us France for an ally. I hoped for good news as regards ourselves, but we have been betrayed by an enemy; we have lost the frigate which I have had a hand in building, and of whose command I was altogether certain for more than a year past. We must now wait for further orders here, and refit the Ranger, and presently get to sea with her instead. I own that it is a great disappointment to us all."

Dickson wore no look of surprise; he was too full of triumph. Lieutenant Simpson was crestfallen. The other officers and men who were near enough to hear looked angry and disturbed. They had been persuaded that they must be rid of the captain before they could follow their own purposes. 'Twas a strange and piteous condition of things aboard the Ranger, and an example of what the poison of lies and a narrow-minded jealousy can do to set honest minds awry. And Paul Jones had himself to thank for much ill will: he had a quick temper, and a savage way of speaking to his fellows. The one thing he could not bear was perfidy, and a bland and double disposition in a man seemed at once to deserve the tread of his angry heel.

The captain was hardly to be seen for a day or two after his return, except in occasional forays of fault-finding. Wallingford was successful in keeping out of his way; the great fact that all his own best hopes had been destroyed dulled him even to feelings of resentment. While suffering his great dismay he could almost forget the cause whence it came, and even pitied, for other reasons, the man who had worn the ring. The first stroke of a bullet only benumbs; the fierceness of pain comes later. Again and again he stood before Mary Hamilton, and lived over the night when he had stood at the window and dared to meet her beautiful angry eyes; again and again he reviewed those gentler moments by the river, when her eyes were full of their old affection, though her words were stern. He had won her plain promise that some day, having served their country, he might return to her side, and clung to that promise like a last hope.

It already seemed a year since the night when Wallingford and the captain had dined together. The steward had interrupted them just as the lieutenant sprung to his feet.

"Must we say good-night, then?" said Paul Jones, protesting. "As for me, I ought to be at my papers. Send me William Earl to write for me," he told the steward. "Thank you for your good company, Mr. Wallingford. I hope we may have many such evenings together."

Yet he had looked after his guest with a sense that something had gone wrong at this last moment, though the steward had found them hand in hand.

The sight of the ring among his possessions, that day when he made ready for the journey to Paris, had given him a moment of deep happiness; he had placed it on his finger, with a certain affectionate vanity. Yet it was a token of confidence, and in some sense a reward. He had been unjust in the beginning to the young lieutenant; he had now come to like and to trust him more than any other man on board the ship. In the exciting days that had followed, rings, and lieutenants, and even so lovely a friend and lady as Miss Mary Hamilton had been forgotten.

Yet at most unexpected moments Paul Jones did remember her, and his heart longed for the moment when they should meet once more, and he might plead his cause. "L'absence diminue les petits amours et augmente les grandes, comuie le vent qui éteint les bougies et rallume la feu."

THE CAPTAIN AT ONCE BEGAN to hasten the work of refitting the Ranger for sea. He gave no explanations; he was more surly in temper, and strangely uncompanionable. Now that they could no longer admire his seamanship in a quick voyage, the sailors rated him for the ship's idleness and their long detention in port. This was not what they had signed for. Dickson now and then let fall a word which showed that he had means of information that were altogether his own; he was often on shore, and seemed free with his money. Lieutenant Wallingford and the surgeon, with some of the other officers, became familiar with the amusements of Nantes; but the lieutenant was observed by every one to be downhearted and inclined to solitary walks, and by night he kept his cabin alone, with no inclination toward company. He had been friendly with every one in the early part of the voyage, like a man who has no fear of risking a kind word. The surgeon, after making unwonted efforts to gain his old neighbor's confidence, ignored him with the rest, until he should come to himself again.

This added to the constraint and discomfort on board the Ranger. She was crowded with men eager enough for action, and yet kept in idleness under a needlessly strict discipline. Simpson, the senior lieutenant, willingly received the complaints of officers and crew, and Dickson's ceaseless insistence that Simpson was their rightful leader began to have its desired effect.

XX

Now are we Friends Again?

"My altar holds a constant flame."

Some dreary days, and even weeks, passed by, and one evening
Wallingford passed the captain's cabin on his way to his own. It had
lately been rough, windy weather in the harbor, but that night the Ranger
was on an even keel, and as steady as if she were a well-built house on shore.

The door was open. "Is that you, Mr. Wallingford? Come in, will
you?" The captain gave his invitation the air of a command.

Wallingford obeyed, but stood reluctant before his superior.

"I thought afterward that you had gone off in something of a flurry,
that night we dined together, and you have avoided any conversation
with me since my return from Paris. I don't like your looks now. Has
anything come between us? Do you repent your confidence?"

"No, I do not repent it," said the lieutenant slowly.

"Something has touched your happiness. Come, out with it! We
were like brothers then. The steward caught us hand in hand; it is long
since I have had so happy an evening. I am grateful for such friendship
as you showed me, when we were together that night. God knows I
have felt the lack of friendship these many days past. Come, sir, what's
your grievance with me?"

"It is nothing that I should tell you. You must excuse me, sir."

The captain looked at him steadily. "Had I some part in it? Then you
are unjust not to speak."

There was great kindness, and even solicitude, in Paul Jones's tone.
Wallingford was moved. It was easier to find fault with the captain
when his eyes were not upon one; they had great power over a man.

"Come, my dear fellow," he said again, "speak to me with frankness;
you have no sincerer friend than I."

"It was the sight of the ring on your finger, then. I do not think you
meant to taunt me, but to see it was enough to rob me of my hope, sir:
that was all."

The captain colored and looked distressed; then he covered his eyes,
with an impatient gesture. He had not a guilty air, or even an air of

provocation; it struck Wallingford at the moment that he wore no look, either, of triumphant happiness, such as befitted the accepted lover of Mary Hamilton.

"You knew the ring?" asked the captain, looking up, after some moments of perplexing silence.

"I have always known it," answered Roger Wallingford; "we were very old friends. Of late I had been gathering hope, and now, sir, it seems that I must wish another man the joy I lived but to gain."

"Sit ye down," said the captain. "I thought once that I might gather hope, too. No man could wish for greater happiness on earth than the love of such a lady: we are agreed to that."

Then he was silent again. The beauty of Mary Hamilton seemed once more before his eyes, as if the dim-lighted cabin and the close-set timbers of the ship were all away, and he stood again on the terrace above the river with the pleading girl. She had promised that she would set a star in the sky for him; he should go back, one day, and lay his victories at her feet. How could a man tell if she really loved this young Wallingford? In the natural jealousy of that last moment when they were together, he had felt a fierce delight in bringing Wallingford away; she was far too good for him,—or for any man, when one came to that! Yet he had come himself to love the boy. If, through much suffering, the captain had not stood, that day, at the very height of his own character, with the endeavor to summon all his powers for a new effort, the scale at this moment would have turned.

"My dear lad, she is not mine," he said frankly. "God knows I wish it might be otherwise! You forget I am a sailor." He laughed a little, and then grew serious. "'T is her ring, indeed, and she gave it me, but 't was a gift of friendship. See, I can kiss it on my finger with you looking on, and pray God aloud to bless the lovely giver. 'T will hold me to my best, and all the saints know how I stand in need of such a talisman!"

"You do not mean it, sir?" faltered Roger. "Can you mean that"—

"Now are we friends again? Yes, I mean it! Let us be friends, Wallingford. No, no, there need be nothing said. I own that I have had my hopes, but Miss Hamilton gave me no promise. If you go home before me, or without me, as well may happen, you shall carry back the ring. Ah no, for 't is my charm against despair!" he said. "I am sore vexed; I am too often the prey of my vulgar temper, but God knows I am sore vexed. Let us be friends. I must have some honest man believe in me, among these tricksters." The captain now bent to his writing, as if he could trust himself to say no more, and waved the lieutenant to be gone. "God help me, and I'll win her yet!" he cried next moment, when he was alone again, and lifted his face as if Heaven must listen to the vow. "Women like her are blessed with wondrous deep affections rather than quick passion," he said again softly. "'T is heaven itself within a heart like that, but Love is yet asleep."

The lights of Nantes and the lanterns of the shipping were all mirrored in the Loire, that night; there was a soft noise of the river current about the ship. The stars shone thick in the sky; they were not looking down on so happy a lover the world over as Roger Wallingford. He stood by the mainmast in the cold night air, the sudden turn of things bewildering his brain, his strong young heart beating but unsteadily. Alas, it was weeks ago that a single, stiffly phrased letter had gone home to his mother, and Mary's own letter was at the bottom of the sea. There was a swift homeward-bound brig just weighing anchor that had ventured to sea in spite of foes, and taken all the letters from the Ranger, and now it might be weeks before he could write again. Oh, distance, distance! how cruel are the long miles of sea that separate those who love, and long to be together!

Later that night, before they turned in, the officers and crew beheld Captain Paul Jones and his lately estranged lieutenant pacing the deck together. They were looked upon with pleasure by some who honored them both, but next day a new whispering was set forward; there was need of suspicion, since this new alliance might mean concerted betrayal, and Paul Jones himself was not above being won over to the Tories, being but an adventurer on his own account. Dickson was as busy as the devil in a gale of wind. His own plots had so far come to naught; he had not set these officers to hate each other, or forced them to compass each other's downfall. On the contrary, they had never really been fast friends until now.

The only thing was to rouse public opinion against them both. It were easy enough: he had promised to meet again the man whom he had met in the tavern the day before,—that messenger of Thornton, who had given hints of great reward if any one would give certain information which was already in Dickson's keeping. That night he shook his fist at the two figures that paced the quarter-deck.

"One of you came out of pride and ambition," he muttered, "and the other to please his lady! We men are here for our own rights, and to show that the colonies mean business!"

XXI

The Captain gives an Order

*"But see how they turn their backs and go out of the city, and how
merrily and joyfully they take the road to Paris."*

The captain was dressed in his best uniform, fresh from its tailor's
wrappings, with all his bright lace and gilt buttons none the worse
for sea damp. With manners gay enough to match, he bade good-
morning to whoever appeared, and paced his twelve steps forward
and back on the quarter-deck like the lucky prince in a fairy story.
Something had happened to make a new pleasure; at any rate, Mr. Paul
Jones was high above any sense of displeasure, and well content with
the warm satisfaction of his own thoughts.

Presently this cheerful captain sent a ship's boy to command the
presence of Mr. Wallingford, and Mr. Wallingford came promptly in
answer to the summons. There was so evident a beginning of some high
official function that the lieutenant, not unfamiliar with such affairs,
became certain that the mayor and corporation of Nantes must be
expected to breakfast, and lent himself not unwillingly to the play.

"You will attend me to Paris, sir," announced the commander. "I shall
wait the delays of our Commissioners no longer. 'If you want a good
servant, go yourself,' as our wise adviser, Poor Richard, has well counseled
us. I mean to take him at his word. Can you be ready within the hour,
Mr. Wallingford? 'T is short notice for you, but I have plenty left of my
good Virginia money to serve us on our way. The boat awaits us."

Wallingford made his salute, and hastened below; his heart beat fast
with pleasure, being a young heart, and the immediate world of France
much to its liking. The world of the Ranger appeared to grow smaller
day by day, and freedom is ever a welcome gift.

When the lieutenant reached his berth the captain's arrangements
had preceded him: there was a sailor already waiting with the leather
portmanteau which Wallingford had brought to sea. The old judge, his
father, had carried it on many an errand of peace and justice, and to
the son it brought a quick reminder of home and college journeys, and
a young man's happy anticipations. The sight of it seemed to change

everything, stained though this old enchanter's wallet might be with sea water, and its brasses green with verdigris. The owner beheld it with complete delight; as for the sailor, he misunderstood a sudden gesture, and thought he was being blamed.

"Cap'n ordered it up, sir; never demeaned hisself to say what for," apologized Cooper.

"Take hold now and stow these things I give you," said the excited lieutenant. "Trouble is, every man on board this ship tries to be captain. Don't wrap those boots in my clean linen!"

"I ain't no proper servant; takes too much l'arnin'," protested Cooper good-naturedly, seeing that the young squire was in a happy frame. "Our folks was all content to be good farmers an' live warm on their own land, till I took up with follerin' the sea. Lord give me help to get safe home this time, an' I won't take the chances no more. A ship 's no place for a Christian."

Wallingford's mind was stretched to the task of making sudden provision for what might not be a short absence; he could hear the captain's impatient tramp on the deck overhead.

"I expect old Madam, your lady mother, and my sister Susan was the last ones to pack your gear for you?" ventured this friend of many years, in a careful voice, and Wallingford gave him a pat on the shoulder for answer.

"We'll speed matters by this journey to Paris, if all goes well," he replied kindly. "Keep the men patient; there are stirrers-up of trouble aboard that can do the crew more harm than the captain, if they get their way. You'll soon understand everything. France cannot yet act freely, and we must take long views."

"Wish 't I was to home now," mourned Cooper gloomily.

"Don't fear!" cried Wallingford gayly, though 't was but a pair of days since he himself had feared everything, and carried a glum face for all the crew to see. "Good-day, Cooper. If anything should happen to me, you must carry back word!" he added, with boyish bravado.

"Lord bless you!" said Cooper. "I figur' me darin' to go nigh the gre't house with any bad tidin's o' you! Marm Susan'd take an' scalp me, 's if I'd been the fust to blame." At which they laughed together, and hurried to the deck.

"'T is high time!" blustered the captain; but once in the boat, he became light-hearted and companionable. It was as if they had both left all their troubles behind them.

"There's Simpson and Sargent and that yellow-faced Dickson leaning over the side to look after us and think how well they can spare us both," grumbled Paul Jones. "I can see them there, whether I turn my head or not. I've set them stints enough for a fortnight, and named this day week for our return. Lay out! lay out!" cried the captain. "Give way, my lads!" and settled himself in the boat.

The wind was fresh; the waves splashed into the gig as they toiled steadily up the river. The walls of the old castle looked grim and high, as they came under the city. In the cathedral abode the one thing that was dear to Wallingford's heart in this strange place,—the stately figure of Anne of Brittany, standing at her mother's feet by the great Renaissance tomb. She wore a look like Mary Hamilton when she was most serious, so calm and sweet across the brow. The young officer had discovered this lovely queen, and her still lovelier likeness, on a dark and downcast day, and had often been grateful since for the pleasure of beholding her; he now sent a quick thought into the cathedral from the depths of his fond heart.

The two travelers, in their bright uniforms, hurried up through the busy town to a large inn, where the captain had ordered his post horses to be ready. Bretons and Frenchmen both cheered them as they passed the market place: the errand of the Ranger was well known, and much spending-money had made most of her ship's company plenty of friends ashore. They took their seats in the post chaise, not without disappointment on Wallingford's part, who had counted upon riding a good French horse to Paris instead of jolting upon stiff springs. There was more than one day, however; the morning was fresh and bright, and there were too many mercies beside to let a man groan over anything.

The thought now struck Wallingford, as if he were by far the elder man, that they might well have worn their every-day clothes upon the journey, but he had not the heart to speak. The captain wore such an innocent look of enjoyment, and of frankly accepting the part of a proven hero and unprotested great man.

"I must order a couple of suits of new uniform from one of their best tailors," said Mr. Paul Jones, only half conscious of his listener. One moment the hardened man of affairs and rough sea bully, at the next one saw him thus; frank, compassionate of others, and amused by small pleasures,—the sentimental philosopher who scattered largess of alms like a royal prince all along the white French roads.

"I go north by Rennes and Vitré, and to Paris by Alençon. I am told the roads are good, and the worst inns passable, while the best are the best," said the little captain, dropping the last of his lofty manner of the quarter-deck, and turning to his companion with a most frank air of good-fellowship. "We can return by the Loire. I hear that we can come by barge from Orleans to Nantes in four days, lying in the river inns by night. I have no love for the road I was so sorry on last month, or the inns that stood beside it."

The young men sat straight-backed and a little pompous in the post chaise, with their best cocked hats bobbing and turning quickly toward each other in the pleasures of conversation. Was this the same Paul Jones who so vexed his ship with bawling voice and harsh behavior, this quiet, gay-hearted man of the world, who seemed to play the princely traveler even more easily than he crowded sail on the Ranger all across the stormy seas,—the flail of whose speech left nobody untouched? He was so delightful at that moment, so full of charming sympathy and keenest observation, that all private grievances must have been dissolved into the sweet French air and the blue heaven over their heads.

"There were others of my officers who might well go to Paris, but I wanted the right gentleman with me now," explained the captain with frankness. "'T is above all a gentleman's place when court matters are in hand. You have some acquaintance with their language, too, which is vastly important. I blessed Heaven last time for every word I knew; 't was most of it hard learnt in my early days, when I was a sailor before the mast, and had but a single poor book to help me. No man can go much in the world over here without his French. And you know Paris, too, Mr. Wallingford, while I am almost a stranger in the streets. I cared not where I was, in my late distresses, though I had longed to see the sights of Paris all my life! My whole heart is in the journey now, tiresome though we may find many a day's long leagues."

"'T is some years since I lived there for a month," said Wallingford modestly; but a vision of all the pleasure and splendor of the great city rose to his mind's eye.

"I have suffered unbelievable torture on that petty ship!" exclaimed Paul Jones suddenly, waving his hand toward the harbor they were fast leaving out of sight. "Now for the green fields of France and for the High Commissioners at Paris! I wish to God my old auntie Jean MacDuff, that was fain to be prood o' me, could see me with my two postilions on the road, this day." And such was the gayety of the moment, and the boyish pride of the little sailor, that his companion fairly loved him for the wish, and began to think tenderly of his own dear love, and of his mother waiting and watching by the riverside at home.

"'Vitré,'" he repeated presently, with fresh expectation,—"'t is a name I know well, but I cannot call to mind the associations; of the town of Rennes I do not remember to have heard."

"I wish that I could have fallen in with their great admiral, Bailli Suffren," said the captain, leaning back in the post chaise, and heaving a sigh of perfect content. "We know not where he sails the sea; but if it chanced that he were now on his way to the fleet at Brest, or going up to Paris from the sea, like ourselves, and we chanced to meet at an inn, how I should beg the honor of his acquaintance! The King ought to put a sailor like that beside him on his throne; as for Bailli Suffren, he has served France as well as any man who ever lived. Look, there are two poor sailors of another sort, fresh from their vessel, too! See how wide they tread from balancing on the decks; they have been long at sea, poor devils!" he grumbled, as the post chaise overtook a forlorn pair of seamen, each carrying a loose bundle on his back. They were still young men, but their faces looked disappointed and sad. Seeing that the captain fumbled in his waistcoat pocket, Wallingford did the same, and two bright louis d'or flew through the morning air and dropped at the sailors' feet. They gave a shout of joy, and the two young lords in the post chaise passed gayly on.

"They'll sit long at the next inn," said Captain Paul Jones. "They were thin as those salt fish we shipped for the voyage, at Newcastle."

"A prime dun fish is a dainty not to be despised," urged Wallingford, true to his local traditions.

"'T is either a dainty, or a cedar shingle well preserved in brine, which is eatable by no man," pronounced the captain, speaking with the authority of an epicure. "We must now deal with their best French dishes while we stay in Paris. Mr. Franklin will no doubt advise us in regard to their best inns. I was careless of the matter in my first visit."

"'T was Poor Richard himself said, 'A fat kitchen makes a lean will,'" laughed Wallingford, "but he is a great man for the proprieties."

XXII

The Great Commissioner

"The Philosopher showeth you the way."

The heads of the high Vitré houses nodded together above their narrow streets, as if to gossip about two unexpected cocked hats that passed below. This uniform of the Continental navy was new enough, but old Vitré had seen many new and strange things since she herself was young. The two officers had an air of proud command about them, and seemed to expect the best rooms at the inn, and the best wines.

"'T was here the famous Marchioness de Sévigné dwelt!" exclaimed Wallingford, with triumph. "My mother often read a book of her letters to my father, on a winter evening. I thought them dull then, but I know now 't was most pretty reading, with something of fresh charm on every page. She had her castle here at Vitré; she was a very great lady," continued the lieutenant, explaining modestly. "She spoke much in her letters about her orange trees, but I think that she was ill at ease, so far from Paris."

"We could visit her to-night, if she were still in Vitré," said the captain. "'T would pass our time most pleasantly, I dare say. But I take it the poor lady is dead, since we have her memoirs. Yes, I mind me of the letters, too; I saw them in a handsome binding once at Arbigland, when I was a lad. The laird's lady, Mrs. Craik, read the language; she had been much in France, like many of our Scottish gentlefolk. Perhaps 't was her very castle that we observed as we came near the town, with the quaint round tower that stood apart."

"'T was the chapel of Madame," said the old French serving man on a sudden, and in good English. "Messieurs will pardon me, but my grandfather was long ago one of her head foresters."

The gentlemen turned and received this information with a politeness equal to that with which it was given.

"'T is a fine country, France," said the little captain handsomely. "Let us fill our glasses again to the glory of France and the success of our expedition." Then, "Let us drink to old England too, Mr. Wallingford, and that she may be brought to reason," he added unexpectedly, when they had drunk the first toast. "There is no such soldier-breeder as England; and as for her sailors, they are the Northmen of old, born again for the glory of a later time."

The next day but two they came into the gate of Paris, and saw the dark prison of the Bastille, the Tour St. Jacques, and the great cathedral of Notre Dame. It was late afternoon, and Paris looked like a greater Vitré, but with higher houses that also nodded together, and a busier world of shops and palaces and churches. Wallingford returned with older eyes to see much that had escaped him as a boy. And to Captain Paul Jones there was a noble assurance in finding the capital city of his adopted country's allies so rich and splendid; above all, so frankly gay. There was none of the prim discretion of those English and Scottish towns with which he was most familiar. Paris was in her prime, and was wholly independent of trifles, like a fine lady who admitted these two admiring strangers to the hospitality of her house, with the unconcern of one whose dwelling was well furnished and well served. The old French kings had gone away one by one, and left their palaces behind them,—the long façades of the Louvre, and the pleasant courts of the Palais Royal, and many another noble pile. Here in Paris, Mr. Benjamin Franklin, the Bon Homme Richard, was bearing his difficult honors as first citizen of a new republic, and living on good terms with the best gentlemen of France. His house, which he had from Monsieur Le Ray de Chaumont, was at the other end of Paris, at Passy, a village beyond the suburbs of the great town; and next morning, the young men, well mounted, rode thither with a groom behind them, and alighted at the Commissioner's door.

Mr. Benjamin Franklin was in the midst of his morning affairs. He was dressed in a suit of reddish-brown velvet, with white stockings, and had laid his white hat beside him on a table which was covered with papers and a few serious-looking books. It was a Tuesday, and he had been to court with the rest of the diplomats, having lately been presented, with the two American Commissioners, his fellows, to his majesty the King.

He rose with a courteous air of welcome, as the young men entered, and looked sharply at them, and then at their uniforms with much indulgent interest.

"You are the representatives of our navy. 'T is a very dignified dress; I am glad to see it,—and to receive its wearers," he added, smiling, while the officers bowed again gravely.

"I was in a poor enough undress at my first visit, and fresh from travel in the worst of weather," said Paul Jones, lowering his voice at the sad remembrance.

"Mr. Wallingford!" and the old Commissioner turned quickly toward the younger guest. "I remember you as a lad in Portsmouth. As for my good friend your honored father, he will be unforgettable to those who knew him. You begin to wear his looks; they will increase, I think, as you gather age. Sit ye down, gentlemen, sit ye down!" and he waved them to two straight chairs which stood side by side at some distance down the room, in the French fashion. Then he seated himself again behind his table, and gave audience.

Captain Paul Jones was occupied for a moment in placing his heavy sword. Wallingford was still looking eagerly toward their host.

"You are very good to remember me, sir," he said. "I counted it a great honor that my father let me attend him that day, at Mr. Warner's dinner. You will be pleased to know that the lightning conductors are still in place on the house, and are much shown to strangers in these days as being of your planning."

The philosopher smiled at his young friend's warmth; there was something most homely and amiable mingled with his great dignity.

"And my friend Mr. John Langdon? I have deeply considered our dispatches from him, and especially the letter from Robert Morris, which agrees in the main with your own ideas, sir," and he bowed to Captain Paul Jones. "And my friend Langdon?" he repeated, looking for his answer to the lieutenant. "Mr. Langdon was very well, sir, though much wearied with his cares, and sent his best remembrances and respects in case I should be so honored as to see you. And also Mr. Nicholas Gilman, of Exeter, who was with him, beside many Portsmouth gentlemen, your old friends."

"Our men at home carry the heaviest burdens," said Mr. Franklin, sighing, "yet I wish every day that I might be at home, as they are."

"My first lieutenant, Mr. Simpson, is the brother-in-law of Major Langdon," said Captain Paul Jones, flushing like a boy as he spoke. He could not help a somewhat uncomfortable sense of being on the quarter-deck of a commander much greater than himself, and an uncertain feeling about their relations that tried him very much, but he wore a manly look and kept to his quietest manners. He had parted from the Commissioner, at their last interview, in deep distress and a high passion.

"You have found Lieutenant Simpson an excellent officer, no doubt, with the large experience of a Portsmouth shipmaster," observed Mr. Franklin blandly. He cast a shrewd look at the captain; but while his firm mouth set itself a little more firmly, there was a humorous gleam of half inquiry, half indulgence, in his wide-set eyes.

"You have spoken him, sir," acknowledged Captain Paul Jones, while with equal self-possession and a touch of deference he waited for the Commissioner to lead the conversation further, and thereby did not displease Mr. Franklin, who had feared an interview of angry accusation and indignant resentment. Wallingford, too, was conscious of great pleasure in his captain's bearing.

There was a pause, and Mr. Franklin looked again at the captain, and bowed slightly from his chair.

"You may say what you have come to say to me, Captain Paul Jones. You can no doubt trust Mr. Wallingford, you see that I have for the moment dismissed my secretary."

"I can trust Mr. Wallingford," answered the captain, holding himself steady, but rising from the chair unconsciously, and taking a step nearer to the table. His new cocked hat was crushed under his arm, and Wallingford could see that the whole figure of the man was in a nervous quiver.

"I can trust Mr. Wallingford," he repeated sternly, "but I am sorry that I cannot say the same of Lieutenant Simpson. I have suffered too much already at his hands through his endeavors to supplant me as commander of the Ranger. He has descended to the poor means of disputing my authority before my crew, and stimulating them in their rebellion and surly feelings. A crew is easily prejudiced against its superiors. You must be well aware, sir, how difficult a proper government may become at sea; 't is a hard life at best for crew or captain, and its only safety is in wise control and decent obedience."

"Do you desire to make formal complaint of your lieutenant? It is hardly my province," said the Commissioner. The amused look had left his eyes, and they were as firm now as if he were a great judge on the bench.

"I respect your anxieties," he added next moment, when he saw that he held the captain in check. "I am not unaware of your high aims, your great disappointment, or your most difficult conditions of the present. But these conditions and the varieties of human nature among so large a ship's company were not unknown to you. The uncongenial man and the self-seeking, unwilling assistant must always be borne with patience, among our fellows. Besides, we pardon anything to those we love, and forgive nothing to those we hate. You may go on, sir."

"The trouble has come in great measure from an open understanding, long before we set sail out of Portsmouth, that I was to be given another frigate immediately upon my arrival, and that Simpson was to take command of the Ranger in my stead," said Paul Jones. "Now that all is over in regard to the Indien, he can fret under the long delay no worse than I, but shows his impatience of my orders at times and seasons when it ill befits him, and most wrongs and debases me; he behaves, on the slightest provocation, as if I had deeply injured him, and gives no reason why. He is my senior in age, which has added much to the difficulty between us. He loses no chance to hint that I am bent on selfish ends; even, I believe, that my principles, my character, may be questioned in this matter. My crew have become sensitive to the fear that I cannot be trusted, owing to my Scottish birth and early life spent upon British vessels,—as if they were any of them of a very different blood and descent! There is a worse man on board than Simpson, a man named Dickson, who, to further his own ends, furthers the lieutenant's. He has insisted from the first that Mr. Wallingford is a Tory spy, and that the Ranger should be in the hands of those who could fill their pockets with prize money. He, and perhaps Simpson himself, bewail their disappointment at discovering that a man-of-war is not the same as a privateer. Their ignorance of statecraft and the laws of naval science and duty seems to make them smile with derision at all proper discipline as if at some pompous horseplay."

The captain's face was red now, and his voice sharpening to undue loudness; but at an anxious gesture from Wallingford he grew quiet again.

"I come to ask you, Mr. Commissioner, if by any means I can further this business and hasten my transfer to another ship; but I must first do what I can with the Ranger. She is unfit for any great action, but we can make a pretty showing in small matters. My head is full of ideas which I should be glad to lay before you. I desire to strike a smart blow at the English coast, to counteract the burnings of our towns at home, and the interference with our shipping, and to stop the prisoning of our sailors.

I can light a fire in England that will show them we are a people to be feared, and not teased and laughed at. I ask you now how far France is ready to help me."

"We have good friends in England still," said the Commissioner slowly. "Some of the best minds and best characters among Englishmen see our question of the colonies with perfect fairness; the common people are in great part for us, too, and I have not yet lost hope that they may win the day. But of late things have gone almost too far for hope. Mr. Wallingford," and he turned abruptly toward the lieutenant, "I must not forget to ask you for your mother's health. I have thought of her many times in her widowhood; she would ill bear the saddest loss that can fall upon any of us, but she would bear it nobly."

The captain felt himself silenced in the very gathering and uplift of his eloquence, when he was only delayed out of kind consideration. Roger Wallingford answered the kind old man briefly and with deep feeling; then the conference went on. The captain was in full force of his honest determination.

"Since I cannot have the Indien, as we well know, what ship can I have?" he demanded. "Shall I do what I can with the Ranger? 'T were far better than such idleness as this. When I have seen my friend the Duke of Chartres again, things may take a turn."

"He can do much for you," answered Franklin. "I have been told that he speaks of you everywhere with respect and affection. These things count like solid gold with the indifferent populace, ready to take either side of a great question."

"I feel sure, sir, that the blow must be struck quickly, if at all," urged the captain. "If nothing is to be expected from France, I must do the best I can with the means in my hand. I must make some use of the Ranger; we have already lost far too much time. They hampered and delayed me in Portsmouth for month upon month, when I might have been effective here."

"When you are as old as I, Captain Paul Jones, you will have learned that delays appear sometimes to be the work of those who are wiser than we. If life has anything to teach us, it is patience; but patience is the hardest thing to teach those men who have the makings of a hero in their breasts." And again he fell into expectant silence, and sat behind his table looking straight at the captain. Wallingford's heart was touched by a recognition of Paul Jones's character, which had been so simply spoken; but that man of power and action took no notice himself, except to put on a still more eager look, and shift his footing as he stood, doing honor from his heart to Mr. Franklin.

"Will you not sit, captain? We have much talk before us. It astonishes me that you should have gained so warm a love for your adopted country," said the Commissioner.

"I have to confess that England has been to me but a cruel stepmother. I loved her and tried to serve her, boy and man," answered the other. "When I went to live in Virginia, I learned to love my new country as a lover loves his mistress. God forgive me if I have sometimes been rash in my service, but Glory has always shone like a star in my sky, and in America a man is sure of a future if it is in his own breast to make one. At home everything is fixed; there are walls that none but the very greatest have ever climbed. Glory is all my dream; there is no holding back in me when I think of it; my poor goods and my poor life are only for it. Help me, sir, help me to get my opportunity. You shall see that I am at heart a true American, and that I know my business as a sailor. Do not join with those who, with petty quibbles and excuses, would hold me back!"

The passion of Paul Jones, the fire and manly beauty in his face, his look of high spirit, would have moved two duller hearts than belonged to his listeners. Mr. Franklin still sat there with his calm old face, and a look of pleasant acceptance in his eyes.

"Yes, you are willing to go forward; the feet of young men are ever set toward danger," he said. "I repeat that we must sometimes be heroes at waiting. To your faith you must add patience. Your life of effort, like mine, must teach you that, but I have had longer to learn the lesson. I shall do all that I can for you. I respect your present difficulties, but we have to live in the world as it is: we cannot refashion the world; our task is with ourselves."

"Quel plaisir!" said the little captain bitterly, under his breath.

The pleasant French room, with its long windows set open to the formal garden, was so silent for a time that at last all three of the men were startled by a footstep coming out of the distance toward them, along the loose pebbles of the garden walk. They could not help the feeling that a messenger was coming from the world outside; but as the sound approached the window they recognized the easy clack of a pair of wooden shoes, and the young gardener who wore them began to sing a gay little French song. Captain Paul Jones moved impatiently, but Mr. Franklin had taken the time for thought.

"My friend Mr. David Hartley, a member of Parliament, who has been my willing agent in what attempts could be made to succor our prisoned sailors, begs me to have patience," he said reflectively. "He still thinks that nothing should persuade America to throw herself into the arms of France; for times are sure to mend, and an American must always be a stranger in France, while Great Britain will be our natural home for ages to come. But I recalled to him, in my answer, the fact that his nation is hiring all the cutthroats it can collect, of all countries and colors, to destroy us. It would be hard to persuade us not to ask or accept aid from any power that may be prevailed with to grant it, for the reason that, though we are now put to the sword, we may at some future time be treated kindly!

"This expects too much patience of us altogether," he continued. "Americans have been treated with cordiality and affectionate respect here in France, as they have not been in England when they most deserved it. Now that the English are exasperated against us we have become odious as well as contemptible, and we cannot expect a better treatment for a long time to come. I do not see why we may not, upon an alliance, hope for a steady friendship with France. She has been faithful to little Switzerland these two hundred years!"

"I cannot find it in my heart to think that our friendship with our mother country is forever broken," urged Wallingford, speaking with anxious solicitude. "The bond is too close between us. It is like the troubles that break the happiness of a family in a day of bad weather; it is but a quarrel or fit of the sulks, and when past, the love that is born in our hearts must still hold us together."

"You speak truly, my young friend," said the old Commissioner; "but we have to remember that the lives of nations are of larger scope, and that the processes of change are of long duration. I think that it may be a century before the old sense of dependence and affection can return, and England and America again put their arms about each other."

Paul Jones fretted in his gilded chair. The carved crest of Monsieur de Chaumont was sharp against his back, and the conversation was becoming much too general.

"Our country is like a boy hardly come to manhood yet, who is at every moment afraid that he will not be taken for a man of forty years," said Mr. Franklin, smiling. "We have all the faults of youth, but, thank God, the faults of a young country are better than the faults of an old one. It is the young heart that takes the forward step. The day comes when England will love us all the better for what we are doing, but it provokes the mother country now, and grieves the child. If I read their hearts aright, there have been those who thought the mother most deeply hurt, and the child most angry. You will have seen much of the Loyalists, Mr. Wallingford, if I mistake not?"

Wallingford colored with boyish confusion. "It would seem most natural, sir, if you take my mother's connection into account," he answered honestly. "She and her family are among those who have been sure of England's distress at our behavior. She is of those who inherit the deepest sentiments of affection toward the Crown."

"And you have been her antagonist?"

The question was kindly put, but it came straight as an arrow, and with such force that Paul Jones forgot his own burning anxiety for the French frigate, and turned to hear Wallingford's answer. All his natural jealousy of a rival in love, and deep-hidden suspicion of a man who had openly confessed himself a conservative, were again roused.

"I have taken oath, and I wear the uniform of our American navy, sir," replied Wallingford quietly. "My father taught me that a gentleman should stand by his word. I was not among those who wished to hasten so sad a war, and I believe that our victory must be the long defeat of our prosperity; but since there is war and we have become independent, my country has a right to claim my service. The captain knows the circumstances which brought me here, and I thank him for giving me his confidence." The young man blushed like a girl, but Captain Paul Jones smiled and said nothing.

"You have spoken like your father's son,—and like the son of Madam Wallingford," added Mr. Franklin. "I must say that I honor your behavior. I trust that your high principle may never fail you, my young friend, but you are putting it to greater strain than if you stood among the Patriots, who can see but one side." The sage old man looked at the lieutenant with a mild benevolence and approval that were staying to the heart. Then a shrewd, quick smile lighted his eyes again.

"You should be one of the knights of old come out on his lady's quest," said Mr. Benjamin Franklin; and the young man, who might have blushed again and been annoyed at the jest, only smiled back as he might have smiled at his own father, whose look had sometimes been as kind, as wise and masterful, as this of the old Commissioner.

Captain Paul Jones was in no mind that this hour should be wasted, even though it was a pleasant thing to see an old man and a young one so happily at home together. He wished to speak again for himself, and now rose with a formal air.

"Sir, I pray you not to condemn me without hearing me. I have my enemies, as you have come to know. I am convinced that at least one of Mr. Lee's secretaries is a British spy. I do not blame England for watching us, but I accuse Mr. Lee. If his fault is ignorance, he is still guilty. I desire also to lay before you my plans for a cruise with the Ranger."

Mr. Roger Wallingford left his own chair with sudden impulse, and stood beside his captain. He was a head taller and a shoulder-breadth broader, with the look of an old-fashioned English country gentleman, in spite of his gold lace and red waistcoat and the cocked hat of a lieutenant of marines.

"I have already reminded you, sir, and the other honorable Commissioners," the captain continued, speaking quickly, "that I have the promise of a better ship than the Ranger, and that my opportunities of serving the Congress must wait in great measure upon the event of that promise being fulfilled. I have also to make formal complaint of the misdemeanors of some members of my present crew. I have fixed upon the necessity of this, and the even greater necessity for money, as our men lack clothes, and we are running short in every way. Our men are clamorous for their pay; I have advanced them a large sum on my own account. And we are already short of men; we must soon take action in regard to the exchange of prisoners toward this end."

"Wait a few moments, Captain," said the Commissioner. "Mr. Deane and Mr. Adams should listen to your reasonable requests and discuss these projects. With your permission, we can dispense with the advice of Mr. Lee. I have here under consideration some important plans of the French Minister of Marine."

There was a happy consciousness in the hearts of both the younger men that they had passed a severe examination not wholly without credit, and that the old Commissioner would stand their friend. There were still a few minutes of delay; and while the captain hastily reviewed his own thick budget of papers, Wallingford glanced often at Mr. Franklin's worn face and heavy figure, remembering that he had lately said that his life was now at its fag-end, and might be used and taken for what it was worth. All the weight of present cares and all the weariness of age could not forbid the habit of kindly patience and large wisdom which belonged to this very great man.

"You are a dumb gentleman!" exclaimed the captain as they came away. "You sat there, most of the time, like an elder of the kirk, but you and Mr. Franklin seemed to understand each other all the better. The higher a man gets, the less he needs of speech. My Lord Selkirk and his mates and my dear Duke of Chartres, they do it all with a nod and a single word, but poor folks may chatter the day through. I was not so garrulous myself to-day?" he said, appealing for approval; and Wallingford, touched by such humility, hastened to assure him that the business of the Ranger had been, in his opinion, most handsomely conducted. The captain's fiery temper might well have mounted its war chariot at certain junctures.

"Listen!" said Paul Jones, as they climbed the long slopes toward Paris and their good horses settled into a steady gait. "I have often been uncertain of you since we came to sea; yet I must have a solid knowledge that you are right at heart, else I could not have had you with me to-day. But you have been so vexingly dumb; you won't speak out, you don't concern yourself!" and the captain swore gently under his breath.

Wallingford felt a touch of hot rage; then he laughed easily. "Poor Dickson will be disappointed if I do not prove a spy in the end," he said. "Look, captain; Mr. Franklin gave me these letters. The packet came for us by the last ship."

The lieutenant had already found time to take a hasty look at two letters of his own; his young heart was heating fast against them at that moment. His mother's prim and delicate handwriting was like a glimpse of her face; and he had seen that Mary Hamilton had also written him in the old friendly, affectionate way, with complete unconsciousness of those doubts and shadows which so shamed his own remembrance.

XXIII

The Salute to the Flag

"Nor deem that acts heroic wait on chance,

* * * * *

The man's whole life preludes the single deed
That shall decide if his inheritance
Be with the sifted few of matchless breed."

In midwinter something happened that lifted every true heart on board. There had been dull and dreary weeks on board the Ranger, with plots for desertion among the crew, and a general look of surliness and reproach on all faces. The captain was eagerly impatient in sending his messengers to Nantes when the Paris post might be expected, and was ever disappointed at their return. The discipline of the ship became more strict than before, now that there was little else to command or insist upon. The officers grew tired of one another's company, and kept to their own quarters, or passed each other without speaking. It was easy, indeed, to be displeased with such a situation, and to fret at such an apparently needless loss of time, even if there were nothing else to fret about.

At last there was some comfort in leaving Nantes, and making even so short a voyage as to the neighboring Breton port of L'Orient, where the Ranger was overhauled and refitted for sea; yet even here the men grumbled at their temporary discomforts, and above all regretted Nantes, where they could amuse themselves better ashore. It was a hard, stormy winter, but there were plenty of rich English ships almost within hand's reach. Nobody could well understand why they had done nothing, while such easy prey came and went in those waters, from Bordeaux and the coast of Spain, even from Nantes itself.

On a certain Friday orders were given to set sail, and the Ranger made her way along the coast to Quiberon, and anchored there at sunset, before the bay's entrance, facing the great curve of the shores. She had much shipping for company: farther in there lay a fine show of French frigates with a convoy, and four ships of the line. The captain scanned these through his glass, and welcomed a great opportunity: he had come upon a division of the French navy, and one of the frigates flew the flag of a rear admiral, La Motte Piqué.

The wind had not fallen at sundown. All night the Ranger tossed about and tugged at her anchor chains, as if she were impatient to continue her adventures, like the men between her sides. All the next day she rode uneasily, and clapped her sailcloth and thrummed her rigging in the squally winter blast, until the sea grew quieter toward sundown. Then Captain Paul Jones sent a boat to the King's fleet to carry a letter.

The boat was long gone. The distance was little, but difficult in such a sea, yet some of the boats of the country came out in hope of trading with the Ranger's men. The poor peasants would venture anything, and a strange-looking, swarthy little man who got aboard nobody knew how, suddenly approached the captain where he stood, ablaze with impatience, on the quarter. At his first word Paul Jones burst with startling readiness into Spanish invective, and then, with a look of pity at the man's poverty of dress in that icy weather, took a bit of gold from his pocket. "Barcelona?" said he. "I have had good days in Barcelona, myself," and bade the Spaniard begone. Then he called him back and asked a few questions, and, summoning a quartermaster, gave orders that he should take the sailor's poor gear, and give him a warm coat and cap from the slop chests.

"He has lost his ship, and got stranded here," said the captain, with compassion, and then turned again to watch for the boat. "You may roll the coat and cap into a bundle; they are quaint-fashioned things," he added carelessly, as the quartermaster went away. The bay was now alive with small Breton traders, and at a short distance away there was a droll little potato fleet making hopefully for the Ranger. The headmost boat, however, was the Ranger's own, with an answer to the captain's letter. He gave an anxious sigh and laid down his glass. He had sent to say frankly to the rear admiral that he flew the new American flag, and that no foreign power had yet saluted it, and to ask if his own salute to the Royal Navy of France would be properly returned. It was already in the last fluster of the February wind, and the sea was going down; there was no time to be lost. He broke the great seal of his answer with a trembling hand, and at the first glance pressed the letter to his breast.

The French frigates were a little apart from their convoy, and rolled sullenly in a solemn company, their tall masts swaying like time-keepers against the pale winter sky. The low land lay behind them, its line broken here and there by strange mounds, and by ancient altars of the druids, like clumsy, heavy-legged beasts standing against the winter sunset. The captain gave orders to hoist the anchor, nobody knew why, and to spread the sails, when it was no time to put to sea. He stood like a king until all was done, and then passed the word for his gunners to be ready, and steered straight in toward the French fleet.

They all understood now. The little Ranger ran slowly between the frowning ships, looking as warlike as they; her men swarmed like bees into the rigging; her colors ran up to salute the flag of his most Christian Majesty of France, and she fired one by one her salute of thirteen guns.

There was a moment of suspense. The wind was very light now; the powder smoke drifted away, and the flapping sails sounded loud overhead. Would the admiral answer, or would he treat this bold challenge like a handkerchief waved at him from a pleasure boat? Some of the officers on the Ranger looked incredulous, but Paul Jones still held his letter in his hand. There was a puff of white smoke, and the great guns of the French flagship began to shake the air,—one, two, three, four, five, six, seven, eight, *nine*; and then were still, save for their echoes from the low hills about Carnac and the great druid mount of St. Michael.

"Gardner, you may tell the men that this was the salute of the King of France to our Republic, and the first high honor to our colors," said the captain proudly to his steersman. But they were all huzzaing now along the Ranger's decks,—that little ship whose name shall never be forgotten while her country lives.

"We hardly know what this day means, gentlemen," he said soberly to his officers, who came about him. "I believe we are at the christening of the greatest nation that was ever born into the world."

The captain lifted his hat, and stood looking up at the Flag.

XXIV

Whitehaven

*"The only happiness a man ought to ask for is happiness
enough to get his work done."*

Early in April the Ranger was still waiting to put to sea. She had
been made ready and trained for action like a single gun, in her
long weeks at Brest. The captain had gone away on a mysterious errand,
afterward reported to be a visit to Amsterdam directed by Mr. Franklin,
who wished for information regarding the affairs of the Commissioners
and the loss of their frigate. Paul Jones carried with him the poor dress
of that Spanish seaman who had hoarded him at Quiberon, and made
good use of the Basque cap and his own sufficient knowledge of the
Spanish language. To Wallingford only he gave any news of the journey,
and it was only Wallingford whom he made his constant companion in
frequent visits to the Duke of Chartres and his duchess, at their country
house near the city.

The Sailor Prince had welcomed this American captain and friend
with all the affection with which he had said farewell in Virginia, and
hastened to present him to his wife, who was not only one of the
most charming of French ladies, and a great-grand-daughter of Louis
Quatorze, but granddaughter of the great Count of Toulouse, that
sailor son of the King, who had won the famous sea fight off Malaga
against the Dutch and English fleets, seventy years before. The beautiful
duchess was quick to recognize a hero. She was most proud of her
seafaring ancestor, and listened with delight to Paul Jones as he spoke
with some French officers of the Malaga victory, and showed his perfect
acquaintance with its strategy. She found him handsome, spirited, and
full of great qualities, and at once gave her warmest friendship to him
and to his cause.

All the degrading side of a sailor's life and hardships, all the distresses
that Paul Jones and Roger Wallingford had known on board the Ranger,
faded away like bad dreams when they stood in her presence. They were
both true gentlemen at heart; they were also servants of their own
country in France; and now every door flew open before their wishes;

the future seemed but one long triumph and delight. Paul Jones, the poor Scottish lad who had steadily followed his splendid vision, had come at last very near to its reality, and to the true joys of an unfailing friendship.

THE RANGER SAILED OUT OF Brest on the 10th of April. There had been an attempt at mutiny on board, but the captain had quelled that, and mastered the deep-laid plot behind it. Once at sea, everything seemed to be at rights again, since the ship was heading toward the English coast. The captain was silent now, as if always brooding upon great affairs, and appeared to have fallen into a calm state of self-possession; his eyes looked unconscious of whatever minor objects were reflected in their quick mirrors. All his irascibility was for the moment gone; his face was thoughtful and even melancholy, with a look as if at last he possessed some secret happiness and assurance. Glory herself had become strangely identified with a beautiful French princess, and he had made a vow to high Heaven that he would some day lay an English frigate at her feet, and show himself worthy of her confidence and most inspiriting sympathy. The captain had spoken to her of all his hard and hopeful life as he had never spoken to any one; she even knew the story of Wallingford, and their relations to Mary Hamilton and to each other. The Duchess of Chartres had listened eagerly, and next day said a word to the lieutenant that made his young heart fairly quiver at such exquisite understanding; to the captain she had spoken only of Glory as they both understood it, and of a hero's task and sacrifice.

The Ranger headed past the Channel and into the Irish Sea. At last she stood over from the Isle of Man until the shores of England were close at hand, behind a shifting veil of fog, and even those among the Ranger's crew whose best dreams were of prizes were not unsatisfied with their prospects. When the gusty wind beat back the fog, they could see the mountains of Cumberland; and the shapes of those solid heights looked well to the eye, after the low lines of the French coast they had left behind. They passed St. Bees Head, keeping well at sea; and the captain did some petty trading with poor fishermen, to learn how things stood now at Whitehaven, and whether there might be frigates in those waters, or any foe too great for so bold a venturer. They were beating against the easterly winds, and steadily nearing the shore. They could see no large-looking ships when the fog lifted, though it was a region where much shipping went and came. There was possible danger of alarm, and that their sailing from Brest had been heralded by treachery. The captain was alive in every nerve, and held himself steady, like a tiger in the night, whose best weapons must be speed and silence.

Wallingford stood long on deck in the late afternoon, leaning against the gun in his wonted place, and troubled by the persistent reluctance of his heart. These were the shores of England, and he was bound to do them harm. He was not the first man who found it hard to fight against the old familiar flag which a few months earlier had been his own. He had once spent a few months in the old country, after his college course had ended,—a boy of eighteen, who looked on at life admiringly, as if it were a play. He had been happy enough in London then, and in some country houses, where old family friends of both his father and his mother had shown him much kindness, and the days had gone by not so unlike the fashion of life at home. The merchants and gentlefolk of New England had long been rich enough to live at ease, and Boston and Portsmouth, with Salem and the harbor towns between, were themselves but tiny Londons in those happier days before the war. Each had a few men of learning and women of the world, and were small satellites that borrowed their lesser light from a central sun. Wallingford knew enough of the solid force and dignity of England to wince at the ignorant talk of the crew about so formidable an enemy, and again his heart grew heavy with regret that this mother and child among the nations had been so rashly drawn into the cruelties of war. The King and those who flattered him were wrong enough, God forgive them! But the great Earl of Chatham, and Mr. Fox, and many another man of authority and power had stood for the colonies. For a moment this heavy young heart grew even heavier with the thought of being the accomplice of France in such a short-sighted business, but next moment Wallingford angrily shook himself free from such fears as these. They were the thoughts that had been born in him, not his own determination: he had come to fight for the colonies, and would trample down both his fears and his opinions once for all on the Ranger's deck. The lieutenant looked down at the solid deck planks where he stood,— they had grown out of the honest ground of his own neighborhood; he had come to love his duty, after all, and even to love his ship. Up went his head again, and his heart was once more hot within him; the only question now was, what did the captain mean to do?

The light began to fade, and evening to fall. The men were heaving the lead, and the captain watched them, listening anxiously as they told their soundings with the practiced drawl and quaint phrases that old seamen use. They could now and then catch a glimpse of small houses on the shore. The ship was evidently in shoal water, and the fog lifted and parted and thickened again, as if a skyful of clouds had dropped upon the sea.

Presently the word was passed to let go the anchor; and the storm of oaths and exclamations which this involved, owing to some unexpected hindrance, grew so tiresome to the lieutenant that he left the place where he had been standing, to go below again.

"Look, look, mon ami!" urged the captain eagerly; and Wallingford turned to see that the fog had driven away, while Paul Jones pointed toward a large town, and a forest of vessels lying in the bay before it,—a huge flock of shipping for such a port. The Irish Sea had emptied itself into Whitehaven, and the wind had gone down; not a sloop or a snow, and not a little brig in a hurry, could put to sea again that April night.

"'T is old Whitehaven," said Paul Jones. "Now I'll show them that they have made an enemy! Now they'll know we are to be feared, not laughed at! I'll put an end to all their burnings in America. I'll harry their own coasts now, and frighten them back into their hills before I'm done. I'll sweep them off their own seas! My chance is in my hand!"

Dickson presented himself at this moment. The captain would not have had him listening, and turned upon him angrily to hear what he had to say.

"Thick as coasters in Portsmouth lower harbor in a northeast blow," commented the unwelcome officer, "but that's no such handsome town as ours."

"'T is a town of three hundred ships, mostly in the coal trade, and ranks close to Newcastle in Northumberland; 't is a town large enough to be charged with six hundred men for his Majesty's navy," and the captain scowled. "We need not take it for a poor fishing village till we have seen it better. A more uncertain coast, from the shifting sands, I do not remember to have known; but I can keep the main channels well enough through long acquaintance," he added, in a lower voice. "Now we are out of this dungeon of fog, thank God, and I shall creep in still and steady as a snail when I get ready."

They could see the gleam of white cliffs now, as the fog rolled up the hills.

"'T is full of poor miners there, burrowing like moles in the dark earth," said the captain pityingly,—"a wretched life for a Christian!"

Then he went to his cabin, and called his officers about him, and gave orders for the night's work.

"I LOVED BRITAIN AS A man may only love his mother country; but I was misjudged, and treated with such bitter harshness and contempt in my younger days that I renounced my very birthright!" said Paul Jones, turning to Wallingford with a strange impulse of sadness when the other men had gone. "I cannot help it now; I have made the break, and have given my whole allegiance to our new Republic, and all the strength of me shall count for something in the building of her noble future. Therefore I fight her battles, at whatever cost and on whatever soil. Being a sailor, I fight as a sailor, and I am here close to the soil that bore me. 'T is against a man's own heart, but I am bent upon my duty, though it cost me dear."

Wallingford did not speak,—his own reluctance was but hardly overcome; he could not take his eyes off the captain, who had grown unconscious of his presence. It was a manly face and bold look, but when at rest there was something of sad patience in the eyes and boyish mouth,—something that told of bafflings and disappointments and bitter hardness in a life that had so breathlessly climbed the steep ladder of ambition. The flashing fire of his roused spirit, the look of eager bravery, were both absent now, leaving in their places something of great distinction, but a wistfulness too, a look hungry for sympathy,—that pathetic look of simple bewilderment which sometimes belongs to dreamers and enthusiasts who do not know whither they are being led.

The wind was down, so that there was no hope, as at first, of the Ranger's running in closer to the harbor, with all her fighting force and good armament of guns. There was still light enough to see that no man-of-war was standing guard over so many merchantmen. The Ranger herself looked innocent enough from shore, on her far anchorage; but when darkness fell they hove up the anchor and crept in a little way, till the tide turned to go out and it was too dangerous among the shoals. They anchored once more, yet at too great a distance. Hours of delay ran by, and when the boats were lowered at last there was hindrance still. Some preparations that the captain had ordered were much belated, to his great dismay; discipline was of no avail; they were behindhand in starting; the sky was clear of clouds now, and the night would be all the shorter.

The officers were silent, wrapped in their heavy boat-cloaks, and the men rowed with all the force that was in them. The captain had the surgeon with him in one boat, and some midshipmen, and the other boat was in charge of Lieutenant Wallingford, with Dickson and Hall.

There were thirty picked seamen, more or less, in the party; the boats were crowded and loaded to the gunwale, and they parted company like thieves in the night to work their daring purposes. The old town of Whitehaven lay quiet; there was already a faint light of coming dawn above the Cumberland Hills when they came to the outer pier; there was a dim gleam of snow on the heights under the bright stars, and the air was bitter cold. An old sea was running high after the late storms, and the boats dragged slowly on their errand. The captain grew fierce and restless, and cursed the rowers for their slowness; and the old town of Whitehaven and all her shipping lay sound asleep.

The captain's boat came in first; he gave his orders with sure acquaintance, and looked about him eagerly, smiling at some ancient-looking vessels as if they were old friends, and calling them by name. What with the stormy weather of the past week, and an alarm about some Yankee pirates that might be coming on the coast, they had all flocked in like sheep, and lay stranded now as the tide left them. There was a loud barking of dogs from deck to deck, but it soon ceased. Both the boats had brought what freight they could stow of pitch and kindlings, and they followed their orders; the captain's boat going to the south side, and Wallingford's to the north, to set fires among the shipping. There was not a moment to be lost.

On the south side of the harbor, where the captain went, were the larger ships, many of them merchantmen of three or four hundred tons burthen; on the north side were smaller craft of every sort, Dutch doggers and the humble coast-wise crafts that made the living of a family,—each poor fish boat furnishing the tool for a hard and meagre existence. On few of these was there any riding light or watch; there was mutual protection in such a company, and the harbor was like a gateless poultry-yard, into which the captain of the Ranger came boldly like a fox.

He ran his boat ashore below the fort, and sent most of her crew to set fires among the vessels, while he mounted the walls with a few followers, and found the sentinels nothing to be feared: they were all asleep in the guardhouse, such was the peace and prosperity of their lives. It was easy enough to stop them from giving alarm, and leave them fast-bound and gagged, to find the last half of the night longer than the first of it. A few ancient cannon were easily spiked, and the captain ran like a boy at Saturday-afternoon bird-nesting to the fort beyond to put some other guns out of commission; they might make mischief for him, should the town awake.

"Come after me!" he called. "I am at home here!" And the men at his heels marveled at him more than ever, now that they were hand to hand with such an instant piece of business. It took a man that was half devil to do what the captain was doing, and they followed as if they loved him. He stopped now in a frenzy of sudden rage. "They have had time enough already to start the burning; what keeps them? There should be a dozen fires lit now!" he cried, as he ran back to the waterside. The rest of the boat's crew were standing where he had left them, and met his reproaches with scared faces: they had their pitch and tar with them, and had boarded a vessel, but the candles in their dark lanterns, which were to start the blaze, had flickered and gone out. Somebody had cut them short: it was a dirty trick, and was done on purpose. They told in loud, indignant whispers that they had chosen an old deserted ship that would have kindled everything near her, but they had no light left. And the sky was fast brightening.

The captain's face was awful to look at, as he stood aghast. There was no sight of fire across the harbor, either, and no quick snake of flame could be seen running up the masts. He stood for one terrible moment in silence and despair. "And no flint and steel among us, on such an errand!" he gasped. "Come with me, Green!" he commanded, and set forth again, running like a deer back into the town.

It took but a minute to pass, by a narrow way, among some poor stone houses and out across a bit of open ground, to a cottage poorer and lower than any, and here Paul Jones lifted the clumsy latch. It was a cottage of a single room, and his companion followed hastily, and stood waiting close behind oil the threshold.

"Nancy, Nancy, my dear!" said the captain, in a gentle voice, but thrusting back a warning hand to keep the surgeon out. "Nancy, ye'll not be frightened; 't is no thief, but your poor laddie, John Paul, that you wintered long ago with a hurt leg, an' he having none other that would friend him. I've come now but to friend you and to beg a light."

There was a cry of joy and a sound of some one rising in the bed, and the surgeon heard the captain's hasty steps as he crossed the room in the dark and kissed the old creature, who began to chatter in her feeble voice.

"Yes, here's your old tinder box in its place on the chimney," said the captain hastily. "I'm only distressed for a light, Mother Nancy, and my boat just landing. Here's for ye till I get ashore again from my ship," and there was a sound of a heavy handful of money falling on the bed.

"Tak' the best candle, child," she cried, "an' promise me ye'll be ashore again the morn's morn an' let me see your bonny eyes by day! I said ye'd come,—I always said ye'd come!" But the two men were past hearing any more, as they ran away with their treasure.

"Why in God's name did you leave the door wide open?" said the surgeon. "She'll die of a pleurisy, and your gold will only serve to bury her!"

There was no time for dallying. The heap of combustibles on one old vessel's deck was quick set afire now and flung down the hatches, and a barrel of tar was poured into the thick-mounting flames; this old brig was well careened against another, and their yards were fouled. There was no time to do more; the two would easily scatter fire to all their neighborhood when the morning wind sprung up to help them, and the captain and his men must put off to sea. There were still no signs of life on the shore or the fort above.

They all gathered to the boat; the oarsmen were getting their places, when all at once there was a cry among the lanes close by, and a crowd of men were upon them. The alarm had been given, and the Ranger's men were pressed hard in a desperate, close fight. The captain stood on the end of the little pier with his pistol, and held back some of the attacking party for one terrible minute, till all his men were in. "Lay out, lay out, my boys!" he cried then from his own place in the stern. There were bullets raining about them, but they were quick out of harm's way on the water. There was not a man of that boat's company could forget the captain's calmness and daring, as they saw him stand against the angry crowd.

The flames were leaping up the rigging of the burning ship; the shore was alive with men; there were crowds of people swarming away up among the hills beyond the houses. There had been a cannon overlooked, or some old ship's gun lay upon the beach, which presently spoke with futile bravado, bellowing its hasty charge when the captain's boat was well out upon the bay. The hills were black with frightened folk, as if Whitehaven were a ruined ant-hill; the poor town was in a terror.

On the other side of the harbor there was no blaze even yet, and the captain stood in his boat, swaying to its quick movement, with anxious eyes set to looking for the other men. There were people running along the harbor side, and excited shapes on the decks of the merchantmen; suddenly, to his relief of mind, he saw the other boat coming out from behind a Dutch brig.

Lieutenant Hall was in command of her now, and he stood up and saluted when he came near enough to speak.

"Our lights failed us, sir," he said, looking very grave; "somebody had tampered with all our candles before we left the ship. An alarm was given almost at once, and our landing party was attacked. Mr. Dickson was set upon and injured, but escaped. Mr. Wallingford is left ashore."

"The alarm was given just after we separated," said Dickson, lifting himself from the bottom of the boat. "I heard loud cries for the guard, and a man set upon me, so that I am near murdered. They could not have watched us coming. You see there has been treachery; our fine lieutenant has stayed ashore from choice."

"That will do, sir!" blazed the captain. "I must hear what you have done with Wallingford. Let us get back to our ship!" And the two boats sped away with what swiftness they could across the great stretch of rough water. Some of the men were regretful, but some wore a hard and surly look as they bent to their heavy oars.

XXV

A Man's Character

"Yet have they still such eyes to wait on them
As are too piercing; that they can behold
And penetrate the Inwards of the Heart."

The men left on board the Ranger, with Lieutenant Simpson in command, who had been watching all these long hours, now saw clouds of smoke rising from among the shipping, but none from the other side of the town, where they knew the captain had ordered many fires to be set among the warehouses. The two boats were at last seen returning in company, and the Ranger, which had drifted seaward, made shift with the morning breeze to wear a little nearer and pick them up. There was a great smoke in the harbor, but the town itself stood safe.

The captain looked back eagerly from the height of the deck after he came aboard; then his face fell. "I have been balked of my purpose!" he cried. "Curse such treachery among ye! Thank God, I've frightened them, and shown what a Yankee captain may dare to do! If I had been an hour earlier, and no sneaking cur had tampered with our lights"—

He was pale with excitement, and stood there at first triumphant, and next instant cursing his hard luck. The smoke among the shipping was already less; the Ranger was running seaward, as if the mountains had waked all their sleepy winds and sent them out to hurry her.

There was a crowd on deck about the men who had returned, and the sailors on the yards were calling down to their fellows to ask questions. The captain had so far taken no notice of any one, or even of this great confusion.

"Who's your gentleman now?" Dickson's voice suddenly rang triumphant, like a cracked trumpet, above the sounds of bragging narrative that were punctuated by oaths to both heaven and the underworld. "Who 's a traitor and a damned white-livered dog of a Tory now? Who dropped our spare candles overboard, and dirtied his pretty fingers to spoil the rest? Who gave alarm quick 's he got his boat ashore, and might have had us all strung up on their English gallows before sunset?"

Dickson was standing with his back against the mast, with a close-shouldered audience about him, officious to give exact details of the expedition. Aloft, they stopped who were shaking out the sails, and tried to hear what he was saying. At this moment old Cooper lowered himself hand over hand, coming down on the run into the middle of the company before he could be stopped, and struck Dickson a mighty blow in the breast that knocked him breathless. Some of Dickson's followers set upon Cooper in return; but he twisted out of their clutch, being a man of great strength and size, and took himself off to a little distance, where he stood and looked up imploringly at the captain, and then dropped his big head into his hands and began to sob. The captain came to the edge of the quarter-deck and looked down at him without speaking. Just then Dickson was able to recover speech; he had nearly every man aboard for his audience.

"You had ten minutes to the good afore Mr. Wallingford follered ye!" bellowed Hanscom, one of the Berwick men who had been in the same boat.

"I saw nothing of the judge's noble son; he took good care of that!" answered Dickson boldly; and there was a cry of approval among those who had suspected Wallingford. They were now in the right; they at last had proof that Wallingford deserved the name of traitor, or any evil name they might be disposed to call him. Every man in the lieutenant's boat was eager to be heard and to tell his own story. Mr. Hall had disappeared; as for Wallingford, he was not there to plead for himself, and his accusers had it all their own way.

"I tell ye I ain't afraid but he's all right! A man's character ought to count for something!" cried Hanscom. But there was a roar of contempt from those who had said from the first that a Tory was a Tory, and that Wallingford had no business to be playing at officer aboard the Ranger, and making shift to stand among proper seamen. He had gone ashore alone and stayed ashore, and there had been a sudden alarm in the town: the black truth stared everybody in the face.

The captain's first rage had already quieted in these few minutes since they had come aboard, and his face had settled into a look of stolid disappointment and weariness. He had given Whitehaven a great fright,—that was something; the news of it would quickly travel along the coast. He went to his cabin now, and summoned Dickson and Hall to make their statements. Lieutenant Hall had no wish to be the speaker, but the fluent Dickson, battered and water-soaked, minutely described the experience of the boat's company. It certainly seemed true enough that Wallingford had deserted. Lieutenant Hall could contradict nothing that was said, though the captain directly appealed to him more than once.

"After all, we have only your own word for what happened on shore," said the captain brutally, as if Dickson were but a witness in court before the opposing attorney.

"You have only my word," said Dickson. "I suppose you think that you can doubt it. At least you can see that I have suffered. I feel the effects of the blows, and my clothes are dripping here on your cabin floor in a way that will cause you discomfort. I have already told you all I can."

"I know not what to believe," answered Paul Jones, after a moment's reflection, but taking no notice of the man's really suffering condition. The captain stood mute, looking squarely into Dickson's face, as if he were still speaking. It was very uncomfortable. "Lieutenant Wallingford is a man of character. Some misfortune may have overtaken him; at the last moment"—

"He made the most of the moments he had," sneered Dickson then. "The watch was upon us; I had hard work to escape. I tried to do my best."

"*Tried!*" roared the captain. "What's *trying*? 'Tis the excuse of a whiner to say he *tried*; a man either does the thing he ought, or he does it not. I gave your orders with care, sir; the treachery began here on hoard. There should have been fires set in those spots I commanded. 'T was the business of my officers to see that this was done, and to have their proper lights at hand. Curse such incompetence! Curse your self-seeking and your jealousy of me and one another!" he railed. "This is what I count for when my work is at the pinch! If only my good fellows of the Alfred had been with me, I might have laid three hundred ships in ashes, with half Whitehaven town."

Dickson's face wore a fresh look of triumph; the captain's hopes were confessedly dashed to ground, and the listener was the better pleased. Hall, a decent man, looked sorry enough; but Dickson's expression of countenance lent fuel to the flames of wrath, and the captain saw his look.

"I could sooner believe that last night's villain were yourself, sir!" he blazed out suddenly, and Dickson's smug face grew a horrid color. The attack was so furious that he was not without fear; a better man would have suffered shame.

"I take that from nobody. You forget yourself, Captain Jones," he managed to say, with choking throat; and then the viper's instinct in his breast made him take revenge. "You should be more civil to your officers, sir; you have insulted too many of us. Remember that we are American citizens, and you have given even Mr. Wallingford good reason to hate you. He is of a slow sort, but he may have bided his time!"

The bravery of the hypocrite counted for much. Paul Jones stared at him for a moment, wounded to the quick, and speechless. Then, "You sneaking thief!" he hissed between his teeth. "Am I to be baited by a coward like you? We'll see who's the better man!" But at this lamentable juncture Lieutenant Hall stepped between, and by dint of hard pushing urged the offending Dickson to the deck again. Such low quarrels were getting to be too common on the Ranger, but this time he was not unwilling to take the captain's part. Dickson was chilled to the bone, and his teeth were chattering; the bruises on his face were swelling fast. He looked like a man that had been foully dealt with,—first well pounded and then ducked, as Hall had once seen an offender treated by angry fishwives in the port of Leith.

There was much heaviness among those Berwick men who stood bravely for Roger Wallingford; one of them, at least, refused to be comforted, and turned his face to the wall in sorrow when the lieutenant's fate was discussed. At first he had boldly insisted that they would soon find out the truth; but there were those who were ready to confute every argument, even that of experience, and now even poor Cooper went sad and silent about his work, and fought the young squire's enemies no more.

XXVI

They have made Prey of Him

"Implacable hate, patient cunning, and a sleepless refinement
of device to inflict the extremest anguish on an enemy,
these things are evil."

While Wallingford insisted that he must carry out the captain's plain instructions to the letter, the moment their boat touched the landing steps Dickson leaped over the side and ran up the pier. He had said, carelessly, that it was no use to risk several lives where one might serve; it was possible that they had been seen approaching, and he would go and play the scout, and select their buildings for firing. Both the lieutenants, Wallingford and Hall, took this breach of discipline angrily; there seemed to be an aggravating desire in Dickson's heart to put himself first now when it would count to his own gain. Their orders had been to leave the boat in his charge while the landing party was away; and in the next few moments, when he had disappeared into the narrow street that led up from the small pier, Wallingford grew uneasy, and went ashore himself. He climbed to the top of the pier, and then heard Dickson's voice calling at no great distance as if for help. As he started to run that way, he shouted to the men below to follow him.

His voice was lost in the noise of waves lapping and splashing about them against the pier; they heard his cry, but could not tell what it meant, or whether they should stay or go. The captain's orders had been strict that all three of the elder officers should not leave the boat at once. Young Hill, the midshipman, a fine brave fellow, now landed; but in the dim light he could see nobody, and returned. The discovery was then made that they had all their kindlings and tar in readiness, but there were no candles left in the two lanterns, and the bag of spare candles and tinder box which the midshipman had in charge was no longer to be found in the boat. It had been laid next the thwart, and in crossing some rough water might have fallen overboard, though nobody could understand the accident.

They could only wait now, in mortification and distress, for Wallingford's return, and some minutes passed in a grievous uncertainty.

The lieutenant had much resented Dickson's show of authority, and feared the ill success of his errand; although he had no liking for the man, it was no time to consider personalities; they were all on duty, and must report to their commander. It was certainly dangerous for a man to venture ashore alone, and the first distant outcry set him running at the top of his speed, expecting the landing party to follow.

Wallingford was light-footed, and as he ran he plainly heard Dickson's voice once more, and then all was silent. He hurried along, keeping close to the walls of warehouses, and came next into a street of common, poor dwellings of the seafaring folk. Then he stopped and listened, and whistled a call familiar enough to Dickson or any man of the Somersworth and Berwick neighborhoods, as if they had strayed from each other hunting in the old York woods. There was no answer, and he turned to go back; he must rejoin his men and attend to duty, and Dickson must take care of himself. There were dark alleys that led from this narrow thoroughfare to the water side; he heard footfalls, and again stood listening in the shelter of a deep doorway, when a group of half-dressed men burst out of a side lane, armed, and with a soldier or two among them. They ran down the street toward the shore, and took a short way round a corner. Wallingford heard a word or two which made him sure they had been given warning; it flashed through his brain that this was Dickson's business and plan for revenge. If their own men were still in the boat or near it,—which seemed likely, since they had not followed him,—they would be safe enough, but danger threatened them all. There was a sound of gathering voices and frightened outcries and slamming doors beyond in the town, as if the whole place were astir, and the morning light was growing fast in the sky, and making a new day in the dark little street. There was nothing for Wallingford to do but to hurry back to the boat as best he might. In some of the neighboring houses they had heard the guard go by, and sleepy heads were appearing to learn the news. The lieutenant made haste. Just as he passed the side passage whence the men had come, Dickson himself appeared through an archway just beyond, and stopped to call, "Watch! Watch! The Yankees are in the town to set it burning! *Watch! Watch!*" he was crying at the top of his lungs, instead of that faint "*Help! Help!*" which had seemed to cry for mercy in Wallingford's ears, and had enticed him into peril of his life.

With one bound Wallingford leaped upon the scoundrel and caught him in a mighty clutch. There was the look of a fiend in Dickson's face, in the dim light, as he turned and saw the man he hated most, and the two clinched in a fury. Then Dickson remembered the straight knife in his belt, and as they fought he twisted himself free enough to get it in his hand and strike; next moment Wallingford was flat on the cobblestones, heavily fallen with a deep cut in his shoulder.

There were men running their way, and Dickson fled before them. He had been badly mauled before the trick of stabbing could set him free; the breath was sobbing out of his lungs from the struggle, but he ran unhindered to the pier end, past the gaping townsfolk, and threw himself into the water, striking out for the boat, which had drawn well away from shore. There was a loud shout at his escape, but he was a good swimmer. They were watching from the boat, and when they saw that Dickson lagged, they drew nearer and dragged him in. It was all in a moment; there was firing at them now from the shore. Hall and the midshipman were at the very worst of their disappointment; they had failed in their errand; the whole thing was a fiasco, and worse.

Then Dickson, though sick and heavy from such an intake of salt water, managed to speak and tell them that Wallingford had waked the town; he must have found the guardhouse at once, for the watch was out, and had even set upon himself as he returned. He had reconnoitred carefully and found all safe, when he heard a man behind him, and had to fight for his life. Then he heard Wallingford calling and beating upon the doors. They might know whether they had shipped a Tory, now! Dickson could speak no more, and sank down, as if he were spent indeed, into the bottom of the boat. He could tell already where every blow had struck him, and a faintness weakened his not too sturdy frame.

Now they could see the shipping all afire across the harbor as they drew out; the other boat's party had done their work, and it was near to broad day. Now the people were running and crying confusion, and boats were putting out along the shore, and an alarm bell kept up an incessant ringing in the town. The Ranger's men rowed with all their might. Dickson did not even care because the captain would give the boat a rating; he had paid back old scores to the lofty young squire, his enemy and scorner; the fault of their failure would be Wallingford's. His heart was light enough; he had done his work well. If Wallingford was not already dead or bleeding to death like a pig, back there in the street, the Whitehaven folk were like to make a pretty hanging of him before sunset. There was one pity,—he had left his knife sticking in the Tory's shoulder, and this caused a moment of sharp regret; but it was a plain sailor's knife which he had lately got by chance at Brest, and there were no witnesses to the encounter; his word was as good as Wallingford's to most men on their ship. He began to long for the moment when the captain should hear their news. "He's none so great a hero yet," thought Dickson, and groaned with pain as the boat lurched and shifted him where he lay like ballast among the unused kindlings. Wallingford had given him a fine lasting legacy of blows.

XXVII

A Prisoner and Captive

"Close at thy side I walk unseen,
And feel thy passion and thy prayer.
Wide separation doth but prove
The mystic might of human love."

The poor lieutenant was soon turned over scornfully by a musket butt and the toe of a stout Whitehaven shoe. The blood was steadily running from his shoulder, and his coat was all sodden with a sticky wetness. He had struck his head as he fell, and was at this moment happily unconscious of all his woes.

"Let him lie, the devil!" growled a second man who came along,—a citizen armed with a long cutlass, but stupid with fear, and resenting the loss of his morning sleep and all his peace of mind. They could see the light of the burning vessel on the roofs above. "Let's get away a bit further from the shore," said he; "there may be their whole ship's company landed and ranging the town."

"This damned fellow 'll do nobody any mischief," agreed the soldier, and away they ran. But presently his companion stole back to find if there were anything for an honest man and a wronged one in this harmless officer's pockets. There were some letters in women's writing that could be of no use to any one, and some tobacco. "'T is the best American sort," said the old citizen, who had once been a sailor in the Virginia trade. He saw the knife sticking fast, and pulled it out; but finding it was a cheap thing enough, and disagreeable just now to have in hand, he tossed it carelessly aside. He found a purse of money in one pocket, and a handsome watch with a seal like some great gentleman's; but this was strangely hooked and ringed to the fob buttons, and the chain so strong that though a man pulled hard enough to break it, and even set his foot on the stranger's thigh to get a good purchase, the links would not give way. The citizen looked for the convenient knife again, but missed it under the shadow of the wall. There were people coming. He pocketed what he had got, and looked behind him anxiously: then he got up and ran away, only half content with the purse and good tobacco.

An old woman, and a girl with her, were peeping through the dirty panes of a poor, narrow house close by; and now, seeing that there was such a pretty gentleman in distress, and that the citizen, whom they knew and treasured a grudge against, had been frightened away, they came out to drag him into shelter. Just as they stepped forth together on the street, however, a squad of soldiers, coming up at double-quick, captured this easy prisoner, whose heart was beating yet. One of them put the hanging watch into his own pocket, unseen,—oddly enough, it came easily into his hand; and after some consideration of so grave a matter of military necessity, two of them lifted Wallingford, and finding him both long and heavy called a third to help, and turned back to carry him to the guard-house. By the time they reached the door a good quarter part of the townsfolk seemed to be following in procession, with angry shouts, and tearful voices of women begging to know if their husbands or lovers had been seen in danger; and there were loud threats, too, meant for the shaming of the silent figure carried by stout yeomen of the guard.

After some hours Wallingford waked, wretched with the smart of his wounds, and dazed by the first sight of his strange lodging in the town jail. There were no friends to succor him; he had not even the resource of being mistaken for a Tory and a friend of the Crown. There were at least three strutting heroes showing themselves in different quarters of the town, that evening, who claimed the honor of giving such a dangerous pirate his deathblow.

Some days passed before the officer in charge of this frightened seaport (stricken with sincere dismay, and apprehensive of still greater disaster from such stealthy neighbors on the sea) could receive the answer to his report sent to headquarters. Wallingford felt more and more the despair of his situation. The orders came at last that, as soon as he could be moved, he should be sent to join his fellow rebels in the old Mill Prison at Plymouth. The Whitehaven citizens should not risk or invite any attempt at his rescue by his stay. But, far from regretting his presence, there were even those who lamented his departure; who would have willingly bought new ribbons to their bonnets to go and see such a rogue hanged, wounded shoulder and all, on a convenient hill and proper gallows outside the town.

NONE OF THE HEAVY-LADEN BARLEY ships or colliers dared to come or go. The fishing boats that ventured out to their business came home in a flutter at the sight of a strange sail; and presently Whitehaven was aghast at the news of the robbery of all my Lady Selkirk's plate, and the astonishing capture of his Majesty's guardship Drake out of Carrickfergus, and six merchantmen taken beside in the Irish Sea,— three of them sunk, and three of them sent down as prizes to French ports. The quicker such a prisoner left this part of the realm, the better for Whitehaven. The sheriff and a strong guard waited next morning at the door of the jail, and Wallingford, taken from his hard bed, was set on a steady horse to begin the long southward journey, and be handed on from jail to jail. The fresh air of the spring morning, after the close odors of his prison, at first revived him. Even the pain of his wound was forgotten, and he took the change gladly, not knowing whither he went or what the journey was meant to bring him.

At first they climbed long hills in sight of the sea. Notwithstanding all his impatience of the sordid jealousies and discomforts of life on board the Ranger, Roger Wallingford turned his weak and painful body more than once, trying to catch a last glimpse of the tall masts of the brave, fleet little ship. A remembrance of the good-fellowship of his friends aboard seemed to make a man forget everything else, and to put warmth in his heart, though the chill wind on the fells blew through his very bones. For the first time he had been treated as a man among men on board the Ranger. In early youth the heir of a rich man could not but be exposed to the flatteries of those who sought his father's favors, and of late his property and influence counted the Loyalists far more than any of that counsel out of his own heart for which some of them had begged obsequiously. Now he had come face to face with life as plain men knew it, and his sentiment of sympathy had grown and doubled in the hard process. He winced at the remembrance of that self-confidence he had so cherished in earlier years. He had come near to falling an easy prey to those who called him Sir Roger, and were but serving their own selfish ends; who cared little for either Old England or New, and still less for their King. There was no such thing as a neutral, either; a man was one thing or the other. And now his head grew light and dizzy, while one of those sudden visions of Mary Hamilton's face, the brave sweetness of her living eyes as if they were close to his own, made him forget the confused thoughts of the moment before.

The quick bracing of the morning air was too much for the prisoner; he felt more and more as if he were dreaming. There was a strange longing in his heart to be back in the shelter and quiet of the jail itself;

there began to be a dull roaring in his ears. Like a sharp pain there came to him the thought of home, of his mother's looks and her smile as she stood watching at the window when he came riding home. He was not riding home now: the thought of it choked his throat. He remembered his mother as he had proudly seen her once in her satin gown and her laces and diamonds, at the great feast for Governor Hutchinson's birthday, in the Province House,—by far the first, to his young eyes, of the fine distinguished ladies who were there. How frail and slender she stood among them! But now a wretched weakness mastered him; he was afraid to think where he might be going. They could not know how ill and helpless he was, these stout men of his guard, who sometimes watched him angrily, and then fell to talking together in low voices. The chill of the mountain cloud they were riding into seemed to have got to his heart. Again his brain failed him, and then grew frightfully clear again; then he began to fall asleep in the saddle, and to know that he slept, jolting and swaying as they began to ride faster. The horse was a steady, plodding creature, whose old sides felt warm and comfortable to the dreaming rider. He wished, ever so dimly, that if he fell they would leave him there by the road and let him sleep. He lost a stirrup now, and it struck his ankle sharply to remind him, but there was no use to try to get it again; then everything turned black.

One of the soldiers caught the horse just as the prisoner's head began to drag along the frozen road.

"His wound's a-bleeding bad. Look-a-here!" he shouted to the others, who were riding on, their horses pressing each other close, and their cloaks held over their faces in the cold mountain wind. "Here, ahoy! our man 's dead, lads! The blood's trailed out o' him all along the road!"

"He's cheated justice, then, curse him!" said the officer smartly, looking down from his horse; but the old corporal, who had fought at Quebec with Wolfe, and knew soldiering by heart, though he was low on the ladder of promotion by reason of an unconquerable love of brandy,—the old corporal dropped on his knees, and felt Wallingford's heart beating small and quick inside the wet, stained coat, and then took off his own ragged riding cloak to wrap him from the cold.

"Poor lad!" he said compassionately. "I think he's fell among thieves, somehow, by t' looks of him; 't is an honest face of a young gentleman's iver I see. There's nowt for 't now but a litter, an't' get some grog down his starved throat. I misdoubt he's dead as t' stones in road ere we get to Kendal!"

"Get him a-horse again!" jeered another man. "If we had some alegar now, we mought fetch him to! Say, whaar er ye boun', ye are sae dond out in reed wescut an' lace?" and he pushed Wallingford's limp, heavy body with an impatient foot; but the prisoner made no answer.

XXVIII

News at the Landing

"What, have the heralds come,
To tell this quiet shore of victories?—

* * * * *

There is a mother weeping for her son!
Like some lean tree whose fruit has dropt, she gives
Her all, to wither in autumnal woe."

There were several low buildings to the east of Colonel Hamilton's house, where various domestic affairs were established; the last of these had the large spinning room in the second story, and stood four-square to the breezes. Here were the wool and flax wheels and the loom, with all their implements; and here Peggy reigned over her handmaidens one warm spring afternoon, with something less than her accustomed severity. She had just been declaring, in a general way, that the idle clack of foolish tongues distressed her ears more than the noise of the loom and wheels together.

There was an outside stairway, and the coveted seat of the young maids who were sewing was on the broad doorstep at the stairhead. You could look up the wide fields to the long row of elms by General Goodwin's, and see what might pass by on the Portsmouth road; you could also command the long green lane that led downhill toward the great house; also the shipyard, and, beyond that, a long stretch of the river itself. A young man must be wary in his approach who was not descried afar by the sentinels of this pretty garrison. On a perfectly silent afternoon in May, the whole world, clouds and all, appeared to be fast asleep; but something might happen at any moment, and it behooved Hannah Neal and Phebe Hodgdon to be on the watch.

They sat side by side on the doorstep, each reluctantly top-sewing a new linen sheet; two other girls were spinning flax within the room, and old Peggy herself was at the loom, weaving with steady diligence. As she sat there, treading and reaching at her work, with quick click-clacks of the shuttle and a fine persistence of awkward energy, she could look across the river to Madam Wallingford's house, with its high elms and rows of shuttered windows. Between her heart and old Susan's there was a bond of lifelong friendship; they seldom met, owing to their respective responsibilities; they even went to different places of worship on Sunday; but they always took a vast and silent comfort in watching for each other's light at night.

It was Peggy's habit to sing softly at her work; once in a while, in her gentlest mood, she chanted aloud a snatch of some old song. There was never but one song for a day, to be repeated over and over; and the better she was pleased with her conditions, the sadder was her strain. Now and then her old voice, weak and uncertain, but still unexpectedly beautiful, came back again so clear and true that the chattering girls themselves were hushed into listening. To-day the peace in her heart was such that she had been singing over and over, with plaintive cadences, a most mournful quatrain of ancient lines set to a still more ancient tune. It must have touched the chords of some inherited memory.

"O Death, rock me asleep"

sang Peggy dolefully;—

"O Death, rock me asleep,
Bring me to quiet rest;
Let pass my weary, guiltless ghost
Out of my care-full breast!"

The girls had seldom heard their old tyrant forget herself and them so completely in her singing; they gave each other a sympathetic glance as she continued; the noisy shuttle subdued itself to the time and tune, and made a rude accompaniment. One might have the same feeling in listening to a thrush at nightfall as to such a natural song as this. At last the poignancy of feeling grew too great for even the singer herself, and she drew away from the spell of the music, as if she approached too near the sad reality of its first occasion.

"My grandmother was said to have the best voice in these Piscataqua plantations, when she was young," announced Peggy with the tone of a friend. "My mother had a pretty voice, too, but 't was a small voice, like mine. I'm good as dumb beside either of them, but there is n't no tune I ever heard that I can't follow in my own head as true as a bird. This one was a verse my grandmother knew,—some days I think she sings right on inside of me,—but I forget the story of the song: she knew the old story of everything." Peggy was modest, but she had held her audience for once, and knew it.

She stopped to tie a careful weaver's knot in the warp, and adjust some difficulty of her pattern. Hitty Warren, who was spinning by the door, trilled out a gay strain, as if by way of relief to the gloom of a song which, however moving and beautiful, could not fail to make the heart grow sad.

"I have a house and lands in Kent,"

protested Hitty's light young caroling voice,—

"And if you'll love me, love me now,
Two pence ha'penny is my rent,
And I cannot come every day to woo!"

Whereupon Hannah Neal and Phebe, who sang a capital clear second, joined in with approval and alacrity to sing the chorus:—

"Two pence ha'penny is his rent,
And he cannot come every day to woo!"

They kept it going over and over, like blackbirds, and Peggy clacked her shuttle in time to this measure, but she did not offer to join them; perhaps she had felt some dim foreboding that her own song comforted. The air had suddenly grown full of spring-time calls and cries, as if there were some subtle disturbance; the birds were in busy flight; and one could hear faint shouts from the old Vineyard and the neighboring falls, where men and boys were at the salmon fishing.

At last the girls were done singing; they had called no audience out of the empty green fields. They began to lag in their work, and sat whispering and chuckling a little about their own affairs. Peggy stopped the loom and regarded them angrily, but they took no notice. All four had their heads close together now over a piece of gossip; she turned on her narrow perch and faced them. Their young hands were idle in their laps.

"Go to your wheel, Hitty Warren, and to your work, the pack of you! I begrech the time you waste, and the meals you eat in laziness, you foolish hussies!" cried Peggy, with distinctness. "Look at the house so short of both sheeting and table gear since the colonel took his great boatload of what we had in use to send to the army! If it wa'n't for me having forethought to hide a couple o' heaping armfuls of our best Russian for the canopy beds, we'd been bare enough, and had to content the gentlefolk with unbleached webs. And all our grand holland sheets, only in wear four years, and just coming to their softness, all gone now to be torn in strips for them that's wounded; all spoilt like common workhouse stuff for those that never slept out o' their own clothes. 'T was a sad waste, but we must work hard now to plenish us," she gravely reproached them.

"Miss Mary is as bad as the Colonel," insisted Hannah Neal, the more demure of the seamstresses, who had promptly fallen to work again. The handsome master of the house could do no wrong in the eyes of his admiring maids. They missed his kind and serious face, even if sometimes he did not speak or look when he passed them at their sewing or churning.

"A man knows nowt o' linen: he might think a gre't sheet like this sewed its whole long self together," said Phebe Hodgdon ruefully, as she pushed a slow needle through the hard selvages.

"To work with ye!" commanded Peggy more firmly. "My eye 's upon ye!" And Hitty sighed loud and drearily; the afternoon sun was hot in the spinning room, and the loom began its incessant noise again.

At that moment the girls on the doorstep cheerfully took notice of two manly figures that were coming quickly along the footpath of the spring pasture next above the Hamilton lands on the riverside. They stooped to drink at the spring in the pasture corner, and came on together, until one of them stood still and gave a loud cry. The two sewing girls beckoned their friends of the spinning to behold this pleasing sight. Perhaps some of the lads they knew were on their way from the Upper Landing to Pound Hill farms; these river footpaths had already won some of the rights of immemorial usage, and many foot travelers passed by Hamilton's to the lower part of the town. A man could go on foot to Rice's Ferry through such byways across field and pasture as fast as a fleet horse could travel by the winding old Portsmouth road.

The two hurrying figures were strangers, and they came to the knoll above the shipyard. They were both waving their hats now, and shouting to the few old men at work below on the river bank.

Peggy was only aware of a daring persistence in idleness, and again began to chide, just as the eager girls dropped their work and clattered down the outer stair, and left her bereft of any audience at all. She hurried to the door in time to see their petticoats flutter away, and then herself caught sight of the excited messengers. There was a noise of voices in the distance, and workmen from the wharves and warehouses were running up the green slopes.

"There's news come!" exclaimed Peggy, forgetting her own weaving as she stumbled over the pile of new linen on the stair landing, and hurried after the girls. News was apt to come up the river rather than down, but there was no time to consider. Some ill might have befallen Colonel Hamilton himself,—he had been long enough away; and the day before there had been rumors of great battles to the southward, in New Jersey.

The messengers stood side by side with an air of importance.

"Our side have beat the British, but there's a mort o' men killed and taken. John Ricker's dead, and John Marr and Billy Lord's among the missing, and young Hodgdon's dead, the widow's son; and there's word come to Dover that the Ranger has made awful havoc along the British coast, and sent a fortin' o' prizes back to France. There's trouble 'mongst her crew, and young Mr. Wallingford's deserted after he done his best to betray the ship."

The heralds recited their tale as they had told it over and over at every stopping-place for miles back, prompting each other at every sentence. From unseen sources a surprising crowd of men and women had suddenly gathered about them. Some of these wept aloud now, and others shouted their eager questions louder and louder. It was like a tiny babel that had been brought together by a whirlwind out of the quiet air.

"They say Wallingford's tried to give the Ranger into the enemy's hands, and got captured for his pains. Some thinks they've hung him for a spy. He's been watching his chance all along to play the traitor," said one news-bringer triumphantly, as if he had kept the best news till the last.

"'T is false!" cried a clear young voice behind them.

They turned to front the unexpected presence of Miss Hamilton.

"Who dared to say this?" She stood a little beyond the crowd, and looked with blazing eyes straight at the two flushed faces of the rustic heralds.

"Go tell your sad news, if you must," she said sternly, "but do not repeat that Roger Wallingford is a traitor to his oath. We must all know him better who have known him at all. He may have met misfortune at the hand of God, but the crime of treachery has not been his, and you should know it,—you who speak, and every man here who listens!"

There fell a silence upon the company; but when the young mistress turned away, there rose a half-unwilling murmur of applause. Old Peggy hastened to her side; but Miss Hamilton waved her back, and, with drooping head and a white face, went on slowly and passed alone into the great house.

THE MESSENGERS WERE IMPATIENT TO go their ways among the Old Fields farms, and went hurrying down toward the brook and round the head of the cove, and up the hill again through the oak pasture toward the houses at Pound Hill. They were followed along the footpath by men and boys, and women too, who were eager to see how the people there, old Widow Ricker especially, would take the news of a son's captivity or death. The very torch of war seemed, to flame along the footpath, on that spring afternoon.

The makers of the linen sheets might have been the sewers of a shroud, as they came ruefully back to their places by the spinning-room door, and let the salt tears down fall upon their unwilling seams. Poor Billy Lord and Humphrey Hodgdon were old friends, and Corporal Ricker was a handsome man, and the gallant leader of many a corn-husking. The clack of Peggy's shuttle sounded like the ticking clock of Fate.

"My God! my God!" said the old woman who had driven the weeping maids so heartlessly to their work again. The slow tears of age were blinding her own eyes; she could not see to weave, and must fain yield herself to idleness. Those poor boys gone, and Madam's son a prisoner, or worse, in England! She looked at the house on the other side of the river, dark and sombre against the bright sky. "I'll go and send Miss Mary over; she should be there now. I'll go myself over to Susan."

"Fold up your stents; for me, I can weave no more," she said sorrowfully. "'T is like the day of a funeral." And the maids, still weeping, put their linen by, and stood the two flax wheels in their places, back against the wall.

XXIX

PEGGY TAKES THE AIR

"And now that an over-faint quietnes
Should seem to strew the house,—"

That evening, in Hamilton House, Mary felt like a creature caged against its will; she was full of fears for others and reproaches for herself, and went restlessly from window to window and from room to room. There was no doubt that a great crisis had come. The May sun set among heavy clouds, and the large rooms grew dim and chilly. The house was silent, but on the river shores there were groups of men and boys gathering, and now and then strange figures appeared, as if the news had brought them hastily from a distance. Peggy had gone early across the river, and now returned late from her friendly errand, dressed in a prim bonnet and cloak that were made for Sunday wear, and gave her the look of a dignitary in humble disguise, so used to command was she, and so equipped by nature for the rule of others.

PEGGY FOUND HER YOUNG MISTRESS white and wan in the northwest parlor, and knew that she had been anxiously watching Madam Wallingford's house. She turned as the old housekeeper came in, and listened with patience as, with rare tact, this good creature avoided the immediate subject of their thoughts, and at first proceeded to blame the maids for running out and leaving the doors flying, when she had bidden them mind the house.

"The twilight lasts very late to-night; you have been long away," said Mary, when she had finished.

"'T is a new-moon night, and all the sky is lit," exclaimed Peggy seriously. "It will soon be dark enough." Then she came close to Mary, and began to whisper what she really had to say.

"'T is the only thing to do, as you told me before I went. Cæsar abased himself to row me over, and took time enough about it, I vowed him. I thought once he'd fetched himself to the door of an apoplexy, he puffed an' blowed so hard; but I quick found out what was in his piecemeal mind, before I heared folks talking on t' other bank. The great fightin' folks that stayed at home from the war is all ablaze against Mr. Roger; they say they won't have no such a Tory hive in the neighborhood no longer! 'Poor Madam! poor Madam!' says I in my mind, and I wrung my hands a-hearin' of it. Cæsar felt bad when he was tellin' of me, the tears was a-runnin' down his foolish ol' black face. He's got proper feelings, if he is so consequential. Likes to strut better 'n to work, I tell 'em, but he's got his proper feelin's; I shan't never doubt that no more," asserted Peggy, with emphatic approval.

"Yes," assented Mary impatiently, "Cæsar is a good man, but he is only one. What shall we do now?" Her voice was full of quivering appeal; she had been long alone with her distressful thoughts.

Peggy's cheeks looked pink as a girl's in her deep bonnet, and her old eyes glittered with excitement.

"You must go straight away and fetch Madam here," she said. "I'd brought her back with me if it had been seemly; but when I so advised, Susan 'd hear none o' me, 'count o' fearin' to alarm her lady. 'Keep her safe an' mistaken for one hour, will ye, so's to scare her life out later on!' says I; but Susan was never one to see things their proper size at first. If they know Madam 's fled, 't will be all the better. I want to feel she's safe here, myself; they won't damage the colonel's house, for his sake or your'n neither; they'd know better than to come botherin' round my doors. I'd put on my big caldron and get some water het, and treat 'em same fashion 's they did in old Indian times!" cried Peggy, in a fury. "I did hear some men say they believed she'd gone to Porchmouth a'ready; and when they axed me if 't was true, I nodded my head and let 'em think so."

Mary listened silently; this excited talk made her know the truth of some fast-gathering danger. She herself had a part to play now.

"I shall go at once," she insisted. "Will you bespeak the boat?"

"Everything's all ready, darlin'," said the good soul affectionately, as if she wished to further some girlish pleasure. "Yes, I've done all I could out o' door. The best boat's out an' layin' aside the gre't warehouse. Cæsar 's stopped down there to mind it, though he begun to fuss about his supper; and there's our own watermen ready to row ye over. I told 'em you was promised to the Miss Lords at the Upper Landing for a card party; I've let on to no uneasiness. You'll consider well your part; for me there's enough to do,—the best chamber warmed aright for Madam, for one thing; an' Phebe's up there now, gettin' over a good smart scoldin' I give her. I'll make a nice gruel with raisins an' a taste o' brandy, or a can o' mulled port, an' have 'em ready; 't will keep poor Madam from a chill. You'll both need comfort ere you sleep," she muttered to herself.

"I wonder if she will consent to come? She is a very brave woman," said Mary doubtfully.

"Darlin', listen to me; she must come," replied Peggy, "an' you must tell her so. You do your part, an' I'll be waitin' here till you get back."

THE LARGE BOAT WHICH WAS Hamilton's river coach and four in peaceful times lay waiting in the shadow of the warehouse to do its errand. The pairs of rowers were in their places: Peggy may have had a sage desire to keep them out of mischief. They were not a vigorous crew, by reason of age; else they would have been, like other good men, with the army. With her usual sense of propriety and effect, Peggy had ordered out the best red cushions and tasseled draperies for the seats. In summer, the best boat spread a fine red and green canopy when it carried the master and mistress down to Portsmouth on the ebb tide. The old boatmen had mounted their liveries, such was Peggy's insistence and unaccountable desire for display, but a plainer craft, rowed by a single pair of oars, was enough for any errand at nightfall, and the old fellows grumbled and shivered ostentatiously in the spring dampness.

Old Cæsar handed Miss Hamilton to her seat with all the more deference. She was wrapped in a cloak of crimson damask, with a hood to it, which her brother loved to see her wear in their gayer days. She took her place silently in the stern, and sat erect there; the men stole a glance at her now and then, and tugged willingly enough at their oars. There were many persons watching them as they went up the stream.

"'T will be a hard pinch to land ye proper at the upper wharves," said the head boatman. "The tide's far out, miss."

"I go to Madam Wallingford's," said Mary; and in the dusk she saw them cast sidewise glances at each other, while their oars lost stroke and fouled. They had thought it lucky that there should be a card party, and their young mistress out of sight and hearing, if the threats meant anything and there should be trouble that night alongshore. Miss Hamilton said nothing further,—she was usually most friendly in her speech with these old servants; but she thanked them in a gentle tone as she landed, and bade them be ready at any moment for her return. They looked at her with wonder, and swore under their breath for mere astonishment, as she disappeared from their sight with hurrying steps, along the winding way that led up to the large house on the hill. As Mary passed the old boathouse, and again as she came near the storehouses just beyond, she could see shadowy moving figures like ghosts, that were gone again in an instant out of sight, crouching to the ground or dodging behind the buildings as they saw her pass. Once she heard a voice close under the bank below the road; but it ceased suddenly, as if some one had given warning. Every dark corner was a hiding place, but the girl felt no fear now there was something to be done. There was no light in the lower story of the great house, but in Madam Wallingford's chamber the firelight was shining, and by turns it darkened and brightened the windows. For the first time Mary felt weak at heart, but there was that within her which could drive out all fear or sense of danger. As she stood on the broad doorsteps, waiting and looking riverward, she smiled to see that Peggy had lighted their own house as if for some high festival. It had a look of cheerfulness and security there beyond the elms; she gave a sigh of relief that was like a first acknowledgment of fear. She did not remember that one person might have come safely from the boat, where two could not go back.

Again she struck the heavy knocker, and this time heard Rodney's anxious voice within, whispering to ask whether she were friend or foe before he timidly unbarred the door.

"THEY TELL ME THERE IS some danger of a mob, my child." Madam Wallingford spoke calmly, as if this were some ordinary news. Mary had found her sitting by the fire, and kissed her cheek without speaking. The room was so quiet, and its lady looked so frail and patient, unconscious that danger already hemmed them in on every side.

"I fear that this house may be burnt and robbed, like the Salem houses," she said. "Poor Rodney and the women are afraid, too. I saw that they were in a great fright, and forced the truth from them. I think my troubles have robbed me of all my strength. I do not know what I must do. I feel very old, Mary, and my strength fails me," she faltered. "I need my son—oh, I have had dreadful news"—

"I have come to take you home with me to-night, dear," answered Mary. "Come, I shall wrap you in my warm red cloak; the night is chilly. These are Peggy's orders, and we must follow them. She would not have you frighted ever so little, if there is any danger. She is making you some hot drink this very minute, and I have brought our steady boat with the four old rowers. They are waiting for us below."

"Good Peggy!" exclaimed Madam Wallingford, who saw the bright smile that lighted Mary's face, and was now rallying all her forces. "She was here herself this afternoon; I wish that I had seen her. We shall not obey her this once; you see that I cannot go. If there is an attack, I must be here to meet it,—the men may hear to reason; if there is no real danger, I am safe to stay," and she cast a fond look about the room.

Mary saw it with compassion; at the same moment she heard cries outside, as if some fresh recruits were welcomed to the gathering fray.

"My safety and the safety of our house lies in my staying here," said the lady, sitting straight in her great chair. "I am not easily made afraid; it is only that my strength failed me at the first. If God sends ruin and death this night, I can but meet it. I shall not go away. You were a dear child to come; you must make my kind excuses to Peggy. Go, now, my dear, and Rodney shall put you in your boat." There was a proud look on Madam Wallingford's face as she spoke.

"I shall stay with you," answered Mary. "Alas, I think it is too late for either of us to go," she added, as her quick ears were aware of strange noises without the house. There was a sharp rapping sound of stones striking the walls, and a pane of glass fell shattering into the room.

"In Salem they took an old man from his dying bed, and destroyed his habitation. He had been a judge and a good citizen. If these be our own neighbors who think me dangerous, I must follow their bidding; if they are strangers, we must be in danger. I wish that you had not come, Mary!"

Mary was already at the window; the shutters were pushed back, and the sweet night air blew through the broken pane upon her face. The heavy sliding shutter caught as she tried to stir it, and she saw that the moving crowd had come close about the house. At the sight of her they gave an angry roar; there were musket shots and a great racket of noise. "Come out, come out," they cried, "and take the oath!"

"So the mob has come already," said Madam Wallingford calmly, and rose from her seat. "Then I must go down. Is it a great company?"

"I could not have believed so many men were left," answered Mary bitterly. "They should be fighting other battles!" she protested, trembling with sudden rage. "Where go you, Madam?" for Madam Wallingford was hurrying from the room. As she threw open the door, all the frightened people of the household were huddled close outside; they fell upon their knees about her and burst into loud lamentations.

They pressed as near their mistress as they could; it was old Rodney and Susan who had kept the others from bursting into the room.

"Silence among ye!" said Madam Wallingford. "I shall do what I can, my poor people. I am going down to speak to these foolish men."

"They have come to rob us and murder us!" wailed the women.

"Rodney, you will go before me and unbar the door!" commanded the mistress. "Susan shall stay here. Quiet this childishness! I would not have such people as these think that we lack courage."

She went down the wide staircase as if she were a queen, and Mary her maid of honor. Rodney was for hanging back from those who pounded to demand entrance, and needed an angry gesture before he took the great bar down and flung the door wide open. Then Madam Wallingford stepped forward as if to greet her guests with dignity, and Mary was only a step behind. There was a bonfire lit before the house, and all the portraits along the paneled hall seemed to come alive in the blazing light that shone in, and to stand behind the two women like a guard.

"What do you wish to say to me?" asked Madam Wallingford.

"The oath! the oath!" they cried, "or get you hence!" and there was a shaking of firebrands, and the heads pressed closer about the door.

"You are Sons of Liberty, and yet you forbid liberty to others," said the old gentlewoman, in her clear voice. "I have wronged none of you." For very sight of her age and bravery, and because she was so great a lady, they fell silent; and then a heavy stone, thrown from the edge of the crowd, struck the lintel of the door, beside her.

"Is there no man among you whom you will choose to speak fairly with me, to tell your errand and whence you come?"

"We are some of us from Christian Shore, and some are Dover men, and some of us are men of your own town," answered a pale, elderly man, with the face of a fanatic; he had been a preacher of wild doctrines in the countryside, and was ever a disturber of peace. "We want no Royalists among us, we want no abettors of George the Third; there's a bill now to proscribe ye and stop your luxury and pride. We want no traitors and spies, neither, to betray the cause of the oppressed. You and your son have played a deep game; he has betrayed our cause, and the penalty must fall."

There was a shout of approval; the mob was only too ready to pour into the house.

"My son has put his name to your oath, and you should know that he has not broken it, if some of you are indeed men of our own town," said the mother proudly, and they all heard her speak. "I can promise that this is true. Cannot you wait to hear the truth about him, or is it only to rob us and make a night of revel you have come? Do not pay sin with sin, if you must hold those to be sinners who are Loyalists like me!"

"Burn the old nest!" cried an impatient voice. "She may be hiding some King's men,—who knows? Stop her prating, and let's to business; we are done with their Royalties," and the crowd pushed hard. They forced the two women and old Rodney back into the hall; and at the sound of heavy trampling, all the women on the stair above fell to shrieking.

Mary put herself before Madam Wallingford for safety's sake, and held up her hand. "Stop, stop!" she begged them. "Let me first take my friend away. I am Mary Hamilton of the Patriots, and you all know my brother. I ask you in his name to let us go in peace."

Her sorrowful face and her beauty for one instant held some of them irresolute, but from the back of the crowd a great pressure urged the rest forward. There was a little hush, and one man cried, "Yes, let them go!" but the wild and lawless, who were for crowding in, would not have it so. It was a terrible moment, like the sight of coming Death. There was a crash; the women were overpowered and flung back against the wall.

Suddenly there was a new confusion, a heavier din, and some unexpected obstacle to this onset; all at once a loud, familiar voice went to Mary's heart. She was crouching with her arms close about her old friend, to shield her from bruises and rough handling as the men pushed by; in the same moment there were loud outcries of alarm without. What happened next in the hall seemed like the hand of Heaven upon their enemies. Old Major Tilly Haggens was there in the midst, with friends behind him, dealing stout blows among those who would sack the house. Outside on their horses were Judge Chadbourne and General Goodwin, who had ridden straight into the mob, and with them a little troop of such authorities as could be gathered, constables and tithing men; and old Elder Shackley in his scarlet cloak; Parson Pike and Mr. Rollins, his chief parishioner, were all there together. They rode among the brawling men as if they were but bushes, and turned their good horses before the house. The crowd quick lost its solid look; it now had to confront those who were not defenseless.

"We are Patriots and Sons of Liberty, all of us who are here!" shouted the minister, in a fine, clear voice. "We are none of us, old or young, for the King, but we will not see a Christian woman and kind neighbor made to suffer in such wise as this. Nor shall you do vengeance upon her son until there is final proof of his guilt."

"We can beat these old parsons!" shouted an angry voice. "To it, lads! We are three to their one!" But the elderly men on horseback held their own; most of them were taught in the old school of fighting, and had their ancient swords well in hand, ready for use with all manly courage. Major Tilly Haggens still fought as a foot soldier in the hall; his famous iron fist was doing work worthy of those younger days when he was called the best boxer and wrestler in the plantations. He came forth now, sweeping the most persistent before him out of the house.

"I'll learn ye to strike a poor lame old man like me! Ye are no honest Patriots, but a pack of thieves and blackguards! The worst pest of these colonies!" he cried, with sound blows to right and left for emphasis. He laid out one foe after another on the soft grass as on a bed, until there was no one left to vanquish, and his own scant breath had nearly left his body. The trampling horses had helped their riders' work, and were now for neighing and rearing and taking to their heels. The town constable was bawling his official threats, as he held one of the weaker assailants by the collar and pounded the poor repentant creature's back. It had suddenly turned to a scene of plain comedy, and the mob was nothing but a rabble of men and boys, all running for shelter, such as could still run, and disappearing down toward the river shore.

The old judge got stiffly from his tall Narragansett pacer, and came into the hall.

"Madam Wallingford's friends stop here to-night," he told the old servant, who appeared from some dark corner. Poor Rodney was changed to such an ashen color that he looked very strange, and as if he had rubbed phosphorus to his frightened eyes. "You may tell your mistress and Miss Hamilton that there is no more danger for the present," added the judge. "I shall set a watch about the house till daylight."

Major Haggens was panting for breath, and leaned his great weight heavily against the wainscoting. "I am near an apoplexy," he groaned faintly. "Rodney, I hope I killed some of those divils! You may fetch me a little water, and qualify it with some of Madam's French brandy of the paler sort. Stay; you can help me get to the dining parlor myself, and I'll consider the spirit-case. Too violent a portion would be my death; 't would make a poor angel of me, Rodney!"

Early in the morning, Judge Chadbourne and his neighbor Squire Hill, a wise and prudent man, went out to take the morning air before the house. They were presently summoned by Madam Wallingford, and spoke with her in her chamber. The broken glass of the window still glittered on the floor; even at sunrise the day was so mild that there was no chill, but the guests were struck by something desolate in the room, even before they caught sight of their lady's face.

"I must go away, my good friends," she declared quietly, after she had thanked them for their service. "I must not put my friends in peril," she said, "but I am sure of your kind advice in my sad situation.

"We wait upon you to say that it would be best, Madam," said the judge plainly. "I hear that New Hampshire as well as Massachusetts has in consideration an act of great severity against the presence or return of Loyalists, and I fear that you would run too much risk by staying here. If you should be proscribed and your estates confiscated, as I fear may be done in any case, you are putting your son's welfare in peril as well as your own. If he be still living now, though misfortunes have overtaken him, and he has kept faith, as we who know him must still believe, these estates which you hold for him in trust are not in danger; if the facts are otherwise"—and the old justice looked at her, but could not find it in his heart to go on.

Madam Wallingford sat pondering the matter with her eyes fixed upon his face, and was for some time lost in the gravest thoughts.

"What is this oath?" she asked at last, and her cheeks whitened as she put the question.

The judge turned to Mr. Hill, and, without speaking, that gentleman took a folded paper from among some documents which he wore in his pocket, and rose to hand it to the lady.

"Will you read it to me?" she asked again; and he read the familiar oath of allegiance in a steady voice, and not without approval in his tone:—

"I do acknowledge the United States of America to be free, independent; and sovereign states, and declare that the people thereof owe no allegiance or obedience to George The Third, King of Great Britain: and I renounce, refuse, and abjure any allegiance or obedience to him; and I do swear that I will, to the utmost of my power, support, maintain, and defend the said United States against the said King George The Third, his heirs and successors, and his or their abettors, assistants, and adherents, and will serve the said United States in the office. . . which I now hold, with fidelity, according to the best of my skill and understanding."

As he finished he looked at the listener for assent, as was his habit, and Judge Chadbourne half rose in his eagerness; everything was so simple and so easy if she would take the oath. She was but a woman,— the oath was made for men; but she was a great land holder, and all the country looked to her. She was the almoner of her own wealth and her husband's, and it were better if she stood here in her lot and place.

"I cannot sign this," she said abruptly. "Is this the oath that Roger, my son, has taken?"

"The same, Madam," answered Mr. Hill, with a disappointed look upon his face, and there was silence in the room.

"I must make me ready to go," said Madam Wallingford at last, and the tears stood deep in her eyes. "But if my son gave his word, he will keep his word. I shall leave my trust and all our fortunes in your hands, and you may choose some worthy gentlemen from this side of the river to stand with you. The papers must be drawn in Portsmouth. I shall send a rider down at once with a message, and by night I shall be ready to go myself to town. I must ask if you and your colleagues will meet me there at my house. . . You must both carry my kind farewells to my Barvick friends. As for me,"—and her voice broke for the first time,—"I am but a poor remainder of the past that cannot stand against a mighty current of change. I knew last night that it would come to this. I am an old woman to be turned out of my home, and yet I tell you the truth, that I go gladly, since the only thing I can hope for now is to find my son. You see I am grown frail and old, but there is something in my heart that makes me hope. . . I have no trace of my son, but he was left near to death, and must now be among enemies by reason of having been upon the ship. No, no, I shall not sign your oath; take it away with you, good friends!" she cried bitterly. Then she put out her weak hands to them, and a pathetic, broken look came upon her face.

"'T was most brotherly, what you did for me last night. You must thank the other good men who were with you. I ask your affectionate remembrance in the sad days that come; you shall never fail of my prayers."

And so they left her standing in the early sunshine of her chamber, and went away sorrowful.

SARAH ORNE JEWETT

An hour later Mary Hamilton came in, bright and young. She was dressed and ready to go home, and came to stand by her old friend, who was already at her business, with many papers spread about.

"Mary, my child," said Madam Wallingford, taking her hand and trembling a little, "I am going away. There is new trouble, and I have no choice. You must stay with me this last day and help me; I have no one to look to but you."

"But you can look to me, dear lady." Mary spoke cheerfully, not understanding to the full, yet being sure that she should fail in no service. There was a noble pride of courage in her heart, a gratitude because they were both safe and well, and the spring sun shining, after such a night. God gives nothing better than the power to serve those whom we love; the bitterest pain is to be useless, to know that we fail to carry to their lives what their dear presence brings to our own. Mary laid her hand on her friend's shoulder. "Can I write for you just now?" she asked.

"I am going to England," explained Madam Wallingford quietly. "Judge Chadbourne and Mr. Hill have both told me that I must go away. . . I shall speak only of Halifax to my household, but my heart is full of the thought of England, where I must find my poor son. I should die of even a month's waiting and uncertainty here; it seems a lifetime since the news came yesterday. I must go to find Roger!"

All the bright, determined eagerness forsook Mary Hamilton's face. It was not that the thought of exile was new or strange, but this poor wistful figure before her, with its frayed thread of vitality and thin shoulders bent down as if with a weight of sorrow, seemed to forbid even the hard risks of seafaring. The girl gave a cry of protest, as if she felt the sharp pain of a sudden blow.

"I have always been well enough on the sea. I do not dread the voyage so much. I am a good sailor," insisted Madam Wallingford, with a smile, as if she must comfort a weaker heart than her own. "My plans are easily made, as it happens; one of my own vessels was about to sail for West Indian ports. It was thought a useless venture by many, but the captain is an impatient soul, and an excellent seaman. He shall take us to Halifax, Susan and me. I thought at first to go alone; but Susan has been long with me, and can be of great use when we are once ashore. She is in sad estate on the ocean, poor creature, and when we went last to Virginia I thought never to distress her so much again."

There was a shining light on the girl's face as she listened.

"I shall go with you, not Susan," she said. "Even with her it would be like letting you go alone. I am strong, and a good sailor too. We must leave her here to take care of your house, as I shall leave Peggy."

Madam Wallingford looked at Mary Hamilton with deep love, but she lifted her hand forbiddingly.

"No, no, dear child," she whispered. "I shall not think of it."

"There may be better news," said Mary hopefully.

"There will be no news, and I grudge every hour that is wasted," said the mother, with strange fretfulness. "I have friends in England, as you know. If I once reach an English port, the way will be easy. When prison doors shut they do not open of themselves, in these days, but I have some friends in mind who would have power to help me. I shall take passage from Halifax for Bristol, if I can; if no better vessel offers, I shall push on in the Golden Dolphin rather than court delay."

Mary stood smiling into her face.

"No, no, my dear," said Madam Wallingford again, and drew the girl closer. "I cannot let you think of such a thing. Your young heart speaks now, and not your wise reflection. For your brother's sake I could not let you go, still less for your own; it would make you seem a traitor to your cause. You must stand in your own place."

"My brother is away with his troop. He begged me to leave everything here, and go farther up the country. The burning of Falmouth made him uneasy, and ever since he does not like my staying alone in our house," insisted Mary.

"There is knowledge enough of the riches of this river, among seamen of the English ports," acknowledged Madam Wallingford. "In Portsmouth there are many friends of England who will not be molested, though all our leaders are gone. Still I know that an attack upon our region has long been feared," she ended wistfully.

"I told my brother that I should not leave home until there was really such danger; we should always have warning if the enemy came on the coast. If they burnt our house or plundered it, then I should go farther up the country. I told Jack," continued Mary, with flushing cheeks, "that I did not mean to leave you; and he knew I meant it, but he was impatient, too. 'I have well-grown timber that will build a hundred houses,' he answered me, and was rough-spoken as to the house, much as he loves it,—'but I shall not have one moment's peace while I think you are here alone. Yet, you must always look to Madam Wallingford,' he said more than once."

"Go now, my dear child; send me Susan, who is no doubt dallying in the kitchen!" commanded the mistress abruptly. "I must not lose a minute of this day. You must do as your brother bade you; but as for doing the thing which would vex him above everything else,—I cannot listen to more words. I see that you are for going home this morning; can you soon return to me, when you have ordered your affairs? You can help me in many small matters, and we shall be together to the last. I could not take you with me, darling," she said affectionately. "'T was my love for you—no, I ought to say 't was my own poor selfishness—that tempted my heart for the moment. Now we must think of it no more, either of us. You have no fellowship with those to whom I go; you are no Loyalist," and she even smiled as she spoke. "God bless you for such dear kindness, Mary. I think I love you far too much to let you go with me."

Mary's face was turned away, and she made no answer; then she left her friend's side, wondering at the firm decision and strong authority which had returned in this time of sorrow and danger. It frightened her, this flaring up of what had seemed such a failing light of life. It was perhaps wasting to no purpose the little strength that remained.

She stood at the window to look down the river, and saw the trampled ground below; it seemed as if the last night's peril were but the peril of a dream. The fruit-trees were coming into bloom: a young cherry-tree, not far away, was white like a little bride, and the pear-trees were ready to follow; their buds were big, and the white petals showing. It was high water; the tide had just turned toward the ebb, and there were boats going down the river to Portsmouth, in the usual fashion, to return with the flood. There was a large gundalow among them, with its tall lateen sail curved to the morning breeze. Of late the river had sometimes looked forsaken, so many men were gone to war, and this year the fields would again be half tilled at best, by boys and women. To country eyes, there was a piteous lack of the pleasant hopefulness of new-ploughed land on the river farms.

"There are many boats going down to-day," reported Mary, in her usual tone; "they will be for telling the news of last night at the wharves in Portsmouth. There will be a fine, busy crowd on the Parade."

Then she sighed heavily; she was in the valley of decision; she felt as if she were near to tearing herself from this dear landscape and from home,—that she was on the brink of a great change. She could not but shrink from such a change and loss.

She returned from her outlook to Madam Wallingford's side.

"I must not interrupt your business. I will not press you, either, against your will. I shall soon come back, and then you will let me help you and stay with you, as you said. When will your brig be ready?"

"She is ready to sail now, and only waits her clearance papers; the captain was here yesterday morning. She is the Golden Dolphin, as I have already told you, and has often lain here at our river wharves; a very good, clean vessel, with two lodgings for passengers. I have sent word that I shall come on board to-morrow; she waits in the stream by Badger's Island."

"And you must go from here"—

"To-night. I have already ordered my provision for the voyage. Rodney went down on the gundalow before you were awake, and he will know very well what to do; this afternoon I shall send many other things by boat."

"I was awake," said Mary softly, "but I hoped that you were resting"—

"If the seas are calm, as may happen, I shall not go to Halifax," confessed the other; "I shall push on for Bristol. Our cousin Davis is there, and the Russells, and many other friends. The brig is timber-laden; if we should be captured"—

"By which side?" laughed Mary, and a sad gleam of answering humor flitted over Madam Wallingford's face.

"Oh, we forget that my poor child may be dead already!" she cried, with sharp agony, next moment. "I think and think of his hurting wounds. No pity will be shown a man whom they take to be a spy!" and she was shaken by a most piteous outburst of tears.

Then Mary, as if the heart in her own young breast were made of love alone, tried to comfort Madam Wallingford. It was neither the first time nor the last.

XXX

Madam goes to Sea

"The paths to a true friend lie direct, though he be far away."

The bright day had clouded over, and come to a wet and windy spring night. It was past eight o'clock; the darkness had early fallen. There was a sense of comfort in a dry roof and warm shelter, as if it were winter weather, and Master Sullivan and old Margery had drawn close to their warm fireplace. The master was in a gay mood and talkative, and his wife was at her usual business of spinning, stepping to and fro at a large whirring wheel. To spin soft wool was a better trade for evening than the clacking insistence of the little wheel with its more demanding flax. Margery was in her best mood, and made a most receptive and admiring audience.

"Well, may God keep us!" she exclaimed, at the end of a story. "'T was as big a row as when the galleries fell in Smock Alley theatre. I often heard of that from my poor father."

Master Sullivan was pleased with his success; Margery was not always so easy to amuse, but he was in no mind for a conflict. Something had made his heart ache that day, and now her love and approval easily rescued him from his own thought; so he went on, as if his fortunes depended upon Margery's favor and frankly expressed amusement.

"One night there was a long-legged apprentice boy to a French upholsterer; this was in London, and I a lad myself stolen over there from Paris with a message for Charles Radcliffe. He had great leanings toward the stage, this poor boy, and for the pride of his heart got the chance to play the ghost in Hamlet at Covent Garden. Well, it was then indeed you might see him at the heighth of life and parading in his pasteboard armor. 'Mark me!' says he, with a voice as if you'd thump the sides of a cask. '*I'll mark you!*' cries his master from the pit, and he le'pt on the stage and was after the boy to kill him; and all the lads were there le'pt after him to take his part; and they held off the master, and set the ghost in his place again, the poor fellow; and they said he did his part fine, and creeped every skin that was there. He'd a great night; never mind the beating that fell to him afterward!"

The delighted listener shook with silent laughter.

"'T was like the time poor Denny Delane was in Dublin. I was there but the one winter myself," continued the master. "He came of a fine family, but got stage-struck, and left Trinity College behind him like a last year's bird's nest. Every woman in Dublin, old and young, was crazy after him. There were plays bespoke, and the fashion there every night, all sparked with diamonds, and every officer in his fine uniform. There was great dressing with the men as you'd never see them now: my Lord Howth got a fancy he'd dress like a coachman, wig and all; and Lord Trimlestown was always in scarlet when he went abroad, and my Lord Gormanstown in blue. Oh, but they were the pictures coming in their coaches! You would n't see any officer out of his uniform, or a doctor wanting his lace ruffles! 'T was my foolish young self borrowed all the lace from my poor mother that she'd lend me, and I but a boy; and then I'd go help myself out of her boxes, when she'd gone to mass. She'd a great deal of beautiful lace, and knew every thread of it by heart. I've a little piece yet that was sewed under a waistcoat. Go get it now, and we'll look at it; 't is laid safe in that second book from the end of the shelf. You may give it to the little lady, when I'm gone, for a remembrance; 't is the only—ah, well; I've nothing else in the world but my own poor self that ever belonged to my dear mother!"

The old master's voice grew very sad, and all his gayety was gone.

"'Deed, then, Miss Mary Hamilton 'll get none of it, and you having a daughter of your own!" scolded Margery, instantly grown as fierce as he was sad. Sometimes the only way to cure the master of his dark sorrows was to make him soothe her own anger. But this night he did not laugh at her, though she quarreled with fine determination.

"Oh me!" groaned the master. "Oh me, the fool I was!" and he struck his knee with a hopeless hand, as he sat before the fire.

"God be good to us!" mourned old Margery, "and I a lone child sent to a strange country without a friend to look to me, and yourself taking notice of me on the ship; 't was the King I thought you were, and you'd rob me now of all that. Well, I was no fit wife for a great gentleman; I always said it, too. I loved you as I don't know how to love my God, but I must ask for nothing!"

The evening's pleasure was broken; the master could bear anything better than her poor whimpering voice.

"You look at a poor man as if he were the front of a cathedral," he chided her, again trying to be merry. But at this moment they were both startled into silence; they both heard the heavy tread of horses before the house.

"Come in, come in, whoever you are!" shouted Master Sullivan, as he threw open the outer door. "Are ye lost on the road, that ye seek light and lodging here?"

The horses would not stand; the night was dark as a dungeon; the heavy rain blew in the old man's face. His heart beat fast at the sound of a woman's voice.

"By great Jupiter, and all the gods! what has brought you here, Mary Hamilton, my dear child?" he cried. "Is there some attack upon the coast? 'T is the hand of war or death has struck you!"

The firelight shone upon Mary's face as she entered, but the wind and rain had left no color there; it was a wan face, that masked some high resolve, and forbade either comment or contradiction. She took the chair to which the master led her, and drew a long breath, as if to assure herself of some steadiness of speech.

A moment later, her faithful friend, Mr. John Lord, opened the door softly, and came in also. His eyes looked troubled, but he said nothing as he stood a little way behind the others in the low room; the rain dropped heavily from his long coat to the floor. The Sullivans stood at either side the fireplace watching the pale lady who was their guest. John Sullivan himself it was who unclasped her wet riding cloak and threw it back upon the chair; within she wore a pretty gown of soft crimson silk with a golden thread in it, that had come home in one of her brother's ships from Holland. The rain had stained the breast of it where the riding cloak had blown apart; the strange living dyes of the East were brightened by the wet. The two old people started back, they believed that she had sought them because she was hurt to death. She lifted her hand forbiddingly; her face grew like a child's that was striving against tears.

"Dear friends, it is not so bad as you think; it is because I am so full of hope that I have come to you," she said to the anxious, kind old faces. There was such a sweetness in the girl's voice, and her beautiful dress was so familiar, so belonging to the old quiet times and happy hospitalities, that the two men felt a sharp pain of pity, and because there was nothing else to do they came nearer to her side. Master Sullivan looked questioningly at young Mr. Lord, but old Margery found instinctive relief in a low, droning sort of moan, which sometimes lifted into that Irish keening which is the voice of fear and sorrow. She was piling all her evening fagots at once upon the fire.

"Speak now!" said the master. "If my old heart knows the worst, it can begin to hope the best. What is it that could not wait for the morning of such a night as this?"

"There is bad news," replied Mary; "there are letters come from the Ranger. They have attacked a large seaport town on the coast of England, and spread great alarm, though their chief projects were balked. They have fought with an English frigate in the Irish Sea, and taken her captive with some rich prizes. Roger Wallingford was left ashore in Whitehaven. They believe on the ship that he tried to betray his companions and warned the town; but he was badly wounded ashore, and thrown into prison. There is a great rising of the Patriots against Madam Wallingford, who is warned to leave the country. They threatened her very life last night." Mary was standing now, and the quick firelight, sprung afresh, made her look like a bright flame. The master made a strange outcry, like a call for hidden help, and looked hastily at the walls of the room about him, as if he sought some old familiar weapons.

"I am going away with her for a time," said Mary, speaking now without any strain or quiver in her voice. "My brother does not need me, since he is with the army, and Mr. Lord knows our business here, if any be left. Peggy can stand bravely for me in the house. Dear master!" and she came close to the old man's side; her young slender body was almost as tall as his; she put her arm about his neck and drew down his head so that he must look into her upturned face. "Dear master," she said, in a low voice, "you told me once that you still had friends in England, if the worst should come to Roger, and I think now that the worst has come."

"You may bring the horses at once," said the master, turning quickly to Mr. Lord. "Stay, Margery; you must light your old lantern and give it him; and I would wrap you well and hold it for him to rub them off with a wisp of thatch, and let them have a mouthful of corn to satisfy their minds."

Mary felt for that one moment as if Hope were like an old frail friend with eyes of living fire; she had known no other father than the master, when all was said. He put her hand gently away from its unconscious clinging hold of his shoulder, and, with a woman's care, took the wet cloak, as he placed her again in his own chair, and spread its dry inner folds to the fire, so that they might warm a little.

Then, without speaking, he went to the shelf of books, and took from one of them a thin packet of papers.

"I am an old man," he said gently. "I have been fearful of all this, and I made ready these things, since it might some day please God to let me die. I have heard of the fray last night, but you will find letters here that will be of service. Come, warm you now by the fire, and put them in the bosom of your gown. I think you will find them something worth; but if you keep their words in your heart or near it, 't will be far the best. And burn them quick if there is need; but you shall read them first, and send their messages by word of mouth, if need be. Listen to me now; there are a few things left for me to say."

The girl's face was full of a sweet relief; she did not thank him, save with one long look, and put the packet where he had bidden her. She looked into the fire as she listened to his counsels, and suddenly was afraid of tears, the errand being safely done.

"Forgive me, sir, for this new trouble!"

She spoke with a different impulse and recognition from any she had known before, and looked brave as a young soldier. This was a friend who knew indeed the world whither she was going.

"Why should you not come to me?" asked the master. "'Men were born for the aid and succor of men,'" he added with a smile. "You do not know your Rabelais, my little lady."

The horses had come up; they trod the ground outside impatiently. She knelt before the old man humbly, and he blessed her, and when she rose she kissed him like a child, and looked long in his face, and he in hers; then she put on her heavy cloak again, and went out into the rainy night.

Next day, in Portsmouth, Madam Wallingford, pale and stately, and Susan, resolute enough, but strangely apathetic, put off into the harbor from Langdon's wharf. They were accompanied to the shore by many friends, whose hearts were moved at so piteous a sight. When the mistress and maid were safe on the deck of the Golden Dolphin, Mary Hamilton stood there before them; the beauty of her young face was like some heavenly creature's.

"I know that you said last night, when I was for bidding you farewell, that you should see me again. I have been thinking all this morning that you had been prevented," whispered Madam Wallingford tenderly. They were long in each other's arms. "I have a few things left to say; it is impossible to remember all proper messages, at such short warning. Let them keep the boat for Miss

Hamilton, until the last moment before we sail," she said to the captain.

"They are heaving up the anchor now," the captain answered. "I must not lose this fair wind to get us out of the river."

Mary was impatient to speak; she cast a smiling glance at Susan, who wore a timid look, not being used to plots, or to taking instructions from any but her mistress.

"Dear friend," cried Mary then, "you must let me have my way! I could not let you go alone. I tried to think as you bade me, but I could not. I am going with you wherever you may go: I think it is my right. You have short time now to give Susan your last charges, as I have given mine to Peggy. I stay with you and Phebe with me, and Susan goes ashore. Please God, some short weeks or months may see us sailing home again up the river, with our errand well done!"

"I could not stand against them, Madam," and Susan looked more apprehensive than triumphant, though she was grateful to Heaven to be spared a voyage at sea. Her mistress was not one to have her own plans set aside. "I listened well, Madam, to all you said to Rodney and the maids. They are good girls, but they need a head over them. And I could do nothing against Miss Mary; for Peggy, that has a love for great ploys to be going on, and the world turned upside down, has backed her from the first."

XXXI

THE MILL PRISON

"Lackyng my love, I goe from place to place."

"'Twixt every prayer he says, he names you once
As others drop a bead."

O ne morning late in spring the yellow primroses were still abloom
on the high moorlands above Plymouth; the chilly sea wind was
blowing hard, and the bright sunshine gave little warmth, even in a
sheltered place. The yard of the great Mill Prison was well defended by
its high stockade, but the wind struck a strong wing into it in passing,
and set many a poor half-clad man to shivering. The dreary place was
crowded with sailors taken from American ships: some forlorn faces
were bleached by long captivity, and others were still round and ruddy
from recent seafaring. There was a constant clack of sharp, angry voices.
Outside the gate was a group of idle sightseers staring in, as if these
poor Yankees were a menagerie of outlandish beasts; now and then
some compassionate man would toss a shilling between the bars, to
be pitifully scrambled for, or beckon to a prisoner who looked more
suffering than the rest. Even a south-westerly gale hardly served to
lighten the heavy air of such a crowded place, and nearly every one
looked distressed; the small-pox had blighted many a face, so that the
whole company wore a piteous look, though each new day still brought
new hopes of liberty.

There were small groups of men sitting close together. Some were
playing at games with pebbles and little sticks, their draughts board
or fox-and-geese lines being scratched upon the hard trodden ground.
Some were writing letters, and wondering how to make sure of sending
them across the sea. There were only two or three books to be seen in
hand; most of the prisoners were wearily doing nothing at all.

In one corner, a little apart from the rest, sat a poor young captain
who had lost his first command, a small trading vessel on the way to
France. He looked very downcast, and was writing slowly, a long and
hopeless letter to his wife.

"I now regret that I had not taken your advice and Mother's and remained at home instead of being a prisoner here," he had already written, and the stiff, painfully shaped words looked large and small by turns through his great tears. "I was five days in the prison ship. I am in sorrow our government cares but little for her subjects. They have nothing allowed them but what the British government gives them. Shameful,—all other nations feels for their subjects except our Country. There is no exchange of prisoners. It is intirely uncertain when I return perhaps not during the war. I live but very poor, every thing is high. I hope you have surmounted your difficulties and our child has come a Comfort to imploy your fond attention. It is hard the loss of my ship and difficult to bare. God bless you all. My situation is not so bad but it might be worse. This goes by a cartel would to God I could go with it but that happiness is denied me. It would pain your tender heart to view the distressed seamen crowded in this filthy prison, there is kind friends howiver in every place and some hours passed very pleasant in spite of every lack some says the gallows or the East Indias will be our dreadful destiny, 't would break a stone's heart to see good men go so hungry we must go barefoot when our shoes is done. Some eats the grass in the yard and picks up old bones, and all runs to snatch the stumps of our cabbage the cooks throws out. Some makes a good soup they say from snails a decent sort that hives about the walls, but I have not come to this I could not go it. They says we may be scattered on the King's ships. I hear the bells in Plymouth Town and Dock pray God 't is for no victory—no I hear in closing 't is only their new Lord Mayor coming in"—

As this was finished there was another man waiting close by, who caught impatiently at the thrice-watered ink, and looked suspiciously to see if any still remained.

"Harbert said 's how I should have it next," grumbled the fellow prisoner, "if so be you've left me any. Who'll car' our letters to the cartel? They want to send a list o' those that's dead out o' the Dolton, an' I give my promise to draw up the names."

There were many faces missing now from the crew of the Dolton brigantine, taken nearly a year and a half before, but there were still a good number of her men left in the prison. Others had come from the Blenheim or the Fancy; some from the Lexington; and the newest resident was a man off The Yankee Hero, who had spent some time after his capture as sailor on a British man-of-war. He was a friendly person, and had brought much welcome news, being also so strong and well fed that he was a pleasant sight to see. Just now he sat with Charles Herbert, of Newbury, in Massachusetts, whom they all called the scribe. For once this poor captive wore a bright, eager look on his scarred face, as he listened to the newcomer's talk of affairs; they had been near neighbors at home. The younger man had been in prison these many months. He was so lucky as to possess a clumsy knife, which was as great a treasure as his cherished bottle of ink, and was busy making a little box of cedar wood and fitting it neatly together with pegs. Since he had suffered the terrible attack of small-pox which had left his face in ruins, and given him a look of age at twenty, his eyesight had begun to fail; he was even now groping over the ground, to find one of the tiny dowels that belonged to his handiwork.

"'T is there by your knee; the rags of your trouser leg was over it," said Titcomb, the new man-of-war's man, as he reached for the bit of wood.

"Who 's this new plant o' grace, comin' out o' hospit'l?" he asked suddenly, looking over Herbert's shoulder, with the peg in his fingers. "'T is a stranger to me, and with the air of a gentleman, though he lops about trying his sea legs, like an eel on 's tail."

"No place for gentlemen here, God help him!" said the young scribe sadly, trying to clear his dull eyes with a ragged sleeve as he turned to look. "No, I don't know who it is. I did hear yisterday that there was an officer fetched here in the night, from the nor'ard, under guard, and like to be soon hanged. Some one off of a Yankee privateer, they said, that went in and burnt the shipping of a port beyond Wales. I overheared the sentinels havin' some talk about him last night. I expect 't was that old business of the Ranger, and nothin' new."

There was a rough scuffling game going on in the prison yard, which made all the sick and disabled men shrink back against the walls, out of danger. The stranger came feebly from point to point, as the game left space, toward the sunny side where the two Newbury men were sitting. As they made room for him, they saw that he was dressed in the remains of a torn, weather-stained uniform; his arm was in a sling, and his shoulder fast bound with dirty bandages.

"You're a new bird in this pretty cage," said poor Herbert, smiling pleasantly. He was a fellow of sympathetic heart, and always very friendly with new-comers.

The stranger returned his greeting, with a distressed glance toward their noisy companions, and seated himself heavily on the ground, leaning back against the palisade. The tumult and apparent danger of finding himself trodden underfoot vexed and confused him in his weakness; presently he grew faint, and his head dropped on his breast. His last thought was a wish to be back in the wretched barracks, where at least it was quiet. At that moment two men pushed their way out of the middle of a quarreling group of playmates, and ran toward him.

"'Tain't never you, sir!" cried one.

"'Tis Mr. Roger Wallingford, too! Don't you think I've got sense enough to know?" scolded the other, both speaking at once, in tones which conveyed much pity and astonishment to the Newbury men's ears.

"By God! it is, an' he's a dyin' man!"

Gideon Warren was a Berwick sailor of the old stock, who had known the lieutenant from a child, and was himself born and reared by the river. "What've them devils used him such a way for?" he demanded angrily. "He looks as ancient as the old judge, his father, done, the week afore he died. What sort of a uniform's this he's got on him?"

The other men looked on, and, any excitement being delightful in so dull a place, a crowd gathered about them quickly, pushing and jostling, and demanding to know what had happened. Warren, a heavily built, kind-faced old mariner, had fallen on his knees and taken the sick man's head on his own ample shoulder, with all the gentleness of a woman. There was more than one old Berwick neighbor standing near The general racket of noise began to be hushed.

"Git him some water, can't ye?" commanded Warren. "I misdoubt we've got no sperits for him. Stand to t' other side, there, some on ye caw-handed cutters, an' keep the sun off'n him!"

"'T ain't no British fightin' gear, nor French neither, that's on him," said Ichabod Lord, as he leaned forward to get a better view of the red waistcoat, and, above all, the gilt buttons of the new prisoner's coat.

"'T is an officer from one o' our own Congress ships; they'd keep such news from us here, any way they could," said young Earl angrily.

"Looks to me different," said the Newbury man who was with Herbert. "No, I'll begretch it's anything more 'n some livery wear and relic o' fashion. 'T is some poor chap they've cotched out'n some lord's house; he mought be American-born, an' they took him to be spyin' on 'em."

"What d' you know o' them high affairs?" returned Warren with indignation. "Livery wear? You ain't never been situated where you'd be like to see none! 'T is a proper uniform, or was one, leastways; there's a passel o' anchors worked on him, and how he ever come here ain't for me to say, but 'tis our young Squire Wallin'ford, son an' heir o' the best gentleman that was ever on the old Piscataqua River.

"When we come away, folks was all certain they had leanin's to the wrong side: his mother's folks was high among the Boston Tories," explained Ichabod Lord wonderingly. "Yet he must ha' been doin' some mischief 'long o' the Patriots, or he'd never been sent here for no rebel,—no, they'd never sent him here; this ain't where they keep none o' their crown jew'ls! Lord! I hope he ain't goin' to die afore he tells some news from the old Lower Landin' an' Pound Hill, an' how things was goin' forrard, when he left home, all up along the Witchtrot road!"

These last words came straight from the depths of an exile's heart, and nobody thought it worth while to smile at the names of his localities; there was hardly a man who was not longing for home news in the same desperate way. A jail was but a jail the world over, a place to crowd a man lower down, soul and body, and England was not likely to be anxious about luxuries for these ship's companies of rebels and pirates, the willful destroyers of her commerce; they were all thought guilty of treason, and deserved the worst of punishment.

THERE WAS A FAINT FLICKER of color now on the stranger's cheeks, and Charles Herbert had brought some water, and was fanning him with a poor fragment of headgear, while some one else rubbed his cold hands. They were all well enough used to seeing men in a swoon; the custom was to lay them close to the wall, if they were in the way, to recover themselves as best they could, but this man with the stained red waistcoat might have news to tell.

"I'll bate my head he's been on the Ranger with Paul Jones," announced Ichabod Lord solemnly, as if he were ready to suffer for his opinions. "That's what 't is; they may have all been taken, too, off the coast."

"Why, 'tis the uniform of our own Congress navy, then!" exclaimed young Herbert, with his scarred cheeks gone bright crimson like a girl's, and a strange thrill in his voice. He sprang to his feet, and the men near him gave the best cheer they could muster. Poor Wallingford heard it, and stirred a little, and half opened his eyes.

"I've above two shillings here that I've airnt makin' of my workboxes: some o' you fellows run to the gates and get a decent-looking body to fetch us some brandy," begged Herbert hastily.

"I'm all right now," said Wallingford aloud; and then he saw whose stout arms were holding him, and looked into a familiar face.

"Good God! we had news at home long ago that you were dead, Warren!" he said with wide-eyed bewilderment.

"I bain't then, so now," insisted the honest Gideon indignantly, which amused the audience so that they fell to laughing and slapping one another on the shoulder.

"Well, I bain't," repeated Warren, as soon as he could be heard. "I've been here in this prison for seven months, and it's a good deal worse 'n layin' at home in Old Fields bur'in' ground, right in sight o' the river 'n all's a-goin' on. Tell us where you come from, sir, as soon 's you feel able, and how long you are from Barvick! We get no sort of news from the folks. I expect you can't tell me whether my old mother 's livin'?" The poor man tried hard to master his feelings, but his face began to twitch, and he burst out crying suddenly, like a child.

"Looks like they've all gone and forgot us," said a patient, pale-faced fellow who stood near. Wallingford was himself again now, and looked with dismay at those who looked at him. Their piteous pallor and hungry-eyed misery of appearance could give but little sense of welcome or comfortable reassurance to a new captive. He was as poor as they, and as lacking in present resource, and, being weak and worn, the very kindness and pity of the arms that held him only added to his pain.

"If I had not come the last of my way by sea," he told them, trying to speak some cheerful hope to such hopeless souls, "I might have got word to London or to Bristol, where I can count upon good friends," but some of the listeners looked incredulous and shook their heads doubtfully, while there were those who laughed bitterly as they strolled away.

"Have you any late news from Captain Paul Jones?" he asked, sitting straight now, though Warren still kept a careful arm behind him. "I was at Whitehaven with him; I belong on the frigate Ranger," and his eyes grew bright and boyish.

"They say that one of her own officers tried to betray the ship," sneered a young man, a late comer to the Mill Prison, who stood looking straight into poor Wallingford's face.

"'T was true enough, too," said Roger Wallingford frankly; "it is by no fault of mine that you see me here. God grant that such treachery made no other victim!"

"They say that the Ranger has taken a mort o' prizes, and sent them back to France," announced the Newbury sailor. "Oh, Lord, yes, she's scared 'em blue ever sence that night she went into Whitehaven! She took the Drake sloop o' war out o' Carrickfergus that very next day."

"I knew there was business afoot!" cried the lieutenant proudly; but he suddenly turned faint again, and they saw a new bright stain strike through the clumsy bandages on his shoulder.

XXXII

THE GOLDEN DRAGON

*"Give where want is silently clamorous, and men's necessities, not
their tongues, do loudly call for thy mercies."*

The less said of a dull sea voyage, the better; to Madam Wallingford
and her young companion their slow crossing to the port of Bristol
could be but a long delay. Each day of the first week seemed like a
week in passing, though from very emptiness it might be but a moment
in remembrance; time in itself being like money in itself,—nothing at
all unless changed into action, sensation, material. At first, for these
passengers by the Golden Dolphin, there was no hope of amusement
of any sort to shorten the eventless hours. Their hearts were too heavy
with comfortless anxieties.

The sea was calm, and the May winds light but steady from the west.
It was very warm for the season of year, and the discouragements of
early morning in the close cabin were easily blown away by the fresh
air of the quarter-deck. The captain, a well-born man, but diffident in
the company of ladies, left his vessel's owner and her young companion
very much to themselves. Mary had kept to a sweet composure and
uncomplainingness, for her old friend's sake, but she knew many
difficult hours of regret and uncertainty now that, having once taken
this great step, Madam Wallingford appeared to look to her entirely for
support and counsel, and almost to forget upon how great an adventure
they had set forth. All Mary's own cares and all her own obligations and
beliefs sometimes rose before her mind, as if in jealous arraignment of
her presence on the eastward-moving ship. Yet though she might think
of her brother's displeasure and anxiety, and in the darkest moments of
all might call herself a deserter, and count the slow hours of a restless
night, when morning came, one look at Madam Wallingford's pale face
in the gray light of their cabin was enough to reassure the bravery of
her heart. In still worse hours of that poor lady's angry accusation of
those whom she believed to be their country's enemies, Mary yet found
it possible to be patient, as we always may be when Pity comes to help
us; there was ever a final certainty in her breast that she had not done

wrong,—that she was only yielding to an inevitable, irresistible force of love. Love itself had brought her out of her own country.

Often they sat pleasantly together upon the deck, the weather was so clear and fine, Mary being always at Madam Wallingford's feet on a stout little oaken footstool, busy with her needle to fashion a warmer head-covering, or to work at a piece of slow embroidery on a strip of linen that Peggy had long ago woven on their own loom. Often the hearts of both these women, who were mistresses of great houses and the caretakers of many dependents, were full of anxious thought of home and all its business.

Halfway from land to land, with the far horizon of a calm sea unbroken by mast or sail, the sky was so empty by day that the stars at night brought welcome evidence of life and even companionship, as if the great processes of the universe were akin to the conscious life on their own little ship. In spite of the cruelty of a doubt that would sometimes attack her, Mary never quite lost hold on a higher courage, or the belief that they were on their way to serve one whom they both loved, to do something which they alone could do. The thought struck her afresh, one afternoon, that they might easily enough run into danger as they came near land; they might not only fall an easy prey to some Yankee privateer (for their sailing papers were now from Halifax), but they might meet the well-manned Ranger herself, as they came upon the English coast. A quick flush brightened the girl's sea-browned cheeks, but a smile of confidence and amusement followed it.

Madam Wallingford was watching her from the long chair.

"You seem very cheerful to-day, my dear child," she said wistfully.

"I was heartened by a funny little dream in broad daylight," answered Mary frankly, looking up with something like love itself unveiled in her clear eyes.

"It is like to be anything but gay in Bristol, when we come to land," answered Madam Wallingford. "I had news in Halifax, when we lay there, that many of their best merchants in Bristol are broken, and are for a petition to Parliament to end these troubles quickly. All their once great trade with the colonies is done. I spent many happy months in Bristol when I was young. 'T was a noble town, with both riches and learning, and full of sights, too; it was a fit town for gentlefolk. I sometimes think that if anything could give back my old strength again, 't would be to take the air upon the Clifton Downs."

"You will have many things to show me," said Mary, with a smile. "You are better already for the sea air, Madam. It does my heart good to see the change in you."

"Oh, dear child, if we were only there!" cried the poor lady. "Life is too hard for me; it seems sometimes as if I cannot bear it a moment longer. Yet I shall find strength for what I have to do. I wonder if we must take long journeys at once? 'T is not so far if Roger should be at Plymouth, as they believed among the Halifax friends. But I saw one stranger shake his head and look at me with pity, as I put my questions. He was from England, too, and just off the sea"—

"There is one thing I am certain of,—Roger is not dead," said Mary. "We are sure to find him soon," she added, in a different tone, when she had spoken out of her heart for very certainty. The mother's face took on a sweet look of relief; Mary was so strong-hearted, so sure of what she said, that it could not help being a comfort.

"Our cousin Davis will be gathering age," Madam Wallingford continued, after a little while. "I look to find her most sadly changed. She had been married two years already when I made my first voyage to England, and went to visit her."

Mary looked up eagerly from her work, as if to beg some further reminiscences of the past. Because she loved Madam Wallingford so well it was pleasant to share the past with her; the old distance between them grew narrower day by day.

"I was but a girl of seventeen when I first saw Bristol, and I went straight to her house from the ship, as I hope we may do now, if that dear heart still remains in a world that needs her," said the elder woman. "She is of kin to your own people, you must remember, as well as to the Wallingfords. Yes, she was glad of my visit, too, for she was still mourning for her mother. Being the youngest child, she had been close with her till her marriage, and always a favorite. They had never been parted for a night or slept but under the same roof, until young Davis would marry her, and could not be gainsaid. He had come to the Piscataqua plantations, supercargo of a great ship of his father's; the whole countryside had flocked to see so fine a vessel, when she lay in the stream at Portsmouth. She was called the Rose and Crown; she was painted and gilded in her cabin like a king's pleasure ship. He promised that his wife should come home every second year for a long visit, and bragged of their ships being always on the ocean; he said she should keep her carriage both on sea and on land. 'T was but the promise of a courting man, he was older than she, and already very masterful; he had grown stern and sober, and made grave laws for his household, when I saw it, two years later. He had come to be his father's sole heir, and felt the weight of great affairs, and said he could not spare his wife out of his sight, when she pleaded to return with me; a woman's place was in her husband's house. Mother and child had the sundering sea ever between them, and never looked in each other's face again; for Mistress Goodwin was too feeble to take the journey, though she was younger than I am now. He was an honest man and skillful merchant, was John Davis; but few men can read a woman's heart, which lives by longing, and not by reason; 't is writ in another language.

"You have often heard of the mother, old Mistress Goodwin, who was taken to Canada by the savages, and who saw her child killed by them before her eyes? They threatened to kill her too because she wept, and an Indian woman pitied her, and flung water in her face to hide the tears," the speaker ended, much moved.

"Oh, yes. I always wish I could remember her," answered Mary. "She was a woman of great valor, and with such a history. 'T was like living two lifetimes in one." The girl's face shone with eagerness as she looked up, and again bent over her needlework. "She was the mother of all the Goodwins; they have cause enough for pride when they think of her."

"She had great beauty, too, even in her latest age, though her face was marked by sorrow," continued Madam Wallingford, easily led toward entertaining herself by the listener's' interest, the hope of pleasing Mary. "Mistress Godwin was the skillful hostess of any company, small or great, and full of life even when she was bent double by her weight of years, and had seen most of her children die before her. There was a look in her eyes as of one who could see spirits, and yet she was called a very cheerful person. 'T was indeed a double life, as if she knew the next world long before she left this one. They said she was long remembered by the folk she lived among in Canada; she would have done much kindness there even in her distress. Her husband was a plain, kind man, very able and shrewd-witted, like most Goodwins, but she was born a Plaisted of the Great House; they were the best family then in the plantation. Oh yes, I can see her now as if she stood before me,—a small body, but lit with flame from no common altar of the gods!" exclaimed Madam Wallingford, after a moment's pause. "She had the fine dignity which so many women lack in these days, and knew no fear, they always said, except at the sight of some savage face. This I have often heard old people say of her earlier years, when the Indians were still in the country; she would be startled by them as if she came suddenly upon a serpent. Yet she would treat them kindly."

"I remember when some of our old men still brought their guns to church and stood them in the pews," said Mary; "but this year there were only two poor huts in the Vineyard, when the Indians came down the country to catch the salmon and dry them. There are but a feeble few of all their great tribe; 't is strange to know that a whole nation has lived on our lands before us! I wonder if we shall disappear in our own turn? Peggy always says that when the first settlers came up the river they found traces of ancient settlement; the Vineyard was there, with its planted vines all run to waste and of a great age, and the old fields, too, which have given our river neighborhoods their name. Peggy says there were other white people in Barvick long ago; the old Indians had some strange legends of a folk who had gone away. Did Mistress Goodwin ever speak of her captivity, or the terrible march to Canada through the snow, when she was captured with the other Barvick folk, Madam?" asked Mary, with eagerness to return to their first subject. "People do not speak much of those old times now, since our own troubles came on."

"No, no, she would never talk of her trials; 't was not her way," protested Madam Wallingford, and a shadow crossed her face. "'T was her only happiness to forget such things. I can see her sitting in the sun with a fescue in her hand, teaching the little children. They needed bravery in those old days; nothing can haunt us as their fear of sudden assault and savage cruelty must have haunted them."

Mary thought quickly enough of that angry mob which had so lately gathered about her old friend's door, but she said nothing. The Sons of Liberty and their visit seemed to have left no permanent discomfort in Madam's mind. "No, no!" said the girl aloud. "We have grown so comfortable that even war has its luxuries; they have said that a common soldier grows dainty with his food and lodging, and the commanders are daily fretted by such complaints."

"There is not much comfort to be had, poor fellows!" exclaimed Madam Wallingford rebukingly, as if she and Mary had changed sides. "Not at your Valley Forge, and not with the King's troops last year in Boston. They suffered everything, but not more than the rebels liked."

Mary's cheeks grew red at the offensive word. "Do not say 'rebels'!" she entreated. "I do not think that Mistress Hetty Goodwin would side with Parliament, if she were living still. Think how they loved our young country, and what they bore for it, in those early days!"

"'T is not to the purpose, child!" answered the old lady sharply. "They were all for England against France and her cruel Indian allies; I meant by 'rebels' but a party word. Hetty Goodwin might well be of my mind; too old to learn irreverence toward the King. I hate some of his surrounders,—I can own to that! I hate the Bedfords, and I have but scorn for his Lord Sandwich or for Rockingham. They are treating our American Loyalists without justice. Sir William Howe might have had five thousand men of us, had he made proclamation. Fifty of the best gentlemen in Philadelphia who were for the Crown waited upon him only to be rebuffed."

She checked herself quickly, and glanced at Mary, as if she were sorry to have acknowledged so much. "Yes, I count upon Mr. Fox to stand our friend rather than upon these! and we have Mr. Franklin, too, who is large-minded enough to think of the colonies themselves, and to forget their petty factious and rivalries. Let us agree, let us agree, if we can!" and Madam Wallingford, whose dignity was not a thing to be lightly touched, turned toward Mary with a winning smile. She knew that she must trust herself more and more to this young heart's patience and kindness; yes, and to her judgment about their plans. Thank God, this child who loved her was always at her side. With a strange impulse to confess all these things, she put out her frail hand to Mary, and Mary, willingly drawing a little closer, held it to her cheek. They could best understand each other without words. The girl had a clear mind, and had listened much to the talk of men. The womanish arguments of Madam Wallingford always strangely confused her.

"Mr. Franklin will ever be as young at heart as he is old in years," said the lady presently, with the old charm of her manner, and all wistfulness and worry quite gone from her face. She had been strengthened by Mary's love in the failing citadel of her heart. "'Tis Mr. Franklin's most noble gift that he can keep in sympathy with the thoughts and purposes of younger men. Age is wont to be narrow and to depend upon certainties of the past, while youth has its easily gathered hopes and quick intuitions. Mr. Franklin is both characters at once,—as sanguine as he is experienced. I knew him well; he will be the same man now, and as easy a courtier as he was then content with his thrift and prudence. I trust him among the first of those who can mend our present troubles.

"I beg you not to think that I am unmindful of our wrongs in the colonies, Mary, my dear," she added then, in a changed voice. "'T is but your foolish way of trying to mend them that has grieved me,—you who call yourselves the Patriots!"

Mary smiled again and kept silence, but with something of a doubtful heart. She did not wish to argue about politics, that sunny day on the sea. No good could come of it, though she had a keen sense that her companion's mind was now sometimes unsettled from its old prejudices and firm beliefs. The captain was a stanch Royalist, who believed that the rebels were sure to be put down, and that no sensible man should find himself left in the foolish situation of a King's antagonist, or suffer the futility of such defeat.

"Will Mistress Davis look like her mother, do you think?" Mary again bethought herself to return to the simpler subject of their conversation.

"Yes, no doubt; they had the same brave eyes and yet strangely timid look. 'T is a delicate, frail, spirited face. Our cousin Davis would be white-headed now; she was already gray in her twenties, when I last saw her. It sometimes seems but the other day. They said that Mistress Goodwin came home from Canada with her hair as white as snow. Yes, their eyes were alike; but the daughter had a Goodwin look, small featured and neatly made, as their women are. She could hold to a purpose and was very capable, and had wonderful quickness with figures; 't is common to the whole line. Mistress Hetty, the mother, had a pleasing gentleness, but great dignity; she was born of those who long had been used to responsibility and the direction of others."

Mary laughed a little. "When you say 'capable,' it makes me think of old Peggy, at home," she explained. "One day, not long ago, I was in the spinning room while we chose a pattern for the new table linen, and she had a child there with her; you know that Peggy is fond of a little guest. There had been talk of a cake, and the child was currying favor lest she should be forgotten.

"'Mrs. Peggy,' she piped, 'my aunt Betsey says as how you're a very capering woman!'

"'What, what?' says Peggy. 'Your aunt Betsey, indeed, you mite! Oh, I expect 't was capable she meant,' Peggy declared next moment, a little pacified, and turned to me with a lofty air. 'Can't folks have an English tongue in their heads?' she grumbled; but she ended our high affairs then, and went off to the kitchen with the child safe in hand."

"I can see her go!" and Madam Wallingford laughed too, easily pleased with the homely tale.

"Ah, but we must not laugh; it hurts my poor heart even to smile," she whispered. "My dear son is in prison, we know not where, and I have been forgetting him when I can laugh. I know not if he be live or dead, and we are so far from him, tossing in the midseas. Oh, what can two women like us do in England, in this time of bitterness, if the Loyalists are reckoned but brothers of the rebels? I dreamed it was all different till we heard such tales in Halifax."

"We shall find many friends, and we need never throw away our hope," said Mary Hamilton soothingly. "And Master Sullivan bade me remember with his last blessing that God never makes us feel our weakness except to lead us to seek strength from Him. 'T was the saying of his old priest, the Abbé Fénelon."

They sat silent together; the motion of the ship was gentle enough, and the western breeze was steady. It seemed like a quiet night again; the sun was going down, and there was a golden light in the thick web of rigging overhead, and the gray sails were turned to gold color.

"It is I who should be staying you, dear child," whispered Madam Wallingford, putting out her hand again and resting it on Mary's shoulder, "but you never fail to comfort me. I have bitterly reproached myself many and many a day for letting you follow me; 't is like the book of Ruth, which always brought my tears as I read it. I am far happier here with you than I have been many a day at home in my lonely house. I need wish for a daughter's love no more. I sometimes forget even my great sorrow and my fear of our uncertainty, and dread the day when we shall come to land. I wish I were not so full of fears. Yet I do not think God will let me die till I have seen my son."

Mary could not look just then at her old friend's fragile figure and anxious face; she had indeed taken a great charge upon herself, and a weakness stole over her own heart that could hardly be borne. What difficulties and disappointments were before them God only knew.

"Dear child," said Madam Wallingford, whose eyes were fixed upon Mary's unconscious face, "is it your dreams that keep your heart so light? I wish that you could share them with the heavy-hearted like me! All this long winter you have shown a heavenly patience; but your face was often sad, and this has grieved me. I have thought since we came to sea that you have been happier than you were before."

"'T was not the distresses that we all knew; something pained me that I could not understand. Now it troubles me no more," and Mary looked at the questioner with a frank smile.

"I am above all a hater of curious questions," insisted the lady. But Mary did not turn her eyes away, and smiled again.

"I can hold myself to silence," said Madam Wallingford. "I should not have spoken but for the love and true interest of my heart; 'twas not a vulgar greed of curiosity that moved me. I am thankful enough for your good cheer; you have left home and many loving cares, and have come with me upon this forced and anxious journey as if it were but a holiday."

Mary bent lower over her sewing.

"Now that we have no one but each other I should be glad to put away one thought that has distressed me much," confessed the mother, and her voice trembled. "You have never said that you had any word from Roger. Surely there is no misunderstanding between you? I have sometimes feared—Oh, remember that I am his mother, Mary! He has not written even to me in his old open fashion; there has been a difference, as if the great distance had for once come between our hearts; but this last letter was from his own true heart, from his very self! The knowledge that he was not happy made me fearful, and yet I cannot brook the thought that he has been faithless, galling though his hasty oath may have been to him. Oh no, no! I hate myself for speaking so dark a thought as this. My son is a man of high honor." She spoke proudly, yet her anxious face was drawn with pain.

Mary laid down her piece of linen, and clasped her hands together strongly in her lap. There was something deeply serious in her expression, as she gazed off upon the sea.

"It is all right now," she said presently, speaking very simply, and not without effort. "I have been grieved for many weeks, ever since the first letters came. I had no word at all from Roger, and we had been such friends. The captain wrote twice to me, as I told you; his letters were the letters of a gentleman, and most kind. I could be sure that there was no trouble between them, as I feared sometimes at first," and the bright color rushed to her face. "It put me to great anxiety; but the very morning before we sailed a letter came from Roger. I could not bring myself to speak of it then; I can hardly tell you now."

"And it is all clear between you? I see,—there was some misunderstanding, my dear. Remember that my boy is sometimes very quick; 't is a hasty temper, but a warm and true heart. Is it all clear now?"

Mary wished to answer, but she could not, for all her trying, manage to speak a word; she did not wish to show the deep feeling that was moving her, and first looked seaward again, and then took up her needlework. Her hand touched the bosom of her gown, to feel if the letter were there and safe. Madam Wallingford smiled, and was happy enough in such a plain assurance.

"Oh yes!" Mary found herself saying next moment, quite unconsciously, the wave of happy emotion having left her calm again. "Oh yes, I have come to understand everything now, dear Madam, and the letter was written while the Ranger lay in the port of Brest. They were sailing any day for the English coast."

"Sometimes I fear that he may be dead; this very sense of his living nearness to my heart may be only—The dread of losing him wakes me from my sleep; but sometimes by day I can feel him thinking to me, just as I always have since he was a child; 't is just as if he spoke," and the tears stood bright in Madam Wallingford's eyes.

"No, dear, he is not dead," said Mary, listening eagerly; but she could not tell even Roger Wallingford's mother the reason why she was so certain.

XXXIII

They come to Bristol

*"The wise will remember through sevenfold births the love of
those who wiped away their falling tears."*

Miss Mary Hamilton and the captain of the Golden Dolphin walked together from the busy boat landing up into the town of Bristol. The tide was far down, and the captain, being a stout man, was still wheezing from his steep climb on the long landing-stairs. It was good to feel the comfort of solid ground underfoot, and to hear so loud and cheerful a noise of English voices, after their four long weeks at sea, and the ring and clank of coppersmiths' hammers were not unpleasant to the ear even in a narrow street. The captain was in a jovial temper of mind; he had some considerable interest in his cargo, and they had been in constant danger off the coast. Now that he was safe ashore, and the brig was safe at anchor, he stepped quickly and carried his head high, and asked their shortest way to Mr. Davis's house, to leave Mary there, while he made plans for coming up to one of that well-known merchant's wharves.

"Here we are at last!" exclaimed the master mariner. "I can find my way across the sea straight to King's Road and Bristol quay, but I'm easy lost in the crooked ways of a town. I've seen the port of Bristol, too, a score o' times since I was first a sailor, but I saw it never so dull as now. There it is, the large house beyond, to the port-hand side. He lives like a nobleman, does old Sir Davis. I'll leave ye here now, and go my ways; they've sarvents a plenty to see ye back to the strand."

The shy and much occupied captain now made haste toward the merchant's counting-room, and Mary hurried on toward the house, anxious to know if Madam Wallingford's hopes were to be assured, and if they should find Mistress Davis not only alive and well, but ready to welcome them. As she came nearer, her heart beat fast at the sight of a lady's trim head, white-capped, and not without distinction of look, behind the panes of a bowed window. It was as plain that this was a familiar sight, that it might every day be seen framed in its place within the little panes, as if Mary had known the face since childhood, and watched for a daily greeting as she walked a Portsmouth street at home. She even hesitated for a moment, looking eagerly, ere she went to lift the bright knocker of the street door.

In a minute more she was in the room.

"I am Mary Hamilton, of Berwick," said the guest, with pretty eagerness, "and I bring you love and greeting from Madam Wallingford, your old friend."

"From Madam Wallingford?" exclaimed the hostess, who had thought to see a neighbor's daughter enter from the street, and now beheld a stranger, a beautiful young creature, with a beseeching look in her half familiar face. "Come you indeed from old Barvick, my dear? You are just off the sea by your fresh looks. I was thinking of cousin Wallingford within this very hour; I grieved to think that now we are both so old I can never see her face again. So you bring me news of her? Sit you down; I can say that you are most welcome." Her eyes were like a younger woman's, and they never left Mary's face.

"She is here; she is in the harbor, on board the Golden Dolphin, one of her own ships. I have not only brought news to you; I have brought her very self," said the girl joyfully.

There was a quick shadow upon the hostess's face. "Alas, then, poor soul, I fear she has been driven from her home by trouble; she would be one of the Loyalists! I'll send for her at once. Come nearer me; sit here in the window seat!" begged Mistress Davis affectionately. "You are little Mary Hamilton, of the fine house I have heard of and never seen, the pride of my dear old Barvick. But your brother would not change sides. You are both of the new party,—I have heard all that months ago; how happens it that the Golden Dolphin brought you hither, too?"

Mary seated herself in the deep window, while Mistress Davis gazed at her wonderingly. She had a tender heart; she could read the signs of great effort and of loneliness in the bright girlish face. She did not speak, but her long, discerning look and the touch of her hand gave such motherly comfort that the girl might easily have fallen to weeping. It was not that Mary thought of any mean pity for herself, or even remembered that her dear charge had sometimes shown the unconscious selfishness of weakness and grief; but brave and self-forgetful hearts always know the true value of sympathy. They were friends and lovers at first sight, the young girl and the elderly woman who was also Berwick-born.

"I HAVE HAD YOUR HOUSE filled to its least garrets with Royalists out of my own country, and here comes still another of them, with a young friend who is of the other party," Mistress Davis said gayly; and the guest looked up to see a handsome old man who had entered from another room, and who frowned doubtfully as he received this information. Mary's head was dark against the window, and he took small notice of her at first, though some young men outside in the street had observed so much of her beauty as was visible, and were walking to and fro on the pavement, hoping for a still brighter vision.

"This is Miss Mary Hamilton, of Barvick," announced the mistress, "and your old friend Madam Wallingford is in harbor, on one of her ships." She knew that she need say no more.

Mr. John Davis, alderman of Bristol and senior warden of his parish church, now came forward with some gallantry of manner.

"I do not like to lay a new charge upon you," said his wife, pleading prettily, "but these are not as our other fugitives, poor souls!" and she smiled as if with some confidence.

"Why, no, these be both of them your own kinsfolk, if I mistake not," the merchant agreed handsomely; "and the better part of our living has come, in times past, from my dealings with the husband of one and the good brother of the other. I should think it a pity if, for whatever reason they may have crossed the sea, we did not open wide our door; you must bid your maids make ready for their comfortable housing. I shall go at once to find the captain, since he has come safe to land in these days of piracy, and give so noble a gentlewoman as his owner my best welcome and service on the ship. Perhaps Miss Hamilton will walk with me, and give her own orders about her affairs?"

Mary stepped forward willingly from the window, in answer to so kind a greeting; and when she was within close range of the old man's short-sighted eyes, she was inspected with such rapid approval and happy surprise that Mr. Alderman Davis bent his stately head and saluted so fair a brow without further consideration. She was for following him at once on his kind errand, but she first ran back and kissed the dear mistress of the house. "I shall have much to tell you of home," she whispered; "you must spare me much time, though you will first be so eager for your own friend."

"We shall find each other changed, I know,—we have both seen years and trouble enough; but you must tell Mrs. Wallingford I have had no such happiness in many a year as the sight of her face will bring me. And dear Nancy Haggens?" she asked, holding Mary back, while the merchant grew impatient at the delay of their whispering. "She is yet alive?" And Mary smiled.

"I shall tell you many things, not only of her, but of the gay major," she replied aloud. "Yes, I am coming, sir; but it is like home here, and I am so happy already in your kind house." Then they walked away together, he with a clinking cane and majestic air, and kindly showing Miss Hamilton all the sights of Bristol that they passed.

"So you sailed on the Golden Dolphin?" he asked, as they reached the water side. "She is a small, old vessel, but she wears well; she has made this port many a time before," said John Davis. "And lumber-laden, you say? Well, that is good for me, and you are lucky to escape the thieving privateers out of your own harbors. So Madam Wallingford has borne her voyage handsomely, you think? What becomes of her young son?"

XXXIV

GOOD ENGLISH HEARTS

"'T is all an old man can do, to say his prayers for his country."

Late that evening, while the two elder ladies kept close together, and spoke eagerly of old days and friends long gone out of sight, John Davis sat opposite his young guest at the fireplace, as he smoked his after-supper pipe.

The rich oak-paneled room was well lit by both firelight and candles, and held such peace and comfort as Mary never had cause to be grateful for before. The cold dampness of the brig, their close quarters, and all the dullness and impatience of the voyage were past now, and they were safe in this good English house, among old friends. It was the threshold of England, too, and Roger Wallingford was somewhere within; soon they might be sailing together for home. Even the worst remembrance of the sea was not unwelcome, with this thought at heart!

The voyagers had been listening to sad tales of the poverty and distress of nearly all the Loyalist refugees from America, the sorrows of Governor Hutchinson and his house, and of many others. The Sewalls and Russells, the Faneuils, and the Boutineaus, who were still in Bristol, had already sent eager messages. Mistress Davis warned her guests that next day, when news was spread of their coming, the house would be full of comers and goers; all asking for news, and most of them for money, too. Some were now in really destitute circumstances who had been rich at home, and pensions and grants for these heartsick Loyalists were not only slow in coming, but pitiful in their meagreness. There was a poor gentleman from Salem, and his wife with him, living in the Davises house; they had lodged upward of thirty strangers since the year came in; it was a heavy charge upon even a well-to-do man, for they must nearly all borrow money beside their food and shelter. Madam Wallingford was not likely to come empty-handed; the heavy box with brass scutcheons which the captain himself had escorted from the Golden Dolphin, late that afternoon, was not without comfortable reassurance, and the lady had asked to have a proper English waiting-maid chosen for her, as she did not wish to bring a weight upon the household. But there were other problems to be faced. This good merchant, Mr. Davis, was under obligations to so old a friend, and he was not likely to be a niggard, in any sense, when she did him the honor to seek his hospitality.

"I must go to my library, where I keep my business matters; 'tis but a plain book room, a place for my less public affairs. We may have some private talk there, if you are willing," he said, in a low voice; and Mary rose at once and followed him. The ladies did not even glance their way, though the merchant carefully explained that he should show his guest a very great ledger which had been brought up from his counting-room since business had fallen so low. She might see her brother's name on many of the pages.

"Let us speak frankly now," he urged, as they seated themselves by as bright a fire of blazing coals as the one they had left. "You can trust me with all your troubles," said the fatherly old man. "I am distressed to find that Madam Wallingford's case is so desperate."

Mary looked up, startled from the peace of mind into which she had fallen.

"Do you know anything, sir?" she begged him earnestly. "Is it likely"—But there she stopped, and could go no further.

"I had not the heart to tell her," he answered, "but we have already some knowledge of that officer of the Ranger who was left ashore at Whitehaven: he has been reported as gravely wounded, and they would not keep him in any jail of that northern region, but sent him southward in a dying state, saying that he should by rights go to his own kind in the Mill Prison. You must be aware that such an unprovoked attack upon a British seaport has made a great stir among us," added the merchant, with bitterness.

Mary remembered the burning of Falmouth in her own province, and was silent.

"If he had been a deserter, and treacherous at heart, as I find there was suspicion," he continued; "yes, even if his own proper feelings toward the King had mastered your lieutenant, I do not know that his situation would have been any better for the moment. They must lack spirit in Whitehaven; on our Bristol wharves the mob would have torn such a prisoner limb from limb. You must remember that I am an Englishman born and bred, and have no patience with your rebels. I see now 't was a calmer judgment ruled their course when they sent him south; but if he is yet in the Mill Prison, and alive, he could not be in a worse place.

This war is costing the King a fortune every week that it goes on, and he cannot house such pirates and spies in his castle at Windsor."

Mary's eyes flashed; she was keeping a firm hold upon her patience. "I think, from what we are told of the Mill Prison, that the King has gone too far to the other extreme," she could not forbear saying, but with perfect quietness.

"Well, we are not here to talk politics," said the alderman uneasily. "I have a deep desire to serve so old and respected a friend as this young man's mother. I saw the boy once when he came to England; a promising lad, I must own, and respectful to his elders. I am ready to serve him, if I can, for his father's sake, and to put all talk of principles by, or any question of his deserts. We have been driven to the necessity of keeping watchers all along the sea-coast by night and day, to send alarm by beacons into our towns. They say Paul Jones is a born divil, and will stick at nothing. How came Colonel Wallingford's son to cast in his lot with such a gallows rogue?"

"If you had lived on our river instead of here in Bristol, you would soon know," Mary answered him. "Our honest industries have long been hindered and forbidden; we are English folk, and are robbed of our rights."

"Well, well, my dear, you seem very clear for a woman; but I am an old man, and hard to convince. Your brother should be clear-headed enough; he is a man of judgment; but how such men as he have come to be so mistaken and blind"—

"It is Parliament that has been blind all the time," insisted Mary. "If you had been with us on that side of the sea, you would be among the first to know things as they are. Let us say no more, sir; I cannot lend myself to argument. You are so kind and I am so very grateful for it, in my heart."

"Well, well," exclaimed the old man again, "let us speak, then, of this instant business that you have in hand! I take it you have a heart in the matter, too; I see that you cherish Madam Wallingford like her own child. We must find out if the lad is still alive, and whether it is possible to free him. I heard lately that they have had the worst sort of small-pox among them, and a jail fever that is worse than the plague itself. 'T is not the fault of the jail, I wager you, but some dirty sailor brought it from his foul ship," he added hastily. "They are all crowded in together; would they had kept at home where they belong!"

"You speak hard words," said the girl impatiently, and with plain reproach, but looking so beautiful in her quick anger that the old man was filled with wonder and delight before his conscience reminded him that he should be ashamed. He was not used to being so boldly fronted by his own women folk; though his wife always had her say, she feared and obeyed him afterward without question.

"I wish that this foolish tea had never been heard of; it has been a most detestable weed for England," grumbled the old merchant. "They say that even your Indians drink it now, or would have it if they could."

"Mr. Davis, you have seen something of our young country," said the girl, speaking in a quiet tone. "You have known how busy our men are at home, how steadily they go about their business. If you had seen, as I did, how they stood straight, and dropped whatever they had in hand, and were hot with rage when the news came from Boston and we knew that we were attacked at Lexington and Concord, you would have learned how we felt the bitter wrong. 'T was not the loss of our tea or any trumpery tax; we have never been wanting in generosity, or hung back when we should play our part. We remembered all the old wrongs: our own timber rotting in our woods that we might not cut; our own waterfalls running to waste by your English law, lest we cripple the home manufacturers. We were hurt to the heart, and were provoked to fight; we have turned now against such tyranny. All we New England women sat at home and grieved. The cannon sounded loud through our peaceful country. They shut our ports, and we could not stand another insult without boldly resenting it. We had patience at first, because our hearts were English hearts; then we turned and fought with all our might, because we were still Englishmen, and there is plenty of fight left in us yet."

"You are beset by the pride of being independent, and all for yourselves," Mr. Davis accused her.

"Our hearts are wounded to the quick, because we are the same New England folk who fought together with the King's troops at Louisburg, and you have oppressed us," said Mary quickly. "I heard that Mr. John Adams said lately—and he has been one of our leaders from the first—that there had not been a moment since the beginning of hostilities when he would not have given everything he possessed for a restoration to the state of things before the contest began, if we could only have security for its continuance. We did not wish to separate from England, and if the separation has come, it is only from our sad necessity. Cannot you see that, being English people, we must insist upon our rights? We are not another race because we are in another country."

"Tut, tut, my dear," said the old man uneasily. "What does a pretty girl like you know about rights? So that's the talk you've listened to? We may need to hear more of it; you sound to me as if Fox had all along been in the right, and knew the way to bring back our trade." He began to fidget in his elbow chair and to mend the fire. "I can't go into all this; I have had a wearying day,"—he began to make faint excuse. "There's much you should hear on England's side; you only know your own; and this war is costing Parliament a terrible drain of money."

"Do you know anything of Lord Newburgh, and where he may be found?" asked Mary, with sudden directness.

"My Lord Newburgh?" repeated Mr. Davis wonderingly. "And what should you want with him? I know him but by name. He would be the son of that Radcliffe who was a Scotch rebel in '45, and lost his head by it, too; he was brother to the famous Lord Darwentwater. 'T was a wild family, an unfortunate house. What seek you at their hands?"

Mary sat looking into the fire, and did not answer.

"Perhaps you can send some one with me toward Plymouth to-morrow?" she asked presently, and trembled a little as she spoke. She had grown pale, though the bright firelight shone full in her face. "The captain learned when we first came ashore that Lord Mount Edgecumbe is likely to be commander of that prison where our men are; the Mill Prison they said it was, above Plymouth town. I did not say anything to Madam Wallingford, lest our hopes should fail; but if you could spare a proper person to go with me, I should like to go to Plymouth."

The old man gazed at her with wonder.

"You do not know what a wild goose chase means, then, my little lady!" he exclaimed, with considerable scorn. "Lord Mount Edgecumbe! You might as well go to Windsor expecting a morning talk and stroll in the park along with the King. 'T is evident enough one person is the same as another in your colonies! But if you wish to try, I happened to hear yesterday that the great earl is near by, in Bath, where he takes the waters for his gout. You can go first to Mr. George Fairfax, of Virginia, with whom Madam Wallingford is acquainted; she has told me that already. He is of a noble house, himself, Mr. Fairfax, and may know how to get speech with these gentlemen: why, yes, 't is a chance, indeed, and we might achieve something." Mr. Davis gave a satisfied look at the beautiful face before him, and nodded his sage head.

"I shall go with you, myself, if it is a fair day tomorrow," he assured her. "I am on good terms with Mr. Fairfax. I was long agent here for their tobacco ships, the old Lord Fairfaxes of Virginia; but all that rich trade is good as done," and he gave a heavy sigh. "We think of your sailors in the Mill Prison as if they were all divils. You won't find it easy to get one of them set free," he added boldly.

Mary gave a startled look, and drew back a little. "I hear the King is glad to ship them on his men-of-war," she said, "and that the Mill Prison is so vile a place the poor fellows are thankful to escape from it, even if they must turn traitor to their own cause."

"Oh, sailors are sailors!" grumbled the old man. "I find Madam Wallingford most loyal to the King, however, so that there is a chance for her. And she is no beggar or would-be pensioner; far from it! If her foolish son had been on any other errand than this of the Ranger's, she might easier gain her ends, poor lady. 'What stands in the way?' you may ask. Why, only last week our own coast was in a panic of fear!" John Davis frowned at the fire, so that his great eyebrows looked as if they were an assaulting battery. He shrugged his shoulders angrily, and puffed hard at his pipe, but it had gone out altogether; then he smiled, and spoke in a gentler tone:—

"Yes, missy, we'll ride to Bath to-morrow, an the weather should be fair; the fresh air will hearten you after the sea, and we can talk with Mr. Fairfax, and see what may be done. I'm not afraid to venture, though they may know you for a little rebel, and set me up to wear a wooden ruff all day in the pillory for being seen with you!"

"I must speak ye some hard words," the old man added unexpectedly, leaning forward and whispering under his breath, as if the solid oak panels might let his forebodings reach a mother's ears in the room beyond. "The young man may be dead and gone long before this, if he was put into the Mill Prison while yet weak from his wounds. If he is there, and alive, I think the King himself would say he could not let him out. There's not much love lost in England now for Paul Jones or any of his crew."

XXXV

A STRANGER AT HOME

"Would that she had told us of the trials of that time, and why it was that her heart rose against the new world and the new manners to which she had come!"

The next morning Miss Hamilton came down dressed in her riding gear, to find her host already in the saddle and armed with a stout hunting crop, which he flourished emphatically as he gave some directions to his groom. The day was fine and clear after a rainy night, with a hearty fragrance of the showery summer fields blowing through the Bristol streets.

They were quick outside the town on the road to Bath. Mary found herself well mounted, though a little too safely for her liking. Her horse was heavy of build, being used to the burden of a somewhat ponderous master; but the lighter weight and easy prompting hand of a young girl soon made him like a brave colt again. The old merchant looked on with approval at such pretty skill and acquaintance with horsemanship as his companion showed at the outset of their journey; and presently, when both the good horses had finished their discreet frolic and settled to sober travel, he fell into easy discourse, and showed the fair rider all the varied interests of the way. It was a busy thoroughfare, and this honored citizen was smiled at and handsomely saluted by many acquaintances, noble and humble. Mr. Davis was stingy of holidays, even in these dull times, but all the gallantry he had ever possessed was glowing in his heart as he rode soberly along in such pleasant company.

The dreary suspense and anxiety of six long weeks at sea were like a half-forgotten dream in the girl's own mind; at last she could set forth about her business. The sorrows of seafaring were now at an end; she was in England at last, and the very heart of the mother country seemed to welcome her; yet a young heart like Mary Hamilton's must needs feel a twinge of pain at the height of her morning's happiness. The fields and hedges, the bright foxglove and green ivy, the larks and blackbirds and quiet robins, the soft air against her cheeks,—each called up some far-inherited memory, some instinct of old relationship. All her elders in Berwick still called England home, and her thrilled heart had come to know the reason.

Roger Wallingford had lived in England. She suddenly understood against her will why he could find it so hard to go to sea in the Ranger to attack these shores, and why he had always protested against taking part in the war. England was no longer an angry, contemptuous enemy, tyrannous and exacting, and determined to withhold the right of liberty from her own growing colonies. All those sad, familiar prejudices faded away, and Mary could only see white clouds in a soft sky above the hazy distance, and hear the English birds singing, and meet the honest English faces, like old friends, as she rode along the road. There was some witchery that bewildered her; it was like some angry quarrel sprung up between mother and child while they were at a distance from each other, that must be quick forgotten when they came face to face. There was indeed some magic touch upon her: the girl's heart was beating fast; she was half afraid that she had misunderstood everything in blaming old England so much, and even stole a quick glance at her companion to see if he could have guessed her strange thoughts.

"'T is a pretty morning," said Mr. Davis kindly, seeing that she looked his way. "We shall reach Bath in proper season," and he let his horse come to a slow walk.

Whether it was the fresh air of the summer day, very strengthening to one who had been long at sea, or whether it was the justice of their errand itself, the weakness of this happy moment quickly passed, and Miss Hamilton's hand eagerly sought for a packet in the bosom of her gown, to see if it were safe. The reason for being on this side the sea was the hope that an anxious errand could be well done. She thought now of Master Sullivan on his bleak New England hillside; of the far blue mountains of the north country, and the outlook that was clearer and wider than this hazy landscape along the Avon; she looked down at the tame English river, and only remembered the wide stream at home that ran from the mountains straight to sea,—how it roared and droned over the great rocky fall near the master's own house, and sounded like the calling sea itself in his ears.

"You may see Bath now, there in the valley," said Mr. Davis, pointing with his big hand and the hunting crop. "'T is as fine a ride from Bristol to Bath as any you may have in England." They stopped their horses, a little short of breath, and looked down the rich wooded country to the bright town below.

"'T is a fine ride indeed," said Mary, patting her horse's neck, and thinking, with uncontrollable wistfulness, of the slenderer and less discreet young Duke at home, and of the old coachman and his black helpers as they always stood by the stable, eager to watch her, with loud cautions, as she rode away. It was a sharp touch of homesickness, and she turned her head so that she could hide her face from sight.

"I'll change with you, my dear, as we ride toward home; I see you are so competent a rider," offered Mr. Davis heartily. "Lightfoot is a steady beast, though I must own you found him otherwise this morning; this chestnut is younger and freer-gaited." He had a strange sense, as he spoke, that Mary was no longer in good spirits. Perhaps the heavy horse had tired her strength, though Lightfoot was as good a creature as any in Bristol, and much admired for his noble appearance.

Mary eagerly protested, and patted the old horse with still greater friendliness and approval as they went riding on toward the town. The alderman sighed at the very sight of her youth and freshness; it would be pleasant to have such a daughter for his own. A man likes young company as he grows older; though the alderman might be growing clumsy on his own legs, the good horse under him made him feel like a lad of twenty. This was a fine day to ride out from Bristol, and the weather of the best. Mr. Davis began to mind him of an errand of business to Westbury on Trym, beyond the Clifton Downs, where, on the morrow, he could show Miss Hamilton still finer prospects than these.

They stopped at last before a handsome lodging in the middle of the town of Bath. Mr. George Fairfax was a Virginian, of old Lord Bryan Fairfax's near kindred, a man of great wealth, and a hearty Loyalist; his mother, a Cary of Hampton, had been well known to Madam Wallingford in their early years. He was at home this day, and came out at once to receive his guests with fine hospitality, being on excellent terms of friendship with the old merchant. They greeted each other with great respect before Miss Hamilton's presence was explained; and then Mr. Fairfax's smiling face was at once clouded. He had been the hope and stay of so many distressed persons, in these anxious days of war, that he could only sigh as he listened. It was evident enough that, however charming this new sufferer and applicant might be, their host could but regret her errand. Yet one might well take pleasure in her lovely face, even if she must be disappointed, as most ladies were, in the hope of receiving an instant and ample pension from the Ministers of His Majesty George the Third.

Mr. Fairfax, with great courtesy, began to say something of his regrets and fears.

"But we do not ask for these kind favors," Mary interrupted him, with gentle dignity. "You mistake our present errand, sir. Madam Wallingford is in no need of such assistance. We are provided with what money we are like to need, as our good friend here must already know. The people at home"—and she faltered for one moment before she could go on. "It was indeed thought best that Madam Wallingford should be absent for a time; but she was glad to come hither for her son's sake, who is in prison. We have come but to find him and to set him free, and we ask for your advice and help. Here is her letter," and Miss Hamilton hesitated and blushed with what seemed to both the gentlemen a most pretty confusion. "I ought to tell you, Mr. Fairfax—I think you should know, sir, that I am of the Patriots. My brother was with General Washington, with his own regiment, when I left home."

Mr. George Fairfax bowed ceremoniously, but his eyes twinkled a little, and he took instant refuge in reading the letter. This was evidently an interesting case, but not without its difficulties.

"The young gentleman in question also appears to be a Patriot," he said seriously, as he looked up at Mr. Davis. "In Miss Hamilton's presence I must drop our usual term of 'rebel.' Madam Wallingford professes herself unshaken in her hereditary allegiance to the Crown; but as for this young officer, her son, I am astonished to find that he has been on board the Ranger with that Paul Jones who is the terror of all our ports now, and the chief pest and scourge of our commerce here in England. 'T is a distressed parent, indeed.

"You have the right of it," said the old British merchant, with great eagerness and reproach. Mr. Davis was not a man who found it easy to take the humorous point of view. "It seems that he was left ashore, that night of the attack upon Whitehaven, in the north, which you will well remember. He was caught by the town guard. You know that we captured one of the Ranger's men? 'Twas this same young officer, and, though badly wounded, he was ordered to the Mill Prison, and is said to have arrived in a dying state. For his mother's sake (and her face would distress any man's heart), I try to believe that he is yet alive and lies there in the jail; but 't is a sorry house of correction that he has come to through his own foolishness. They say he is like to have been hanged already."

"Good God! what a melancholy story, and all England thinking that he deserves his fate!" exclaimed Fairfax. "I cannot see how anything can be done."

"There is but one gleam of hope," said Mr. Davis, who had not sat among the Bristol magistrates in vain. He spoke pompously, but with some kindness for Miss Hamilton, who was listening sadly enough, the eager bravery of her face all gone; their last words had been very hard to bear. "There is one thing to add. The story reached America, before these good friends left, that young Mr. Wallingford was suspected by many persons on board the Ranger of still holding to his early Loyalist principles. They openly accused him of an effort to betray the ship into our hands. If this is true"—

"It is not true!" interrupted Miss Hamilton, and both the gentlemen looked a little startled. "No, it is not true," she repeated more calmly. "It is not a proper plea to make, if he should never be set free."

"We must think of his mother; we are only reviewing the situation in our own fashion," said the elder man, frowning a stern rebuke at her. But she would have her way.

"Mr. Davis has been very kind in the matter," she continued. "When we were speaking together, last night, he told me that Lord Mount Edgecumbe was now in Bath, and would have great influence about the American prisoners."

"That is true," said Mr. Fairfax politely; "but I do not possess the honor of his lordship's acquaintance, and I fear that I have no means of reaching him. He is in bad health, and but lately arrived in Bath to take the waters."

"Miss Hamilton has brought letters"—

"I have some letters, given me by an old friend at home," acknowledged Mary. "The writer was very sure that they would be of use to us. Do you happen to know anything of Lord Newburgh, sir, and where he may be found?"

"Lord Newburgh?" repeated the Virginian eagerly, with a quick shake of his head and a sudden frown, though there was again a twinkle of merriment in his eyes. Mary's best hopes suddenly fell to the ground. She was aware as she had not been before upon how slight a foundation these best hopes might have been built. She had always looked up to Master Sullivan with veneration; the mystery of his presence was like an enchantment to those who knew him best. But he had been a long lifetime in America; he might have written his letters to dead men only;

they might be worth no more than those withered oak leaves of last year that were fluttering on the hedges, pierced by a new growth.

There was a pause. Mr. Fairfax's face seemed full of pity. Miss Hamilton began to resent his open show of sympathy.

"I am strangely inhospitable!" he exclaimed. "We were so quick at our business that I forgot to offer you anything, sir, and you, Miss Hamilton, after your morning's ride! No, no, it is no trouble. You will excuse me for a moment? I am like to forget my good bringing up in Virginia, and my lady is just now absent from home."

Mr. Fairfax quickly left the room. The alderman sat there speechless, but looking satisfied and complacent. It certainly did make a man thirsty to ride abroad on a sunshiny morning, and his ears were sharp-set for the comfortable clink of glasses. The heavy tray presently arrived, and was put near him on a card table, and the old butler, with his pleasant Virginian speech, was eager in the discharge of hospitality; Mr. Fairfax being still absent, and Mary quite at the end of her courage. She could not take the cool draught which old Peter offered her with respectful entreaties, as if he were Cæsar, their own old slave; she tried to look at the hunting pictures on the wall, but they blurred strangely,—there was something the matter with her eyes.

"What noble Jamaica spirits!" said Mr. John Davis, looking at the ceiling with affected indifference as his glass was being replenished. "Did your master grow these lemons on his own plantations in Virginia? They are of a wondrous freshness," he added, politely, to repeat his approval of such an entertainment. "Miss Hamilton, my dear, you forget we must take the long ride back again to Bristol. I fear you make a great mistake to refuse any refreshment at good Peter's hands."

The door was thrown open and Mr. Fairfax made a handsome, middle-aged gentleman precede him into the room.

"I was afraid that I should miss this noble friend," he said gayly; "he might have been taking advantage of so fine a morning, like yourselves. Here is my Lord Newburgh, Miss Hamilton; this is Lord Newburgh himself for you! You must have heard of the Honorable Mr. Davis, of Bristol, my lord?—one of their great merchants. I have told you already that Miss Hamilton brings you a letter, and that she hopes for your interest with my Lord Mount Edgecumbe. My dear Miss Hamilton, this gives me great pleasure! When you said that you had brought such a letter, I was sure at last that there was one thing I could do for you."

Lord Newburgh gravely saluted these new acquaintances, taking quick notice of the lady's charm, and smiling over his shoulder at Mr. Fairfax's excited manner. He waved his hand in kind protest to check Peter's officious approach with the tray of glasses.

"So you have a letter for me, from America, Miss Hamilton?" he asked bluntly; and she put it into his hand.

Lord Newburgh gave a curious look at the carefully written address, and turned the folded sheet to see the seal. Then he flushed like a man in anger and bit his lip as he looked at the seal again, and started back as he stood close by the window, so that they all saw him. Then he tore open Master Sullivan's letter.

"It is dated this very last month!" he cried. "My God! do you mean to tell me that this man is still alive?"

XXXVI

My Lord Newburgh's Kindness

*"Thus says my King: Say thou to Harry of England, though we
seemed dead, we did but sleep."*

W hat man?" asked Mr. Fairfax and Mr. Davis, with eager
curiosity, seeing such astonishment upon his face; but Lord
Newburgh made them no answer until he had read the letter and
carefully folded it again. They saw his hands tremble. He stood
looking blankly at the two men and Miss Hamilton, as if he were in
doubt what to say.

"'T is like one risen from the dead," he told them presently, "but
what is written here is proof enough for me. There are some things
which cannot be spoken of even after all these years, but I can say this:
't was a friend of my poor father, Charles Radcliffe, and of his brother,
Darwentwater,—one of their unlucky company sixty years ago. There
are high reasons, and of State too, why, beyond this, I must still keep
silence. Great heavens, what a page of history is here!" and he opened
the letter to look at it once more.

"Mount Edgecumbe will not believe me," he said, as if to himself.
"Well, at least he knows something of those old days, too; he will be
ready to do what he can for such a petitioner as this, but we must be
careful. I should like to speak with Miss Hamilton alone, if you will
leave us here together, gentlemen," said Lord Newburgh, with quiet
authority; and Mr. Fairfax and the alderman, disappointed, but with
ready courtesy, left them alone in the room.

"Do you know the writer of this letter, madam?" demanded Lord
Newburgh; and he was so well aware of the girl's beauty that, while he
spoke, his eyes scarcely left her face. "'T is true he speaks your name
here and with affection, but I cannot think his history is known."

Mary smiled then, and answered gently to her life-long acquaintance
with the master and her deep love for him, but that his early life was a
matter of conjecture to those who had longest been her neighbors. Lord
Newburgh saw with approval that she knew more than she was ready
to confess.

"He has followed the great Example,—he has given his life for his friend," said Lord Newburgh, who showed himself much moved, when she had finished speaking. "They should know of this among our friends in France; by God's truth, the King himself should know but for his present advisers! I must say no more; you can see how this strange news has shaken me. He asks a thing difficult enough; he has broken his long silence for no light reason. But Mount Edgecumbe will feel as I do,—whatever he asks should be promised him; and Mount Edgecumbe has power in Plymouth; even with Barrington reigning in the War Office he is not likely to be refused, though Barrington is a narrow soul, and we can give no reasons such as make our own way plain. Your man shan't stay in the Mill Prison, I can promise you that, Ranger or no Ranger!"

Lord Newburgh smiled now at Miss Hamilton, as if to bring a look of pleasure to so sweet a face, and she could not but smile back at him.

"I shall do my part of this business at once," he said, rising. "I passed Mount Edgecumbe on my way here; he'll swear roundly at such a request. He fears again that his great oaks must go down, and his temper is none of the best. The Earl is an old sailor, my dear Miss Hamilton, and has a sailor's good heart, but this will stagger him well. You say that Madam Wallingford, the young man's mother, is now in Bristol?" and again he looked at the letter. "Stay; before I speak with the Earl I should like to hear more of these interesting circumstances. I must say that my own sympathies are mainly with your party in the colonies. I believe that the King has been made a tool of by some of his ministers. But I should not say this if you are one of the Loyalist refugees. Why, no, my dear!" He checked himself, laughing. "'T is a strange confusion. I cannot think you are for both hound and hare!"

It was near an hour later when Mr. Fairfax fumbled at the latch to see if he might be of service, and was politely though not too warmly requested to enter. Mr. John Davis had grown fretful at their long delay, but Miss Hamilton and Lord Newburgh were still deep in their conversation. The young lady herself had been close to her brother's confidence, and was not ignorant of causes in this matter of the war. Lord Newburgh struck his fist to the table with emphatic approval, as he rose, and told the two gentlemen who entered that he had learned at last what all England ought to know,—the true state of affairs in America.

The Virginia Loyalist looked disturbed, and showed some indifference to this bold announcement.

"Come, Fairfax," cried the guest gayly, "I shall have arguments enough for ye now! I can take the Patriot side with intelligence, instead of what you have persisted in calling my ignorant prejudice."

"'T is your new teacher, then, and not your reasoning powers," retorted Fairfax; and they both fell to laughing, while Mary fell to blushing and looking more charming than before.

"Well, Miss Hamilton, and is your business forwarded? Then we must be off; the day is well squandered already," said John Davis.

"I shall first take Miss Hamilton to our good housekeeper for a dish of tea before she rides home," protested the host kindly. "I am grieved that my lady is not here; but our housekeeper, Mrs. Mullet, can offer the dish of tea, if so stern a Boston Patriot does not forbid. You will try the Jamaica spirits again yourself, sir? A second glass may be better than the first, Mr. Alderman!"

"I shall speak with my friends as to these Plymouth affairs, and do my best for you," Lord Newburgh kindly assured Miss Hamilton, as they parted. "You shall see me in Bristol to-morrow. Ah, this letter!" and he spoke in a low voice. "It has touched my heart to think that you know so well our sad inheritance. My poor father and poor Darwentwater! Every one here knows their melancholy fate, their 'sad honors of the axe and block;' but there were things covered in those days that are secrets still in England. *He speaks of the Newgate supper to me! . . .'Twas he himself who saved. . . and only a lad*" . . . But Mary could not hear the rest.

"I must see you again," he continued, aloud. "I shall have a thousand questions to put to you, and many messages for your old Master Sullivan (God bless him!) when you return. I offer you my friendship for his sake," and Lord Newburgh stood with bared head beside the horse when Miss Hamilton had mounted. "We have pleasant Dilston Hall to our home no more these many years; we Radcliffes are all done, but at Slindon you shall be very welcome. I shall wait upon Madam Wallingford to-morrow, and bring her what good comfort I can."

THE ALDERMAN WAS WARMED BY Mr. Fairfax's hospitalities, and rode beside his young guest as proudly as if he were the lord mayor on high holiday. The streets of Bath were crowded with idle gentlefolk; it was a lovely day, and many people of fashion were taking the air as well as the famous waters. This was a fine sight for a New England girl, and Mary herself was beheld with an admiration that was by no means silent. Their horses' feet clacked sharply on the cobblestones, as if eager to shorten the homeward road, and the young rider sat as light as her heart was, now the errand was done. It was a pretty thing, her unconsciousness of all admiration: she might have been flitting along a shady road under the pines at home, startling the brown rabbits, and keeping a steady hand on the black Duke's rein to be ready for sudden freaks. She did not see that all along by the pump room they were watching her as she passed. She was taking good news to Bristol; Lord Newburgh had given his word of honor that Roger Wallingford should be pardoned and set free. Was not his mother a great lady, and heartily loyal to the Crown? Was there not talk of his having been suspected of the same principles on board the American privateer? It must be confessed that Lord Newburgh's face had taken on a look of amused assurance when these facts were somewhat unwillingly disclosed; they were the last points in the lieutenant's history which Mary herself woidd have willingly consented to use, even as a means of deliverance from captivity, but, unknown to her, they had won an easy promise of freedom.

"She's a rebel indeed, but God bless me, I don't blame her!" laughed the noble lord, as he reflected upon their conversation. It was not in his loyal heart to forget his heritage. Whatever might fall out in the matter of those distressed seamen who now suffered in the Mill Prison, no man could fail of pleasure in doing service for such sweet eyes as Miss Mary Hamilton's. There were some private reasons why he could go boldly to ask this great favor, and Lord Mount Edgecumbe was as good as master of the town of Plymouth, both by land and sea, and responsible for her concerns. "I'll make him ride with me to Bristol tomorrow to see these ladies," said Lord Newburgh from a generous heart. "'T will be a sweet reward, he may take my word for it!"

XXXVII

The Bottom of these Miseries

*"Let us pray that our unconscious benefactions outweigh
our unconscious cruelties!"*

The order for Lieutenant Wallingford's release was soon in hand,
but the long journey across country from Bristol to Plymouth
seemed almost as long as all the time spent in crossing the sea. From the
morning hour when the two elder ladies had watched Miss Hamilton
and her kind old cavalier ride away down the narrow Bristol street, with
a stout man servant well mounted behind them, until the day they were
in sight of Plymouth Hoe, each minute seemed slower than the last. It
was a pretty journey from inn to inn, and the alderman lent himself
gayly to such unwonted holidays, while Mary's heart grew lighter on
the way, and a bright, impatient happiness began to bloom afresh in her
cheeks and to shine in her eyes.

They reached Plymouth town at nightfall, and Mary was for taking
fresh horses and riding on to the Mill Prison. For once her face was
dark with anger when the landlord argued against such haste. He was
for their taking supper, and assured the travelers that not even the
mayor of Plymouth himself could knock at the jail gate by night and
think to have it opened.

Miss Hamilton turned from such officious speech with proud
indifference, and looked expectantly at her companion.

"It is not every night they will have a pardon to consider," she said
in a low voice to Mr. Davis. "We carry a letter from my Lord Mount
Edgecumbe to the governor of the prison. We must first get speech
with the guard, and then I have no fear."

The innkeeper looked provoked and wagged his head; he had
already given orders for a bountiful supper, and was not going to let a
rich Bristol merchant and two persons beside ride away without paying
for it.

"We shall not be long away," said Mary, pleading. If she had known
of the supper, she would have added that they might bring back
another and a hungrier guest than they to sit at table. The alderman was

irresolute; he was ready to succor a distressed prisoner, being a good Christian; but he was hungry now, and they had been riding all day at a quicker pace than he might have followed if alone. His man servant, just come into the inn parlor to wait for orders, stole a meaning glance at him; and they were two against one.

"No, no, my dear; 't is a good bit further, and most likely we should have our ride in vain. I know the rules of such places, from our Bristol laws at home. The governor will most likely be here in the town. Rest you now, and let us make a good supper, and start again betimes in the morning." Then, seeing how disappointed and even determined her face grew, and that she looked very tired, "I am an old man, you must remember," he added kindly. "I fear that I am spent to-night, and can do no more without resting."

She was silent then, and crossed the room to stand by the window. There was a voice in her heart that begged her to persist, to go on alone, if need be, and not let herself be hindered in her quest. It was still light out of doors; the long twilight of the English summer was making this last step of her great adventure a possibility. She sighed; the voice within still warned and pleaded with her. "Who are you?" the girl said wonderingly. "Who are you that comes and helps me? You are not my own thought, but some one wiser than I, who would be my friend!" It was as if some unseen ministering spirit were face to face with her, bringing this insistent thought that she hardly dared refuse to take for guidance.

She gazed out of the window. Sunset clouds were brightening the whole sky; an afterglow was on the moorland hills eastward above the town. She could hear the roar of the ocean not far away; there were cheerful voices coming up the street, and the citizens were all abroad with their comfortable pipes and chatter.

"Get me a fresh horse and a man to follow," said Miss Hamilton, turning again to face the room. The landlord himself was laying the white cloth for supper. Matthew, their old groom, was stiffly kneeling and pulling off his master's riding boots, and they all three looked at her in dismay.

"Our own horses are done, miss," said Matthew, with decision.

"I have none I can let you to-night from my stable," the landlord seconded. "There was a review to-day of our raw recruits for America, and I had to empty every stall. The three best horses are returned with saddle galls from their clumsy ignorance," he protested boldly.

Mary glanced at Mr. Davis, and was still unconvinced; but all her determination was lost when she saw that the old man was really fatigued. Well, it was only one night more, and she must not insist. Perhaps they were right, and her ride would be in vain. At least she could send a messenger; and to this proposal the landlord readily acceded, since, useless or not, it would be a shilling in his pocket, and a slow boy could carry the letter which the young lady made such haste to write.

She stopped more than once, with trembling fingers and trembling heart. "Dearest Roger," and the written words made her blush crimson and hold her face closer to the paper. "Dearest Roger, I would that I might come to you to-night; but they say it is impossible. Your mother is in Bristol, and awaits you there. Mr. John Davis has brought me hither to the Crown Inn. In the morning we shall open the prison door for you. Oh, my dear Roger, to think that I shall see you at last!"

"When can we have the answer back?" she asked; and the landlord told her, smiling, that it would be very late, if indeed there were any answer at all, and reminded her, with insolent patience, that he had already told her they would not open their prison gates, for Lords or Commons, to any one who came by night.

"You may send the answer by one of your maids to the lady's room," commanded the Bristol magnate, in a tone that chased the servile smile from the inn-keeper's face.

WHEN MARY WAKED, THE MORNING sun was pouring in at her window, and there was no word of any answer. Old Matthew had spoken with the young messenger, and brought word that he had given the letter to one of the watch by the gate, who had taken the money, and promised to do his best to put the message into Mr. Wallingford's hands that night when they changed guard.

"WE MIGHT HAVE BEEN HERE last night; why, 't is but a step!" said John Davis, as they drew near the dismal prison next morning; but his young companion made no answer. He could not guess what happy fear mingled with her glad anticipation now, nor how her certainties and apprehensions were battling with each other.

Matthew's own horse and another that he led for Mr. Wallingford were weighted with provisions, so that he trudged afoot alongside. It was easy to hear in Plymouth town how the American prisoners lacked such things, and yet Mary could hardly wait now to make the generous purchase which she had planned. She could not know all that Matthew had learned, and told his master in whispers in the stable yard.

As they rode nearer to the prison a flaw of wind brought toward them all the horrible odors of the crowded place, like a warning of the distress and misery within. Though it was so early, there were many persons standing outside the gates: some of them were jeering at the sad spectacle, and some talking in a friendly way with the men who stood within. Happily, it was not only a few compassionate Americans who had posted themselves here to give what they could of food and succor, but among the Plymouth folk themselves many a heart was wrung with pity, and one poor old body had toiled out of the town with a basket of food to smuggle through the bars; cakes and biscuit of a humble sort enough, but well flavored with love. Mary saw her take thread and needles out of her pocket, and sit down on the ground to mend some poor rags of clothing. "My own lad went for a sailor," she said, when they thanked her and called her "mother."

There was long delay; the guards pushed back the crowd again and again; one must stand close to see the sights within. All at once there was a cry and scuffling among the idlers, as some soldiers came riding up, one of them bringing an old horse with a man thrown across the saddle and tied down. As they loosed him he slid heavily to the ground as if he were dead, and the spectators closed about him.

Mary Hamilton could only look on in horror and apprehension. Her companion was in the midst of the pushing crowd.

"'T was a prisoner who escaped last night and has been retaken," he said hastily, as he returned to her side. "You may stay here with Matthew, my dear, while I take our letters and go in. I see that it is no place for you; they are like wild beasts."

"I must go, too," said Mary; "you will not forbid me now. Good heavens!" she cried aloud. "Now that they stand away from the gate I can see within. Oh, the poor prisoners! Oh, I cannot bear their sick faces! They are starving, sir! These must be the men who had the fever you told me of. I wish we had brought more wine and food to these poor fellows! Let us go in at once," she cried again, and was in a passion of pity and terror at the sight.

"Let us go in! Let us go in!" she begged. "Oh, you forget that they are my own countrymen! I cannot wait!"

The guard now returned with a message, and the alderman gave his bridle to the groom. Mary was afoot sooner than he, and had run to the gate, pushing her way among the idle sightseers to the heavy grating. They were calling from both sides of the gate to old Matthew, who was standing with the horses, to come up and give them what he had brought. Mary Hamilton felt as if she were among wolves: they did not listen; they did not wait to find what she had to say. "For love of God, give me a shilling for a little 'baccy, my lady," said one voice in her ear. "I'll fetch them the'baccy from the town, poor boys; they lack it most of anything, and he'll drink the money!" protested an old beggar woman at her side. "Go in? They'll let no ladies in!" and she gave a queer laugh. "And if you're once in, all you'll pray for is to be out again and forget the sight."

THE GOVERNOR WAS IN HIS room, which had a small grated window toward the prison yard; but there was a curtain before it, and he looked up anxiously to see if this were close drawn as his early guests entered. This task of jailer was a terrible duty for any man, and he swore under his breath at Lord Mount Edgecumbe for interfering with what at best was an impossible piece of business. If he had seen to it that they had decent supplies for the prison, and hanged a score of their purveyors and contractors, now, or had blown the whole rotten place into the air with his fleet guns, 't were a better kindness!

The clerk stood waiting for orders.

"Show them in, then, these people," he grumbled, and made a feint of being busy with some papers as Miss Hamilton and her escort appeared. The governor saw at once that the honorable Mr. Davis was a man of consequence.

"My Lord Mount Edgecumbe writes me that you would make inquiries for a prisoner here," said the old soldier, less roughly because the second guest proved to be a lady and most fair to see. She looked very pale, and was watching him with angry eyes. As she had crossed the prison yard, she had seen fewer miseries because her tears had blinded her. There had been one imploring voice calling her by her own name. "Stop, Miss Hamilton, stop, for God's sake!" some one had cried; but the guard had kept the poor prisoners off, and an attendant hurried her along by force when she would gladly have lingered. The horror of it all was too much for her; it was the first time she had ever been in a jail.

"I am fearful of your sad disappointment, madam," said the governor of the prison. "You wished to see Lieutenant Roger Wallingford. I grieve to say"—He spoke kindly, but looked to ward Mary and stopped, and then, sighing heavily, turned his eyes toward Mr. Davis with a kind of relief.

"He is not dead, I hope, sir?" asked the old man, for Mary could not speak. "We have the order for his release."

"No, he is not dead to any certain knowledge," explained the governor, more slowly than before, "but he was one of a party that made their escape from this prison last night; 't was through one of their silly tunnels that they dig. They have some of them been shot down, and one, I hear, has just been taken and brought in alive; but Wallingford's name is not among any of these." He turned to some records, and then went to the grated window and looked out, but pulled the curtain across it impatiently as he came away. "You brought his pardon?" the governor then asked brusquely. "I should think he would be the last man for a pardon. Why, he was with Paul Jones, sir; but a very decent fellow, a gentleman, they tell me. I did not see him; I am not long here. This young lady had best go back to the inn," and he stole a look at Mary, who sat in despairing silence. A strange flush had replaced her first pallor. She had thought but a moment before that she should soon look again into Roger Wallingford's face and tell him that he was free. On the end of the governor's writing table lay the note that she had written with such a happy heart only the night before.

XXXVIII

Full of Straying Streets

*"Nona ne souffrons quo dans la mesure où nous co-opérons
à nos souffrances."*

"His age saw visions, though his youth dream'd dreams."

The town of Bristol was crowded with Loyalist refugees: some who had fled the colonies for honest love of their King, and some who believed that when the King's troops had put down the rebellion they should be well rewarded for holding to his cause. They were most of them cut off from what estates they may have had, and were begging for pensions from a government that seemed cruelly indifferent. Their sad faces fairly shadowed the Bristol streets, while many of them idled the day through, discussing their prospects with one another, and killing time that might have been lived to some profit. The disappointment of their hope was unexpected, and an England that showed them neither sympathy nor honor when they landed on her shores, glowing with self-sacrifice, was but a sad astonishment. England, their own mother country, seemed fallen into a querulous dotage, with her King's ministers so pompous in their stupid ignorance and self-consequence, and her best statesmen fighting hard to be heard. It was an age of gamester heroes and of reckless living; a poor page of English history was unfolded before their wistful eyes. These honest Loyalists were made to know the mortified feelings of country gentlefolk come unheralded to a city house that was busy with its splendors on a feast day, and impatient of what was inopportune. Worse than this, though Judge Curwen and other loyal Americans of his company were still hopeful of consideration, and of being warmly received by England as her own true children, they were oftener held guilty of the vexing behavior of their brothers, those rebels against English authority whom they had left behind. Something to Mary's wonder, Madam Wallingford would have few of them to friend. She was too great a person at home to consent even now to any social familiarity on the score of political sympathies. She was known to have brought much money, and it was made easy for her to share this with one and another distressed acquaintance or friend's friend; but while this was done with generosity, she showed herself more and more impatient of their arguments, even of those plaints which were always ready, and the story of such grievances as had led them into exile.

"I am too ill and sad to listen to these things," she said often, even to her friends the Pepperrells, who came from London to visit her. "I only know my country's troubles through my own sorrow." She begged them at last to find poor Roger's grave, so she might go there to pray for him; 't was all that she could do. "Oh no," she would say mournfully to those who looked for her assent to their own views of the great situation, "do not expect me to understand you. I am only a mother, and all my life is done!"

The Bristol streets were busy as Miss Hamilton came walking through the town, and the bells were ringing for a holiday. She was deep in anxious thought, and kept steadily on her way toward the abbey church, without even a glance at a tradesman's window or a look at the people she met. Life was filled with new anxieties. Since the day when they had left Plymouth they could find no trace of Roger Wallingford, beyond the certainty that he had made his escape with some fellow prisoners through a tunnel which they had been for many days digging under the prison wall. There had been a light near the opening in the field outside, and a guard set, but six men had gone out of the narrow hole and crawled away. It was a windy night, and the lantern light and shadows wavered on the ground and hid them. Two were shot and killed, but two were captured and brought back at once, while another was shot and got away, stumbling and falling often, and bleeding like a slaughtered creature, as the watch could see next morning by daylight. This poor fellow had escaped to the moors; there was a pool of blood in a place where he must have hidden for some hours among the furze bushes. There was so large a bounty paid for any escaped traitors and felons like these, who might be brought back alive to the Mill Prison, that the poor moorland folk back of Plymouth were ever on the quest. Roger Wallingford might have been that bleeding man. They would not dare to keep together; his companion might have left him dying or dead somewhere in the lonely waste country that stretched miles away above the prison. His fate was sure if he should be captured; he was not a man to yield his life too easily. There were some carefully worded notices posted,—broadsides which might easily reach the eyes of such fugitives if they ventured into any of the Devon towns near by; but they might well have starved to death by this time in the deserts of Dartmoor. One sailor beside the lieutenant had succeeded in making his escape.

Mary Hamilton had left her lady pale and in tears that morning, and all her affectionate solicitude had been in vain.

There was some relief in finding herself afoot in the fresh air. For the first time she wondered if they must yield all their hopes and think of going home. It must be so if they should come to know that Roger was really dead, and her heart stopped as if with a sudden shock. Alas, next moment she remembered that for poor Madam Wallingford there was no safe return; her son was not yet disproven of Tory crimes. If there were any chance of sailing, the poor lady was far too ill and feeble in these last days. The summer, the little that was left of it, looked long and dreary; the days were already growing short. There had not come a word from home since they sailed.

There was no longer much use in riding abroad on futile quests, and in these last days most persons had ceased to ask if there were any news of the lieutenant. Week after week had gone by, and his mother's proud courage was gone, while her bodily strength was fast failing. Lord Newburgh and Mr. Fairfax, even Lord Mount Edgecumbe himself, had shown very great kindness in so difficult a matter, and Mary never let them go away unthanked for any favors which it could only be a happiness for any man to bestow. The gift and spell of beauty were always hers, and a heart that was always ready to show both gratitude and affection. She might not speak these things, but she was instant in giving the sweetest recognition to the smallest service that she might discover.

The abbey church of St. Augustine was cool and dim as Mary Hamilton went in, with a drooping head and a heavy heart. Her courage had never before seemed so utterly to fail. She had passed two forlorn Royalists at the gatehouse who were talking of their pensions, and heard one of them say, "If I were safe home again I'd never leave it, principles or no principles!" and the words rang dull and heavy in her ears. She sat down on an old stone bench in the side aisle; the light came sifting down to the worn stone pavement, but she was in shadow, behind a great pillar that stood like a monstrous tree to hold the lofty roof. There was no one in sight. The lonely girl looked up at a familiar old Jacobean monument on the wall, with the primly ruffed father and mother kneeling side by side with clasped hands, and their children kneeling in a row behind them down to the very least, in a pious little succession. They were all together there in comfortable safety, and many ancient tablets covered the walls about them with the names and virtues of soldiers and sailors, priests and noblemen, and gallant gentlemen of Old England with their children and their good wives.

"They have all won through," whispered Mary to herself. "They have all fought the long battle and have carried care like me, and they have all won through. I shall not be a coward, either," and her young heart rose; but still the tears kept coming, and she sat bowed in the shadow and could not lift her head, which until lately had faced the sun like a flower. She sat there, at last, not thinking of her present troubles, but of home: of old Peggy and the young maids who often sang at their pleasant work; the great river at full tide, with its wooded shores and all its points and bays; the fishing weirs in the distance; the slow, swaying flight of the eagles and the straight course of the herons overhead. She thought of the large, quiet house facing southward, and its rows of elms, and the slender poplars going down the garden terraces; she even heard the drone of the river falls; she saw the house standing empty, all the wide doors shut to their old hospitality. A sense of awful distance fell upon her heart. The responsibility and hopelessness of her errand were too heavy on her young heart. She covered her face and bent still lower, but she could not stop her tears.

There came the sound of footsteps up the nave: it might be the old verger in his rusty gown, or some sightseer stopping here and there to read an inscription. Poor Mary's tears would have their way: to one of her deep nature weeping was sad enough in itself; to cry for sorrow's sake was no common sorrow. She was safe in her dim corner, and thought little of being seen; she was only a poor girl in sore trouble, with her head sunk in her hands, who could not in any way concern a stranger. The wandering footsteps stopped near by, instead of going on and entering the choir. She noticed, then, in a dull way, the light echo of their sound among the arches overhead.

"My God!" said a man's voice, as if in great dismay.

The speaker stepped quickly to Mary's side, and laid his hand gently on her shoulder. She looked up into the face of Captain Paul Jones of the Ranger.

XXXIX

Mercy and Manly Courage

"Look on his honour!
That bears no stamp of time, no wrinkles on it;
No sad demolishment nor death can reach it."

"O my dear better Angel and my star,
My earthly sight needs yours, your heavenly, mine!"

The captain's eyes were full of tears; it was no sign that he lacked manliness. To find Miss Hamilton in England, to find her alone and in piteous despair, was the opportunity of his own heart. He could not but be startled into wondering silence; the event was too astonishing even for one so equal to emergencies; but he stood ready, with beating heart and sure sense of a man's abundant strength, to shelter her and to fight against the thing that troubled her, whatever it might be. Presently he seated himself by Mary's side, and took her hand in his and held it fast, still without speaking. She was the better for such friendliness, and yet wept the more for his very sympathy.

The captain waited until her passion of tears had spent itself. It was a pity she could not watch his compassionate face; all that was best and kindest in the man was there to see, with a grave look born of conflict and many grievous disappointments. To see Paul Jones now, one could not but believe him capable of the sternest self-command; he had at least the unassuming and quiet pride of a man who knows no master save himself. His eyes were full of womanly tenderness as he looked down at the pathetic bowed head beside him. Next moment they had a keen brightness as he caught sight of a tablet on the abbey wall to some Bristol hero long dead,—the gallant servant, through many perils by sea and land, of Anne his Queen: it was a record that the captain's heart could perfectly understand.

"Calm yourself now, my dearest girl," he said at last, with gentle authority. "I must not stay long beside you; I am always in danger here. I was not unknown in Bristol as a younger man."

Mary lifted her head; for a moment the sight of his face helped to put her own miseries quite out of mind. Her ready sympathy was quickly enough roused when she saw how Paul Jones had changed. He had grown much older; years might have passed instead of months since that last evening he had spent in America, when she had seen him go away with his men by moonlight down the river. Now more than ever he might easily win the admiration of a woman's heart! She had half forgotten the charm of his voice, the simple directness of his eyes and their strange light, with something in his behavior that men called arrogance and willful rivalry, and women recognized as a natural royalty and irresistible, compelling power. To men he was too imperious, to women all gentleness and courtesy.

"You are in disguise!" she exclaimed, amazed at his courage. "How do you dare, even you, to be here in Bristol in broad day?" and she found herself smiling, in spite of her unchecked tears. The captain held a rough woolen cap in his hand; he was dressed in that poor garb of the hungry Spanish sailor of Quiberon, which had so often done him good service.

"Tell me what has brought you here," he answered. "That is by far the greatest wonder. I am no fit figure to sit beside you, but 't is the hand of God that has brought us here together. Heaven forbid that you should ever shed such bitter tears again!" he said devoutly, and sat gazing at her like a man in a day dream.

"Sometimes God wills that we shall be sorry-hearted; but when He sends the comfort of a friend, God himself can do no more," answered the girl, and there fell a silence between them. There was a sparrow flying to and fro among the pillars, and chirping gayly under the high roof,—a tiny far-fallen note, and full of busy cheer. The late summer sunshine lay along the floor of that ancient house of God where Mary and the captain sat alone together, and there seemed to be no other soul in the place.

Her face was shining brighter and brighter; at last, at last she could know the truth, and hear what had happened at Whitehaven, and ask for help where help could be surely given.

"But why are you here? You must indeed be bold, my lord captain!" she ventured again, in something very like the old gay manner that he knew; yet she still looked very white, except for her tear-stained eyes. "There were new tales of your seafaring told in the town only yesterday. I believe they are expecting you in every corner of England at once, and every flock of their shipping is dreading a sight of the Sea Wolf."

"I do my own errands,—that is all," replied the captain soberly. "My poor Ranger is lying now in the port of Brest. I am much hampered by enemies, but I shall presently break their nets. . . I was for a look at their shipping here, and how well they can defend it. There is a well-manned, able fish-boat out of Roscoff, on the Breton coast, which serves me well on these expeditions. I have a plan, later, for doing great mischief to their Baltic fleet. I had to bring the worst of my ship's company with me; 't is my only discomfort," said Paul Jones, with bitterness. "I have suffered far too much," and he sighed heavily and changed his tone. "I believe now that God's providence has brought me to your side; such happiness as this makes up for everything. You remember that I have been a sailor all my life," he continued, as if he could not trust himself to speak with true feeling. "I have been acquainted since childhood with these English ports."

"You did not know that I had come to Bristol?" said Mary. "Oh yes, we have been here these many weeks now," and she also sighed.

"How should I know?" asked Paul Jones impatiently. "I am overwhelmed by such an amazing discovery. I could burst into tears; I am near to being unmanned, though you do not suspect it. Think, dear, think what it is to me! I have no discretion, either, when I babble my most secret affairs aloud, and hardly know what I am saying. I must leave you in a few short moments. What has brought you here? Tell me the truth, and how I may safely manage to see you once again. If you were only in France, with my dear ladies there, they would love and cherish you with all their kind hearts! 'T is the Duchess of Chartres who has been my good angel since I came to France, and another most exquisite being whom I first met at her house,—a royal princess, too. Oh, I have much to tell you! Their generous friendship and perfect sympathy alone have kept me from sinking down. I have suffered unbelievable torture from the jealousy and ignorance of men who should have known their business better, and given me every aid."

"I am thankful you have such friends as these ladies," said Mary, with great sweetness. "I am sure that you have been a good friend to them. Some knowledge of your difficulties had reached us before we left home; but, as you know, intercourse is now much interrupted, and we were often uncertain of what had passed at such a distance. We hear nothing from home, either," she added mournfully. "We are in great distress of mind; you could see that I was not very cheerful. . . I fear in my heart that poor Madam Wallingford will die."

"Madam Wallingford!" repeated the captain. "You cannot mean that she is here!" he exclaimed, with blank astonishment. His tone was full of reproach, and even resentment. "Poor lady! I own that I have had her in my thoughts, and could not but pity her natural distress," he added, with some restraint, and then burst forth into excited speech: "There is no need that they should make a tool of you,—you who are a Patriot and Hamilton's own sister! This is arrant foolishness!"

He sprang to his feet, and stood before Miss Hamilton, with his eyes fixed angrily upon her face. "If I could tell you everything! Oh, I am outdone with this!" he cried, with a gesture of contempt.

"Captain Paul Jones," she said, rising quickly to confront him, "I beg you to tell me everything. I cannot believe that Roger Wallingford is a traitor, and I love his mother almost as if she were my own. I came to England with her of my own wish and free will, and because it was my right to come. Will you tell me plainly what has happened, and why you do not take his part?"

The captain's quick change from such deep sympathy as he had shown for her tears to a complete scorn of their cause could only give a sad shock to Mary Hamilton's heart. He was no helper, after all. There came a dizzy bewilderment like a veil over her mind; it seemed as if she felt the final blow of Fate. She had not known how far she had spent her strength, or how her very homesickness had weakened her that day.

"I fear it is true enough that he betrayed us at Whitehaven," said Paul Jones slowly, and not unmindful of her piteous look. "I could not bring myself to doubt him at first; indeed, I was all for him. I believe that I trusted him above every man on board. I was his champion until I found he had been meddling with my papers,—my most secret dispatches, too; yes, I have proof of this! And since then some of the stolen pages have found their way into our enemies' hands. He has not only betrayed me, but his country too; and worst of all in men's eyes, he has sinned against the code of honor. Yet there is one thing I will and must remember: 't is never the meanest men who serve their chosen cause as spies. The pity is that where success may be illustrious, the business asks completest sacrifice, and failure is the blackest disgrace. 'Tis Wallingford's reward. I loved him once, and now I could stand at the gallows and see him hanged! Perhaps he would say that he acted from high motives,—'t is ever a spy's excuse; but I trusted him, and he would have ruined me."

"I do not believe that he is guilty," declared Mary Hamilton, with perfect calmness, though she had drawn back in horror as she heard the last words and saw such blazing anger in Paul Jones's eyes. "You must look elsewhere for your enemy," she insisted,—"for some other man whose character would not forbid such acts as these. If Roger Wallingford has broken his oath of allegiance, my faith in character is done; I have known him all my life, and I can answer for him. Believe me, there is some mistake." Her eyes did not fall; as the captain held them straight and answerable with his own she met the challenge of his look, and there came a beautiful glow of pity and gentleness upon her face.

The captain gave a long sigh.

"I am sure that you are mistaken," she said again, quietly, since he did not speak. "We are now in great trouble, and even despair, about Mr. Wallingford, and have been able to get no word from him. We have his pardon in hand; it would make you wonder if I told you how it came to us. Your lieutenant was left most cruelly wounded on the shore at Whitehaven, and was like to die on the long journey to Plymouth jail where they sent him. How he has lived through all his sufferings I do not know. I have seen the Mill Prison, myself; they would not even let us speak with those who knew him among our poor captives. The night before we reached the prison he had escaped; there were some men shot down who were of his party. We can get no trace of him at all. Whether he is dead on the great moors, or still alive and wandering in distress, no one can tell. This does not look as if he were a spy for England; it were easy to give himself up, and to prove such a simple thing, if only to be spared such misery. I am afraid that his mother will soon fade out of life, now that, after all these weeks, she believes him dead. She thought he would return with us, when she saw us ride away to Plymouth, and the disappointment was more than she could bear."

The bitter memory of that morning at the Mill Prison was like a sword in Mary's heart, and she stopped; she had spoken quickly, and was now trembling from head to foot. "I thought, when I saw your face, that you would know how to help us find him," she said sorrowfully, under her breath.

"If I have been wrong," exclaimed the captain, "if I have been wrong, I should give my life to make amends! But all the proofs were there. I even found a bit of one of my own papers among his effects,—'t was in a book he had been reading. But I hid the matter from every one on board; I could not bear they should know it. Dickson's word was their mainstay at first; but that counted worse than nothing to me, till there were other matters which fully upheld his account."

"Dickson has always been a man mistrusted and reproached," protested Miss Hamilton, with indignation. "There is a man for you whose character would not forbid such treachery! You must know, too, that he has a deep hatred for the Wallingfords, and would spare no pains to revenge himself."

The captain stood doubtful and dismayed. "I have gone over this sad matter by day and by night," he said; "I do not see where I could be mistaken. I went to the bottom of my evidence without regard to Dickson, and I found proof enough. I hate that man, and distrust him, yet I can find little fault with his service on the ship; and when I have been surest of catching him in a lie, he always proves to have told the exact truth, and wears a martyr's air, and is full of his cursed cant and talk of piety. Alas, I know not what can be done at this late day."

"Did you never think that Dickson could put many a proof like your bit of paper where your eyes alone could fall upon it?" asked Mary. "I remember well that he has tried more than once to cast blame upon others when he himself was the sinner. He has plenty of ability; 't is his bad use of it that one may always fear."

The captain moved restlessly, as if conscious of her accusation. "Many believed Wallingford to be a Tory on the ship," he answered. "They were jealous and suspicious of his presence; but Dickson, who has warped Simpson's honest mind against me, may also have set his energies to this. If we could only find Wallingford! If we could only hear his own story of that night! In all this time he should have sent some word to me, if he were innocent. If I were free, I'd soon know what they learned from him in the prison; he must have spoken openly with some of the Portsmouth men who are there. What can we do?" the speaker ended, in a different tone altogether, making a direct appeal to Mary. "If I have fallen a dupe to such a man as Dickson in this matter, I shall never recover from the shame. You would never forgive me. Alas, how can I ask the question that my heart prompts! You are most unhappy," said Paul Jones, with exquisite compassion. "Is it because of Wallingford alone? Oh, Mary, is there no hope for me? You have had my letters? You cannot but remember how we parted!"

She looked at him imploringly.

"Tell me," said the captain. "I must ask a question that is very hard for me. I believe that you love this unfortunate officer, and desire his safety beyond everything else. Is it not true?"

Mary waited only a moment before she spoke.

"Yes, it is true," she said then. "I know now that we have always belonged to each other."

"Alas for my own happiness!" said the captain, looking at her. "I thought when we parted that last night"—He groaned, his words faltering. "Oh, that I had only spoken! Glory has been a jealous mistress to me, and I dared not speak; I feared 't would cost me all her favor, if my thoughts were all for you. It seems a lifetime ago. I could throw my hope of glory down at your feet now, if it were any use. I can do nothing without love. Oh, Mary, must you tell me that it is too late?"

The captain's voice made poignant outcry to the listener's heart. The air seemed to quiver in strange waves, and the walls of the abbey seemed to sway unsteadily. The strong, determined soul before her was pleading for an impossible happiness. Even better than he could know, she knew that he lacked a woman's constant love and upholding, and that, with all his noble powers, his life tended toward ruin and disappointment. She stood there, white and wistful; her compassionate heart was shaken with pity for his loneliness.

There was a change on the man's dark face; he took one step toward her, and then was conscious of a strange separation between them. Mary did not move, she did not speak; she stood there as a ghost might stand by night to pity the troubles of men. She knew, with a woman's foresight, the difference it would make if she could only stand with love and patience by his side.

"There must be some one to love you as it is in your heart to love," she told him then. "God bless you and give you such a happiness! You are sure to find each other in this sad world. I know you will! I know you will!"

One of the great bells began to ring in the tower, and its vibrations jarred her strangely; she could hardly hinder herself now from a new outburst of tears, and could not think clearly any more, and was trembling with weakness.

"I must go home if I can," she whispered, but her voice was very low. "I cannot get home alone—No, no, I must not let you be so kind!"

He placed her gently on the stone bench, and she leaned back heavily with his arm about her, thankful for some protecting affection in her brief bewilderment. She could not but hear his pitying, endearing words as her faintness passed; the poor girl was so breathless and weak that she could only throw herself upon his mercy. There was even an unexpected comfort in his presence,—she had been so much alone with strangers; she forgot everything save that he was a friend of her happier days. And as for the captain, he had held her in his arms, she had turned to him with touching readiness in her distress; nothing could ever rob his heart of the remembrance.

He watched her with solicitude as her color came back, and lingered until he saw that she was herself again. They must part quickly, for he could not venture to be seen with her in the open streets.

"You have convinced me that I may have been wrong about Wallingford," he said impulsively. "I shall now do my best to aid you and to search the matter out. I shall see you again. Your happiness will always be very dear to me. I can but thank Heaven for our being here together, though I have only added something to your pain. Perhaps these troubles may not be far from their solution, and I shall see you soon in happier hours."

He kissed her hand and let it go; his old hope went with it; there must be a quick ending now. A man must always resent pity for himself, but his heart was full of most tender pity for this overburdened girl. There had been few moments of any sort of weakness in all the course of her long bravery,—he was sure enough of that,—and only loved her the more. She had been the first to show him some higher things: it was not alone her charm, but her character, her great power of affection, her perfect friendship, that would make him a nobler lover to his life's end.

She watched him as he went away down the nave toward the open door; the poverty of such disguise and the poor sailor's threadbare dress could not hide a familiar figure, but he was alert no more, and even drooped a little as he stood for one moment in the doorway. He did not once look back; there were people in the church now, and his eyes were bent upon the ground. Then he lifted his head with all the spirit that belonged to him, stepped out boldly from the shadow into the bright daylight beyond, and was gone.

The old verger crossed over to speak with Mary; he had learned to know her by sight, for she came often to the abbey church, and guessed that she might be one of the exiles from America.

"'T was some poor sailor begging, I misdoubt. There's a sight o' beggars stranded in the town. I hope he would not make bold to vex you, my lady?" asked the dim-eyed old man, fumbling his snuffbox with trembling hands. "I fell asleep in the chapter room."

"'T was some one I had known at home," Miss Hamilton answered. "He is a good man." And she smiled a little as she spoke. It would be so easy to cause a consternation in the town. Her head was steady now, but she still sat where the captain left her.

"'T is a beautiful monyment,—that one," said the verger, pointing up to the kneeling figures in their prim ruffs. "'T is as beautiful a monyment as any here. I've made bold to notice how you often sits here to view it. Some o' your Ameriky folks was obsarvin' as their forbears was all buried in this abbey in ancient times; 't would be sure to make the owd place a bit homely."

The bells were still chiming, and there were worshipers coming in. Mary Hamilton slipped away, lest she should meet some acquaintance; she felt herself shaken as if by a tempest. Paul Jones had gone into fresh danger when he left her side; his life was spent among risks and chances. She might have been gentler to him, and sent him away better comforted.

She walked slowly, and stood still once in the street, startled by the remembrance of her frank confession of love; the warm color rushed to her pale face. To have told the captain, when she had never told Roger himself, or his mother, or any but her own heart! Yet all her sorrows were lightened by these unconsidered words: the whole world might hear them now; they were no secret any more.

There were busy groups of people about the taverns and tobacco shops, as if some new excitement were in the air; it might be that there was news from America. As Mary passed, she heard one man shout to another that John Paul Jones, the pirate, had been seen the day before in Bristol itself. An old sailor, just landed from a long voyage at sea, had known him as he passed. There was word, too, that the Ranger had lately been sighted again off Plymouth, and had taken two prizes in the very teeth of the King's fleet.

XL

The Watcher's Light

"There's no deep valley but near some great hill."

L ate that night Mary Hamilton sat by the window in her sleeping closet, a quaint little room that led from the stately chamber of Madam Wallingford. Past midnight, it was still warm out of doors, and the air strangely lifeless. It had been late before the maid went away and their dear charge had fallen asleep; so weak and querulous and full of despair had she been all the long day.

The night taper was flickering in its cup of oil, but the street outside was brighter than the great room. The waning moon was just rising, and the watcher leaned back wearily against the shutter, and saw the opposite roofs slowly growing less dim. There were tall trees near by in the garden, and a breeze, that Mary could not feel where she sat, was rustling among the poplar leaves and mulberries. She heard footsteps coming up the street, and the sound startled her as if she had been sitting at her window at home, where footsteps at that time of night might mean a messenger to the house.

The great town of Bristol lay fast asleep; it was only the watchman's tread that had startled the listener, and for a moment changed her weary thoughts. The old man went by with his clumsy lantern, but gave no cry nor told the hour until he was well into the distance.

There was much to think about at the end of this day, which had brought an unexpected addition to her heart's regret. The remembrance of Paul Jones, his insistence upon Wallingford's treachery, a sad mystery which now might never be solved, even the abruptness of the captain's own declaration of love, and a sense of unreality that came from her own miserable weakness,—all these things were new burdens for the mind. She could not but recognize the hero in this man of great distinction, as he had stood before her, and yet his melancholy exit, with the very poverty of his dress, had somehow added to the misery of the moment. It seemed to her now as if they had met each other, that morning, with no thoughts of victory, but in the very moment of defeat. Their hopes had been so high when last they talked together. Again there came to her mind the anxiety of that bright night when she had stood pleading with Roger Wallingford on the river shore, and had thrown down her challenge at his feet. How easy and even how happy it all seemed beside these dreadful days! How little she had known then! How little she had loved then! Life had been hardly more than a play beside this; it was more dramatic than real. She had felt a remote insincerity, in those old days, in even the passionate words of the two men, and a strange barrier, like a thin wall of glass, was always between her heart and theirs. Now, indeed, she was face to face with life, she was in the middle of the great battle; now she loved Roger Wallingford, and her whole heart was forever his, whether he was somewhere in the world alive, or whether he lay starved and dead among the furze and heather on the Devon moors. She saw his white face there, as if she came upon it in the shadows of her thoughts, and gave a quick cry, such was the intensity of her grief and passion; and the frail figure stirred under its coverlet in the great room beyond, with a pitiful low moan like the faint echo of her own despair.

The sad hour went by, and still this tired girl sat by the window, like a watcher who did not dare to forget herself in sleep. Her past life had never been so clearly spread before her, and all the pleasant old days were but a background for one straight figure: the manly, fast-growing boy whom she played with and rebuffed on equal terms; the eager-faced and boyish man whom she had begun to fear a little, and then to tease, lest she should admire too much. She remembered all his beautiful reticence and growing seriousness, the piety with which he served his widowed mother; the pleading voice, that last night of all, when she had been so slow to answer to his love. It was she herself now who could plead, and who must have patience! How hard she had been sometimes, how deaf and blind, how resistant and dull of heart! 'T was a girl's strange instinct to fly, to hide, to so defeat at first the dear pursuer of her heart's love!

Again there was a footstep in the street. It was not the old watchman coming, for presently she heard a man's voice singing a country tune that she had known at home. He came within sight and crossed the street, and stood over the way waiting in shadow; now he went on softly with the song. It was an old Portsmouth ballad that all the river knew; the very sound of it was like a message:—

> "The mermaids they beneath the wave,
> The mermaids they o'er my sailor's grave,
> The mermaids they at the bottom of the sea,
> Are weeping their salt tears for me.

"The morning star was shining still,
'T was daybreak over the eastern hill"—

He began the song again, but still more softly, and then stopped.

Mary kept silence; her heart began to beat very fast. She put her hand on the broad window-sill where the moonlight lay, and the singer saw it and came out into the street. She saw the Spanish sailor again. What had brought the captain to find her at this time of night?

She leaned out quickly. "I am here. Can I help you? Is there any news?" she whispered, as he stood close under the window, looking up. "You are putting yourself in danger," she warned him anxiously. "I heard the people saying that you have been seen in Bristol, this morning as I came home!"

"God be thanked that I have found you awake!" he answered eagerly, and the moon shone full upon his face, so that she could see it plain. "I feared that I should have to wait till daylight to see you. I knew no one to trust with my message, and I must run for open sea. I have learned something of our mystery at last. Go you to the inn at Old Passage to-morrow night,—do you hear me?—to the inn at Old Passage, and wait there till I come. Go at nightfall, and let yourself be unknown in the house, if you can. I think—I think we may have news from Wallingford."

She gave a little cry, and leaned far out of the window, speaking quickly in her excitement, and begging to hear more; but the captain had vanished to the shadows whence he came. Her heart was beating so fast and hard now that she could not hear his light footsteps as he hurried away, running back to the water-side down the echoing, paved street.

SARAH ORNE JEWETT

XLI

An Offered Opportunity

*"Neither man nor soldier.
What ignorant and mad malicious traitors!"*

"License, they mean, when they cry Liberty."

The Roscoff fishing smack lay in the Severn, above Avon mouth, and it was broad day when Captain Paul Jones came aboard again, having been rowed down the river by some young Breton sailors whom he had found asleep in the bottom of their boat. There would be natural suspicion of a humble French craft like theirs; but when they had been overhauled in those waters, a day or two before, the owner of the little vessel, a sedate person by the name of Dickson, professed himself to be an Englishman from the Island of Guernsey, with proper sailing papers and due reverence for King George the Third. His crew, being foreigners, could answer no decent Bristol questions, and they were allowed to top their boom for the fishing grounds unmolested, having only put into harbor for supplies.

The Roscoff lads looked at their true captain with mingled sleepiness and admiration as he took the steersman's place. He presently opened a large knotted bundle handkerchief, and gave them a share of the rich treat of tobacco and early apples within; then, seeing that they kept their right course, he made a pillow of his arm and fell sound asleep.

As they came under the vessel's side the barking of a little dog on board waked him again with a start. He looked weary enough as he stood to give his orders and watch his opportunity to leap from the boat, as they bobbed about in the choppy sea. All was quiet on deck in the bright sunlight; only the little French dog kept an anxious lookout. The captain gave orders to break out their anchor and be off down channel, and then turned toward the cabin, just as Dickson made his appearance, yawning, in the low companion way.

Dickson had found such life as this on the fisherman very dull, besides having a solid resentment of its enforced privations. None of the crew could speak English save Cooper and Hanscom, who had come to hate him, and would not speak to him at all except in the exercise of duty. He knew nothing of the Breton talk, and was a man very fond of idle and argumentative conversation. The captain had been ashore now for thirty-six long hours, and his offended colleague stood back, with a look of surly discontent and no words of welcome, to let the tyrant pass. The captain took a letter out of his pocket and gave it to him, with a quick but not unfriendly glance, as if half amused by Dickson's own expression of alarm as he turned the folded paper and looked at its unbroken seal. He mumbled something about a tailor's bill, and then insisted that the letter could not be meant for him. He did not seem to know what it would be safe to say.

"Come below; I wish to speak with you." The captain spoke impatiently, as usual, and had the air of a kingbird which dealt with a helpless crow. "We are in no danger of being overheard. I must speak with you before you read your letter. I have chanced upon some important information; I have a new plan on foot."

"Certainly, sir," replied Dickson, looking very sour-tempered, but putting a most complaisant alacrity into his voice.

"The news was given me by a man who succeeded in making his escape from the Mill Prison some months since, and who came to Bristol, where he had old acquaintants; he is now at work in a coppersmith's shop," explained the captain. "He has been able to help some of his shipmates since then, and, under the assumed character of an American Loyalist, has enjoyed the confidence of both parties. 'T will be a dangerous fellow to tamper with; I have heard something of him before. I doubt if he is very honest, but he turns many a good sound penny for himself. Lee believes that all his spies are as trusty as Ford and Thornton, but I can tell you that they are not." The captain's temper appeared to be rising, and Dickson winced a little. "I know of some things that go on unbeknownst to him, and so perhaps do you, Mr. Dickson; this man has advised me of some matters in Bristol this very night, about which I own myself to be curious. He says that there are two men out of the Mill Prison who may be expected in, and are hoping to get safe away to sea. It would be a pretty thing to add a pair of good American sailors to our number without the trouble of formal exchange. So I must again delay our sailing for France, and I shall leave you here to-night, while I go to inspect the fugitives. There are special reasons, too, why I wish to get news from the prison."

The captain seemed excited, and spoke with unusual frankness and civility. Though Dickson had begun to listen with uneasiness, he now expressed approval of such a plan, but ventured at the same time to give an officious warning that there might be danger of a plot among the Bristol Loyalists. They would make themselves very happy by securing such an enemy as John Paul Jones. But this proof of sagacity and unselfishness on Dickson's part the captain did not deign to notice.

"I shall pass the day in fishing, and toward night take another anchorage farther up the channel," he continued. "There are reasons why prudence forbids my going into the Avon again by boat, or being seen by day about the Bristol quays. I shall run farther up the Severn and land there, and ride across by Westbury, and over the downs into Bristol, and so return by daybreak. I have bespoken a horse to wait for me, and you will see that a boat is ready to take me off in the morning."

Dickson received these instructions with apparent interest and an unconscious sigh of relief. He understood that the captain's mind was deeply concerned in so innocent a matter; there was probably no reason for apprehension on his own part. The next moment his spirits fell, and his face took on that evil color which was the one sign of emotion and animosity that he was unable to conceal. There was likely to be direct news now from the Mill Prison; and the grievous nightmare that haunted Dickson's thoughts was the possible reappearance of Roger Wallingford.

Once or twice he swallowed hard, and tried to gather courage to speak, but the words would not come. The captain passed him with a scowl, and threw himself into the wretched bunk of the cabin to get some sleep.

"Captain Jones," and Dickson boldly followed him, "I have something important which I must say"—

"Will not you read your letter first?" inquired the captain, with unaccustomed politeness. "I am very much fatigued, as you might see. I want a little sleep, after these two nights."

"We are alone now, sir, and there is something that has lain very heavy on my mind." The man was fluent enough, once his voice had found utterance.

The captain, with neither an oath nor a growl, sat up in his berth, and listened with some successful mockery of respect, looking him straight in the face.

"That night,—you remember, sir, at Whitehaven? I have come to be troubled about that night. You may not recall the fact that so unimportant a person as I stood in any real danger on such an occasion of glory to you, but I was set upon by the town guard, and only escaped with my life. I returned to the Ranger in a suffering condition. You were a little overset by your disappointment, and by Mr. Wallingford's disappearance and your suspicions of his course. But in my encounter,— you know that it was not yet day,—and in the excitement of escaping from an armed guard, I fear that I fought hand to hand with Wallingford himself, taking him for a constable. He was the last of them to attack me, when I was unable to discriminate,—or he, either," added Dickson slyly, but with a look of great concern. "The thought has struck me that he might not have been disloyal to our cause, and was perhaps escaping to the boat, as I was, when we fell into such desperate combat in that dark lane. It would put me into an awful position, you can see, sir. . . I may be possessed of too great a share of human frailty, but I have had more than my share of ill fortune. I have suffered from unjust suspicions, too, but this dreadful accident would place me"—

"You thought to save your life from an unknown enemy?" the captain interrupted him. "You struck one of your own party, by mischance, in the dark?" he suggested, without any apparent reproach in his voice.

"Exactly so, sir," said Dickson, taking heart, but looking very mournful.

"Yet you told us that Mr. Wallingford alarmed the guard?"

"I could suspect nothing else, sir, at the time; you heard my reasons when I returned."

"Never mind your return," urged Paul Jones, still without any tone of accusation. "'T was long after the gray of the morning, it was almost broad day, when I left the shore myself at Whitehaven, and a man might easily know one of his shipmates. 'T was a dark lane, you told me, however," and his eyes twinkled with the very least new brightness. "If we should ever see poor Wallingford again, you could settle all that between you. I can well understand your present concern. Do you think that you did the lieutenant any serious damage before you escaped? I recall the fact that you were badly mauled about the countenance."

"I fear that I struck him worst in the shoulder, sir," and Dickson shifted his position uneasily, and put one hand to the deck timber above to hold himself steady, now that they were rolling badly with the anchor off ground. "I know that I had my knife in my hand. He is a very strong fellow, and a terrible man to wrestle with,—I mean the man whom I struck, who may have been Wallingford. I thought he would kill me first."

"I wish you had bethought yourself to speak sooner," said the captain patiently. "'T is a thing for us to reflect upon deeply, but I can hear no more now. I must sleep, as you see, before I am fit for anything. Do not let the men disturb me; they may get down channel to their fishing. If they succeed as well as yesterday, we shall soon make the cost of this little adventure."

He spoke drowsily, and drew the rough blanket over his head to keep the light away.

Dickson mounted to the deck. If he had known how easy it would be to make things straight with the captain, how much suffering he might have spared himself! You must take him in the right mood, too. But the captain had an eye like a gimlet, that twisted into a man's head.

"Wallingford may never turn up, after all. I wish I had killed him while I was about it," said Dickson to himself uneasily. "It may be all a lie that he was sent to Plymouth; it would be such a distance!" There was something the matter with this world. To have an eye like Paul Jones's fixed upon you while you were trying to make a straight story was anything but an assistance or a pleasure.

The captain was shaking with laughter in the cabin as Dickson disappeared. "What a face he put on the smooth-spoken hypocrite! His race is run; he told me more than he needed," and Paul Jones's face grew stern, as he lay there looking at the planks above his head. "He's at the bottom of the hill now, if he only knew it. When a man's character is gone, his reputation is sure enough to follow;" and with this sage reflection the captain covered his head again carefully, and went to sleep.

Unaware of this final verdict, Dickson was comfortably reading his letter on the deck, and feeling certain that fortune had turned his way. His mind had been made up some days before to leave the Ranger as soon as he got back to France, even if he must feign illness to gain his discharge, or desert the ship, as others had done. He had already a good sum of money that had been paid him for information useful to the British government, and, to avoid future trouble, proposed to hide himself in the far South or in one of the West Indian Islands. "My poor wife would gain by the change of climate," said the scoundrel, pitying himself now for the loss of friendship and respect from which he felt himself begin to suffer, and for those very conditions which he had so carefully evolved.

He started as he read the brief page before him; the news of the letter was amazingly welcome. It was written by some one who knew his most intimate affairs. The chance had come to give up the last and best of those papers which he had stolen from the captain's desk. For this treasure he had asked a great price,—so great that Thornton would not pay it at Brest, and Ford's messenger had laughed him in the face. Now there was the promise of the money, the whole noble sum. Word of his being with Paul Jones had somehow reached Bristol. The crafty captain had been unwise, for once, in speaking with this make-believe coppersmith, and the play was up! The writer of the letter said that a safe agent would meet Mr. Dickson any night that week at seven o'clock, at the inn by Old Passage, to pay him his own price for certain papers or information. There was added a handsome offer for the body of Paul Jones, alive or dead, in case he should not be in custody before that time. The letter was sealed as other letters had been, with a device known among Thornton's errand runners.

"Old Passage!" repeated the happy Dickson. "I must now find where that place is; but they evidently know my present situation, and the inn is no doubt near!"

He stepped softly to the cabin hatchway, and looked down. The captain's face was turned aside, and he breathed heavily. The chart of that coast was within easy reach; Dickson took it from the chest where it lay, since it was an innocent thing to have in hand. There was all the shore of the Severn and the Bristol Channel, with the spot already marked nearest Westbury church where the captain was likely to land; and here beyond, at no great distance, was Old Passage, where a ferry crossed the Severn. He should have more than time enough for his own errand and a good evening ashore, while Paul Jones was riding into Bristol, perhaps to stay there against his will. For the slight trouble of ripping a few stitches in his waistcoat seams and taking out a slip of paper, Dickson would be rich enough at that day's end.

"Yes, I'll go to the southward when I reach America, and start anew," he reflected. "I've had it very hard, but now I can take my ease. This, with the rest of my savings, will make me snug."

He heard the captain move, and the planks of the berth creak in the stuffy cabin. They were running free before the east wind, and were almost at the fishing grounds.

XLII

The Passage Inn

"The Runlet of Brandy was a loving Runlet and floated
after us out of pure pity."

Just before nightfall, that same day, two travel-worn men came riding
along a country road toward Old Passage, the ancient ferrying-place
where travelers from the south and west of England might cross over
into Wales. From an immemorial stream of travel and the wear of
weather, the road-bed was worn, like a swift stream's channel, deep
below the level of the country. One of the riders kept glancing timidly
at the bushy banks above his head, as if he feared to see a soldier in the
thicket peering down; his companion sat straight in his saddle, and
took no notice of anything but his horse and the slippery road. It had
been showery all the afternoon, and they were both spattered with mud
from cap to stirrup.

As they came northward, side by side, to the top of a little hill, the
anxious rider gave a sigh of relief, and his horse, which limped badly and
bore the marks of having been on his knees, whinnied as if in sympathy.
The wide gray waters of the Severn were spread to east and west; the
headland before them fell off like a cliff. Below, to the westward, the
land was edged by a long line of dike which walled the sea floods away
from some low meadows that stretched far along the coast. Over the
water were drifting low clouds of fog and rain, but there was a dull gleam
of red on the western sky like a winter sunset, and the wind was blowing.
At the road's end, just before them, was a group of gray stone buildings
perched on the high headland above the Severn, like a monastery or
place of military defense.

As the travelers rode up to the Passage Inn, the inn yard, with all
its stables and outhouses, looked deserted; the sunset gust struck a last
whip of rain at the tired men. The taller of the two called impatiently
for a hostler before he got stiffly to the ground, and stamped his feet as
he stood by his horse. It was a poor tired country nag, with a kind eye,
that began to seek some fondling from her rider, as if she harbored no
ill will in spite of hardships. The young man patted and stroked the poor

creature, which presently dropped her head low, and steamed, as if it were winter weather, high into the cool air.

The small kitchen windows were dimly lighted; there was a fire burning within, but the whole place looked unfriendly, with its dark stone walls and heavily slated roof. The waters below were almost empty of shipping, as if there were a storm coming, but as the rider looked he saw a small craft creeping up close by the shore; she was like a French fishing boat, and had her sweeps out. The wind was dead against her out of the east, and her evident effort added to the desolateness of the whole scene. The impatient traveler shouted again, with a strong, honest voice that prevailed against both wind and weather, so that one of the stable doors was flung open and a man came out; far inside the dark place glowed an early lantern, and the horses turned their heads that way, eager for supper and warm bedding. There seemed to be plenty of room within; there was no sound of stamping hoofs, or a squeal from crowded horses that nipped their fellows to get more comfort for themselves. Business was evidently at a low ebb.

"Rub them down as if they were the best racers in England; give them the best feed you dare as soon as they cool,—full oats and scant hay and a handful of corn: they have served us well," said Wallingford, with great earnestness. "I shall look to them myself in an hour or two, and you shall have your own pay. The roan's knees need to be tight-bandaged. Come, Hammet, will you not alight?" he urged his comrade, who, through weariness or uncertainty, still sat, with drooping head and shoulders, on his poor horse. "Shake the mud off you. Here, I'll help you, then, if your wound hurts again," as the man gave a groan in trying to dismount. "After the first wrench 't is easy enough. Come, you'll be none the worse for your cropper into soft clay!" He laughed cheerfully as they crossed the yard toward a door to which the hostler pointed them.

The mistress of the inn, a sharp-looking, almost pretty woman, suddenly flung her door open, and came out on the step to bid them good-evening in a civil tone, and in the same breath, as she recognized their forlorn appearance, to bid them begone. Her house was like to be full, that night, of gentlefolk and others who had already bespoken lodging, and she had ceased to take in common wayfarers since trade was so meagre in these hard times, and she had been set upon by soldiers and fined for harboring a pack of rascals who had landed their run goods from France and housed them unbeknownst in her hay barn.

They could see for themselves that she had taken down the tavern sign, and was no more bound to entertain them than any other decent widow woman would be along the road.

She railed away, uncontradicted; but there was a pleasant smile on Wallingford's handsome face that seemed to increase rather than diminish at her flow of words, until at last she smiled in return, though half against her will. The poor fellow looked pale and tired: he was some gentleman in distress; she had seen his like before.

"We must trouble you for supper and a fire," he said to the landlady. "I want some brandy at once for my comrade, and while you get supper we can take some sleep. We have been riding all day. There will be a gentleman to meet me here by and by out of Bristol," and he took advantage of her stepping aside a little to bow politely to her and make her precede him into the kitchen. There was a quiet authority in his behavior which could not but be admired; the good woman took notice that the face of her guest was white with fatigue, and even a little tremulous in spite of his calmness.

"If he's a hunted man, I'll hide him safe," she now said to herself. It was not the habit of Old Passage Inn to ask curious questions of its guests, or why they sometimes came at evening, and kept watch for boats that ran in from mid-channel and took them off by night. This looked like a gentleman, indeed, who would be as likely to leave two gold pieces on the table as one.

"I have supper to get for a couple o' thieves (by t' looks of 'em) that was here last night waiting for some one who did n't come,—a noisy lot, too; to-night they'll get warning to go elsewhere," she said, in a loud tone. "I shall serve them first, and bid them begone. And I expect some gentlefolk, too. There's a fire lit for 'em now in my best room; it was damp there, and they'd ill mix with t' rest. 'T is old Mr. Alderman Davis a-comin' out o' Bristol, one o' their great merchants, and like to be their next lord mayor, so folks says. He's not been this way before these three years," she said, with importance.

"Let me know when he comes!" cried Wallingford eagerly, as he stood by the fireplace. There was a flush of color in his cheeks now, and he turned to his companion, who had sunk into a corner of the settle. "Thank God, Hammet," he exclaimed, "we're safe! The end of all our troubles has come at last!"

The innkeeper saw that he was much moved; something about him had quickly touched her sympathy. She could not have told why she shared his evident gratitude, or why the inn should be his place of refuge, but if he were waiting for Mr. Davis, there was no fault to find.

"You'll sleep a good pair of hours without knowing it, the two of you," she grumbled good-naturedly. "Throw off your muddy gear there, and be off out o' my way, now, an' I'll do the best I can. Take the left-hand chamber at the stairhead; there's a couple o' beds. I've two suppers to get before the tide turns to the ebb. The packet folks 'll soon be coming; an' those fellows that wait for their mate that's on a fishing smack,—I may want help with 'em, if they're 's bad 's they look. Yes, I'll call ye, sir, if Mr. Davis comes; but he may be kept, the weather is so bad."

Hammet had drunk the brandy thirstily, and was already cowering as if with an ague over the fire. Wallingford spoke to him twice before he moved. The landlady watched them curiously from the stair-foot, as they went up, to see that they found the right room.

"'T is one o' the nights when every strayaway in England is like to come clacking at my door," she said, not without satisfaction, as she made a desperate onset at her long evening's work.

"A pair o' runaways!" she muttered again; "but the tall lad can't help princeing it in his drover's clothes. I'll tell the stable to deny they're here, if any troopers come. I'll help 'em safe off the land or into Bristol, whether Mr. Alderman Davis risks his old bones by night or not. A little more mercy in this world ain't goin' to hurt it!"

XLIII

They follow the Dike

"There's not a fibre in my trembling frame
That does not vibrate when thy step draws near."

E arly in the morning of that day, when Mr. John Davis had been returning from a brief visit to his counting-room, he was surprised at being run against by a disreputable looking fellow, who dashed out of a dirty alley, and disappeared again as quickly, after putting a letter into his hand. The alderman turned, irate, to look after this lawless person, and then marched on with offended dignity up the hill. When he had turned a safe corner he stopped, and, holding his stout cane under his arm, proceeded to unfold the paper. He had received threats before in this fashion, like all magistrates or town officials; some loose fellow warned off, or a smuggler heavily fined, would now and then make threats against the authorities.

The letter in his hand proved to be of another sort. It might be dingy without, but within the handwriting was that of a gentleman.

"Dear Sir," he read slowly, "my father's old friend and mine,—I ask your kind assistance in a time of great danger, and even distress. I shall not venture to Bristol before I have your permission. I am late from prison, where I was taken from an American frigate. At last I have found a chance to get to Chippenham market as a drover, and I hope to reach Old Passage Inn (where I was once in your company) early in the night on Friday. Could you come or send to meet me there, if it is safe? I know or guess your own principles, but for the sake of the past I think you will give what aid he needs to Roger W——, of Piscataqua, in New England. Your dear lady, my kinswoman, will not forget the boy to whom she was ever kind, nor will you, dear sir, I believe. I can tell you everything, if we may meet. What I most desire is to get to France, where I may join my ship. This goes by a safe hand."

The reader struck his cane to the sidewalk, and laughed aloud.

"What will little missy say to this?" he said, as he marched off. "I'll hurry on to carry her the news!"

Miss Hamilton ran out to meet the smiling old man, as she saw him coming toward the house, and was full of pretty friendliness before he could speak.

"You were away before I was awake," she said, "and I have been watching for you this half hour past, sir. First, you must know that dear Madam Wallingford is better than for many days, and has been asking for you to visit her, if it please you. And I have a new plan for us. Some one has sent me word that there may be news out of the Mill Prison, if we can be at the inn at Passage to-night. I hope you will not say it is too far to ride," she pleaded; "you have often shown me the place when we rode beyond Clifton"—

Mr. Davis's news was old already; his face fell with disappointment.

"It was a poor sailor who brought me word," she continued, speaking more slowly, and watching him with anxiety. "Perhaps we shall hear from Roger. He may have been retaken, and some one brings us word from him, who has luckily escaped."

The old merchant looked at Mary shrewdly. "You had no message from Wallingford himself?" he asked.

"Oh no," said the girl wistfully; "that were to put a happy end to everything. But I do think that we may have news of him. If you had not come, I should have gone to find you, I was so impatient."

Mr. Davis seated himself in his chair, and took on the air of a magistrate, now that they were in the house. After all, Roger Wallingford could know nothing of his mother or Miss Hamilton, or of their being in England; there was no hint of them in the note.

"I suppose that we can make shift to ride to Passage," he said soberly. "It is not so far as many a day's ride that you and I have taken this year; but I think we may have rain again, from the look of the clouds, and I am always in danger of the gout in this late summer weather. Perhaps it will be only another wild-goose chase," he added gruffly, but with a twinkle in his eyes.

"If I could tell you who brought the news!" said Mary impulsively. "No, I must not risk his name, even with you, dear friend. But indeed I have great hope, and Madam is strangely better; somehow, my heart is very light!"

The old man looked up with a smile, as Mary stood before him. He had grown very fond of the child, and loved to see that the drawn look of pain and patience was gone now from her face.

"I wish that it were night already. When can we start?" she asked.

"Friday is no lucky day," insisted Mr. John Davis, "but we must do what we can. So Madam's heart is light, too? Well, all this may mean something," he said indulgently. "I must first see some of our town council who are coming to discuss important matters with me at a stated hour this afternoon, and then we can ride away. We have searched many an inn together, and every village knows us this west side of Dorset, but I believe we have never tried Old Passage before. Put on your thick riding gown with the little capes; I look for both rain and chill."

THE WEATHER LOOKED DARK AND showery in the east; the clouds were gathering fast there and in the north, though the sun still fell on the long stretch of Dundry. It had been a bright day for Bristol, but now a dark, wet night was coming on. The towers of the abbey church and St. Mary Radcliffe stood like gray rocks in a lake of fog, and if he had been on any other errand, the alderman would have turned their horses on the height of Clifton, and gone back to his comfortable home. The pretty chimes in the old church at Westbury called after them the news that it was five o'clock, as they cantered and trotted on almost to the borders of the Severn itself, only to be stopped and driven to shelter by a heavy fall of rain. They were already belated, and Mr. Davis displeased himself with the thought that they were in for a night's absence, and in no very luxurious quarters. He had counted upon the waning moon to get them back, however late, to Bristol; but the roads were more and more heavy as they rode on. At last they found themselves close to the water-side, and made their two horses scramble up the high dike that bordered it, and so got a shorter way to Passage and a drier one than the highway they had left.

The great dike was like one of the dikes of Holland, with rich meadow farms behind it, which the high tides and spring floods had often drowned and spoiled in ancient days. The Severn looked gray and sullen, as they rode along beside it; there were but two or three poor fishing craft running in from sea, and a very dim gray outline of the Welsh hills beyond. There was no comfortable little haven anywhere in view in this great landscape and sea border; no sign of a town or even a fishing hamlet near the shore; only the long, curving line of the dike itself, and miles away, like a forsaken citadel, the Passage Inn stood high and lonely. The wind grew colder as they rode, and they rode in silence, each lamenting the other's discomfort, but clinging to the warm, unquenchable hope of happiness that comforted their hearts. There were two or three cottages of the dikekeepers wedged against the inner side of the embankment, each with a little gable window that looked seaward. One might lay his hand upon the low roofs in passing, and a stout bench against the wall offered a resting-place to those travelers who had trodden a smooth footpath on the top of the dike.

Now and then the horses must be made to leap a little bridge, and the darkness was fast gathering. Down at the cottage sides there were wallflowers on the window-sills, and in the last that they passed a candle was already lighted, and bright firelight twinkled cheerfully through the lattice. They met no one all the way, but once they were confronted by a quarrelsome, pushing herd of young cattle returning from the salt sea-pasturage outside. There was a last unexpected glow of red from the west, a dull gleam that lit the low-drifting clouds above the water, and shone back for a moment on the high windows of the inn itself, and brightened the cold gray walls. Then the night settled down, as if a great cloud covered the whole country with its wings.

HALF AN HOUR LATER MR. JOHN Davis dismounted with some difficulty, as other guests now in the inn had done before him, and said aloud that he was too old a man for such adventures, and one who ought to be at home before his own good fire. They were met at the door by the mistress of the inn, who had not looked for them quite so early, though she had had notice by the carrier out of Bristol of their coming. There was a loud buzz of voices in the inn kitchen; the place was no longer lonely, and an unexpected, second troop of noisy Welsh packmen and drovers were waiting outside for their suppers, before they took the evening packet at the turn of tide. The landlady had everything to do at once; one of her usual helpers was absent; she looked resentful and disturbed.

"I'd ought to be ready, sir, but I'm swamped with folks this night," she declared. "I fear there'll be no packet leave, either; the wind's down, and the last gust's blown. If the packet don't get in, she can't get out, tide or no tide to help her. I've got your fire alight in the best room, but you'll wait long for your suppers, I fear, sir. My kitchen's no place for a lady."

"Tut, tut, my good lass!" said the alderman. "We'll wait an' welcome. I know your best room,—'t is a snug enough place; and we'll wait there till you're free. Give me a mug of your good ale now, and some bread and cheese, and think no more of us. I expect to find a young man here, later on, to speak with me. There's no one yet asking for me, I dare say? We are before our time."

The busy woman shook her head and hurried away, banging the door behind her; and presently, as she crossed the kitchen, she remembered the young gentleman in the rough clothes upstairs, and then only thanked Heaven to know that he was sound asleep, and not clamoring for his supper on the instant, like all the rest.

"I'll not wake him yet for a bit," she told herself; "then they can all sup together pleasant, him and the young lady."

Mr. Davis, after having warmed himself before the bright fire of coals, and looked carefully at the portrait of his Majesty King George the Third on the parlor wall, soon began to despair of the ale, and went out into the kitchen to take a look at things. There was nobody there to interest him much, and the air was stifling. Young Wallingford might possibly have been among this very company in some rough disguise, but he certainly was not; and presently the alderman returned, followed by a young maid, who carried a tray with the desired refreshments.

"There's a yellow-faced villain out there; a gallows bird, if ever I saw one!" he said, as he seated himself again by the fire.

Mary Hamilton stood by the window, to watch if the captain might be coming. It was already so dark that she could hardly see what might happen out of doors. She envied her companion the ease with which he had gone out to take a look at the men in the great kitchen; but Paul Jones would be sure to look for her when he came; there was nothing to do but to wait for him, if one could only find proper patience. The bleak inn parlor, scene of smugglers' feasts and runaway weddings, was brightened by the good fire. The alderman was soon comforted in both mind and body, and Mary, concealing her impatience as best she could, shared his preliminary evening meal, as she had done many a night, in many an inn, before. She had a persistent fear that Paul Jones or his messenger might come and go away again, and she grew very anxious as she sat thinking about him; but as she looked up and began to speak, she saw that the tired old man could not answer; he was sound asleep in his chair. The good ale had warmed and soothed him so that she had not the heart to wake him. She resigned herself to silence, but listened for footsteps, and to the ceaseless clink of glasses and loud clatter of voices in the room beyond. The outer door had a loud and painful creak, and for a long time she heard nobody open it, until some one came to give a loud shout for passengers who were intending to take the packet. Then there was a new racket of departure, and the sound of the landlady angrily pursuing some delinquent guest into the yard to claim her pay; but still Mr. Davis slept soundly. The poor woman would be getting her kitchen to rights now; presently it would be no harm to wake her companion, and see if their business might not be furthered. It was not late; they really had not been there much above an hour yet, only the time was very slow in passing; and as Mary watched Mr. John Davis asleep in his chair, his kind old face had a tired look that went to her affectionate heart. At last she heard a new footstep coming down the narrow stairway into the passage. She could not tell why, but there was a sudden thrill at her heart. There was a tumult in her breast, a sense of some great happiness that was very near to her; it was like some magnet that worked upon her very heart itself, and set her whole frame to quivering.

XLIV

The Road's End

"In sum, such a man as any enemy could not wish him worse than to be himself."

*"I found him in a lonely place:
Long nights he ruled my soul in sleep:
Long days I thought upon his face."*

After the packet went there were three men left in the kitchen, who sat by themselves at a small table. The low-storied, shadowy room was ill lighted by a sullen, slow-burning fire, much obscured by pots and kettles, and some tallow candles scattered on out-of-the-way shelves. The mistress of the place scolded over her heap of clattering crockery and heavy pewter in a far corner. The men at the table had finished their supper, and having called for more drink, were now arguing over it. Two of them wore coats that were well spattered with mud; the third was a man better dressed, who seemed above his company, but wore a plausible, persistent look on his sallow countenance. This was Dickson, who had been set ashore in a fishing boat, and was now industriously plying his new acquaintances with brandy, beside drinking with eagerness himself at every round of the bottle. He forced his hospitality upon the better looking of his two companions, who could not be made to charge his glass to any depth, or to empty it so quickly as his mate. Now and then they put their heads together to hear a tale which Dickson was telling, and once burst into a roar of incredulous laughter which made the landlady command them to keep silence.

She was busy now with trying to bring out of the confusion an orderly supper for her patient guests of the parlor, and sent disapproving glances toward the three men near the fire, as if she were ready to speed their going. They had drunk hard, but the sallow-faced man called for another bottle, and joked with the poor slatternly girl who went and came serving their table. They were so busy with their own affairs that they did not notice a man who slipped into the kitchen behind them, as the Welshmen went out. As the three drank a toast together he crossed to the fireside, and seated himself in the corner of the great settle, where the high back easily concealed his slight figure from their sight. Both the women saw him there, but he made them a warning gesture. He was not a yard away from Dickson.

The talk was freer than ever; the giver of the feast, in an unwonted outburst of generosity, flung a shilling on the flagged floor, and bade the poor maid scramble for it and keep it for herself. Then Dickson let his tongue run away with all his discretion. He began to brag to these business acquaintances of the clever ways in which he had gained his own ends on board the Ranger, and outwitted those who had too much confidence in themselves. He even bragged that Captain John Paul Jones was in his power, after a bold fashion that made his admiring audience open their heavy eyes.

"We're safe enough here from that mistaken ferret," he insisted, after briefly describing the ease with which he had carried out their evening plans. "You might have been cooling your heels here waiting for me the whole week long, and I waiting for my money, too, but for such a turn of luck! If I did n't want to get to France, and get my discharge, and go back to America as quick as possible without suspicion, I'd tell you just where he landed, and put him into your hands like a cat in a bag, to be easy drowned!"

"He's in Bristol to-night, if you must know," Dickson went on, after again refreshing himself with the brandy; "we set him ashore to ride there over Clifton Downs. Yes, I might have missed ye. He's a bold devil, but to-night the three of us here could bag him easy. I've put many a spoke in his wheel. There was a young fellow aboard us, too, that had done me a wrong at home that I never forgave; and that night at Whitehaven I've already told ye of, when I fixed the candles, after I got these papers that you've come for, I dropped some pieces of 'em, and things that was with 'em, in my pretty gentleman's locker. So good friends were parted after that, and the whole Whitehaven matter laid to his door. I could tell ye the whole story. His name's Wallingford, curse him, and they say he's got a taste o' your Mill Prison by this time that's paid off all our old scores. I hope he's dead and damned!"

"Who 's your man Wallingford? I've heard the name myself. There's a reward out for him; or did I hear he was pardoned?" asked one of the men.

"'T was a scurvy sort o' way to make him pay his debts. I'd rather ended it man fashion, if I had such a grudge," said the other listener, the man who had been drinking least.

Dickson's wits were now overcome by the brandy, hard-headed as he might boast himself. "If you knew all I had suffered at his hands!" he protested. "He robbed me of a good living at home, and made me fail in my plans. I was like to be a laughingstock!"

The two men shrugged their shoulders when he next pushed the bottle toward them, and said that they had had enough. "Come, now," said one of them, "let's finish our business! You have this document o' one Yankee privateersman called Paul Jones that our principal's bound for to get. You've set your own thieves' price on it, and we're sent here to pay it. I'm to see it first, to be sure there's no cheat, and then make a finish."

"The paper's worth more than't was a month ago," said Dickson shrewdly. His face was paler than ever, and in strange contrast to the red faces of his companions. "The time is come pretty near for carrying out the North Sea scheme. He may have varied from this paper when he found the writing gone, but I know for a fact he has the cruise still in mind, and 't would be a hard blow to England."

"'T is all rot you should ask for more money," answered the first speaker doggedly. "We have no more money with us; 't is enough, too; the weight of it has gallded me with every jolt of the horse. Say, will you take it or leave it? Let me but have a look at the paper! I've a sample of their cipher here to gauge it by. Come, work smart, I tell ye! You'll be too drunk to deal with soon, and we must quick begone."

Dickson, swearing roundly at them, got some papers out of his pocket, and held one of them in his hand.

"Give me the money first!" he growled.

"Give us the paper," said the other; "'t is our honest right."

There was a heavy tramping in the room above, as if some one had risen from sleep, and there was a grumble of voices; a door was opened and shut, and steady footsteps came down the creaking stair and through the dark entry; a moment more, and the tall figure of a young man stood within the room.

"Well, then, and is my supper ready?" asked Wallingford, looking about him cheerfully, but a little dazed by the light.

There was a smothered outcry; the table was overset, and one of the three men sprang to his feet as if to make his escape.

"Stand where you are till I have done with you!" cried the lieutenant instantly, facing him. "You have a reckoning to pay! By Heaven, I shall kill you if you move!" and he set his back against the door by which he had just entered. "Tell me first, for Heaven's sake, you murderer, is the Ranger within our reach?"

"She is lying in the port of Brest," answered the trapped adventurer, with much effort. He was looking about him to see if there were any way to get out of the kitchen, and his face was like a handful of dirty wool. Outside the nearest window there were two honest faces from the Roscoff boat's crew pressed close against the glass, and looking in delightedly at the play. Dickson saw them, and his heart sank; he had been sure they were waiting for Paul Jones, half a dozen miles down shore.

"Who are these men with you, and what is your errand here?" demanded Wallingford, who saw no one but the two strangers and his enemy.

"None of your damned business!" yelled Dickson, like a man suddenly crazed; his eyes were starting from his head. The landlady came scolding across the kitchen to bid him pay and begone, with his company, and Dickson turned again to Wallingford with a sneer.

"You'll excuse us, then, at this lady's request," he said, grinning. The brandy had come to his aid again, now the first shock of their meeting was past, and made him overbold. "I'll bid you good-night, my hero, 'less you'll come with us. There's five pounds bounty on his head, sirs!" he told the messengers, who stood by the table.

They looked at each other and at Dickson; it was a pretty encounter, but they were not themselves; they were both small-sized men, moreover, and Wallingford was a strapping great fellow to tackle in a fight. There he stood, with his back against the door, an easy mark for a bullet, and Dickson's hand went in desperation a second time to his empty pocket. The woman, seeing this, cried that there should be no shooting, and stepping forward stood close before Wallingford; she had parted men in a quarrel many a time before, and the newcomer was a fine upstanding young gentleman, of a different sort from the rest.

"You have no proof against me, anyway!" railed Dickson. He could not bear Wallingford's eyes upon him. His Dutch courage began to ebb, and the other men took no part with him; it was nothing they saw fit to meddle with, so far as the game had gone. He still held the paper in his hand.

"You have n't a chance against us!" he now bellowed, in despair. "We are three to your one here. Take him, my boys, and tie him down! He's worth five pounds to you, and you may have it all between ye!"

At this moment there was a little stir behind the settle, and some one else stepped out before them, as if he were amused by such bungling play.

"I have got proof enough myself now," said Captain Paul Jones quietly, standing there like the master of them all, "and if hanging 's enough proof for you, Dickson, I must say you've a fair chance of it. When you've got such business on hand as this, let brandy alone till you've got it done. The lieutenant was pardoned weeks ago; the papers wait for him in Bristol. He is safer than we are in England."

Wallingford leaped toward his friend with a cry of joy; they were in each other's arms like a pair of Frenchmen. As for Dickson, he sank to the floor like a melted candle; his legs would not hold him up; he gathered strength enough to crawl toward Wallingford and clutch him by the knees.

"Oh, have pity on my sick wife and little family!" he wailed aloud there, and blubbered for mercy, till the lieutenant shook him off, and he lay, still groaning, on the flagstones.

The captain had beckoned to his men, and they were within the room.

"Give me my papers, Dickson, and begone," he said; "and you two fellows may get you gone, too, with your money. Stay, let me see it first!" he said.

They glanced at each other in dismay. They had no choice; they had left their pistols in their holsters; the business had seemed easy, and the house so decent. They could not tell what made them so afraid of this stern commander. The whole thing was swift and irresistible; they meekly did his bidding and gave the money up. It was in a leather bag, and the captain held it with both hands and looked gravely down at Dickson. The other men stared at him, and wondered what he was going to do; but he only set the bag on the table, and poured some of the yellow gold into his hand.

"Look there, my lads!" he said. "There must be some infernal magic in the stuff that makes a man sell his soul for it. Look at it, Dickson, if you can! Mr. Wallingford, you have suffered too much, I fear, through this man's infamy. I have doubted you myself by reason of his deviltries, and I am heartily ashamed of it. Forgive me if you can, but I shall never forgive myself.

"Put this man out!" said the captain loudly, turning to his sailors, and they stepped forward with amusing willingness. "Take him down to the boat and put off. I shall join you directly. If he jumps overboard, don't try to save him; 't were the best thing he could do."

Dickson, wretched and defeated, was at last made to stand, and then took his poor revenge; he sent the crumpled paper that was in his hand flying into the fire, and Paul Jones only laughed as he saw it blaze. The game was up. Dickson had lost it, and missed all the fancied peace and prosperity of the future by less than a brief half hour. The sailors kicked him before them out of the door; it was not a noble exit for a man of some natural gifts, who had undervalued the worth of character.

The captain took up the bag of gold and gave it back to the men. "This is in my power, but it is spies' money, and I don't want such!" he said scornfully. "You may take it to your masters, and say that Captain John Paul Jones, of the United States frigate Ranger, sent it back."

They gave each other an astonished look as they departed from the room. "There's a man for my money," said one of the men to the other, when they were outside. "I'd ship with him to-night, and I'd sail with him round the world and back again! So that's Paul Jones, the pirate. Well, I say here's his health and good luck to him, Englishman though I be!" They stood amazed in the dark outside with their bag of money, before they stole away. There was nothing they could do, even if they had wished him harm, and to-morrow they could brag that they had seen a hero.

THE MISTRESS OF THE INN had betaken herself to the parlor to lay the table for supper. Mr. Alderman Davis had just waked, hearing a fresh noise in the house, and the lady was bidding him to go and look if the captain were not already come. But he first stopped to give some orders to the landlady.

The two officers of the Ranger were now alone in the kitchen; they stood looking at each other. Poor Wallingford's face was aged and worn by his distresses, and the captain read it like an open book.

"I thank God I have it in my power to make you some amends!" he exclaimed. "I believe that I can make you as happy as you have been miserable. God bless you, Wallingford! Wait here for me one moment, my dear fellow," he said, with affection, and disappeared.

Wallingford, still possessed by his astonishment, sat down on the great settle by the fire. This whole scene had been like a play; all the dreary weeks and days that had seemed so endless and hopeless had come to this sudden end with as easy a conclusion as when the sun

SARAH ORNE JEWETT

comes out and shines quietly after a long storm that has wrecked the growing fields. He thought of the past weeks when he had been but a hunted creature on the moors with his hurt comrade, and the tread of their pursuers had more than once jarred the earth where their heads were lying. He remembered the dull happiness of succeeding peace and safety, when he had come to be wagoner in the harvest time for a good old farmer by Taunton, and earned the little money and the unquestioned liberty that had brought him on his way to Chippenham market and this happy freedom. He was free again, and with his captain; he was a free unchallenged man. Please God, he should some day see home again and those he loved.

There was a light footstep without, and the cheerful voice of an elderly man across the passage. The kitchen door opened, and shut again, and there was a flutter of a woman's dress in the room. The lieutenant was gazing at the fire; he was thinking of his mother and of Mary. What was the captain about so long in the other room?

There was a cry that made his heart stand still, that made him catch his breath as he sprang to his feet; a man tall and masterful, but worn with hardships and robbed of all his youth. There was some one in the room with him, some one looking at him in tenderness and pity, with the light of heaven on her lovely face; grown older, too, and struck motionless with the sudden fright of his presence. There stood the woman he loved. There stood Mary Hamilton herself, come to his arms—Heaven alone knew how—from the other side of the world.

XLV

With the Flood Tide

"Swift are the currents setting all one way."

No modern inventions of signals of any kind, or fleet couriers, could rival in swiftness the old natural methods of spreading a piece of welcome news through a New England countryside. Men called to each other from field to field, and shouted to strangers outward bound on the road; women ran smiling from house to house among the Berwick farms. It was known by mid-morning of a day late in October that Madam Wallingford's brig, the Golden Dolphin, had got into Portsmouth lower harbor the night before. Madam Wallingford herself was on board and well, with her son and Miss Mary Hamilton. They were all coming up the river early that very evening, with the flood tide.

The story flew through the old Piscataqua plantations, on both sides of the river, that Major Langdon himself had taken boat at once and gone down to Newcastle to meet the brig, accompanied by many friends who were eager to welcome the home-comers. There were tales told of a great wedding at Hamilton's within a month's time, though word went with these tales, of the lieutenant's forced leave of absence, some said his discharge, by reason of his wounds and broken health.

Roger Wallingford was bringing dispatches to Congress from the Commissioners in France. It was all a mistake that he had tried to betray his ship, and now there could be no one found who had ever really believed such a story, or even thought well of others who were so foolish as to repeat it. They all knew that it was Dickson who was openly disgraced, instead, and had now escaped from justice, and those who had once inclined to excuse him and to admire his shrewdness willingly consented to applaud such a long-expected downfall.

The evening shadows had begun to gather at the day's end, when they saw the boat come past the high pines into the river bay below Hamilton's. The great house was ready and waiting; the light of the western sky shone upon its walls, and a cheerful warmth and brightness shone everywhere within. There was a feast made ready that might befit the wedding itself, and eager hands were waiting to serve it. On the terrace by the southern door stood Colonel Hamilton, who was now at home from the army, and had ridden in haste from Portsmouth that day, at noon, to see that everything was ready for his sister's coming. There were others with him, watching for the boat: the minister all in silver and black, Major Haggens, with his red cloak and joyful countenance, the good old judge, and Master Sullivan, with his stately white head.

Within the house were many ladies, old and young. Miss Nancy Haggens had braved the evening air for friendship's sake, and sat at a riverward window with other turbaned heads of the Berwick houses, to wait for Madam Wallingford. There was a pretty flock of Mary Hamilton's friends: Miss Betsey Wyat and the Lords of the Upper Landing, Lymans and Saywards of old York, and even the pretty Blunts from Newcastle, who were guests at the parsonage near by. It was many a month since there had been anything so gay and happy as this night of Mary's coming home.

Major Langdon's great pleasure boat, with its six oarsmen, was moving steadily on the flood, and yet both current and tide seemed hindering to such impatient hearts. All the way from Portsmouth there had been people standing on the shores to wave at them and welcome them as they passed; the light was fast fading in the sky; the evening chill and thin autumn fog began to fall on the river. At last Roger and Mary could see the great house standing high and safe in its place, and point it out to Madam Wallingford, whose face wore a touching look of gratitude and peace; at last they could see a crowd of people on the lower shore.

The rowers did their best; the boat sped through the water. It was only half dark, but some impatient hand had lit the bonfires; the company of gentlemen were coming down already through the terraced garden to the water-side.

"Oh, Mary, Mary," Roger Wallingford was whispering, "I have done nothing that I hoped to do!" But she hushed him, and her hand stole into his. "We did not think, that night when we parted, we should be coming home together; we did not know what lay before us," he said with sorrow. "No, dear, I have done nothing; but, thank God, I am alive to love you, and to serve my country to my life's end."

Mary could not speak; she was too happy and too thankful. All her own great love and perfect happiness were shining in her face.

"I am thinking of the captain," she said gently, after a little silence. "You know how he left us when we were so happy, and slipped away alone into the dark without a word. . .

"Oh, look, Madam!" she cried then. "Our friends are all there; they are all waiting for us! I can see dear Peggy with her white apron, and your good Rodney! Oh, Roger, the dear old master is there, God bless him! They are all well and alive. Thank God, we are at home!"

They rose and stood together in the boat, hand in hand. In another moment the boat was at the landing place, and they had stepped ashore.

A Note About the Author

Sarah Orne Jewett (1849–1909) was a prolific American author and poet from South Berwick, Maine. First published at the age of nineteen, Jewett started her career early, combining her love of nature with her literary talent. Known for vividly depicting coastal Maine settings, Jewett was a major figure in the American literary regionalism genre. Though she never married, Jewett lived and traveled with fellow writer Annie Adams Fields, who supported her in her literary endeavors.

A Note from the Publisher

Spanning many genres, from non-fiction essays to literature classics to children's books and lyric poetry, Mint Edition books showcase the master works of our time in a modern new package. The text is freshly typeset, is clean and easy to read, and features a new note about the author in each volume. Many books also include exclusive new introductory material. Every book boasts a striking new cover, which makes it as appropriate for collecting as it is for gift giving. Mint Edition books are only printed when a reader orders them, so natural resources are not wasted. We're proud that our books are never manufactured in excess and exist only in the exact quantity they need to be read and enjoyed.

Discover more of your favorite classics with Bookfinity™.

- Track your reading with custom book lists.
- Get great book recommendations for your personalized Reader Type.
- Add reviews for your favorite books.
- AND MUCH MORE!

Visit **bookfinity.com** and take the fun Reader Type quiz to get started.

Enjoy our classic and modern companion pairings!

9 781513 279893